Mature Content Disclaimer:
This book contains some sex and violence.

The Jada-Drau

Sandie Bergen

Enjoy!
Sandie

Dedication

This book is dedicated to Steve Shumka, massage therapist, swordsman, bowmaker, and friend. It takes a good friend to teach you how to torture and kill a person, and Steve has done a wonderful job. Without him this book would never have seen the light of day.

This is a work of fiction. All characters and events in this book are products of the author's imagination or are used fictitiously. There is some mature content in this book.

THE JADA-DRAU

Edited by Sandy Fetchko and Loretta Sylvestre
Cover art by Ron Leming
Cover design and layout by Stephen Blundell.

Published February, 2011 in print
Ebook edition published Summer, 2011

ISBN: 978-0-9829295-6-8

Marion Margaret Press
Headquarters:
1312 16th St
Orange City, FL 32763
Business Office:
PO Box 245
Hebron, NE 68370

email: publisher@marionmargaretpress.com

www.marionmargaretpress.com

Acknowledgements

I'm a firm believer that no book is written completely solo. Every writer has a person, either currently in their life or somewhere in the shadow of their past, that has influenced or helped in some manner. I'm no exception.

Thank you to the following people for their input, suggestions, helpful reviews, and general support: Diana Cacy Hawkins, Sharon Partington, Loretta Sylvestre, Sandy Fetchko, Sheila Hanson, and everyone at OWW who stopped by to have a look.

Another thank you goes to two talented gentlemen, Ron Leming and Stephen Blundell, who created and designed the cover art. Well done.

A big thank you to my family, immediate and extended, who provided encouragement and support. Last, but hardly least, thank you to my long suffering husband Charlie and my children, Amanda and Aaron, who put up with me staring into space when I should have been paying attention to the discussion at hand, who suffered with my 'Just one more minute!' as I struggled to finish a chapter. Hugs and love to you all.

Chapter One

Summer, the year 410, Ardaeli Reckoning

A wayward summer breeze drifted through the window, ruffling pristine ivory curtains. Cool, late afternoon air dried sweat from the brow of the woman lying on the bed too late to provide any respite. With a sigh of relief, the midwife pulled a small, mewling bundle from the bloody linen sheets. Councillor Rymon let loose the breath he'd held. The child was alive; unfortunately, the same couldn't be said for the mother.

The midwife cleaned the child's mouth of birthing fluid while her assistant laid a clean sheet over the mother's body, covering a once pretty face now distorted into a frightening visage by the throes of a horrific death. Rymon shivered despite the heat of the day. His ears still echoed with Lady Islara's screams; bad enough when the child wouldn't come, ten times worse when Saulth, Lord of the principality of Bredun, ordered his mistress cut open to save the babe. Rymon prayed to the goddess Talueth that Islara could finally find peace. Now if only…

"'Tis a girl, m'lord." The midwife's voice trembled as she wrapped the newborn in a clean blanket. Rymon's heart sank.

The woman held the infant close to her breast, taking a step backwards, away from Lord Saulth. He faced the fireplace, both hands splayed over the grey stones. His fingers curled, as if trying to pull the rock from the mortar. He slammed a fist against the chimney. Rymon winced.

"A *girl*!" Saulth spat the word. "Not the one promised to me. More time lost!"

"My Lord." Rymon braced himself for the coming onslaught, but the words had to be spoken. "The scroll does not say it must be a boy." Lord Saulth spun, his lean features twisted in rage. "What use is a girl to my plans, Rymon? Tell me that!"

"I... I..." Rymon gulped. No more words found their way past his constricting throat; none that could soothe his lord's anger, anyway. Only time had a chance. Time, and for blessed Aja to roll his divine dice in their favour for a change.

Saulth strode to the door of the bedchamber and yanked it open, startling the guards on the other side. He paused in the doorway, then said, "Kill it. It is of no use to me."

"No, m'lord! Please! She's done nothin'!" the midwife cried, clutching the child and turning from her lord.

"And will do nothing! Useless, like all her gender." Saulth moved back into the room, heading for the midwife and the infant.

Without thought, Rymon stepped in his path, holding up his hands. "Please, My Lord! Wait and see! She may yet be the one you seek. The scroll gives no hint as to the gender of the..."

A powerful backhand sent Rymon sprawling, crashing into the stone wall of the bedchamber. The tapestry he hit did little to cushion him. Pain exploded in his left arm and hip. Saulth reached his side in seconds, pulling Rymon up by the front of his tunic.

"I have read the scroll. A thousand times." Saulth's calm voice belied his anger. "Do not presume to know more than I do."

"I do not, My Lord! I only wish to remind you that all is not clear! There…" Rymon gulped and licked his lips, forcing his voice to come out as more than a croak. "There is the missing part. It may reveal additional information. If you kill the child, and she proves to be the one…" He tried to shrug. "What would it hurt to keep her? At least until we know for sure."

Saulth let him drop to the ground. Rymon stifled a groan. *I am too old for this!* He glanced at the midwife still cowering in the corner near the bed, her assistant beside her. What the woman thought she could do if Saulth tried to take the babe, Rymon didn't know.

"Five years I searched for the pieces of the scroll." The Lord of Bredun's pride might be mollified, but his anger still raged. "Another two to interpret the four I did find, three more to track down a woman with enough of the Blood in her to fulfill the requirements, and this is what I get. A female!"

Saulth moved toward the women. The midwife turned away from him, sheltering the child, while her assistant tried to protect them both. Two grey-haired women against a trained fighter, who also happened to be their lord. Brave, but foolish. Rymon struggled to his feet helpless to assist them even if he dared. He fought to remain standing, grasping the wall to steady himself.

Just before reaching them, Saulth spun toward the window. He stood, feet apart, his hands behind his back. Long moments passed while he stared at the city of Valda spread below him, a living tapestry of stone and wood. Beyond the city, green and gold plains stretched to the steep purple-white mountains of Dunvalos Reach, a distant, hazy backdrop. Rymon didn't need to look out the window to know what Saulth saw; he'd spent the better part of the last three days leaning on the casement, trying to ignore Islara's pain.

No one moved; the women too afraid to remind their lord they were there, Rymon too weary in body and spirit. Why the babe didn't make a sound, only Talueth knew.

Rymon shifted his weight from his sore leg. He'd seen forty-seven summers, and yet he felt twice that old, all due to an illness he'd suffered as a child. Lord Saulth's tall, straight body darkened the window for what seemed an eternity. Nineteen years younger, Saulth was blessed with a health and vigour Rymon had never known. *Life is hardly fair, but at least I have had a life.* He prayed that the girl would have the same chance.

The women didn't move. They appeared to barely breathe. Their fear showed on their faces, in their stance. It was plain they thought their Lord harsh and cruel, but Rymon knew Saulth did what he felt he must in order to save Ardael, their beloved homeland.

"I was so sure," Saulth whispered.

Rymon started, Saulth's voice slicing like a sword through his thoughts. He pushed himself away from the wall and limped closer to his lord, closer to the women. Saulth continued to stare into the darkness the window showed him. When had the sun set?

"Where did I go wrong?" Saulth spoke to the burgeoning night. Rymon kept his silence. "I performed the ritual exactly as instructed every time I lay with Islara. It should have worked."

Saulth turned from the window, his face set. "We are running out of time, Rymon. Our country is in danger, but the fools on the council will not listen to me, and I dare not tell them about the scroll. The idiots would only laugh. The Jada-Drau is our one hope, but he must be born soon. If not, Ardael will perish and Bredun along with it."

Rymon shuffled his way between Saulth and the women, resting a hand against the window frame for support. His arm and hip ached, but he forced the pain aside.

"Find me another woman of the Blood, Rymon, and quickly."

"My Lord, it was difficult enough to retrieve this one." She'd been found far to the south and had cost Saulth much in both money and men to steal her away from her father.

"How many others were traced back to the Old Ones?" Saulth folded his arms, transfixing Rymon with his gaze.

Why does he ask? He knows the answer. "Ten, My Lord, only three of child bearing age, but they are even farther away than…"

"Then I suggest you send for them now," Saulth said, his eyes piercing Rymon's soul.

"All three, My Lord?" Saulth's wife, the mother of his two other children, would have a fit. Islara was bad enough, but three concubines? "Lady Saybra…"

"Saybra will complain, but she will not risk her position. If I had known the Jada-Drau's mother had to be of the Blood, I never would have married her."

Only when Saulth had located and translated the second part of the scroll, and the last to be found so far, had he discovered the Jada-Drau was to be one born of the Blood, a descendant of the Old Ones. They discovered Saulth himself bore some of that blood, through his mother's line, fuelling his desire to father the Jada-Drau. Rymon had witnessed the wrath of his lord when the details of the mother's lineage was discovered, for Saulth and Saybra had been married for two years and his first child, a son, already born.

Saulth unfolded his arms and strode to the door. Rymon motioned to the women to remain still, then joined his lord. The babe had yet to cry, and he wondered if there was something wrong with her. Just what the poor thing needed, with no mother and a father who didn't want her.

"The Jada-Drau must be born as soon as possible if we are to have any chance of saving this wretched country," Saulth said. He stopped in the open doorway. "Retrieve the women, Rymon. Now."

The infant chose that moment to whimper, then let loose with a full blown wail. The midwife tried to soothe her while choking back tears. Saulth looked in their direction, a scowl deepening the worry lines on his forehead. Rymon's heart skipped a beat. He stared at the man he'd served for eight years, willing him to let the child be.

"I already have a daughter. Aja only knows why I need another." The Lord of Bredun paused a moment, the expression on his face hard, cruel. Rymon feared his lord's next words. "It may live."

Rymon sagged against the curtained wall.

Saulth waved a finger in the child's direction. "But only under these conditions. There is a small storeroom near the kitchen that holds sacks of flour and potatoes. Have them moved. It will live there. Find a wet nurse. No one is to teach it anything beyond what is necessary for safety and cleanliness. If it proves to be the Jada-Drau, I will teach it what it needs to know. I do not want to see it, and I especially do not want to hear it."

The midwife gasped; her assistant uttered a quiet oath. Saulth left the room.

"My Lord!" Rymon called after him. "What shall we call her?"

Saulth's callous voice echoed back from the hallway. "It will have no name until it has earned one."

Rymon closed his eyes. A harsh sentence for merely being born female, but at least the girl would live. For now.

"Councillor Rymon?" The newborn's wails threatened to drown out the midwife's tremulous voice. She stuck the knuckle of her little finger in the child's mouth. Sucking noises replaced the cries.

Rymon hobbled back to the women, his left leg a solid ache from knee to hip, his arm not much better. There'd be colourful bruising, not to mention the other aches and pains that had yet to manifest.

The midwife nodded to her assistant, who pulled back the cloth shadowing the child's face. A cap of black fuzz covered her head. Eyes closed, she sucked greedily at the midwife's finger. The babe seemed tiny, even for a newborn, but Rymon knew little of these things, with no wife or family of his own.

How can one so small cause such problems? Rymon rubbed the stubble on his chin. The past three days had been long and hard. Food, a bath, and sleep would improve matters, but the child had to be looked after first.

"Do you know of any blue eyes in Lord Saulth's family?" the midwife asked.

Rymon had grown up in Bredun castle and had studied Saulth's ancestry extensively while searching for traces of the Blood. "I have never heard of any. Why?"

"Lady Islara was of the Calleni. They only have brown eyes, like Lord Saulth."

"And?" Rymon wondered what she was getting at. They both knew there was no question that Saulth was the babe's father.

"The child's eyes are blue."

Rymon gently pulled back one of the tiny girl's eyelids. Bright blue, just as the midwife said. The child began to fuss and he removed his hand.

"It could be chance, or the colour may change as she grows older. 'Tis happened before," the assistant said.

Rymon nodded. *Or it could be a sign of the Jada-Drau. I simply do not know. If only we could get the missing piece of the scroll, it might hold some clue.*

"There's a woman who lives near Fish Market Square. Her own babe died of fever not four days ago," the assistant offered. "I'm sure I can talk her into nursin' this little one."

"Send for her," Rymon said. "And keep the child hidden from sight. The less Lord Saulth is reminded she is around, the better it will be for her. I will check in when I can."

The midwife nodded. He took up Saulth's former position at the window, finding small comfort in the familiar scene. The two women prepared a bath for the child, then the assistant left to find the wet nurse.

Blue eyes. The one Rymon had seen was bright and clear. Their pieces of the scroll hadn't mentioned eye colour. The child seemed normal, but would she prove to be the Jada-Drau? Only time, and possibly the missing fragment, *might* reveal the truth.

Chapter Two

Spring, the year 426, Ardaeli Reckoning

She trailed her fingers along the length of the hall, the roughness of the wall lifting the tips, then letting them sink where one grey stone met another. Hard rock gave way to softness when her roaming touch found one of the pictures on cloth.

"Pit- chur," she said, repeating the word Rani taught her so long ago. Her fingers lingered here, gliding slow and gentle over the threads. First up and down, where it felt smoothest, then from side to side, the colourful fibres shifting at her touch.

The cloth, cool and soft when she set her cheek against it, had a quiet, clean scent. Stone had a different smell, cold and dull; an old scent, almost not there. This picture had been here only a short time, not like some of the others. They smelled old too, though in a different way than the stone. Sometimes, if she breathed too deep near them, they made her sneeze.

Her fingers wandered over the things in the tapestry, dark colours blending with light. "Teree". She knew that word. She held Baybee up so she could see too.

Then came her favourite. "Horz. Man." The man sat on the horse. There was a picture of a horse in the Book, though it looked different. Rani had said horses could be many colours. Rani knew lots of things, things she wished she knew. One leg, then two. A little space, then three and four.

She sighed, hugging Baybee tight, wishing Rani would come back. It was long and long since she'd sat on her lap, looking at the pictures in the Book, saying the words, colours, and numbers. The tapestry ended and she lifted her heels to move on. She always walked on her toes when out of her room, careful not to make a noise.

Her fingers found more stone, then the wood of a door. Wood had a louder smell than the cloth pictures. This wood was dark; others were lighter colours and had their own smells. Wood felt different than stone, different than the threads of the cloth. Sometimes smooth, sometimes rough, she had to be careful around wood. It could bite and leave a piece of itself in her finger.

She stopped in front of the door, listening. No one was near. Lifting the latch, she pushed the door open. Slow, so slow. Sometimes it made noise. She sat Baybee down by the door. Taking a candle from a shelf, she stepped back into the hall. Standing on her toes, and stretching up, she could just reach the flame of the candle that sat on the wall. She touched the wick of her candle to the flickering light, waiting for it to take hold. Wax dripped to the floor and she pulled back, righting the candle, letting the tiny flame grow. It had taken lots of tries before she could do it without hurting herself.

Satisfied the candle would stay lit, she re-entered the room and closed the door. Her toes curled into the softness of the carpet, but she didn't linger. Instead, she set the candle on a table near the smooth wall, the place she could see through. The cloths over it were pulled back tonight. A rare opportunity to look at the picture in it. Sometimes a light showed her many things. Other times, the light hid from her and the things were only shadows.

She shivered and rubbed her arms. When she felt warmer, she reached out to the heavy, dark green cloth. Back and forth, she rubbed the fabric between her thumb and first two fingers. If she moved it just right, the fibres shifted, not like the thin cloth of her dress, nor that of the pictures on the walls. These fibres stood up straight. A dress made of this would be nice and warm.

Some nights it was cold here by the clear wall, sometimes not. Tonight she could breathe close to it and make the picture cloudy. Warm or cold, if the cloths were pulled back, she'd look; especially on a night like tonight, when the light shone full, making the room bright in a way the candle didn't. If the cloths weren't pulled back, she wouldn't touch them, except to feel their softness. *He* seemed to know when she did, and then *he* would hurt her.

When it was warm, she couldn't spend so long looking at the Books, not if she wanted to stand where the big light sometimes came in the kitchen. The big light came sooner then, and with it, people. She had to be back in her room before the people saw her.

The cloud her breath made faded and she looked into the strange picture in the wall she could see through. This was a special picture.

She'd thought long and long on this one. Rani had talked about a place called Outside, beyond the door in the kitchen. This had to be Outside. No other pictures she'd seen had things that moved. The big things never moved, but sometimes people and other things did. Tonight, only one shape stirred amongst the big things below. A dog. She smiled and ran to get Baybee. Baybee liked dogs too.

"Dawg," she whispered, and held Baybee up to see.

The dog tilted its head and let out a long, mournful sound. It did that sometimes. If it did it too long, a person came out of one of the things and hit it.

Her smile faded. Hitting was hurt. Hurt was bad. She knew about hurt. *He* hurt her sometimes, when she went too far from her room. Other times, there was no reason. She hugged Baybee again.

Not wishing to think those thoughts, she took a last look at the picture in the clear wall, picked up the candle, then turned, digging her toes into the carpet. There were Books to look at. Only a few had pictures, but she'd opened them all at least once.

On a table in the middle of the room sat something made of the same stuff as the Books, only it didn't have the hard things on the front and back. It was always here, always on the table. It laid flat, in four pieces, with no pages to turn. A piece of it was missing; a piece in the middle. There was a picture in one corner. What it was, she didn't know. She felt like she should. It seemed to call to her sometimes. It made her feel nice. Some nights she spent a long time looking at it, tracing the wavy, curly lines that were *wuhds*, but not tonight.

She walked to the long shelves near the fireplace. Red coals still glowed, and, if she sat near enough, their heat warmed her feet. Her fingers touched the edges of the Books, each smooth, yet hard. She pulled one out. This Book she hadn't looked at for a while. There should be a picture in the middle of it, a picture of two people.

She sat Baybee on the warm stone of the fireplace and settled herself beside her. Keeping her feet near the coals, she turned the pages of the Book. After a short time, her toes began to tingle, the leftover warmth from the fire spreading into her feet and up her legs.

Yes, there was the picture. Two people. One like *him*, the one who hurt her, but this one smiled, a smile like Rani had.

"Look, Baybee." She held the picture up for her to see. "Man." Her finger jabbed at the image. "Man. Man."

She showed Baybee the second picture, the person who looked more like Rani. "Wo-man." She repeated this word twice as well. She stared at the picture for a long time before choosing another book.

* * * *

The candle sputtered, drawing her attention from the marks on the pages that were *wuhds*. She glanced at the clear wall. The round light had gone and it wasn't as dark as it should be. The red coals in the fireplace had long disappeared.

She gasped and leapt to her feet. The big light was coming! She closed the book and replaced it on the shelf, making sure it looked like it hadn't been touched. She grabbed Baybee. A puff of breath extinguished the now stubby candle and she returned it to its place near the door. A quick peek showed no one in the hall. She closed the door and ran on tiptoes to the stairs.

Her breath echoed off the stone. Tapestries flashed by, but she couldn't take the time to touch them, to wonder at their mysteries. At the top of the stairs, she stopped again to listen. Hearing nothing, she flew down them and turned at the bottom, hugging the stone. She had to keep out of the view of the *mans* who stood by the big doors on the other side of this room, so much bigger than hers or the room the Books lived in. Another turn, a short run down the hall, and she was outside her door. She paused, listening. The people who came to the kitchen weren't there yet. She ran to the door that led to Outside and placed her ear against it.

No sound of people coming. She relaxed.

All kinds of things could be found here in the kitchen, wondrous things she had no *wuhds* for. Big round things hung from the roof, sat on shelves or the floor, while smaller things rested on tables and other shelves.

"Kep stir-ring. No, no. You burn it. Fool. Motha musta futter a mool," she said, walking to the big table in the middle of the room. These were only some of the *wuhds* she heard coming from the kitchen. So many *wuhds* she didn't have things for, and so many things she didn't have *wuhds* for.

She looked at the floor in front of the fireplaces. Her pictures were still there, drawn from the grey and white stuff the fire left behind. The pictures would be gone when she woke up, they always were, so she had to make sure she put them back again. She tried to make her pictures the same as those in the Book, but they never turned out quite right.

'Black and Grey cat' and 'Orange and White cat' were nowhere to be seen. They both were there when she woke up and she'd cuddled them before she ate. Sometimes they liked to be cuddled, sometimes they didn't. Cats would come and cats would go. They were many different colours, but they all looked like the cat in the Book. She wondered where the cats went when they weren't here anymore.

Her tummy made noise and she returned to the table where the remainder of her food sat. She'd eaten some before she ventured up to the Book room, saving the rest for now, a thing she'd learned to do so she didn't go to bed with a noisy tummy.

The people in the kitchen always left her food. Rani said it was just for her and it made her happy, that people would leave food for her. She tried to talk to the people when Rani didn't come back, but they shoved her into her Room, making shushing noises. She'd cried many times and hit the door, but they didn't come—except for *him*. Rani had always come when she cried. She'd stopped crying long and long ago. *He* might come and hurt her if she made too much noise.

Dipping a ladle into a water barrel near one of the tables, she drank once, then twice, then let Baybee have some. A candle sat on the table and she used a nearby wall candle to light it. Walking as quickly as she could without making the flame go out, she entered her Room. She put Baybee on the bed before setting the candle carefully on the floor. Returning to the kitchen, she folded up the cloth the food sat on and ran back to her Room, reaching her door just as a person opened the one that led to Outside.

She closed her door quietly, then listened a moment. The person hadn't heard her, so she plunked herself down on the blankets that made up her bed. She spread out the cloth with her food and propped Baybee against the wall. Rani had given her Baybee long and long ago. She loved Baybee; Baybee liked to listen when she spoke the *wuhds*. Reaching under her pillow, she pulled out Rani's Book. *He'd* taken it away, long and long ago, but she'd found it in the Book Room.

Choosing an apple from the food on the cloth, she said, "A-pull." She took a bite and then offered some to Baybee. "A-pull. A-pull." She opened the Book to the first page, careful to use the hand not holding the food. "Teree." She traced the outline of the picture, the page cool and smooth beneath her fingers. These pictures, and those in the other Books, didn't feel like the ones in the hall. There were no threads to touch.

She repeated the *wuhd* twice more. Rani had said she needed to say them often or she'd forget. Just before she went to sleep, every time, she'd say the *wuhds* in the Book. She didn't forget.

"Horz," was the next one. Then *b-ird, dee-ur,* cow and the rest. Last was dog, though this dog didn't look quite the same as the one that made noise in the picture on the wall she could see through.

When all the *wuhds* had been repeated three times and the last of the food gone, she wiped her fingers on her clothes and tucked the Book back under her pillow. She slipped out of her dress and hung it on the peg on the door, beside the other one. In the corner near the door sat the *nesses*. She squatted over it and peed, just as Rani had shown her long and long ago.

The *nesses* was quite the wonder. She used it when she was awake, but when she woke up, the pot was empty and clean. She sighed, wishing she could find out what happened to what she left in the *nesses*, as well as many other wonders she didn't know—such as where her dresses came from. They got smaller, and tighter, and then they'd disappear, a bigger one in its place. Two new ones had appeared not long ago. Her front had grown and she had trouble breathing in the old ones. One of the dresses was very big. The other was prettier, with a different kind of cloth, on the edges of the neck and sleeves, that had holes in it and formed a nice pattern.

She finished with the *nesses*, crawled under her blankets, tucked Baybee in beside her and blew the candle out. Resting the back of her head on her hands, she thought about Rani, and the last time she'd seen her. The scene still played in her mind as if it had happened only a short time ago.

He had come when Rani was reading the picture Book to her and Baybee. *He* was angry and had made a lot of noise, said many *wuhds* she didn't know. Rani cried and shoved her in the corner, blocking her from him. One of the guards grabbed Rani by her hair and pulled her from the Room.

That was the last time she'd seen Rani, the first time she remembered *him*, and the first time *he* had hurt her. She cried and cried, but it didn't make *him* stop. Now, when *he* hurt her, she tried hard not to cry. That only made *him* hit harder.

She snuggled into the blankets, hugging Baybee, and rubbed the cloth between her fingers, her body warming the blankets so they would warm her back, and pretended she sat on Rani's lap, cuddled into her arms.

"Rani," she whispered. "Rani. Rani."

A tear wandered down her cheek and into the pillow. She would never forget.

* * * *

Rymon sat near the fire, leaning closer to its budding heat, using his cane for support. The servant had just lit the fire, piling the wood high, but it would be a while before the heat escaped the fireplace. The night had been cold and these days his bones refused to warm up.

Lord Saulth bent over the table, leaning on his hands while staring at the scroll. A guard stood at his elbow, his body rigidly at attention.

"You watched her through the hole last night, Caden?"

"Yes, My Lord. Briefly."

Saulth turned his head toward the guard. "Only briefly?"

Caden swallowed hard enough that Rymon heard it from where he sat. "I feared she would hear me. She has in the past. It is only a matter of time before she finds one of us."

Saulth grunted, then turned his attention back to what lay on the table. Relief flashed across Caden's young face.

"Did she touch the scroll?" Saulth asked.

"No, My Lord. She only looked at it, then leafed through some books."

The guard appeared to be trying to grow a moustache, without much success. Rymon rubbed his chin. He'd never had a problem with that, though he hated a beard. His fingers rasped on grey stubble. Saulth's demand for his presence hadn't allowed time to remove it. Lord

Saulth's black hair showed mere touches of silver at the temples, whereas Rymon's had lost most of the original brown. Time was running out, in more ways than one.

"She went nowhere else?" Saulth's voice held more chill than the unusually cold spring morning.

"No, My Lord."

Saulth slammed his fist on the table, missing the scroll. Caden jumped. It hadn't done much for Rymon's heart either. He took a few careful breaths to slow its beating.

Lord Saulth stood straight, folding his arms across his chest. "If you only watched her briefly, how do you know where she did and did not go?"

Caden's face paled. "I…I… The other guards, My Lord! I asked them to keep an eye out for her so I could help Guard-Commander Tajik with the new recruits on night duty." Beads of sweat outshone the few hairs on his upper lip.

"So you could dice with the new recruits you mean." Saulth's dark eyes narrowed. "I am well aware of your penchant for gambling, Caden." He unfolded his arms and leaned on the table, his attention once more on the scroll. "Half rations and double weapons practice for a week. Perhaps then your arms will be too tired to lift dice."

"Yes, My Lord! Thank you, My Lord!" Caden almost spun on his heel, but stopped himself. Rymon would have been just as eager to retreat with such a light punishment.

Saulth made him sweat a while longer, then said, "Dismissed."

Caden strode on silent feet to the library door, taking care to close it quietly.

"Young fool." Saulth straightened once more and took the chair beside Rymon. When settled, he said, "She could have gone anywhere. Right out of the castle, perhaps. He would not have known. If he was not such a good swordsman I would have had him flogged as well."

"She will be sixteen this summer," Rymon pointed out. "Her curiosity is natural. She wants to learn things, to explore the world around her." *At least he's stopped calling her 'it'.*

"I cannot let her do that. If she is the Jada-Drau, which I doubt, I need a clean piece of parchment upon which my lessons will be written. I do not need her picking up ridiculous ideas from the staff or, Aja save me, Iridia and her gaggle of friends who think money is for wasting on frivolities."

Saulth stared into the flickering flames for several minutes before shifting his eyes to Rymon, his gaze steady, cold; the same look he'd had the day Islara died, the day this daughter was born. Rymon shivered.

"She is not the one," Saulth stated, with more conviction than he'd shown in the past. "Her powers should have manifested by now…shown some sign that she is other than what she appears, an ordinary girl. I had hoped letting her near the scroll would trigger something. Eight years and all she does is trace the letters."

He leaned back into the chair, steepling his fingers. "I am thinking of having her throat slit while she sleeps. She would never even know it. An entire herd of cattle could charge through her room and she would not wake up. I have never seen such a deep sleeper."

Rymon's blood chilled, as it did every time Saulth threatened to kill her. If Saulth found something no longer useful, he disposed of it. *Not just no longer useful. A failure.* Something the lord couldn't abide, not in others, not in himself. Killing the girl would remove that failure, with no chance of her coming back to flaunt it in his face.

Rymon's stomach churned. "The innocent, carefree sleep of a child," he said, surprised he could keep his voice calm. "As for her powers, the scroll says they will manifest at her maturity."

Saulth held up his hand. "The exact words are 'The Jada-Drau's full powers will appear at his coming of age'."

That's where the break occurred. "Part of the word is missing, My Lord. It may not be 'he'. And who knows what the coming of age is for one of pure Blood." The poor girl didn't deserve to die just because it seemed she wasn't what Saulth wanted. Rymon had to make his lord see reason, again.

"I am one of the Blood. Do not forget that." Saulth's eyes glittered black in the firelight. "I came of age at the same time as the other boys. She has had her moon blood for more than two years now and no sign of any powers."

Rymon well remembered the night the girl began her bleeding. She had run through the halls naked, screaming her lungs inside out.

Fortunately, Saulth had been away at a Lords' Council meeting Rymon was unable to attend. The women of the kitchen took care of her.

He'd told his lord only that her moon blood had started, not the circumstances, and Saulth had shown no desire to know the details.

Rymon closed his eyes briefly, searching for the words that would penetrate Saulth's resolve without making him angry. "However, you are not one of pure Blood as the Jada-Drau is prophesied to be. There may be a difference."

Saulth stared into the flames, his fingers steepled once more. He tapped them together while he thought. "There may be," he conceded. "But I doubt it. A female is useless to me. I said that at her birth and many times since. I need a warrior, not an emotion-ridden girl who will faint at the first sight of battle, hesitate to take the lives she must, or bat her eyes at the first handsome man she sees. I doubt she could even lift a sword let alone use one."

Rymon held his tongue. *And what use a warrior against the tornadoes and floods that plague us now?*

Bredun's master pushed himself out of the chair, then brushed imaginary dirt from his black velvet tunic. "All right, Rymon. You win, again. She may continue to live. So long as she behaves herself. And if her powers manifest, I will take her to my breast, shower her with affection and gifts, and teach her what she will need to know to save us all."

Rymon nodded despite the sarcasm, hiding his relief. Leaning heavily on his cane, he struggled to his feet. The fire blazed hot now, though little of the warmth made it through to his bones.

"When do you leave for the council, My Lord?" Another bone of contention between them. Rymon deeply wished his deteriorating health would allow him to travel. For the first time, Saulth's son, Meric, would accompany him; and probably cause more trouble than be of any assistance.

Saulth's expression darkened. "As soon as the pass allows Cenith to leave Dunvalos Reach. Two weeks at least." A single grunt displayed his attitude toward the young Lord of Dunvalos Reach, another principality in Ardael. "If that fool Zhiri had not blundered, the last piece of the scroll would have been in my hands months ago. The council would have been none the wiser and we might have some hint that she is, or is not, the Jada-Drau. Cenith, like his idiot father before him, has no idea what he possesses. If I had not sent Tajik with the delegation to Tiras over those iron shipments, I would still be looking for it. We are lucky they did not destroy it out of ignorance, and that Tajik recognized the writing."

"Ifan would never have destroyed it, and I doubt his son will. They regard it as a curious family heirloom. Just another of the mountain people's peculiarities. If it has been passed down through the family, it is sacred." Rymon hobbled closer to the fire, watching for any sparks that might land on his woolen trousers. "What punishment do you think the council will deliver?"

Saulth's thin lips curled in a snarl. "Something ridiculous that will tie my hands when I most need them free."

"And if they decide you were responsible for Ifan's death?" Rymon held his hands out to the warmth, praying it would take the chill from his blood. A linen shirt over a long sleeved woolen undershirt and thick trousers, all covered with a velvet tunic and wool robe did little to hold back the cold. Rymon wondered if he could make it through another winter.

"That they cannot prove. There is no worry there. It was an accident. Eagle's Nest Pass is dangerous that late in the fall."

Saulth spoke of Ifan's death as if he were discussing the latest fashion in Edara. The horrible part of it was, all the lords had a common ancestor in Rigen, the last king of Ardael. It was he who had broken the country into six principalities to stop the squabbling of his sons—they could all rule, though they were permitted no title higher than lord. Little had gone right since, although to the best of Rymon's knowledge, war had never been openly contemplated, and murder of another lord unheard of, until Saulth decided to take matters into his own hands. Rymon turned his backside to the fire.

"I will go to the council," Saulth said. "If they decide I am guilty, I will tell them it was a mistake, take my punishment and come home. My new bride will be here in a month's time. I do not wish to keep her waiting." He took a last look at the scroll and strode out the door.

Rymon sat heavily in the chair, his breath escaping in a wheeze. *Talueth, let me live long enough to see this through. Someone has to keep him in check.* The goddess of hearth, home, and health had been absent from this castle over the years.

Of the three women Saulth had taken after the girl's birth, not one had produced a living child. One proved barren and, after suffering years of Saulth's ridicule, had thrown herself from her third floor window. The other two were finally sent home in disgrace, their lives ruined. Who would wed them now?

Lady Saybra had succumbed to a growth in her belly not two winters past, leaving Saulth free to actually marry this one. Rymon snorted in disgust. The girl was seventeen, the same age as Iridia, Saulth's daughter by Saybra.

Doesn't that say something? That none of those women's babes lived? The Jada-Drau has been born and is sleeping in a storeroom near the kitchen with no idea of who, or what, she is. But he will not listen.

Time dripped away, more so now than sixteen years ago. It would be almost a year before this new wife could give birth, another fifteen to twenty for the child to mature, provided it survived and turned out to be the Jada-Drau. Saulth would be fifty-nine at best, and Rymon himself… Another winter like this past one and he doubted he'd even be alive.

Rymon leaned forward, closer to the heat. "Guard!"

The man stuck his head in the door.

"More wood, and have some food and tea sent up."

"Yes, Your Excellency." The door creaked closed.

Leaning his cane against his knee, Rymon held his hands out to the fire. No time remained to raise another child. Trouble was imminent, of that he was sure; so many of the portents had come to pass. Rising tension in the principalities, violent floods everywhere except Dunvalos Reach; devastating tornadoes in Bredun and Mador; strange creatures attacking outlying homesteads in Amita and Kalkor; gigantic waves wiping out fishing villages in Mador and Sudara; the death of a mountain lord—though that last one had come true through Saulth himself.

No doubt lingered in Rymon's mind that the Jada-Drau would be needed, or that the girl sleeping below was the one prophesied. He just hoped he could convince his lord of that, and soon.

Chapter Three

The mountain pony picked its way through the last section of the narrow dirt trail. Cenith glanced back at the dozen soldiers following him, and at the turn in the path far above and behind them; the place where his father and seven guards had died over five cold months ago. An early avalanche, Daric and the surviving soldiers said.

A thick layer of crisp snow covered his father's body, watched over by Shadow Mountain. A peak eternally shrouded in white, it gazed down at the lesser mountains surrounding it like a king, rarely without its crown of cloud. It would be at least another month before they could recover Ifan. Perhaps a proper funeral would set Cenith's heart to rest.

He turned back to the view before him…Councillor Daric's broad back, weaving with his pony's sure steps. The hilt of the great sword strapped across his back kept time like an upright pendulum.

With the afternoon sun in Cenith's face, and Daric in his midnight blue military uniform, the councillor appeared a dark shadow against the spring green of the scrub ridges bordering the plains of Bredun. No new green would show in Tiras, Cenith's home high in the mountains, for another two or three weeks. He closed his eyes a moment, the warmth of the sun chasing away the last of the mountain chill.

Once the path opened wide enough, Daric slowed his pony to allow Cenith to ride beside him. "If you keep craning your neck, you'll end up with a crick so bad you'll be looking backwards for a week," Daric said, his usual half-smile giving life to a face chiselled from the rock of the mountains surrounding them. Born in Callenia, far to the south, he now called Dunvalos Reach home.

"I still find it hard to believe Father died there. That spot isn't known for avalanches."

"So you think someone caused it just to murder your father?" Daric asked, his sarcasm not lost on Cenith.

"Of course not!" Just the thought of one lord having another killed brought the chill back. Yet, that's exactly what had crossed Cenith's mind during the long, cold winter nights since his father's death. "Well, maybe I have."

Daric chuckled. "And more than once or twice, I'd say. Keep thinking that way, even if it isn't true. If your father was murdered, whoever did it may be after you as well. It never hurts to be wary."

And I thought I was overly suspicious. "I wish he'd listened to me when I told him not to go to that council meeting. It was too late in the season. The snow was already falling when he left, heavier when he started back." The weather had remained unusually cold, blocking Eagle's Nest and Black Crow Passes, preventing Cenith from leaving Tiras sooner.

Council meeting called on Saulth's behalf. Weather anomalies and attacks from the north, was all the message had said. Several meetings on the same topics had already been held. Why one more? His father had wondered the same thing and had told Cenith he'd winter at the guard station if the weather didn't permit him returning home.

"I don't know why he didn't just stay down here instead of trying the pass. I never thought Father would become addled with age, but maybe that's what happened." Cenith didn't really believe it, but it remained the only logical explanation.

"As I've said all winter, there must have been a reason. Ifan wasn't a foolish man, nor was he addled. He felt it important to attend the meeting and equally important to make it home," Daric countered. "And go easy on that 'age' business. Your father was younger than I am."

Cenith hoped his chuckle didn't sound as forced to Daric's ears as it did to his. "If he was murdered, why? Never in Ardael's history has one lord tried to kill another."

Daric held up his hand. "No lord has tried to kill another *that we know of*. We only know no one has succeeded or been caught in the attempt. And I can think of a reason one of the lords might want you and your father dead. There are rich veins of gold and silver in the mountains of Dunvalos Reach and just as many unscrupulous men who would love to get their hands on them."

Cenith snorted. "Plenty of gold, yes, but buried so deep in frozen rock it can only be chipped out during summer. And trying to find a path wide enough to get it to Tiras is just as difficult." Lead, zinc, copper, coal, and iron mines dotted the steep hills, but gold and silver provided most of the income. His people lived comfortably, no one went without the basic needs, but he hardly considered his principality wealthy. Everyone worked for what they had.

"Nonetheless, people have killed for less. Whatever happened, for whatever reason, we'll find out nothing until we reach Edara. And possibly not even then."

Cenith sighed. Daric had a point, but more than just his father's death preyed on Cenith's mind. "Then there's this whole business of that Bredun man trying to steal the scrap of old parchment. I can't figure out what Saulth would want with it."

"Another problem for which I have no answer. If the thief had had the decency to live after Kian ran him through with his sword, we might have found out."

Kian, Daric's oldest son and Cenith's best friend, had been on guard duty that night. It was only due to Kian's watchfulness, and the skill learned from his father, that the thief was stopped. The only link they had to Saulth was a Bredun badge taken from the dead thief's under-tunic.

The attempted robbery brought Cenith and his companions out of the mountains as soon as the pass was cleared. The trip had been slow and dangerous, but the situation had to be dealt with. Some of the lords wanted Saulth punished, others wished only to know what the parchment held. Cenith couldn't tell them. No one he knew could read the ancient script.

The courier birds were busy these last few weeks. With no way in or out of the Reach during winter, pigeons were the only method of communication Cenith had with the other lords. Of necessity, the messages were curt, but at least it gave him some idea of important events occurring in the rest of the country.

Two more turns in the steep path brought them out of the pass and close to the guard station where they would trade their mountain ponies for the bigger, swifter steeds needed for the trip to Edara. A warm wind and the neighing of corralled horses greeted their arrival. Rail fences ran in neat, orderly rows, keeping the horses, a few dozen cows, and several pigs and goats from roaming. The peaked roofs of the buildings glistened in the morning sun, evidence of the rain that had fallen during the night. They'd hoped to make the guard station the night before, but had run out of light; negotiating the narrow trails on a dark, rainy night would have been foolish.

A child's shout brought three men out of the guardhouse. Thirty Dunvalos Reach guards called this scattered collection of buildings home. Each served five years and was permitted to bring their families with them. The result resembled a settlement with a large guardhouse attached to a long stable, several smaller buildings where the families lived, a couple of barns, and other structures holding food and supplies for men and animals.

A handful of children of various sizes ran to meet them. Daric signalled a dismount. The Calleni's long legs almost allowed him to just stand up and let the pony walk out from underneath him.

"Lord Cenith! It's Lord Cenith!" one boy shouted back to the guardhouse. "And Councillor Daric! Daric's here!"

In no time, grinning, noisy children surrounded them. Several guards tried to shoo the kids away. The little mob bounced and pulled at Cenith's and Daric's sleeves to hurry them along.

"My Lord, I'm sorry for the intrusion," said Aleyn, the captain of the station. "Yesterday's rain kept them indoors with no outlet for their rambunctiousness."

If Cenith remembered correctly, three of the hoard were Aleyn's. He laughed, a hearty one that helped lift his mood. "Don't worry about it. It's good to hear them. The trip has been too quiet."

Daric harrumphed. "Didn't you say not three hours into the journey how much you enjoyed the quiet?"

"Well, that was four days ago."

They all laughed. Daric stopped to pull a small leather bag out of his pack and the children gravitated to him, grubby hands held out. The councillor reached into the bag, and, one at a time, passed a hard candy to the clamouring children.

When each child had a sweet, Daric said, "Now run off and tell the little ones to come see me when we get to the guardhouse. If you behave yourselves, there'll be another on the return journey." Whoops of delight accompanied the retreating pack.

"You've done this before," Cenith said. "They were expecting it." He realized this was the first time he'd travelled out of the mountains with Daric. When his father had taken him to council meetings, Daric, as guard-commander, had always stayed behind to look after Tiras. Now Ors, the new guard-commander, had that responsibility.

Daric chuckled. "You don't have ten children and not learn a thing or two." He tucked the candy back into his saddlebag and they continued the walk to the guardhouse.

Cenith shook his head. Daric never ceased to surprise him. Six foot eight and powerfully built, Daric could be the meanest bastard ever born. Yet, when it came to children he had a heart as soft as down. Just one reason Cenith had chosen him as councillor after Halen died with Ifan, Cenith's father.

Hot food and a warm fire greeted them in the guardhouse. Cenith intended to spend the night at the station before beginning the week long journey to Edara. It offered a chance for him to put his feet up and listen to the recent news.

The rest of the afternoon passed quickly. Cenith and Daric now sat with Aleyn in the captain's house, listening to the wind howl. The warm breeze had turned coat quickly, bringing the threat of more rain with it.

"Saulth is to be married again?" Daric raised an eyebrow. "Didn't he just get rid of the last of his mistresses?"

"He did," Aleyn answered. "I hear this one is actually eager for the joining. She's seventeen and the daughter of a merchant from eastern Syrth. That's quite a rise in station."

"Syrth!" Cenith almost choked on his mulled wine.

"Over the mountains steep and drear, Across the river, wide and clear, 'Tis then you shall draw near, To Syrth, a land rich with honeyed beer." Daric's deep baritone echoed in the rafters of the captain's house. The song was an old one, and popular in the taverns lucky enough to carry the favoured brew.

"Isn't that a bit far to go for a bride?" Cenith asked. "I'm sure there are plenty of women right here in Ardael who would be willing to marry him. Though Talueth only knows why they'd want that miserable old..."

Daric cleared his throat. "We're safe here, My Lord, but you should practice caution where your tongue is concerned."

"You're right," Cenith sighed. "But that man annoys me, and not just because he had one of his men break into the keep."

"That may be, but he's a lord, and who knows who might be listening once we leave this station."

Cenith nodded and took another sip of his wine, properly chastised. The talk turned to other things and the evening passed too quickly.

Later that night, Cenith lay awake in the room set aside for the use of the Lord of Dunvalos Reach. Thoughts of his father, Saulth, and the scrap of parchment now locked away, turned in his mind, one blending into another. Did Saulth have his father killed? Or was it really just an accident? What did the parchment have to do with it? His father's death and the attempted theft had occurred only eight days apart. There had to be a connection.

Somewhere in Cenith's musings, sleep found him.

* * * *

Saulth slowed his horse to a walk, his son and the soldiers trailing him following suit. As they drew nearer to Edara, people, wagons, and carriages prevented faster travel. Limestone walls, domes, and towers of the capital of the principality of Mador shone in stark contrast to the backdrop of green rolling hills and the bright blue of White Deer Lake. The noonday sun shone through coloured glass, casting rainbows on tiled roofs and high walls.

He welcomed the warmth. The steady rain of the last four days had forced them to hide under oiled cloaks while riding, though water still managed to seep past the seams. Rain had pelted sideways, invading their hoods and dripping down to soak their leather jerkins and the wool tunics underneath. At least they arrived at the city dry.

Edara had been the capital of the old country of Ardael. *Before that idiot Rigen broke it apart.* The entire country should have been Saulth's to rule. With Rymon's help he'd discovered not only his mother's ancestry, but that of his father as well. The other lords could also trace their ancestry back to Rigen, but only he could claim descent from the eldest son. Only he had the true right to rule Ardael. That fact had to be kept quiet, for now. If the Jada-Drau wasn't born soon, there'd be no Ardael to rule; it would be difficult enough to keep the country in one piece while the Jada-Drau grew up.

"Where will we be staying, Father?" Meric asked, his normally petulant voice subdued.

"In the Hall of Maegden. It holds the council chambers as well as apartments for the lords." The building also housed the main place of worship for Maegden, Father of the Gods, an elaborate affair of sculpted marble, limestone, wood, and coloured glass. A ludicrous waste of time, money, and labour, but, even though the thing had been built over six hundred years ago when Ardael was whole, replacing it made even less sense.

"How far is it? I want a bath and some wine to wash the dust from my throat."

"In the centre of the city," Saulth said, clenching his teeth. Aja had rolled the Dice of Fate against him with regards to Meric.

Saulth had never introduced his heir to the council, though all the other lords had brought their sons on many occasions. He preferred Rymon's quiet, subtle ways to Meric's whiny selfishness, but his councillor hadn't fared well this winter and travel would only make matters worse. Rymon might be a sentimental old fool, but he knew his way around the machinations of the council. Teaching that to a son who cared only for girls, hawks, and wine proved difficult. Perhaps a rich offering to both Aja's and Talueth's temples would see his fortune change in other ways. Meric never would.

They rode through gilded gates, Mador's banner waving lazily overhead—a white fish swimming on an alternating green and gold wavy background. The guards, overdone in ivory and gold uniforms, waved them through. This section of Edara housed the nobles and wealthier merchants, and guards stood prominently on every corner. They were less noticeable in the North and South Quarters and not to be found at all in the East, also known as the Docks.

There, the dregs and riff-raff of Edara lived in houses too old to stand straight or on the winding, alley-ridden streets if they couldn't afford those rude shelters. Dozens of brothels sold cheap comfort, though a man was likely to go home with more than just a smile on his face.

Meric craned his neck left and right, absorbing his first look at Edara, the Jewel of Ardael. His eyes lingered on two girls who spoke near an elaborate fountain, then on a woman walking with two men. Saulth shook his head; the colourful awnings, busy markets, and talented street musicians held little interest to Meric.

Almost anything could be purchased in Edara, provided one had the money. Stopping Meric from finding the pleasures he wanted would be more than merely difficult, but Saulth had to make sure his son stayed clear of diseased whores. Miscreant Meric might be, but Saulth had no other male heir; at least until he fathered the Jada-Drau. Proper ladies of night delights would cost more, but could be brought into the Hall in secret and carried a significantly less chance of passing on disease.

Soon, the main street opened up to reveal the Hall of Maegden, a walled, two story, sprawling affair complete with carved pillars and a large central dome covering the temple itself. Copper roofs, green with age, adorned sparkling limestone walls with bright green and gold trim. The Hall sat like a gaudy toad in the middle of a landscaped plaza.

They entered the Hall courtyard and guided their horses to the stables, the soldiers waiting outside for their turn. Expert hands took the steeds while others whisked their belongings away to their rooms. Not a word was spoken. Just as it should be.

Saulth let his eyes adjust to the gloom. The floors were clean. Tack and gear hung on the walls in orderly rows. Many of the roomy stalls held contented animals. Also as it should be. A quick count of coloured livery showed the other lords in presence.

"Lord Cenith has made it down from the mountains," Meric said, nodding at a dark blue and silver saddle blanket hanging over a nearby stall. "I still do not understand why he would accuse you of trying to steal something, especially with Tiras snowed in. How could anyone…"

Saulth grabbed Meric's arm and spun him around before releasing him. "Keep your mouth shut on that subject," he hissed in his son's ear. No stable hands stood close, but one couldn't be too careful. "Let me handle it."

Meric frowned, but after one look at Saulth's face he closed his mouth.

Once outside the stable, Saulth gripped Meric's arm again and pulled him around the corner. "You will keep silent on any political matter. If someone asks you a question, just shrug and say 'It is Maegden's will'. Discuss wine, women, and birds to your heart's content, but leave the important matters to me. Understood?"

Meric winced and tried to pull out of Saulth's grip. "Yes, Father. I will do as you say."

"Good." Saulth released his son's arm and straightened his jerkin. He strode to where his soldiers waited.

"Navid, have your men settle their horses. I want them assigned shifts. Two will accompany me at all times when I am outside my rooms. Two will stand guard at the door."

The guard-captain bowed. "Understood, My Lord." He pointed to two of the guards, who passed their reins to those closest to them.

Turning on his heel, Saulth motioned to Meric. Guard-Captain Navid's crisp commands, and the sharp rapping of the guards' boots, followed them into the Hall.

* * * *

Cenith stepped back into the shadows of the Hall's antechamber, his eyes following Saulth. The Lord of Bredun strode across the wide, colonnaded room as if he owned the place, his son following meekly behind. At least, Cenith took the young man to be Saulth's son. He'd never met the Bredun lord's heir, but he had the same dark hair, thin face, and tall, lean body as his father.

His foot came down on something hard and Cenith bumped into one of the columns.

"Ouch."

Cenith jumped forward a step. The 'column' turned out to be Daric, the 'something hard', his councillor's foot.

"Sorry," Cenith said. "I didn't hear you."

"I don't understand why we have to wear these ridiculous cloth shoes. There's nothing wrong with a good pair of leather boots."

"Lorcan complained they marked the marble floors."

Daric snorted. "They've survived for over six hundred years, why worry about them now?"

Cenith shrugged. "Who knows? Old age and senility?" He returned his gaze to Saulth's retreating back.

A grunt was Daric's only response.

"Aren't you supposed to be meeting with the other councillors?"

Saulth disappeared into the dim light of the long corridor leading to the lords' apartments. The click of his boot heels echoed his arrogance. He'd refused the felt shoes a servant tried to give him.

"We finished. I had no idea it could take half a day for four grey-haired men to decide whether to start the lords' meeting with or without Saulth."

Cenith looked into Daric's dark eyes. "Weren't there five of you?"

"I made my position clear within the first minute. The others had to spend the rest of the morning bantering back and forth like broody hens. I finally put an end to it." Daric jerked his head in the direction of the apartments, then stepped back, allowing Cenith to lead the way.

"Walk beside me," Cenith said. "I can't talk to you when you're a step behind."

"As you command, My Lord." Daric's eyes danced with humour.

Cenith scowled. "You can save that nonsense for the benefit of the other lords. Do I want to know how you managed to put an end to the councillor's bickering?" Cenith had attended one of those meetings with Halen, who thought it would be a good education. It had proved even more boring than the Lords' meetings.

Daric folded his hands behind his back, his expression bland. "I slammed my fist on the table."

Cenith stopped mid-stride. Daric took two more steps before halting.

"You slammed your fist on the table?"

Daric nodded once. Cenith trusted him more than anyone now alive, but perhaps he'd made a mistake in naming him his councillor. The former Calleni mercenary had learned many things in his life, some of which he'd passed on to Cenith. Diplomacy didn't sit high on the list.

"And that settled the issue?"

"Partly. I believe it was the crack I put in the table that convinced them more."

Cenith opened his mouth, then closed it again. He blinked. Twice. A quick glance showed no one nearby. Still, he leaned close to Daric. "You put a crack in the councillor's table? It must be two inches thick!"

Daric shrugged. "It was old. I looked at the edge where I was seated. Someone had scratched a woman's name and a suggestion on what the engraver wanted to do to her. It bears several other marks of a similar nature. Not to mention a surface with more scars than I have."

Cenith groaned. "The table was built for the first council meeting, just after Ardael was split. It's over four hundred years old!" *We'll be kicked out. Sent back to Dunvalos Reach in shame.*

"Long past time they replaced it then." Daric gave him a short bow and indicated they should proceed to the apartment. "The vote finally ended with one councillor saying we should wait for Lord Saulth and three seeing things my way. Now that Saulth has arrived, it's a dead issue and most of the morning was wasted."

A servant carrying a cloth-covered tray exited a corridor. She curtseyed to Cenith. Daric gave her a nod. Cenith resisted acknowledging her. It wasn't accepted practice in most of Ardael. When she'd passed, he paused to admire her trim figure and the pleasing sway of her hips.

"If you're feeling the need for some feminine company, I know a place not far from here. It's clean and so are the ladies." A smirk tinted Daric's voice, but the man's face remained passive.

Cenith's cheeks warmed, despite the fact he'd visited brothels many times in the past. He was about to deny his need when Esryn, Lord of Sudara, stepped out of the same corridor the servant had, his councillor, Payden, one step behind. Esryn stood almost as tall as Cenith, but even he looked short next to Daric. Though grey of hair, the eastern lord kept his lean body in shape. The only other lord to bother with that was Saulth.

"Cenith, how good to see you again. Dreadful news about your father." Esryn shook his hand until Cenith felt sure it would break off. "Terrible accident, a waste. Ifan had so much to offer the council, especially in these trying times." Esryn and Ifan had found common ground in their mutual dislike of Saulth and distrust of the other lords.

Cenith's tongue thickened, preventing words from forming. His father's death still affected him that way. He nodded instead.

"Not that I don't think you'll do an adequate job, you understand," Esryn was quick to add. "But your father had a way of calming some of the other lords that will be missed."

"I understand," Cenith said, forcing the words out. "I look forward to the council meeting…" He realized he had no idea exactly when it was scheduled for. That was one of the items discussed amongst the councillors.

Esryn laughed and clapped Cenith's shoulder. "I don't doubt you do. Tomorrow's meeting is going to be anything but routine. I must admit I will enjoy watching Saulth squirm."

Cenith made himself smile, while telling the emerging butterflies in his stomach to flutter somewhere else. He'd have to confront Saulth in front of the other lords. Esryn might enjoy it, but Cenith most certainly wouldn't.

"I will see you tomorrow, if not before," Esryn said. "I am off to take in the sights of the city." He made a show of winking, and Cenith knew exactly which sights he'd be seeing.

His father had told him the lords looked forward to these meetings simply to get away from their wives and enjoy someone else's company. It was Ifan himself who'd taken Cenith to his first brothel, in this very city, though his father had abstained. As far as Cenith knew, he'd touched no woman since the death of his mother.

Cenith nodded farewell and headed once more for his apartments, Daric one step behind, until the Sudara lord disappeared from sight. One long stride brought the councillor back in line with him.

"Don't be fooled by Esryn's past alliance with your father." Daric kept his voice low and ran a slow hand through his short, iron-grey hair, blocking what he said further from those they passed. "He may despise Bredun's lord, but his councillor was the one who wished to wait for Saulth."

"Perhaps it's because he wants to 'enjoy watching Saulth squirm'."

"Perhaps." Daric didn't sound convinced.

Forgotten words, spoken in his father's voice, bubbled up from Cenith's memory. *A viper's smile and mesmerizing eyes can sway a man, but remember, son, a viper has no hands with which to offer true friendship.*

"Each lord has their own plans for the future of Ardael," Daric continued. "Ones that would see them gain and others lose."

"Father said the same thing many times."

They turned left into the next corridor, the whuff of felt shoes on marble floor echoing around them.

Daric set a firm hand on Cenith's shoulder, stopping him. "Nothing has changed in that respect for four hundred years. Keep alert tomorrow. Watch the other lords' eyes. They can be good indicators of what's happening behind them."

"You'll be with me." Cenith's butterflies scattered to new areas of his stomach.

"Yes, but it'll be difficult to give you the advice you need in a room with the same men you wish to discuss."

"What time does the meeting start?" Cenith asked.

"Right after breakfast." Daric indicated they should continue.

At least Cenith's entire day wouldn't be ruined. Perhaps he could look into buying some clothes. Every spring saw new materials and styles. Cenith hadn't liked most of last year's fashions; maybe something would appeal this year. He flexed his shoulders, pulling the light material of his shirt taut. The long winter months offered the perfect opportunity to hone his fighting skills, which added more muscle. He'd reached his full height, but not girth, and still outgrew his clothes.

They turned right, then left again. Two guards stood outside a nearby door. Their green and gold uniforms marked them as soldiers of Bredun. Cenith moved to the other side of the corridor, then chided himself for a fool.

"He frightens you."

Daric's calm voice helped Cenith soothe his frayed nerves. Still, he picked up the pace until they turned the next corner, left this time.

"I hate to admit it, but yes, he does."

"Then he's already won half the battle." Daric's voice hardened. "He's only a man. Nothing more. Don't let him get to you. He'll sense your fear and pounce like a desert cat on a pocket gopher too far from his hole."

Cenith sighed. *Easy words to say, but…* A final right turn brought them to his chambers. The soldiers standing guard, Varth and Ead, snapped to attention. Cenith waved them away, tired of the pretentious, counterfeit protocol. "You two have been there long enough. Somebody else can have a turn at being bored to tears."

Varth's hazel eyes danced. "Thank you, My Lord," they said as one, and broke into wide grins. The pair saluted, fist to chest, bowed again, and strode in the direction of the barracks to arrange for their replacements.

Daric opened the door and motioned Cenith to stay outside. He checked both the adjoining rooms, then the carpet in front of the two tall windows and the door leading to the garden. Daric had sprinkled a special powder on the thick carpet in front of the door and windows before they left that morning. They could take no chances with the solitary piece of evidence they had from the attempted robbery.

Daric waved Cenith in and headed for the sideboard nestled against the wall between the windows, and the wine bottle and glasses resting there.

Rich red velvet hung in thick folds from elaborate windows. Chairs, foot stools, small useless tables, and massive shelves holding boring books littered the room. The two bedrooms were no better. Tasteless paintings in gaudy frames covered walls washed in pale mauve. The effect was enough to send the butterflies in Cenith's stomach on a proper rampage. He sniffed, and followed a pleasant odour to a covered tray on a table near the fire.

"Any sign of intruders?" Cenith pulled back the cloth on the tray. Roast chicken, warm brown bread, thick butter, and a plate of sliced fruit lived up to the scent's promise. He sat in one of the overstuffed chairs and picked up a slice of orange. Cramming it in his mouth, he sucked the sweet juice. It had been such a long winter.

Daric shook his head. "The powder is undisturbed. Before coming to find you, I took the liberty of ordering a bite to eat," he said, pouring them both some wine.

"I'd ask Talueth to grant you many children, but she's already done that," Cenith said, helping himself to the chicken.

"A simple thank you will suffice." Daric passed him a goblet.

"Thank you." Cenith swirled the crimson liquid before sampling it. The light fruity flavour tasted far better than the strong red provided for them. "I see you also managed to find some decent wine. Pleasant. From Cambrel?"

Daric nodded. "It's much better than that swill Lorcan brews. If the meetings weren't held in his principality, I'm sure we'd be provided with something better."

"Like Bredun's white?" Cenith couldn't resist a smirk, or more of the chicken.

Daric raised his goblet in mock salute. "Now that used to be a good wine, until Saulth got his hands on it."

"Actually, I think the miserable weather is responsible. Cambrel wine has become impossible to get since the Asha River flooded their best vineyards. How did you manage to find it?" Cenith laid down a thick layer of butter on a slice of the bread.

"One can find anything if one only knows where to look..."

"…and if one has the appropriate funds," Cenith said, finishing the Calleni saying while rubbing his thumb and index finger together.

"How hard am I going to have to work my miners this summer to pay for it?" Cenith took a bite of the bread, reveling in its simplicity.

He'd had quite enough of the fancy food and overdone sauces served in the dining hall, and he'd only been here two days.

Daric chuckled. "Harder than usual. I bought you two cases and this bottle." He shrugged. "I was afraid I might not be able to get it by the time we leave. My supplier had only a few left."

"Where are the boxes?"

"Under my bed. We can divide the bottles between the fourteen of us for the journey home. We won't be in quite the rush that we were in to get here."

Daric drained his goblet and poured himself another. At that rate, there wouldn't be any bottles left to take home. Cenith swallowed more of the wine, swishing it around his mouth to get the most flavour, then took another bite of bread.

The trip to Edara had been horrendous. Not only had the Asha River, the border between Ardael and Cambrel, flooded, the Kalemi River, running down the middle of the country, had overflowed its banks. The road from the guard station to Edara followed the Kalemi and was washed out for most of its length, delaying their journey by three days. Daric had found them an alternate route that involved dodging two tornadoes, sleeping in the rain in copses instead of the flooded way stations, and eating cold meals for fear of attracting bandits to the fire.

Daric moved away from the window and took the other chair, the one Cenith's father had always sat in. He helped himself to some bread. "How did your meeting with Urik go?"

Cenith grunted, pushing back the memories. "He only wanted me to turn over Kol Mine to him for nothing. He seems to think I should be grateful to him for taking the mining of it off my hands."

The councillor pulled a leg off the chicken and bit deep. While chewing, he tugged on a low stool with his foot, bringing it close enough to stretch out his long legs, sinking deeper in the chair when he did.

"What did you tell him?" he asked around the chicken.

"That I wanted a hide of cattle every fall while the mine is in production, as well as ten percent of the profits," Cenith said. Amita's lord had turned purple at the conditions.

Daric almost choked on the chicken. He sat up and drained the rest of his wine. "One hundred cows? Every fall? I imagine that didn't go over well."

"I'm tired of eating poultry, rabbit, and mutton all winter. Some beef will be a nice change and those cows will allow some others in Dunvalos Reach a treat as well. It's not like I asked for breeding stock. And, no, he was not receptive at first, especially when I told him he was only renting the mine, not buying it. When I said the extra money might possibly be used to buy hard lumber and grain from him, he was more amenable."

Daric laughed and relaxed back into the soft chair. He crossed his feet on the stool and resumed eating. "By Cillain, your father would be proud," he said, invoking his Calleni god.

Cenith's cheeks warmed and a sense of pride beat the butterflies into submission. "Urik seemed satisfied. I'm sure both the lumber and grain will rise in price, especially in light of the problems with the weather, but I'm hoping the deal will show the others that Dunvalos Reach mines aren't there just for the taking."

Daric stopped chewing. "But Kol Mine isn't really in Dunvalos Reach."

Though most of the mine lay in Cenith's principality, the entrance actually sat a quarter mile from the deliberately vague border. Mountain tradition placed ownership with the entrance. "Urik doesn't know that. Are you going to tell him?"

Daric laughed again.

Chapter Four

Cenith plucked a newly-opened red rose from a bush near the fountain. He breathed deep, drinking in the rich, sweet scent. Roses bloomed for such a short time in the mountains, one of the reasons he enjoyed walking in the Lord's Garden. That, and the wondrous variety of flowers, bushes, and small trees that couldn't grow in Dunvalos Reach. The trickle of the fountain reminded him of the many streams and rivulets of home. The day birds had quieted, while the night ones awoke, chirping their greeting to what they considered morning.

He straightened and glanced back to the door leading to his apartment. *I wonder if Daric has finished his prayers yet.* The Calleni worshipped one god and one goddess, as opposed to the five gods and three goddesses of the Ardaeli. Daric set aside time every morning to honour the goddess Niafanna, and every evening to pray to Cillain. The duties of the Ardaeli gods were many and varied. Cenith found it difficult to understand how only one god and one goddess could do it all.

When asked, Daric would smile and say it was because his gods were stronger than those of Ardael and therefore able to do more. It had led to many evenings of lively debate by the fireside.

Ifan had never pressured Daric to worship the gods of Ardael. He said a man was born under the influence of the deities of his home and it would be wrong to try to change him. If a man felt his gods had let him down, then he was perfectly right in choosing to worship others, but that was the man's decision, not anyone else's, even his lord's. Cenith couldn't argue with that, though he enjoyed the discussions with Daric.

The sun disappeared behind the garden wall and Cenith decided Daric had had enough time for worship. He strode to the door and opened it. The councillor sat cross-legged in front of the fireplace, a blue cloth spread out before him. On it lay a lock of dark hair tied with a gold thread, a small, jagged piece of metal, and a strange rock, no bigger than Cenith's thumbnail. Cenith started to close the door, resigned to waiting a while longer.

Daric waved him inside. "I'm finished." He stared at the objects on the cloth. "I've never told you what these are."

Cenith shook his head, then said, "No," when he realized the Calleni couldn't see him. He'd watched Daric perform the ritual every morning and every night of their journey, but had never found the courage to ask what the objects represented. The contents of a Calleni's worship pouch were sacred.

"I'm now your councillor, not just your weapons instructor and commander of the guard. It's right you should know." He pointed to the lock of hair. "This belonged to my mother. You know she was a whore."

"Yes." Cenith held his breath. This was an important honour Daric bestowed on him.

Daric held up the piece of metal, though he continued to face the fire. "This is part of the first dagger I ever broke. It represents my father. Mother liked to believe the man who sired me was a warrior. She wished it, and so it shall be."

Judging by Daric's size, it was quite likely the truth.

The Councillor picked up the lock of hair in his left hand and held the two objects side by side. "Together, my mother and father gave me life, even if they didn't intend it. All that I am, all that I shall be, I owe to them, for I would have been nothing without them."

Daric set the hair on the cloth and put the metal splinter on top of it. He lifted the stone and held it out to the fire. Shiny specks embedded in it glinted in the flickering light.

"This stone fell from the sky. I saw it fall and dug it out of the ground. It's a gift from Cillain, and I use it to worship him who made the sky, the waters, the ground we walk on." He placed the stone on top of the hair and metal. "My parents gave me life, Cillain gave me a wonderful world to live in. With these things, I honour them."

The Calleni folded the cloth over the objects and stood, turning to face Cenith, a fey look in his dark eyes. "If you have questions, you may ask."

Cenith took a much needed breath. "Only one. What do you use to worship the goddess?"

"The hair, the piece of dagger, and the caul from my birthing. My mother had it dried. It's still in my pouch. I only use it for morning worship."

"Caul?" Cenith had never heard the word. Something pricked his finger. The pain reminded him he still held the rose. He set it on the table by the wine and sucked the tiny cut.

"A membrane that sometimes encloses a child's head at birth. It's considered lucky, even to your mountain people, though your lowlanders just throw it away. Three of my children were born with one. I had them dried for their prayer pouches. Niafanna is the giver of life and the taker of life. Cillain created the world, but she created the life that brightens it. The caul is life and luck, as is Niafanna."

When Daric's life was done, Niafanna would see him safely to her side to await rebirth. The Calleni had no hell, the Ardaeli had three—Abyss, Frost, and Char—in accordance to the severity of a man's sins. Daric's people didn't look forward to death, but they didn't fear it either. Shival, the Ardaeli goddess of death, was one to be feared. It was she who would hold your soul in her hand, to discern how much it weighed. If light, the soul would rise to sit at Maegden's side. If heavy, it would be sent to one of the hells. Which one depended on the weight.

"Thank you, Daric. I know how important it is to you."

His councillor nodded and strode to his room. He returned a few moments later, carrying their cloaks. "As I said earlier, I know a brothel not far from here. You need to relax, and, from what I hear, Niela's ladies have an expert touch."

Cenith laughed and took his cloak. Perhaps some feminine company was just what he needed after all.

****

The day merchants had retired, and the night sellers already set up when Cenith and Daric left the Hall. Hawkers called to anyone who passed close, offering food and entertainment. The farther one travelled from the West Quarter, the more illicit the goods. Cenith had heard it mentioned that young boys and girls could be bought near the docks. The thought turned his stomach. Lorcan forbade weapons on his streets, but Daric had insisted Cenith wear a dagger concealed in the small of his back. One never knew.

Daric scared off overzealous hawkers with a dark look, while Cenith perused goods displayed on narrow tables. They passed three intersections before Daric indicated they should turn left. Cenith had seen nothing to interest him, and there were no sellers on this street, so he turned his attention to the buildings overhanging the shadowed road.

Some bore signs indicating the type of wares they sold…clothing, armour, food. Others had only strong-looking men standing outside open doors, the light spilling out providing a crude illumination. Girls with little or nothing on sat in upstairs windows calling to those walking by. They whistled and waved to attract his attention. Cenith waved back, even blew a kiss or two, but he let Daric make the decision, trusting his judgement.

Cenith was about to ask how much farther they had to go, when a commotion in a nearby doorway drew his attention; a woman crying and a man shouting. Before Cenith could react, an airborne body slammed into him, knocking him to the ground. The two landed in a heap in the street, Cenith on the bottom. An instant later, the person on top of him rose. Cenith sucked air into his crushed lungs.

He shook his vision clear, then leapt up, dagger in hand, searching for whoever had run into him. It didn't take long; the object of his search dangled from Daric's fist.

"I demand you let me down, you oaf!" said the squirming man.

Daric ignored him. "Are you all right, Lord Cenith?"

"I think my nether regions might bear a bruise tomorrow, but I'm otherwise unhurt." He tucked his dagger back into the hidden belt sheath.

A bulky man, followed by a crying woman, exited the doorway. The woman clutched a cloth, stained red with blood, to her naked breast. Her only article of clothing, a short, diaphanous skirt, left little to the imagination.

"He bit me!" the woman cried, her voice shrill.

The man in Daric's grip attempted to twist enough to punch his captor. When that didn't work, he tried kicking. The Calleni was having none of it and shook him. "Settle down and I might think about releasing you. You're lucky Lord Lorcan doesn't allow swords on his streets or you'd be skewered."

A string of ripe curses set Cenith's ears burning. Daric shook the man again and threatened to cuff him. The man gave up his struggle, resigned to muttering.

"If ya put 'im down, sir, I'll take care of 'im," said the man who accompanied the woman. "He's drunk. Thinks 'e's Lord Saulth's son."

Cenith studied the man more closely. The cut and material of his disheveled clothes declared him a noble. Bloodshot brown eyes stared out of a thin face decorated with an equally thin attempt at a goatee. Despite the change and condition of his attire, that face belonged to the young man who had followed Saulth into the Hall.

"I believe he *is* Lord Saulth's son," Cenith said.

The big man leaned over and peered into the young man's face. "Guess mebbe 'e does look a little like Lord Saulth."

Saulth must have frequented this place in the past. He obviously wasn't here now, though. Cenith wondered what the Bredun lord's reaction would be to his son's speedy ejection from a brothel.

"What wouldja' like me ta do with 'im, m'lord?"

Toss him in the nearest dung heap. It would be an improvement. A tempting thought. Instead of voicing his wish, Cenith looked to Daric for an answer.

"Master Meric should be escorted back to the Hall, but if we take the time to do that, then your evening is ruined, Lord Cenith."

"It would be an honour to escort the young lord, m'lord," the brothel guard said, adding a deep bow.

"We'd appreciate it," Daric said. "Ensure you have a good grip on him. So he doesn't fall and hurt himself, you understand."

The guard chuckled. "Of course, sir."

Daric set Meric on his feet. The young man straightened his tunic. His hands shook, whether from the alcohol he reeked of or fear of Daric, Cenith couldn't say.

"My father will hear of this!" he said, taking a couple of staggering steps. Then again, maybe it was anger.

"Then he'll also hear how you abused this young lady," Daric said.

"Young lady! She's a whore!"

"Nonetheless, she doesn't deserve cruelty."

Cenith recognized the iron tone in Daric's voice. If he had any wisdom at all in that alcohol-ridden brain, Meric would turn tail for the Hall.

Saulth's son had no time to display further foolishness. The brothel guard took him firmly by the arm and dragged him up the street, Meric cursing him all the way.

When they'd turned the corner, Cenith looked back to the young woman. Another guard exited the doorway. Cenith blinked. It was the same man who'd just left. His eyes glanced to the corner where the two had disappeared, then back to the guard. Maybe that fall had done more than just bruise his hip.

"Didn't you...?"

The guard bowed. "Twas my twin brother, m'lord."

"Oh. I see. Good." Cenith cleared his throat.

"I apologize for the young lord's rudeness and idiocy," Daric said, giving the woman a short bow.

She fluttered her eyelashes and smiled. "I can reward you proper m'lords. I can do you both and give you a grand time. Together if you'd like. I'm sure my boss would give you a reduced price."

The girl's voice didn't have the rough peasant accent of the guards and Cenith briefly wondered where she'd come from.

"A generous offer," Daric said, "but we have an engagement elsewhere."

"Too bad." She gave the Calleni a look that said she'd be more than willing to entertain him for free.

The guard ushered her back inside. "You need that bite looked after, Laisa."

She winked at them both and the door closed. Daric indicated they should continue.

"Do you think Meric will tell his father?" Cenith asked.

"It depends on several things, I suppose," Daric said, keeping a watchful eye on the doors they passed. "If he's still conscious when he arrives at the Hall; if he remembers what happened in the morning; and if his father really cares."

"I suppose we'll find out eventually."

Daric stopped outside an establishment, sedate when compared to the other brothels they'd passed. "I'm sure we will. This is the place."

They stepped inside.

****

Cenith rubbed his eyes. Galim's droning voice recited the prayers mandatory to opening the Lords' Council Meeting. The Mador councillor's voice sounded as thin as he was, a complete opposite to Lorcan's corpulence. It grated on Cenith's nerves and he resisted the urge to shudder.

His gaze wandered around the Lords' Meeting Room, more pleasing than most of the Hall. Pale yellow walls reflected the light of a hundred candles set in wall sconces and in the circular chandelier hanging from the oak-panelled ceiling. More oak covered the floor, producing a soothing effect he wished he could transfer to his apartment. Cenith wondered if it was done deliberately in an effort to calm the lords. Some of the meetings he'd attended with his father had deteriorated into insult sessions.

A young clerk sat at a small pine desk in the corner to Cenith's left. Quill in hand, he hunched over the parchment in front of him, ready to record the meeting's events.

The other lords shuffled their feet, stifled coughs, or cleaned their fingernails. Their councillors stood behind them, equally bored. Except for Saulth. He sat alone, rigid, hands folded in his lap. Esryn examined his nails, every now and then digging something out from underneath one. Lorcan and Urik squatted in their chairs like toads, pudgy fingers tapping or scratching pot bellies. Jylun stroked his long white beard, his hawk eyes studying each of the lords. A former warrior of some merit, he'd let himself go over the past several years, though he stayed far from Urik and Lorcan's proportions.

Cenith rubbed his eyes again and shifted in his chair; his bottom already felt numb. He'd stayed out far later than planned the previous night, but Tisha proved to be great company and he'd been reluctant to leave her warm comfort. Daric had remained downstairs, declining the offers of several ladies. He said he was married and that was that. It would hurt Elessa if she found out, not to mention the guilt he'd have to carry. Cenith wondered what it was like to love someone that much. He planned on finding out, someday.

They'd returned to the apartment to discover someone had entered through the door to the garden. The guards in the hallway hadn't heard a thing. Cenith's heart almost pounded out of his chest, but Daric had calmly patted a pocket in his jerkin and pulled out the badge, reassuring Cenith that their only bit of evidence of the attempted robbery in Tiras remained safe.

Galim's drone came to an end and a clerk struck the gong standing near the door, jerking Cenith from his musings. A quiet chuckle sounded from behind him. He turned and grimaced at Daric.

"So opens the eight hundred and eighty third session of the Ardaeli Lord Council." Galim tapped his staff on the oak floor.

Lorcan cleared his throat and picked up a piece of parchment from the top of a stack Galim had placed in front of him. He held it at arm's length, squinting as he perused the contents.

"First up is the matter of Dunvalos Reach accusing Bredun of attempted theft of a..." Lorcan squinted harder, "...a scrap of old parchment."

The butterflies in Cenith's stomach returned, dancing faster and faster until they rivaled the tornadoes they'd run from in Bredun.

Lorcan looked up, his chubby fingers dropping the parchment to the table. "What makes you think Saulth tried to steal this parchment, Cenith?"

All five lords turned their attention to him. The marble table had six sides so no lord would be set above another. Lorcan only ran the proceedings because the meetings were held in his principality.

Then why do I feel like I'm on trial?

Cenith resisted looking to Daric for support. He had to do this on his own or the other lords would never respect him. He tried to ignore Saulth, who sat directly to his right. Fortunately, the table sides were wide enough that each of the lords sat more than two arm lengths apart. Bredun's Lord, arms folded, his face like stone, altered his gaze to some spot on the far wall.

Cenith still felt like they were laughing at him. "The theft occurred eight days after my father was killed..."

"What has that got to do with it?" Jylun of Kalkor asked. He sat to Cenith's left, between Urik and Lorcan. Jylun, though the same height as Urik, made the Amita lord look shorter than his real height.

"I'm merely setting the time frame," Cenith said, keeping his tone cool and calm. "It was the middle of the night and one of my guards heard a noise in my study. He knew I was asleep and went to investigate. He came across a man, dressed in dark clothing…"

"What has his clothing got to do with it?" Jylun leaned forward, resting on his elbows, fingers laced together.

Cenith gritted his teeth. "If you will let me continue, I will tell you."

Jylun cocked his bushy white eyebrows and sat back, a scowl crumpling his face.

"For Maegden's sake, Jylun," Urik said. "Let the boy finish, you can ask questions later." He waved a pudgy hand in Cenith's direction.

Cenith nodded. "Thank you. As I was saying, the thief had been caught in my study. He tried to escape, but my guard was able to stop him. He then attacked my guard and was killed."

"The guard or the thief?" Jylun folded his arms across his belly and smirked.

"The thief," Cenith said, through clenched teeth. He forced himself to relax. *Watch their eyes*, Daric had said; he didn't need to watch Jylun's eyes to know where he stood. He risked a side glance at Saulth. The man hadn't moved, nor had his expression changed. How could Cenith judge him when his face, and eyes, showed all the emotion of stone?

Jylun harrumphed. "Shame. Never know the truth now."

"I do have a piece of evidence," Cenith said. "When the thief's cloak and jerkin were removed, he wore a tunic underneath bearing this patch."

Saulth unfolded his arms and sat forward, his interest finally piqued. Cenith turned to Daric, who reached into his pocket and pulled out the piece of torn cloth. He placed it on the table in front of Cenith and stepped back. The badge displayed a gold wheat sheaf entwined by grape vines, on a green background.

"That's definitely your patch, Saulth," Esryn said, a light tone to his voice.

"It is." Saulth reached over to pick it up, then stopped. He looked at Cenith. "May I?"

He can't destroy it now. That would prove his guilt. Cenith nodded.

Saulth leaned back in his chair again, examining the patch. "It is genuine." He tossed it back on the table. "But it proves nothing."

"But…" Cenith started.

"Anyone could have stolen a tunic. They are easy enough to come by." Saulth crossed his arms. "A tunic tossed carelessly aside while the soldier enjoys a short fling with a barmaid..." He shrugged. "It happens."

Cenith wished he could punch Saulth's haughty sneer down his throat. He clenched his fists under the table.

"This is inconclusive," Lorcan said. "Unless you can come up with something better than that…"

"Someone broke into my apartment last night," Cenith said, playing his last game chip. Gasps echoed off the limestone walls.

"Through the garden door. And he wore boots." Cenith nodded in Saulth's direction. "He's the only lord who has refused to wear the cloth shoes. Him, his son, and his soldiers."

"Unheard of!" "Preposterous!" The other four lords jumped to their feet.

Jylun narrowed his hard eyes. "How do you know someone broke in? You were down in whore town getting your dagger polished."

Cenith's cheeks burned. *Maegden's balls! How did he know?* He forced himself to concentrate. "My councillor has a special powder he sprinkled on the carpet."

"*Councillor*!" Jylun spat. "Nothing but a jumped up, filthy Calleni mercenary."

"Jylun, shut up," Esryn said. "No one told you who to choose as councillor." He nodded for Cenith to continue.

Cenith clasped his hands together to keep them from shaking, hiding them under the table. "Daric sprinkled powder in front of the outside door and the windows. When we came back from town, there was a footprint in the powder in front of the garden door. We entered through the hall door. The print wasn't that of a cloth shoe, but a nailed boot."

"There is one way to solve this," Esryn put in, a smug smile on his lined face. "We send our councillors to Cenith's room to see the footprint."

"I have no councillor with me," Saulth said, his voice tight.

Esryn shrugged. "Not our fault. You can go with them, if you like."

Saulth glowered. "I will trust the judgement of your councillors."

Esryn nodded and the councillors left, Daric with them, leaving Cenith in a cage of hungry wolves. Saulth sat, his elbows resting on the table, fingers steepled, staring at the patch. Jylun fixed Cenith in his glare and refused let go. Esryn cleaned his nails, humming a tune, while Urik drummed thick fingers on the tabletop. Lorcan leaned over his parchments, shuffling through them. After an eternity, the councillors returned.

"It is as Lord Cenith has stated," Galim said.

The other councillors nodded their agreement and took their places behind their respective lords. Cenith felt safer with Daric at his back.

"There you go," Esryn said, with a short wave of his hand.

"It does not prove a thing." Saulth's hard voice cut through the ensuing murmur. "Anyone can throw on a pair of boots. Why would I want to break into Cenith's rooms?"

Esryn leaned toward Saulth. "Maybe you thought Cenith brought the parchment with him. Or perhaps you suspected he had evidence that you needed to destroy."

Saulth snorted. "And maybe lightning will strike where you sit. It would make as much sense. I did not order anyone to steal that parchment, whatever it is, and I am not the one who broke into Cenith's rooms." He spread his hands out. "There is no real evidence to state otherwise."

Cenith's heart sank. He'd hoped to at least pin this small crime on Saulth. He couldn't prove Saulth had his father killed, didn't even dare mention it, but this…?

Esryn smiled and sat back. "Then why did you first ask Ifan to sell the parchment to you and threaten him when he said no?"

The other lords leapt to their feet. Cenith joined them. Saulth stood, his chair crashing to the floor. He pounded both fists on the table. "That is not true! Who told you that lie?"

Cenith's heart leapt into his throat. *That's why Father wanted to make it home! To protect the parchment!* Why didn't he tell Daric? The answer came to him as quick as the question. He would have confided in Halen, his councillor; Daric had only been guard-commander then.

"Ifan explained everything," Esryn continued, "before he left. Before you had him killed."

Now the councillors joined in the uproar. All shouted accusations and disbeliefs. Spittle flew from Saulth's mouth as he denied everything. Cenith could have kissed the Sudara lord. Never could he have even thought of giving voice to that suspicion.

"Sit down," Daric said in his ear. "You must not say a word about this. Let Saulth and Esryn battle it out. When order is restored, be careful what you say."

He leaned back and Cenith sat, glad to do so. More than just his hands shook.

"Silence!" Lorcan's loud voice echoed off the oak rafters, bounced back from the walls. "I will have silence!"

"I demand you show me evidence!" Saulth spat.

"Sit!" Lorcan bellowed. "Everyone sit so we can discuss this properly."

Saulth picked up his chair, slamming it upright. When all had settled once more, Lorcan said, "Esryn, what evidence do you have that Ifan was murdered? We were told it was an early avalanche."

"In a place not known for avalanches? And after he refused to sell that parchment to Saulth, who had shown he wanted it badly enough to threaten him? Then eight days later, Cenith's study is broken into and the very object Saulth wanted is almost stolen. The intruder in Cenith's apartment is another nail in the shoe." Esryn leaned forward, resting his hands on the table. "Use the brains Talueth gave you! Saulth is guilty of not only trying to steal the parchment, but of murdering Ifan and breaking into Cenith's room to try to cover it up."

"Those are serious accusations," Urik said. "With very little proof."

"With no proof!" Saulth said. "He is making this up! You all know we have never gotten along. This is just an attempt to see me deposed!"

"What is on that parchment, Saulth? Why do you want it so bad?" Esryn asked.

"How would I know what is on it? I have never seen it, you idiot!"

"The man who broke into my study wore a Bredun patch on his sleeve," Cenith said. "The footprint on the carpet in my apartment was that of a boot. You and your retinue are the only ones who refuse to wear the cloth shoes. I know, in here…" He pointed to his heart, "…you're responsible for both incidents."

Saulth sneered. "Is that why you left my son to be escorted home by common dock trash? Revenge for imagined slights? Meric could have been beaten, robbed, even killed. Did you help him? No, you waved it off and carried on with your amusements."

"Disgraceful!" Jylun said.

The lords added their own mutters, but Cenith's anger took control. "Since when am I responsible for that no-good, wine-sodden, vicious piece of offal that sprang from your loins! If he'd been beaten senseless, it would be nothing less than he deserved!"

Saulth turned purple, but before he could respond, Lorcan motioned them both to silence. "That has nothing to do with the business at hand." He gave them a moment to regain composure, then said, "Cenith, what do you have to say, officially, about this latest accusation?"

Good question. He took a moment to find the words. He had to be careful here. As much as he wanted to join in Esryn's accusation, the simple fact remained that there was no evidence. If he gave in to his emotions and declared Saulth guilty, the other lords would never respect him or his judgement.

Gritting his teeth, he said, "I know my father died in an avalanche, and the circumstances are strange. Perhaps when my father's body is recovered, something will come to light. Until then…I just don't know." *I desperately wish I did!*

Saulth sat back in his chair, his elbows resting on the arms, fingers linked, his annoyingly cool and calm demeanour once more in place. Oddly enough, Esryn did the same, imitating Saulth, except for a small smile on his face.

"Has all the evidence been brought forward?" Lorcan asked.

Cenith nodded, as did Esryn.

"Then a decision must be reached." Lorcan stood. "Cenith, Saulth, as the accuser and the accused, you must leave the room while we decide. Your councillors may remain to ensure all is fair."

Saulth glowered at Lorcan, who shrugged and said, "It is not our fault you do not have one."

"I will ensure all is fair on Saulth's side," Jylun said.

"Thank you," Saulth said, not a trace of genuine appreciation in his voice. He stood and strode out of the room.

Cenith pushed back his chair, wondering what Saulth had on Jylun. A rich trade agreement perhaps? He left the council chamber and was ushered into a small room nearby. He could see no sign of Saulth in the corridor. The two guards who were his constant companions stood outside another door, a Mador soldier with them. One of Lorcan's guards also waited outside Cenith's door, preventing him from leaving.

Wine sat on a nearby table, as well as a bowl of fruit, but Cenith's butterflies rebelled at the thought of anything intruding on their domain. He sat in a chair by the fireplace, wondering what the decision would be. They would have to see that Saulth was guilty of the attempted robbery, if nothing else.

And what will they do about it? That was the real question. The lords had always shown reluctance in imposing punishments on each other. The possibility of reprisal was too great.

Cenith wondered if he'd only made a fool of himself in front of the other lords. Perhaps he should have kept the aborted theft to himself. He had to admit, the patch didn't offer much in the way of evidence.

Maybe if he'd said nothing, Saulth would have tried again and Cenith could have obtained the proof he needed. *Or lost the parchment.*

Why does he want that old scrap anyway? No one can read the script. I just don't understand. The butterflies flapped their wings harder and faster as time dragged on. Then the guard opened the door.

"A decision has been reached, My Lord."

He took a deep breath and followed the guard to the Council Room. Daric stood behind Cenith's chair, his face dark with anger. Jylun gloated. Cenith's heart sank. Saulth was already seated, his expression unreadable.

When Cenith had taken his seat, Lorcan cleared his throat. "We have made our decision. The evidence regarding the possibility of Ifan's murder is based on hearsay alone. We cannot accept it."

Esryn shrugged. Cenith wasn't surprised. It had been a small hope.

"The evidence regarding the attempted robbery and the intruder in Cenith's rooms is circumstantial at best," Lorcan continued. "There is simply not enough proof."

Saulth smiled, a colder one Cenith had never seen. It sent a shiver down his spine. That was that, then. Saulth would get away with everything.

"However," Lorcan said, "these are troubled times. We cannot have feuding between two principalities. We must stand together and help each other. The tornadoes, floods, and everything that's gone wrong in the last few years weakens us as a unified nation. If we cannot pull together, we will be ripe for invasion. It is rumoured that the Tai-Keth have their eye on us again." The horse-lords had attacked out of the northeast fifteen years earlier and reaped death and destruction wherever they went.

Lorcan's eyes shifted back and forth between Cenith and Saulth.

"Therefore, it is our judgement that Cenith will wed Saulth's daughter as soon as possible, thereby joining the two families."

Cenith jumped to his feet. "*Married!* But I don't want to get married! I don't even know the girl!"

Four lords turned scowls of disapproval on him. Even Esryn. Saulth just sat, his arms folded, a narrowing of his eyes the only indication he'd heard what Lorcan said.

"You'll get to know her soon enough when you bed her," Jylun said. A smug smile cracked his hard face.

"That is unimportant." Lorcan frowned, his white eyebrows almost meeting over the deep crease between them. "Marriages of state are arranged all the time. This one will put a stop to this nonsense so we can concentrate on how to feed and care for those made homeless by this damned peculiar weather." He rested his arms on a belly at least as big as Urik's. "You will marry the girl, bed her, and get an heir. After that, if you don't like her…" he shrugged, "…find yourself a mistress."

Daric rested his hand on Cenith's shoulder and gently pushed him back into his seat. Cenith glanced back at him. Sympathy showed in a face still set in anger.

"Saulth, are you in agreement?" Lorcan asked.

The lord of Bredun nodded once, his expression unchanged except for his eyes. The lines of tension around them had disappeared. *He agrees with this!* Cenith had to wonder why.

"The documents are being drawn up as we speak." Lorcan made a point of shuffling the parchments in front of him. "Now to other business."

Cenith sat staring at Lorcan. *What the hell just happened? Saulth was the one who committed the crimes and I'm punished for it!* Saulth certainly didn't appear upset by the announcement. Then a thought struck him, but he'd have to wait to talk to Daric.

Chapter Five

Cenith barely heard the next part of the meeting. He had fingers and toes, but he couldn't feel them; he couldn't feel anything. *I want to fall in love. I want to know the kind of love Daric and Elessa have. I want to choose for myself.* The chances of that had just been snatched away, unless Saulth's daughter proved to be of a strikingly different personality than her father or Meric.

His father and mother had fallen in love the first time they met. She'd been part of a trade delegation from distant Syrth. His mother had come to barter and, when the delegation left, had remained behind, wife to the lord of Dunvalos Reach. Cenith had only heard about the love his parents shared since his mother died five years after his birth. He'd always dreamt of that kind of love. Now his dreams lay shattered.

The voices of the lords droned on as they discussed trade agreements and ensured there'd be enough food for the winter. Daric shoved parchments in front of him and pressed a quill into his hand. Cenith had to trust that whatever he signed had Daric's approval. He couldn't make out the words. They all swam together. More parchments replaced those and he signed them, pressing his signet ring—three mountains in a circle, the symbol of Dunvalos Reach—into the blob of red wax Daric provided.

Cenith had to pull his attention away from the disaster his life had become. He closed his eyes and took a deep breath. He felt so dead inside even the butterflies had abandoned him. When he opened his eyes again, it was to see Lorcan squinting at him.

"If you are tired, boy, perhaps you should spend less time with the ladies when you know there is work to do."

Jylun chuckled, but a glare from Esryn's eagle eyes silenced him. The meeting continued, with the talk turning to ways to compensate for the treacherous weather.

"I don't know why both rivers had to flood," Jylun complained. "As if the tornados weren't enough."

Lorcan shot him a glare. "It all happened just to annoy you." He returned his attention to the rest of the council. "I have enough grain in storage to last a year. Even so, I'm ordering my people to tighten their belts."

"We could always bring it in from elsewhere," Urik suggested, stifling a yawn.

Amita, Bredun, Mador, and Kalkor were hit the hardest. Problem was, those were the principalities who fed Dunvalos Reach. 'Elsewhere' appeared the path to follow for Cenith.

"We could always turn to rice," Esryn said, with an odd smile that indicated he didn't really care where anyone else found their grain. It made Cenith wonder if he had plenty in storage as well.

Other ideas were bandied around until Lorcan put a halt to that part of proceedings. "Next on the agenda, the Tai-Keth, who've been rattling their swords across the river again."

The council decided that more military units, one thousand men from each principality, would be sent to the northeast, the border with Tai-Keth, to stop any thought of incursion by the horse-lords. The Chance River, which formed the border, was deep and violent, but the resourceful Tai-Kethians had found ways across in the past.

Now that winter had gone, the strange creatures that had crept out of the Northern Forest vanished. Some resembled bears, others wolves, with the exception that they stood on two legs like men. The only explanation for their appearance seemed to be increased snow and cold weather in the far north, forcing them to look for food to the south. Two winters now they'd terrorized northern Amita.

"When winter comes again," Lorcan said, "the soldiers guarding the border with Tai-Keth could move to protect Urik's principality."

Urik of Amita grunted his approval and the topic changed to the over-sized waves that had killed hundreds of people on the coasts of Sudara and Mador. They now claimed more lives as plague took hold. There were too many bodies for the survivors to bury. The fishing business had almost collapsed since the waves had destroyed most of the boats. Other than passing on their sympathies, the lords had no suggestions for Esryn and Lorcan.

Hundreds of Ardaeli died from flash floods. Innumerable tornadoes took more lives and added their part in ruining crops. If these disasters continued for another two or three years, the threat of starvation would prove all too real. Ardael, the land of three rivers, rich and bountiful, now lay in dire peril, and there was nothing anyone could do except pick up the pieces.

Maegden's altars burned night and day with offerings of grain, incense, and expensive herbs and spices. There were mutterings of offering lambs and calves. Cenith wondered how long it would be until someone suggested using the Tai-Kethian method of worship—human sacrifice.

The subject of the broken councillor's table came up, attracting Cenith's full attention. The Council hastily decided a new one should be built. No one looked at Daric during the short discussion and Cenith quietly sighed in relief.

"Now then," Lorcan said, shuffling the parchments into some kind of order. "That is all I have on the agenda." He paused a moment before asking, "Is there anything else?"

Four pairs of eyes looked to Saulth, as if daring him to say something. Cenith wondered if it had anything to do with the meeting Bredun's lord had called in the fall.

"Yes," Saulth said, "there is."

The lords groaned as one and Esryn slammed a fist on the table. "Not again! Haven't we heard enough of this tripe?"

"Are the tornadoes tripe? Are the thousands of lives already lost, tripe?" Saulth's voice sounded calm.

Cenith risked a glance at him. The man seethed.

"And you think having one lord standing over all of us will stop the tornadoes and floods? Bah!" Esryn sat back, folding his arms, his expression black.

"We all know who you want as that lord, Saulth," Urik said. His dark eyes, almost buried by flesh, flashed in anger.

Saulth sat forward, his hands gripping the edge of the table. "There must be one lord! It is the only way Ardael can survive! Even now you talk of sending soldiers to the border with Tai-Keth, yet I know the ones you send will be the dregs, the trouble makers, those who are soldiers only because they are incapable of anything else. And why? Because none of you trusts the other. No one wants to be left short-handed, just in case, even though in all the history of Ardael, no lord has attacked another."

Saulth stood, keeping his grip on the table. "You are weak, all of you. Four old men and a boy who has not yet learned to wipe his nose!"

Cenith almost checked to see if his nose was running, then cursed himself for a fool.

"You talk of pulling together, working as one." Spittle flew from Saulth's mouth. "You could not find your tarse if a whore unbuttoned your britches and tugged it out for you!"

Cenith hastily wiped a drop from his cheek and shifted so he leaned nearer to Urik. The old man smelled, but he didn't spit when he talked. Daric positioned himself closer to Saulth, partially blocking Cenith.

"*I* am the only one capable of saving this country from total destruction!" Saulth continued. "When the floods have reached your castles, the tornadoes have whisked away your wives and children, you will come to me on your knees!"

Cenith recoiled from the sheer arrogance of the man. Saulth spat on the marble table and strode to the doors. He yanked them open with such force they flew back to the walls and bounced forward, almost closing by themselves. They missed hitting Saulth. He'd already left, his boot heels clicking on the floor, those of his two guards echoing their lord's. No one said a word until the sound faded completely.

Esryn pushed his chair back. "I really wish you had listened to me. I did not lie when I told you what Ifan said. Saulth has ambitions far beyond what is right and just."

Cenith sunk down in his chair, wishing he could slide all the way under the table. Directly, and indirectly, he was the cause of this.

Lorcan sighed, resting his hands on his belly. "We went over all that. With no solid proof, there is little matter if we believe you or not. If we decide a lord's guilt based on what another lord says, not only would we accomplish less than we already do, we would open the door to total pandemonium. Urik would accuse you of stealing a shipment of lumber, Jylun a herd of cows."

Jylun opened his mouth and Lorcan held up his hand. "And I am not saying either of you did. I am merely stating an example. The point is, it would not stop, and this country really would fall apart."

"Oh, I know," Esryn said, rising to his feet. "I just hate dealing with that contemptuous ass. Shival would do us all a favour by collecting his soul sooner than later. The sheer weight of it will send it straight to Char's bottom."

Cenith had to agree. Lorcan started to speak, but Esryn signalled to Payden and the Sudara lord left, the whiff-whuff of his shoes a much quieter echo than Saulth's boots.

"It is well past lunch time, and I, for one, am famished," Urik said, heaving his round bulk out of the chair.

Cenith couldn't help thinking it a good thing all the chairs were made of sturdy oak. They would surely have collapsed under Urik's and Lorcan's weight long ago.

"Sounds like a grand idea," Lorcan said. "Would you like some company?"

Urik waddled over to Mador's lord and clapped him on the shoulder. "A good meal always goes down better with good conversation."

The two headed out, followed by their councillors and the clerk. That left only Jylun and his councillor, Illian, a lean, tight faced man with his nose so high in the air one could see right up his nostrils. Not a pleasant sight.

Jylun pushed his chair back, taking his time about it. The scrape of wood on wood grated on Cenith's overwrought nerves.

The Kalkor lord stood and smiled. Also not a pleasant sight. "Let me be the first to wish you well in your upcoming marriage."

"Shut up. I think you've caused enough damage for one day." Daric placed a firm hand on his shoulder and Cenith bit back what he really wanted to say.

Jylun gave him a mock bow and said, "You are a sore loser. Boy." He strode through the door, Pruneface tagging along behind.

I wish they'd stop calling me 'boy'. I'm taller than any of them. "What happened, Daric? I feel like I've been blown away by one of Saulth's tornadoes."

"A good analogy I suppose. This certainly isn't how I'd expected the situation to be resolved." The Calleni pulled Urik's chair closer and sat down, leaning on his knees. "I did everything I could to make them change their minds. I'm sorry it wasn't enough."

"It's hardly your fault," Cenith said. "Who came up with the idea?"

"Urik."

Urik. That figures. "Getting back at me for the trade agreement?"

Daric shrugged. "Possibly."

Cenith heaved a heavy sigh. "I don't want to get married. Especially to Saulth's daughter." He still couldn't believe it. This had to be a bad dream.

Daric laced his fingers together and looked at them a moment before responding. "You're a lord now. What you want and what you have to do are quite often two very different things."

"Then why do the other lords seem to get their way all the time?"

"Seem is the proper word. Saulth hardly got his way today."

Cenith sat up straight, turning to face his councillor. "And yet, he didn't appear upset by the judgement. I think I might know why."

Daric cocked an eyebrow. Cenith had no idea how he did that; he'd practiced in front of a mirror for hours, but couldn't lift just one.

"Not here," Daric said. "Let's go to the apartment. It's private there."

Cenith nodded and they headed for the heavy doors leading out of the meeting room. The symbols of the six principalities were inlaid on both sides, in and out. Done in thin pieces of varying types of wood, the lighter shades of the symbols stood out in stunning contrast to the dark oak of the doors. In a building decorated with the eye of a blind man, these were a thing of beauty.

"Daric?"

"Yes?"

"What did I sign?"

* * * *

The sky blue chair perched like a toad on the dark green carpet, surrounded by pale mauve walls and red curtains. Cenith slouched in it, trying not to throw up.

A still full glass of wine sat at his elbow, a tray with thick slices of beef drowned in rich gravy near it. The warm bread didn't smell as good as yesterday. Cenith's butterflies refused to let him even think of eating.

He looked over his copies of the documents he'd signed. The first was the trade agreement with Urik. Daric had done an excellent job of putting it together. He'd even added the stipulation that Dunvalos Reach would provide an assistant to Urik's overseer, ostensibly to council his untrained miners on tried and true techniques and provide assistance in unforeseen circumstances. In actual fact, he'd ensure Cenith received his ten percent.

A unit of soldiers would also be in attendance to protect the miners against the denizens of the mountains. Other than cave vipers and the odd bear or mountain cat that would attack if threatened, the only danger was a bite on the ankle by a silver fox or enduring a cuffing by an irate badger. For some reason, the creatures that attacked Amita shunned Cenith's mountains. Urik didn't need to know that either.

The second was the marriage agreement. He stared at it like a death warrant; which it might well be if Saulth's daughter proved to be anything like her father. *How can I bed someone like that? If she even remotely looks like Saulth, I'll never be able to give her a child. My tarse will shrivel and that'll be the end of it.*

Cenith scanned the document once more. Something was missing. "Why is the girl's name not here? Mine is." In fact, it was there four times. *Cenith, son of Ifan, and Lord of Dunvalos Reach*. Hers only said *The daughter of Saulth, Lord of Bredun*.

"I assume the clerk who penned it didn't know her name and was in too much of a hurry to find out." Daric sat beside him, his legs stretched out to the fire. "It was all done and over faster than a desert sand squall. If I remember correctly, her name is Iridia." Daric forked another thick slice of beef onto his plate. At least the food wasn't going to waste.

"Iridia." Cenith braved a sip of the wine. Matters had improved; he could actually taste it. "Cenith and Iridia. Hmmmm." He took another sip. "Iridia and Cenith."

Daric chuckled around the food in his mouth.

Cenith set his glass down. "I don't like the sound of it, but…" He shrugged. He might as well accept it; refusing would only add more tension to a country ripe with it. "Did anyone say when the wedding is supposed to occur?"

"Anytime within the next month. The details were left to you and Saulth."

Cenith sighed. "So soon? I suppose I should talk to Saulth, since the ceremony will have to be held in Valda."

Daric picked up the unused plate, placed two slices of beef on it, scraped butter over a piece of bread and passed it to Cenith. "You need to eat." When Cenith had taken the plate and cut into the meat, Daric said, "In the meeting room, you said you thought you knew why Saulth seemed agreeable to the marriage."

Cenith chewed his meat and swallowed before answering. "I think it's another way of getting to the parchment. He has his daughter steal it for him."

"How is she supposed to get it to him? A city bred girl won't be able to make it out of the mountains."

"I'll be very surprised if she doesn't bring retainers with her, possibly even a few of Saulth's guards. There are ways, and Saulth is sneaky enough to think of a few I haven't." Cenith picked up a small knife from the tray, added more butter to his bread and took a big bite. Daric smiled. "I too, had thought of that. Once again, your father would be proud. What do you plan on doing about it?"

Cenith licked butter from his fingers. "I just might have an idea."

* * * *

Saulth stared out the open door leading to the garden. Behind him, two of his guards packed his and Meric's belongings, stacking the saddlebags by the inside door. Urik, Jylun, and Esryn travelled in carriages with wagons lugging more clothing and useless paraphernalia than they needed. Ifan had also travelled light, as did his son.

Cenith. Saulth smiled. Things had turned out much better than expected. He hadn't been proven innocent, but the lords couldn't prove him guilty either. It mattered little in the end, and now he had a good excuse to put a man inside Tiras keep, one capable enough to steal the parchment. After all, his daughter would need guards of her own to ensure her safety on the trip to the mountains. His man merely had to bide his time, wait for the right moment.

Once Saulth had the final section, he could put the last piece of the puzzle together. With the complete scroll, and the Jada-Drau, he could bring them before the Council and show those fools he was right. There can only be one lord in Ardael, and that lord had to be him.

Saulth's smile faded. It all had to happen soon. Ardael might not last long enough for the Jada-Drau to come of age. Surely this time the ritual would work.

His thoughts wandered back to the first time he'd performed the ceremony described in the scroll. The woman had tried to run, her screams ringing off the rafters in her bedchamber. He finally had to bind her and stuff a gag in her mouth. Every night Saulth followed the scroll's instructions. His mistress eventually gave up resisting him and lay like a dead thing while he did what was necessary…until her moon blood failed to come.

The girl in the room near the kitchen was the result. Saulth scowled. Rymon had insisted he wait to see if she proved to be the Jada-Drau. So far, she'd only proved a nuisance. He tapped his forefinger against his lips. *Perhaps there is a way to force the power out of her. Provided it is there to force out.*

A thump, a crash, and a curse pulled Saulth away from his thoughts. He turned his back to the garden door.

"Who put that bag there!" Meric cried.

"I'm sorry, Master Meric. Your father ordered us to pack your things," one of the guards said.

"You could have killed me!" Meric stumbled out of his room, wearing only a pair of linen small breeches, pushing the guard before him. "I should have you horse-whipped!"

Meric's dark hair stuck up in all directions, his eyes brown drops lost in pools of bloodshot white, rimmed by red.

Saulth scowled. "I am the only one who will do any horsewhipping. Straighten up, or you might find yourself on the receiving end." He nodded to the guard to continue packing. "I do not care how you spend your time with a whore, I only care that you do it discreetly. I told you I would find someone suitable and bring her here. But no, you could not wait for me to finish my business at the temples."

Meric fell into one of the chairs by the fireplace. "I thought you were in a meeting." He peered at the packs by the door. "We going somewhere?"

"The meeting is over and we are going home." Saulth folded his arms. "If we leave now, it should give us a day's grace before Petrella arrives."

Meric sat up. "Home! We just got here!"

"You have been here long enough to make a complete ass of yourself. I have concluded my business and now it is time to go home and prepare for the weddings."

"Weddings? Who else is getting married?" Meric leapt to his feet, stumbled, and fell back into the chair. "Not me, is it? I do not want to get married!"

Saulth grimaced. "Relax, fool. Your sister is marrying Cenith." For once, his son couldn't find anything to say.

The guard came out of Meric's room. "Everything is packed except for a change of clothes for the young master," he said, giving Saulth a half bow.

"Take everything out to the stable and get it loaded. Tell Navid I want to leave within the hour."

After the guards left, Meric made himself comfortable in the chair. "Iridia will not be happy. She had her eye on that grandson of Jylun's who came to visit last summer."

"She will do as I say. She is, at least, slightly better at that than you are." Saulth unfolded his arms and closed the garden door, shutting off the chirping of birds and insects, and the heady scent of the flowers. "Besides, Jylun's grandson will be lord someday. Cenith is a lord now."

"I did not think Cenith was old enough to get married," Meric said. He picked up a small knife from Saulth's dinner tray and cleaned a fingernail with it.

"He is a year younger than you." Saulth stepped toward the table between the two windows and poured himself a glass of wine.

"Nineteen?" Meric grunted. "Looks younger."

"Nineteen or not, he is Lord of Dunvalos Reach and Iridia's betrothed. Witnessed, signed, and done." Saulth sat in the other chair by the fire and used his wine glass to indicate the remains of the meal. "I suggest you get cleaned up, dressed, and have something to eat. Once we start out, we are not stopping until dark."

Meric opened his mouth, but the words were cut off by a knock on the door.

"Enter," Saulth said.

One of the guards stuck his head in. "Lord Cenith and Councillor Daric to see you, My Lord."

"Probably come to make the arrangements," Saulth said to Meric. "Keep your mouth shut."

Meric sat back farther in the chair and tucked his legs in, looking as if he wanted to hide, which was likely given his attire. Or perhaps he disliked the idea of facing them after what had occurred the night before. No matter either way.

"Let them in." Saulth remained seated, his wineglass in hand. He'd be able see them well enough from his chair.

Cenith entered first, followed by the barbarian he had chosen as councillor. Ludicrous. The man was a mercenary, little more than a common thief and murderer. It would serve Cenith right if the Calleni slit his throat in the night and took his place as Lord of the Mountains.

The man even declined to wear the traditional long robe of a councillor, sleeveless and open in the front, in the colours of the lord he served. He chose instead to wear a padded midnight blue leather jerkin, trimmed in silver, with shoulder patches in the sky blue and white of Dunvalos Reach, the uniform he'd worn as Ifan's guard-commander. He didn't wear the great sword that usually hung at his back since no weapons were permitted in Maegden's Hall, nor on Edara's streets. At least not visible ones. Saulth wondered how many blades the Calleni had secreted about his person.

Daric leaned against the now closed door, looking far too relaxed for the dark expression on his hard, lined face. Saulth refused to acknowledge him.

"We have some decisions to make," Cenith said. He rubbed a finger behind his right ear before smoothing down the back of his collar-length brown hair.

The boy stayed close to the Calleni. That, and the fidgeting, screamed his fear. Saulth smiled. He enjoyed playing with little pigeons.

"I imagine you would prefer to get this over with as quickly as possible. I am sure you have responsibilities in Tiras, now that spring has arrived in the mountains."

"Uh, yes. I would like to go home soon." Cenith tried to look into the other chair but seemed reluctant to move his feet. Instead, his eyes travelled the room. They settled on the remaining packs. "You're leaving already?"

"Yes." Saulth twirled his wine glass. "As soon as my son chooses to dress himself." He looked at Cenith over the rim and allowed himself a smile, to tempt the boy into relaxing his guard. "I am getting married again, in eight days."

"I'd heard that. I didn't realize it was so soon. Congratulations." Cenith's voice sounded anything but sincere. He clasped his hands, then unclasped them. The mountain boy tried to look anywhere but at him.

Saulth nodded in mock acknowledgement, never taking his eyes off Cenith. "Come in ten days. That will allow me time to enjoy my new wife before my daughter gets married."

"Ten…days?" Cenith gulped.

"Better to get it over with than dwell on something you cannot change. Leave all the details to me. Perhaps you could spend the next few days choosing a wedding gift for your bride or acquiring a suitable marriage outfit. Something in blue perhaps? Or grey, a light shade that matches your eyes?"

Meric pretended to vomit. Saulth ignored him.

Cenith squirmed under Saulth's steady gaze. "Well, if there's nothing else, I should let you finish your packing." He backed toward the door, bumping into Daric.

Saulth resisted a chuckle. The boy looked more nervous now than when he came in. "I look forward to having you as my son-in-law. I am eager to prove to you that I am not responsible for the terrible things that have happened in Dunvalos Reach of late. We are to be family, and I am sure Iridia will be pleased with the husband Aja has chosen for her." Not that the God of Fate actually had anything to do with it. Saulth lifted his glass in salute.

"Uh, thank you."

The Calleni opened the door and stood back, letting Cenith exit first. Daric's black look hadn't faded one iota. The door had almost closed behind them, when Cenith stepped back in.

"I almost forgot, I wanted to let you know something," Cenith said. His body straightened and he looked at Saulth with a courage and determination he'd not shown a few moments ago. "That scrap of parchment you want so badly?"

The sudden change in Cenith's demeanour threw Saulth off. "I...I told you, I do not..."

"I don't care what you said in the meeting. I know you were behind the attempted theft." Cenith's voice had changed as well, firm and confident. "As soon as I return to Tiras, I'm destroying it. That will put an end to the matter." He smiled, his lips a cold, hard line. "After all, I don't want it causing problems between my wife and me. I should also let you know that I've made the other lords aware of my intention. If anything happens to me, or anyone in my party, while we're at Valda, the other lords will know the truth and you will be dealt with."

Saulth squeezed the stem of his goblet. Cenith disappeared behind the door, only to reappear an instant later. "Oh, by the way, have a nice journey."

Saulth jumped out of the chair and threw the goblet at Cenith. The thin glass shattered against the closing door. "You goat-loving, tarse-sucking son of a worm!"

He shook his fist at the door. "Shival hear me! I swear I will see that swine-futtering mountain turd and his overblown desert ass-licker through all three hells! Even if I have to drag them there myself!"

Saulth picked up the decanter of wine and threw it at the fireplace. Fire sizzled where liquid spattered. Glistening shards flew in all directions. A piece landed on the hearth, a drop of wine cradled in a curve in the glass. It shone red as blood.

Saulth clenched his fists, staring at the drop. "It will be Cenith's blood."

Meric, eyes wide, cowered in the chair.

Chapter Six

Saulth adjusted the collar of his sleeveless, gold velvet tunic and examined his reflection in the full length mirror standing in his sitting room. A shirt of white samite covered his arms, its lace frill peeking out of the tunic at his neck. Dark green, fine wool breeches met black leather, knee high boots. His valet had just left. Saulth now waited on Rymon.

He tugged on the lace decorating the cuffs of the shirt and turned to examine the side view. Rows of green wheat sheaves lined the edges of the tunic, reversing the colours on his banner. A dark green cape matching his breeches would finish off his wedding attire.

Smoothing down a recalcitrant lock of black hair, he took another look in the mirror. The grey at his temples had increased and a short search found a few elsewhere. Saulth patted his flat stomach. Two hours every morning spent in weapons practice with his men proved beneficial in more ways than one.

A knock sounded on the door.

"Come in."

Rymon entered, leaning heavily on his cane. He settled his thin, robe-wrapped, body into the chair nearest the fire.

"All is ready for tonight?" Saulth asked, taking a last look in the mirror.

"It is. The beeswax candles are set up in your bedchamber. The myrrh, mistletoe, seed grains, and acorns are in jars by the fireplace. I have hidden the bone knife in the drawer of the bedside table." Rymon paused, staring at the fire.

"And?"

The councillor sighed. "The unborn piglet is in a box in the coldroom. It will be placed under your bed just before you and the lady retire for the night."

"The other items?" Saulth smoothed the front of his tunic, then reached for a small wooden box on the table beside the mirror.

Rymon grimaced. "The rope and gag are in the wardrobe, on the floor."

Saulth rummaged through the jewellery in the box before choosing a gold brooch in the shape of a wheat sheaf. His mother had given it to his father on the day of their wedding. It seemed fitting.

He closed the lid. "Good. I want everything to be perfect. With luck, I will not require the rope and gag. The Syrthians are a barbarian people. It is said they perform blood sacrifices at all their festivals, especially their spring fertility ceremony." Saulth donned the cape and fastened it with the brooch. "She should not be too upset with this one."

Saulth faced Rymon and held his cape out to either side. "Well? How do I look?"

"Like a lord on his marriage day," Rymon said, bowing his head. "The lady will be impressed."

Saulth smiled. "Is my bride ready?"

"Ready and waiting, My Lord, as are your guests."

"Then walk with me, Rymon. I want the festivities over with as soon as possible. My blood is up and I wish to enjoy my new wife for more than just the ritual."

Rymon pushed himself out of the chair and accompanied him to the castle temple. Only Edara had individual shrines to the gods. The other cities in Ardael had one temple with seven chambers. Each lord had their own temple in their castle, some more elaborate than others.

Saulth's ancestors had designed the one in Valda to be simple and tasteful, which suited Saulth.

They passed the main doors to the temple and entered a small waiting room adjoining the main chamber. Brother Dayfid, dressed in heavy, multi-coloured brocade robes, stood in the opposite doorway, watching the guests take their seats. He turned and bowed when Saulth entered, his broad face wearing his usual piously vapid smile.

Meric leaned against the open door, gazing at the seated guests. Saulth had forbidden him any wine since their return. As a result, he looked at least half way presentable in his new tunic and trousers, made of the same dark green wool as Saulth's breeches.

"Your bride awaits you in the sanctuary, My Lord," Brother Dayfid said.

"Rymon, tell Petrella we are ready and then take your seat." *Let us get this over with.*

Rymon bowed and exited through the same door they'd come in, taking the back way to the sanctuary. Brother Dayfid slid by Meric and made his way to the front of the main chamber. Saulth joined his son at the door, scanning the crowd.

Iridia sat with two of her friends in the front row chatting like a magpie. *Probably discussing her own wedding.* She had pouted on hearing the news, but changed her mind when Meric told her what Cenith looked like. Iridia's eyes had lit up like a cat's at night. Saulth had to admit, the mountain boy was good looking, tall and well built, but Saulth couldn't help wondering if Meric may have overdone it.

The rest of the well wishers consisted of his dukes, the thegn of the city, the more prosperous merchants of Valda, and their wives. Not enough to overcrowd the main chamber, but sufficient to make Petrella feel important. More guests were invited to the dinner afterwards. He'd have been happier with just his children and Rymon.

Two young soldiers stood at attention holding their long trumpets at their sides, another concession to his new wife. The instruments were rarely on key and only served to grate on Saulth's nerves.

At the front of the chamber stood a semi-circle of seven stone pedestals, each supporting a statue of a god or goddess. Dayfid stood directly in front of the center one, Talueth, Goddess of Home and Family, her hand resting on her pregnant belly. Saulth's eyes slid to the three deities standing to her right: Aja, God of Fate and Luck, his dice cupped in his right hand; Keana, Goddess of Agriculture and Commerce, three stalks of wheat in her arms; and Siyon, God of War, Duty and Honour, holding his golden spear as if to throw it.

On her left stood Tailis, Master of the Seas, Lakes and Rivers, pouring water from a jar; Ordan, God of Fire and Smithing, his hammer poised to strike; and Shival, Mistress of Death and Revenge, cold and beautiful, a well-crafted heart resting on her open palm.

On the back wall, above the statues, hung a golden sun. Stylized rays surrounded a disc carved into the likeness of a man's face smiling beatifically down on the worshippers—Maegden, Father of the Gods, Lord of the Sky.

Saulth sneered. Not a one of Ardael's gods or goddesses had done anything about the dilemma his country now faced. Part of the ritual to sire the Jada-Drau involved prayers to heathen deities. If Ardael's gods could do nothing, Saulth had no reservations about praying to those who could possibly help.

Rymon emerged from the sanctuary and shuffled across the chamber to his seat. Trumpets blared and the chatter of the guests ceased. Petrella stepped from the shadows of the sanctuary, followed by one of her ladies who would stand as her witness. She took small measured steps until she stood in front of Dayfid. The mangled tune the trumpeters played ended and Saulth breathed a sigh of relief.

Dayfid turned his back on bride and guests and held his arms up to the golden sun. "Maegden, hear my prayer. Look down upon us, your children, your worshippers, those who honour you. We humbly ask for your blessing on the two who are to be joined as one. We beseech you to stop the floods and tornadoes that plague our principality…"

The priest's prayer continued, but Saulth paid little attention. Petrella's lush figure drew his eye. The girl's face left much to be desired too round, her eyes small, and her mouth too wide. The face paint her ladies had applied didn't appear to have much of an effect. What lay beneath the form fitting gown, however, held more appeal.

The swell of her breasts peered over the top of the green velvet dress, a lighter shade than he wore. Delicate ivory lace covered the gown from neck to floor. Saulth had no idea how much her father had paid for it. He hoped she wouldn't expect dresses like that all the time. Emeralds and amber glistened in the fine net she wore over her light brown hair. Matching gems dangled from her ears and encircled her white throat.

Of all his mistresses, Islara had been the prettiest. The desert rose had more spirit as well. If only that useless girl-child hadn't forced him to cut her open. His eyes strayed in the direction of the store room where the girl slept. *Perhaps I should have ordered her door bolted. She's become too curious of late.*

Dayfid's drone ended and he turned back to face the crowd. "Petrella, daughter of Wister of Syrth, do you come freely and openly to this marriage?"

A traditional question, but irrelevant. The papers were signed months ago; the girl couldn't say no, even if she wanted to. All the marriage needed to be legal was the blessing of the gods. The ceremony was merely for show; an excuse to buy expensive clothing and eat and drink too much.

"I come of my own free will." Though Petrella spoke Ardaeli well, her voice had a nasal quality to it that Saulth found annoying. Not that it really mattered, he wasn't marrying her for her lilting tone.

"Do you declare before Talueth that you are a virgin? Untouched by the hand of man?"

"I do declare that I am pure and innocent of man's touch."

Rymon had done an excellent job of coaching the girl in the two days since her arrival. Marriage customs in Ardael differed greatly from those in Syrth.

Dayfid nodded in Saulth's direction. He stepped out of the vestibule, Meric behind him as his witness. Saulth stood to his bride's left, careful not to touch her. She didn't yet belong to him, not in the eyes of the gods. Dayfid turned his back and intoned more prayers to the deities.

Facing them once more, the priest asked, "Saulth, Lord of Bredun, do you come freely and openly to this marriage?"

"I come of my own free will." *And in the hopes that this one will give me the means to salvage my country.*

Dayfid bowed to each of them and said, "May Aja's dice roll in your favour, may Keana see your home filled with the fruits of the harvest, may Siyon hold your duty to each other in his hands, may Talueth grant you healthy children, may Tailis provide you with the water of life, may Ordan's fire keep you warm, and may Shival grant you long lives. Your hands please."

Saulth raised his right hand palm up, Petrella her left, just above his, palm down. "Take my hand," he said. "I will protect and honour you."

Petrella laid a shaky hand upon his. "Thank you, My Lord. I will obey and honour you in return."

Dayfid raised his arms again. "It is Maegden's will that man and woman live together according to his law, that they bear and raise children to worship him and his kin. Maegden, through me, sends his blessing to Lord Saulth and Lady Petrella. These two are joined as one. May you enjoy a long and fruitful life together."

The priest pulled two small bags out of his robes and handed one to Meric, the other to Petrella's companion. The witnesses opened them and pulled out a handful of seeds and grains. They tossed them over

Saulth and Petrella. The crowd stood and clapped, cheering their good wishes.

Saulth let go of Petrella's hand and they turned to face the crowd. Taking his new wife's hand once more, he said, "Come, my friends. It is time to celebrate. A feast awaits."

More cheers accompanied them down the center aisle. Meric offered his arm to the other witness and followed. The trumpeters lifted their instruments to their lips, but Saulth cut them off with a gesture. He led Petrella out of the temple and to the Lord's Hall, eager to finish the festivities and begin the ritual.

* * * *

She opened her eyes to darkness. Reaching for Baybee, she sat up. Noise from the kitchen told her it wasn't yet time to wake. Then why did she?

Yawning, she rolled over, hugging Baybee to her. She tried to sleep, but sleep wouldn't come. She stood and held her hand out to the wall. Two steps to the basket that held the things she needed when the red time came. She didn't like the red time. Sometimes she hurt a lot and just wanted it to go away. Three steps to the nesses. It was empty again, but not for long.

"Nesses." She said the *wuhd* three times. When she finished, she counted five steps to the door and the dresses hanging there. Her fingers found the one with the pretty cloth on it. She pulled the dress over her head and let it fall around her, saying 'dress' and 'door' three times as well.

The noise in the kitchen had still not gone away, so she went back to her bed and felt for her *br-uss*, using it just as Rani had taught her. As she worked the tangles out of her hair, she said the *wuhds* belonging to the things around her.

"Blan-ket. Pill-ow. Br-uss." Her tummy made noise and she wished the people in the kitchen would go.

She finished her hair, then felt around above her bed for a stick to clean her teeth. Another search found Baybee and she cuddled her until the sounds from the kitchen died away. Waiting a short time more, she stepped to the door and opened it.

The kitchen was quiet, but noise came from elsewhere. She tilted her head. Sounds of people talking and others she hadn't heard in long and long echoed down the hall from the big room. She moved into the hall and stepped on something soft; a towel, with a piece of soap on it.

They wanted her to have a bath. She frowned. The noise needed to be looked at. She didn't have time for a bath, not if she wanted to look at the Books and the noise. Then she remembered the one time she'd decided not to take a bath. *He* had come and hurt her.

She sighed, looking again in the direction the noise came from, before heading into the kitchen. Food waited for her. She sat in the chair and spooned up what was in the bowl. It was hot and good.

While she ate, she thought about the noise she'd heard. She'd heard it two times before; one long ago, and one long and long ago. People had been in the big room, some holding things that made noise, some eating, and others doing things she didn't know. It was wonderful, the *wo-mans* in pretty dresses, the nice noises coming from the things the *mans* held…

There was no time for drawing *pit-churs* by the fire; too much to do. She scraped the bowl clean and ran back for the towel and soap. The bathtub sat in a small room off the kitchen, near one of the fireplaces. There was a time when the tub was bigger, now she could barely sit in it.

Rani had shown her how to use the soap and how to wash her hair. When Rani didn't come anymore, one of the *mans* called *gard* watched over her, though they didn't do that anymore. The *gards* never talked to her, and she'd always hurried in case they might hurt her.

She stuck her hand in the water. It was clean and warm. This was another wonder. The water looked different when she finished; yet it was always clean when she started.

Taking off her dress, she set it on the floor, away from the water so it wouldn't get wet. Sitting with her knees drawn up, she wet the soap and spread it over her body. She rubbed quickly, not bothering with her hair. There was no time. She rinsed the soap off and stepped out of the bathtub. The air always felt colder when she was wet, and she dried herself as fast as she could. She shivered, but decided not to sit by the fire as she usually did after a bath.

Slipping on her dress once more, she ran back to her room for Baybee. Baybee liked pretty dresses too. She crept down the hall to a different set of stairs than she usually used. These ones took longer to get to, and longer to get back to the big room, but this way she wouldn't be seen by the people.

She tip-toed along the upstairs hall, past the stairs she usually used, until she came to a wide place where pieces of wood sat side by side with enough space in between for her to look through.

"Shhhh," she said to Baybee. Crouching down, she moved away from the stone wall enough to see without being seen. She knelt by the first space and held Baybee tight to her chest.

Wo-mans in brightly coloured dresses moved around the big room, while *mans* held their hands, then let them go. She wished she knew what they were doing. Rani had never told her about moving this way.

One, two, three, four, five, six *mans* in a corner of the room held the things that made noise. Some had things held up to their mouths, others used their fingers and hands to make noise. She sighed, wishing she could make noise like that. She wanted to go down to the big room and move like the *wo-mans*. They all smiled and looked happy. She wanted to be happy too.

A sound came from behind her and she twisted around. A man, a *gard*, stood there. His face didn't look nice.

* * * *

Buckam kissed Lina's sweet lips, full from their recent passion. He adjusted his breeches and re-tied the laces before helping her arrange her clothing.

"Can't ya stay? Just a few more minutes? The weddin's over. His lordship's been sung off t' bed wi' his wife. What could 'appen now?" she asked.

"You know I cannot. I am on duty and already late," Buckam said, taking her by the shoulders. "And plenty could happen. There are more drunken guests out there than sober ones." He hated lying to her. The guards assigned to watching the girl drew lots on special nights and he'd lost.

Only eight guards shared that duty, all of them sworn to secrecy on threat of death. Buckam had been chosen as one of the eight because he knew how to move quietly, a talent taught him by an uncle who loved to hunt barefoot and without the benefit of dogs and flushers.

The guards had no clue to her identity or why Saulth treated her the way he did. They were to watch her through the hidden passages, then report to Saulth in the morning, no questions asked. The kitchen staff all knew of her; they kept her fed, cleaned her clothes, and filled her bath, but not a one of them would talk to him about her.

Buckam gave Lina one last kiss before opening the store room door and heading down the hall, his thoughts now on the mysterious girl. Not even five feet tall, and so thin and pale she looked ill even though in the year he'd watched her he couldn't remember her catching so much as a cold. Buckam had thought her only about nine or ten until her dress had grown tight enough to reveal the breasts of a girl much older than that.

Buckam entered another storage room, shifted a barrel on the back wall, pushed a loose stone, and stood back. A four foot high section of stone wall slid back far enough to allow him entry. He ducked and slipped inside the tunnel. A small torch and flint lay on a small shelf above his head. He lit it, then pushed on the back of the door. It closed as silently as it opened.

To the right lay the path to the girl's room. Buckam didn't need the torch to find his way, he just hated walking into spider webs. When he came to his destination, he extinguished the torch and set it on the floor. At this time of night, she'd be out of her room. A quick peek through a small peephole showed the open door, and her absence.

Buckam carried on the few steps to the kitchen. That's where she should be, eating, having her bath, or drawing pictures on the hearth. He looked out the peephole into the kitchen. This one gave him a good view of two of the fireplaces and one of the long tables. She wasn't there. He listened for sounds coming from the rest of the kitchen and where she took her bath. Silence. Hurrying back to her room, he opened the secret door and slipped through there to the kitchen, then into the bath room. Puddles of water lay on the floor with a piece of soap and a wet towel, but no girl.

It must be later than I thought. Could she have already gone to the library? Buckam took the back stairs two at a time until he reached the second floor. He found the library dark and empty. His heart thudded in his chest. *Where could she be? Where would she go?* She always went to the library; she never went anywhere else.

Buckam needed help. Now. Before anyone found out. *Caden!* His friend and the only one he could trust to say nothing to Guard-Commander Tajik. Never one to miss a good time, Caden would be at the party indulging in food, wine, and the attentions of a girl.

Buckam ran to the Lord's Hall, his heart beating faster than his footsteps. Despite the late hour, people still crowded the dance floor and gathered near the food and wine tables. Music rang off the thick beams two stories above them, dark with age and years of drifting smoke from the huge fireplace on the far wall.

Buckam kept back until he spotted Caden's sandy brown head near the food table. Caden's companion confused him. His friend stood not next to a girl, but Tarlis, one of the new recruits, one that everyone hated. No wonder Caden had no girl on his arm. If Tarlis stuck to his side, none would come close. The man annoyed the servant girls to the point where they refused to come anywhere near the guards' quarters for fear of running into him. Tarlis had arrived last month with the other new recruits. In that time, he'd managed to get himself tossed into a cell for drunkenness and brawling no less than three times. Somehow, Buckam had to get Tarlis away from Caden. He couldn't discuss the girl with him around.

Buckam made his way through the crowd, keeping an eye on Caden as he dodged and wove through the revellers. Caden took a filled plate and cup to the last step of the main staircase, Tarlis following with a slice of bread and a goblet. Judging by his stagger, the horse-faced man had already had too much to drink.

Buckam managed to catch Caden's eye before he sat down. Caden set his plate and cup on the step and waited for him.

"I need to talk to you in private," Buckam said.

Tarlis forced himself between them. "Whatever ya 'ave t' say t' Caden, ya can say t' me. We're all guards after all, ain't we?"

Buckam scowled. "This is our business, not yours."

"Yer on duty, that makes it guard business," Tarlis said, washing the last of the bread down with the wine.

"Go find a girl to bother," Buckam said, turning away from him.

Tarlis tossed his empty goblet on the stairs, his right hand already curling into a fist. Buckam groaned inside. Tarlis not only stood taller, but had more muscles than a mule, particularly between his ears. *I do not need this!*

"I think I saw that girl you wanted head upstairs, Tarlis," Caden said.

"Where?" Tarlis' head whipped around and he peered into the gloom at the top of the staircase.

"Up there." Caden shoved the man toward the stairs.

Tarlis stumbled on the first step. Caden grabbed Buckam's arm and made for the door leading to the kitchen. He pulled him around the corner and dragged him to the girl's room, pushing him up against the wall near the open door. "What are you doing? You are supposed to be watching the girl!"

"That is what I came to tell you," Buckam said, his heart still pounding. "I cannot find her!"

"Were you not at your post when she woke up?"

Buckam looked at his feet. "No."

Caden cuffed him on the shoulder. "What were you doing?"

"Lina wanted to see me before my shift. We got a little carried away, but I thought it would be all right." Buckam tried to keep the panic out of his words, and failed. If Tajik found out, he'd receive a beating at the very least. "The kitchen staff worked late and she does not come out until they leave. It is her bath night. And she has to eat. And she always plays in the ashes before she goes to the library."

"Did you check the library? Maybe she is already there."

"I did, and no, she is not," Buckam said, wiping his sweaty palms on his breeches. "Where else would she go?"

Caden paced the hall to the kitchen and back, running his fingers through his hair as he thought. He jerked to a stop and grabbed Buckam's arm. "Come on."

"Where are we going?"

"To the balcony overlooking the Lord's Hall. I bet she is watching the festivities!" Caden ran down the hall, past the main staircase and up the servant's stairs, Buckam a step behind. They turned the corner leading to the balcony in time to see Tarlis grab the front of the girl's dress and drag her from the corner she cowered in.

"Maegden futter me! I am dead!" Buckam cried, passing Caden.

"No! No hurt! No bad!" The girl's voice sounded quieter than Buckam thought it should, given the circumstances.

"Let her go!" Buckam reached out to pull Tarlis' arm away from the girl. The horse-faced guard refused to release her and Buckam only succeeded in ripping the front of her dress.

Tarlis snarled. "She's mine! Go find yer own!"

"You do not know what you are doing!"

Tarlis hauled off and punched Buckam in the face. He stumbled back, hit the wall, and lost his footing. His face, and the back of his head, exploded in pain. He put his hand to his nose. Blood streamed between his fingers.

"Tarlis, let her go," Caden said, approaching him cautiously. "You have no idea of the trouble we are all going to be in if you do not."

"Ya think yer better'n me just 'cause yer a nobleman's son!" Tarlis stuck a grubby finger in Caden's face. "Well yer not! I found 'er first. She's mine!"

Tarlis yanked, tearing off the front portion of the dress. The girl fell to the floor. She scooted farther into the corner, clutching her doll to her now naked chest. Before Caden could utter another word, Tarlis' fist flashed toward him. He dodged, but the move put him off balance and he fell backwards into the balcony railing.

Buckam struggled to get his feet under him. Tarlis growled and, fast as a mountain cat, leapt on Caden. The railing splintered, then broke.

"Caden! No!" Buckam dove, skidding across the floor, trying to catch his friend's legs.

He missed. Screams echoed as Buckam watched, heart pounding and helpless, as the two fell to the hall floor below.

Chapter Seven

Saulth sat in the chair by the fire, playing with the empty wine goblet in his hand. The subtle scent of beeswax purified the air. Petrella dropped the last of her clothing to the floor, then tried to cover herself with her hands.

"No," he said. "Let me look at you." *Your body is more pleasing than your face.*

His wife put her arms at her side, eyes fixed on a spot on the thick carpet. Her heavy breasts sagged only a little, drawing his gaze down to her narrow waist and full hips; hips that should bear a child easily. Saulth made her stand before him, her lovely bosom rising and falling with her quick breaths, until he could take no more.

He set the goblet on the table and stood, holding his arms out to either side. "Undress me."

Petrella stepped out of the puddle her clothes made. Saulth's tunic went first, followed by the white shirt. He sat again and she pulled his boots off. Once more Saulth stood, and, with shaking hands, Petrella undid the laces on his breeches. With trepidation in her eyes, she pushed them down past his hips, then had to crouch to take them off the rest of the way.

Saulth laid his hand on her shoulder, leaving it there until she had removed his linen small breeches. She gasped and turned away at the sight of his manhood. He gripped her chin, forcing her to face him.

"Kiss it."

Petrella stared, unmoving. Saulth squeezed her chin harder, not enough to bruise, but sufficient to let her know she would obey him. She bestowed a quick kiss on the foreskin and he let her go. Any more than that and it would end too soon. He'd teach her how to pleasure him another time.

"Lay down on the bed, but do not put the blankets over you." A clean sheet lay on the coverlet. Petrella had asked him why. He gave her no answer; she'd find out soon.

"I must perform a fertility ritual. Do you want a baby?" The girl nodded. "Then you must do as I say or the gods will not look favourably upon us."

Eyes wide, Petrella nodded again.

Saulth stooped in front of the fireplace and opened the six tiny jars containing the myrrh, mistletoe, acorns, and grains of barley, wheat, and oats. One by one, he emptied them into the fire, laying a pungent aroma over that of the beeswax.

"This is an offering to the gods. You must wait while I say the prayers."

Saulth faced the fire and spoke in a whisper. The words were ancient, the original language that of the scroll, a language learned from pieces of other parchments found over the years; the first from a wizened old man who had sold him the original section of the Jada-Drau scroll many years ago.

"Niafanna, Giver of life, Taker of life. Cillain, Ruler of the skies, the earth, the water. Hear me Mother and Father of all."

Most of the scroll consisted of how to perform the ritual and the prayers to these heathen gods, but Saulth had memorized them long ago and the words slid off his tongue. "Our need is great. The land cries out to you, your people cry out to you. Save us, beautiful Niafanna. Save us, Cillain, the brave and strong. Send us the Jada-Drau that all may be put to rights once more."

Six times Saulth repeated the prayer. When he finished, he stood and joined Petrella, though he only sat on the edge of the bed. Saulth ran his fingers lightly down her throat, her breasts, her stomach. She trembled at his touch.

"Your body is pleasing to me."

She gave him a hesitant smile. "Thank you, My Lord."

Saulth kissed her, tracing the path his fingers had taken, lingering longer at her breasts and the join of her thighs. Petrella shuddered and gasped again, moaned when his tongue found her hidden treasure.

He pulled back. Business first. "I must now do something that you might find distasteful, but if we are to have a child together it must be done. Understood?"

Petrella's pale blue eyes widened. She nodded. Saulth reached over to the bedside table and opened the drawer. He pulled out the bone knife and the girl's eyes widened even more.

"I am not going to hurt you," he said. "I only require a drop of your blood and mine."

Saulth pushed the tip of the knife into his thumb just hard enough to draw forth a tiny bead of blood. "See? Now give me your hand."

Petrella obeyed and he repeated the procedure on her. She only jumped a little.

"Hold your thumb up to mine."

She did as told and he touched his wound to hers. Saulth spread their mixed blood onto the blade of the knife then set it on the table.

"This part can be even more frightening, but you must remember, I will not harm you. You are to bear my child and that is important to me."

"Y...yes, My Lord."

Saulth leaned over and kissed her lips, touching and caressing her until she moaned again. "Now close your eyes. Do not open them until I tell you, no matter what you feel. Understood?" This had failed with all the others, but, why not try?

"Yes, My Lord." Petrella closed her eyes.

Saulth crouched by the bed and pulled out the wooden box Rymon had placed there. Wrapped in a linen cloth lay the piglet taken from its mother's belly before its time. The mother's blood had been washed from it and it lay in his hand, pink and pitiful. He laid the cold little body on Petrella's belly. She gasped.

"Do not open your eyes," he commanded.

His wife said nothing, though her chest heaved. In fear? Anticipation? Saulth didn't know, but the sight had a remarkable effect on him. He picked up the knife again and, whispering more prayers to Niafanna and Cillain, sliced into the piglet. Thick, red blood oozed over white skin. Petrella sucked in a breath.

"Oooh, My Lord! That tickles!" She opened her eyes, stared at the mess on her stomach, and screamed.

"Siyon's sword! You foolish woman!"

Petrella tried to jump off the bed. The piglet slid onto the floor. Saulth gritted his teeth, and backhanded Petrella, stunning her into submission.

"Do not move, or I *will* hurt you." He strode to the wardrobe and retrieved the rope and gag he'd hoped not to use.

Petrella whimpered, but stayed still. Saulth tied her wrists and ankles to the posts of the wide bed, then stuffed the gag in her mouth. Her whimpers turned to muffled sobs. Her cheek blossomed red.

Saulth retrieved the piglet from the floor, praying to any god who would listen that not too much of the blood was lost. He picked up the knife one more time and resumed cutting, whispering the prayers. When the piglet lay open from throat to crotch, and the prayers done, he spread the body wide, then smeared the blood over Petrella's breasts, belly, and goddess mound.

She tried to scream, her eyes white with fear. Saulth set the knife aside and positioned himself over her. He'd waited quite long enough to claim his wife. With the body of the piglet compressed between them, Saulth took Petrella's maidenhood.

When finished, he slid off her to lie on the bed, catching his breath. Petrella still cried and tried to twist out of her bonds. Saulth rolled off the other side of the bed and returned to the fireplace. He added more logs and waited until they caught fire.

He strode to his wife's side and removed the piglet from her belly. Reaching between her legs, he scooped up some of the result of what they'd just done. He mixed his seed and her virgin blood with that of the piglet, then wrapped the entire mess in a linen cloth. His wife's eyes followed his every move.

Back to the fireplace he went and tossed the bloody bundle on the burning logs. The acrid odour turned his stomach. He opened the window to clear the air. Petrella gave up trying to free herself. She coughed into her gag and Saulth kept an eye on her in case she vomited. When the smell faded, he closed the window. She shivered from fright, or the cold. Perhaps both.

A ewer of water and a basin sat on a table on the other side of the room. Saulth washed himself, then Petrella, kissing and licking her after he'd removed the blood. Tears ran down her face and into the pillow, and yet she trembled when he touched her. Saulth smiled and set the basin and cloth aside. He removed her gag, but not the ropes.

"Now was that so bad?"

"It was disgusting!" she cried.

"Nonetheless, it was necessary. You will get used to it."

"Used to it! You mean we have to do that again?" Petrella renewed her battle with the ropes.

"Once every night until you are with child," he said, stroking the red mark on her face. "A special child. Our child."

His caress moved to her breasts. "I am going to untie you and prove to you that I can be a good lover. Without the ritual."

Saulth covered her mouth with his, stroking and caressing until she calmed. He untied her, helped her to her feet, and sat her in the chair. She drank some wine he gave her, refusing to look at the burnt remains on the fire, while he removed the bloody sheet from the bed.

Laying her down once more, Saulth made love to Petrella, taking care not to spill his seed inside her—that had to be reserved for the ritual. When done, he held her until she fell asleep, bundled up to her neck in blankets.

Niafanna, Cillain, anyone who will listen. Will you please let this one be the Jada-Drau?

Saulth let out a long, slow breath, content in body if not in mind. As he drifted toward sleep, he heard a quiet knock. Had he dreamt it? The knock came again.

"My Lord…" Rymon's muffled voice sounded from the sitting room.

Saulth left his warm bed and threw on a robe. He opened the door to Rymon's distressed face.

"I apologize for disturbing you, My Lord. I waited as long as I dared."

"What is so important that you had to disrupt my wedding night?" Anger coloured his words, but Rymon wouldn't disturb him without a good reason.

"There has been a…an incident."

* * * *

Saulth stood at the library window looking down at the practice yard below, and the bloody mess tied to the pole in the center of it.

Tarlis had been warned more than once about his behaviour. Perhaps the manner of his death would be a lesson to those of similar mind. All the guards not on duty were forced to watch, especially that fool Buckam. His punishment would be meted out by Saulth himself, after he dealt with the third party involved in this disaster.

Sleep had avoided him for a long time and when he woke at dawn he made love to Petrella again to calm his nerves. When finished, he cautioned her against speaking of the ritual to anyone. He told her it would lose effectiveness and they would have to perform it more to compensate. With luck, she'd already be pregnant. The silly girl believed him and swore she'd keep quiet, fear once again widening her eyes. He wondered if there was any way of making them stay that wide, it improved her looks.

Tarlis' screams rang off the castle walls, then muffled when a soldier sewed the doomed guard's own genitals into his mouth. Word travelled quickly of his attempt at rape, turning most of the guard against him. Uncaring hands removed the man from the pole and laid him in a wagon. Tarlis writhed on the straw, the skin gone from his back—just one of the things Saulth had ordered done to him. The idiot guard would be hoisted above the city's north gate, a warning to all. With the amount of blood lost, he wouldn't live to see the sun set.

The wagon disappeared through the rear gate and Saulth turned away from the window. Rymon sat in his usual place by the fire, his gaunt face whiter than the sheet that had covered the bed during the ritual.

"I am going to have breakfast with Petrella." Saulth had instructed his wife to stay in their rooms on the other side of the castle. She'd been upset enough with the ritual. He didn't want her watching Tarlis' punishment. "I want Buckam and a whip brought to the storeroom. He can witness another result of his dereliction."

Rymon nodded, but didn't move.

Saulth snorted in disgust and left the room, confident his orders would be carried out.

* * * *

Just outside the girl's door, Rymon awaited Saulth's arrival, leaning heavily on his cane. Buckam stood in shackles beside him, his face as pale as Rymon imagined his own to be. The soldier's pallor made the purple and black of his broken nose stand out like coal in a snowdrift. The two guards accompanying him looked little better.

Rymon's gut churned, not only at what Saulth had done to Tarlis, but what he planned for the girl. A beating, for certain, but he'd never whipped her before. He'd always used a wide leather belt that didn't break the skin. Rymon prayed to Talueth and Maegden both that Saulth didn't plan on whipping her to death.

The kitchen staff went about their business, their normal bustle and chatter subdued. Furtive glances toward the storeroom told him they were just as afraid. Clicking boot heels announced Saulth's arrival. Rymon closed his eyes a moment, praying once more for divine intervention.

Saulth waved his hand in the direction of the door. "Open it."

One of the guards slid back the bolt. The light from the hallway spilled into the room, illuminating a small form huddled under the blankets on the floor. Rymon shook his head. Innocence would let a child sleep anywhere, anytime. Though close to sixteen, she remained a child in almost every way, forbidden access to the knowledge she needed to understand the world around her.

"Bring him." Saulth entered first, followed by the guards leading Buckam. He tossed one of them a length of rope. "Tie her wrists then slip the rope over that sausage hook."

The guard pulled the girl from her bed. Her eyes flew open and she blinked in the light. It took her a moment to realize what Saulth intended. By that time, her wrists were bound.

"No! No hurt! No hurt! *Puh-leece!*" she cried, her voice shrill with fright.

Rymon gritted his teeth against the pitiful plea. The guard pulled up on the rope, lifting it over the curved metal jutting from the ceiling. She hung, naked, her feet well off the ground, twisting her wrists in the rope, desperate to escape.

"Pull her hair off her back," Saulth said.

The guard did as commanded, then stepped back.

"You have been told not go wandering." Saulth cracked the short whip against the wall, the echo a sick harbinger of what was to come.

She kicked her feet and squirmed harder. "No hurt! No bad! No hurt!"

"I have lost two guards because of you." The whip cracked. A red streak appeared on her back, stark against the white skin. Saulth struck again, leaving a matching line across her buttocks.

The poor waif sucked in air and screamed. Heart wrenching. Soul ripping. Rymon moved closer to the wall, needing something to lean against. He stepped on a soft object tangled in her blankets.

"I have to beat one of my guards because of you and your dammed female curiosity!"

Crack! Another line emerged on her back, this one higher up. Her screams intensified.

Rymon looked down at what he'd stepped on. A doll. Button eyes hung from worn threads, the stitched-on smile a mockery in light of the beating its owner suffered.

Three more times the whip cracked. Blood dripped down her back, her buttocks, her legs. She stopped begging. Rymon picked up the doll, clutching it as if it would save him from this horror. The doll's mismatched eyes stared at him. *Stop this! You can stop this!* Rymon could swear the smile widened.

The girl cried now, tears running in rivers down a delicate face twisted in pain. She rarely cried when Saulth beat her, but this proved too much for the brave child. She kicked and squirmed until the rope surrounding her wrists turned red, slick with her blood.

Ten times Saulth struck her. Ten bleeding lines marred her back and buttocks. He raised his arm for another swing. Buckam threw up, his vomit running down his chin and hitting his chest before splashing to the floor. The sharp, bitter smell of bile mingled with that of the girl's blood.

Rymon gagged, almost losing what little he had in his stomach. "Please! My Lord! You will kill her!"

"Shut up, Rymon! Or I will beat you as well!" Madness glinted in eyes as dark as his heart. "She is not the one!" Saulth struck again and again. "She does not fight back!"

Fifteen lines crossed and crisscrossed. One strike crept around to the front, biting into her right breast. She screamed loud and long when that one hit. Eighteen. The girl's bladder let go, adding the pungent scent of urine to the nauseating brew.

"If she was the one, Rymon, would she put up with this? No!" Saulth split her skin again.

She hung limp, not reacting to the blow.

Rymon fell to his knees. "Please! I beg of you! For mercy! For pity!"

Saulth raised his arm for one more swing...and stopped. Whether by choice, by divinity, or exhaustion, Rymon couldn't tell.

"Bah!" Saulth tossed the whip to the floor. His anger deflated; the madness receded.

Not only Rymon sighed in relief. Buckam sobbed.

"You are weak. All of you," Saulth said, his voice as cold as death. "Tie him to the post and bring the whip. He is next." Bredun's lord strode out of the room, the sharp click of his boots cracking like the whip on the girl's back.

The guards dragged Buckam through the door, he couldn't stand on his own. Neither could Rymon; he stayed on his knees, staring at the blood, the damaged body dangling from the ceiling. Did she still live? He couldn't find the strength to check for himself.

"Yer…Yer Excellency?" A man's voice came from the kitchen.

"You may enter. Please. Does she still breathe?"

A middle aged man shuffled in; the chief cook, Lacus. He stepped around the vomit and reached his hand up to the girl's throat.

"She lives, Yer Excellency. Her heartbeat is strong, though Talueth only knows why." He motioned to someone standing in the doorway.

Another man came in, a younger one; Rymon's eyes blurred at Lacus' news and he couldn't see who. They lifted the girl off the hook and laid her, stomach down, on the blankets. Other hands helped Rymon to his feet.

The women took over. Clean cloths and basins of warm water were brought, both for the girl and to clean the floor. Lacus and the other man helped Rymon to a chair in the kitchen. He still held the doll. Someone pressed a cup into his empty hand.

"Some wine, Yer Excellency. Ya look like ya need it," Lacus said.

"Thank you." Rymon took a sip.

The cracking of a whip and a man's cry came through the open kitchen door. Rymon counted. Ten lashes for Buckam. Bad enough, but only ten? Nineteen for the girl and Saulth had wanted to deliver more. He emptied his cup; Lacus refilled it. The women finished their task and brought the basins of bloody water through the kitchen to dispose of outside.

"How is she?" Rymon asked, pulling himself together.

"She's tough, that one, for all that ya could spit thru 'er," Lacus said.

"Poor little thing." One of the women shook her head. "She deserves none o' it."

"It is Lord Saulth's decree and not up to us to question the why of it." It took a moment for him to realize he'd said those words.

Rymon looked at the doll in his hand, at the accusing eyes, the fixed smile. He'd become no more than this doll, a puppet. Helping Saulth bring the prophecy to fruition was his life's work. *For what?* To see his country ravaged by nature gone mad. To watch his lord, the man he'd once honoured and respected, become just as insane.

Rymon passed the doll to one of the women. "Fix her eyes. I have done what I can."

Chapter Eight

Fields of young grain rolled over the gentle swell of Bredun's hills, blending with those containing beans and hemp, broken only by fenced rows of grape vines and the odd copse of trees. It still looked too flat. Cenith missed the variegated peaks and lush valleys of home, the drumming of a ruffled grouse calling for a mate, aspen groves heady with the scent of wild roses.

The soldiers rode single file, Keev in the lead carrying the banner of Dunvalos Reach; three purple-blue mountains, capped in white, on a sky blue background. Sunlight glinted off highlights in the soldier's sandy brown hair. Cenith and Daric travelled side by side, just behind him.

The past ten days had vanished in a blur. Besides solidifying trade deals with the other principalities, Cenith had taken Saulth's patronizing advice and scoured the shops for a wedding outfit. A black short sleeved tunic made of fine velvet and matching light wool trousers rode in his saddle bag. Silver trim adorned the tunic, which would be worn over a dove grey silk shirt. This year's fashion tended toward frills and lace for men. He passed on those.

Daric questioned his choice of colour, but Cenith countered that he felt like he was attending his own funeral, not his wedding. He'd also chosen a respectable gift for the girl; he couldn't blame her that her father had been spawned by a dung beetle and a weasel crossed with a badger. A necklace of star sapphires trimmed with diamond chips lay in the same bag with the new outfit. Artisans in Dunvalos Reach could have made it for less money than he paid, but he needed it now.

They crested a low ridge. Valda, capital of Bredun, sprawled before them. Cenith had seen glimpses of it most of the day as the green hills rose and fell. Now it lay in full view. The early afternoon sun highlighted windows in Saulth's castle, seated on a rise in the center of the city. Gold and green banners, lining city walls and adorning castle towers, pointed the direction the wind blew. People, carts, and carriages flowed into and out of the north gate like autumn leaves on a lazy stream.

The Asha River flowed like sludge in the background, swollen with winter runoff from Cenith's mountains. Logs, branches, and other flotsam, some suspiciously resembling bloated animal bodies, hurried along with the current. Flooded buildings near the river and the remains of a bridge showed just how high the water had risen. The entire city would be waist deep in water if it hadn't been built on a series of low, escalating hills.

The closer they rode to Valda, the heavier the crowd became. More people entered than left, most shabby peasants carrying their belongings in sacks or wrapped in blankets; refugees from the flooding and tornadoes. At Daric's signal, the twelve soldiers split into two groups, half rode in front of Cenith and Daric, half behind.

"I wonder if Saulth has calmed down yet," Cenith said.

Daric chuckled. "For all his pretence at outward calm and reserve, he can put a wet desert cat to shame."

Cenith had passed Saulth's quarters after the Lord of Bredun had left. The door stood open while servants carried out a broken chair and table. Others cleaned up glass from the smashed garden door. He couldn't help but feel at least partially responsible and had offered to pay for the damage. Lorcan waved off the idea. Apparently it wasn't the first time.

Something red, black, and skin-coloured hung above the gate, jerking Cenith out of his thoughts. He squinted into the sun. The black portion moved. His gut lurched. "Tell me that isn't what I think it is."

Daric's eyes shifted from scanning the crowd to where Cenith pointed. A low rumble escaped his throat. "It is, or was, a man."

They rode closer. A young boy threw a stone at the body and the squabbling crows scattered. Cenith's skin turned cold. He shivered. Reining in his horse brought the others to a halt. "Where are his tarse and nuggets?"

A nauseating, red-brown smear, coated in flies, was all that remained between the dead man's legs. With him spread eagled, his knees bent, and feet nailed to the wall, one couldn't help but see the damage. Ropes held up his arms, causing his head to hang forward, staring down with empty eye sockets at those entering and exiting the city. The crows settled again, resuming their perches on the dead man's arms, head, and knees.

"Looks like they're sewed into his mouth," Daric said. "If I'm not mistaken, his back has been flayed and his eyelids cut off. The crows would have taken his eyes first. He probably wasn't dead yet when that happened, otherwise there wouldn't have been so much blood. You can see where the damage caused by the birds differs from that of the knife."

How could Daric sound so calm? Cenith's stomach turned over. The butterflies that had plagued him in Edara hid their cowardly heads. Their fluttering would have been a relief over the current turmoil afflicting his gut.

"What could he have done to deserve this?" Cenith couldn't even imagine what would make Saulth order this done to any man. *And I'm about to enter the lair of this madman? I must be mad myself.*

"Word is, sorr, 'e tried t' rape a kitchen drudge."

The voice drew Cenith's gaze down to his left knee and the hunchbacked old man next to it. His yellow-white hair stuck up like dandelion fluff from a scalp sprinkled with brown blotches. The fellow had to twist his head at an odd angle to look up at him. Daric shifted his bay closer, then leaned down, giving him a look that made it plain that if the man hurt Cenith, Daric would hurt him ten times worse.

The man backed away. "Don't mean no 'arm, sorr. 'Twas just that th' young man asked a question."

"I don't abide with rape, but isn't that a little drastic?" Cenith asked.

The man scratched his crotch with fingers that looked more like the feet on the crows fighting over the body. Cenith hesitated to think what sort of creatures shared the man's dirty cotton pants or his baggy brown tunic. Fortunately, the wind blew from the right.

"His Lordship didn't think so. He was one 'o 'is guards too."

"Here! Get away, you!" One of the gate guards scurried toward them, the point of his short sword directed at the old man. The raggedy fellow held up his hands and shuffled backwards.

"Don't mean no 'arm. Was just talkin'!" He hobbled away, blending into a group of peasants leaving the city.

"Sorry, m'lord," the guard said. He wore the same green and gold uniform as the guards Saulth had brought to Edara; with the addition of a green felt cap. "The floods are bringin' all kinds o' riff-raff t' th' city."

"Is it true that this man was killed for trying to rape a kitchen drudge?" A serious crime, but Cenith still had trouble believing the man deserved this.

"Hard to say, m'lord. I can't see that severe a punishment over a mere drudge. Some are sayin' it must've been his Lordship's daughter who was attacked t' deserve that, but I can't say really. The guards at th' castle ain't talkin'."

If it was Iridia, Cenith could understand the punishment, though he hardly condoned it. Still, he kept his eyes on the Bredun soldier and not the mess hanging on the wall.

The guard sheathed his sword. "Yer banner declares ya of Dunvalos Reach. Yer Lord Cenith?"

"I am."

"Yer expected at th' castle, m'lord. Follow this street, takin' no turns. It leads straight t' Castle Hill." Four streets led away from the gate. The guard pointed to the correct one.

"Thank you."

"Yer welcome, m'lord." The guard tipped his cap and returned to his post.

Daric led the way, instructing their soldiers to surround Cenith. People sat on the sidewalks, their possessions clutched in their arms; thin, dirty children slumped beside them. Eyes empty of hope watched them pass, while merchants with more food than they could sell in a day clamoured for Cenith's attention.

Why doesn't Saulth help these people? Bredun had suffered severe flooding on both its north and south borders, as well as devastating tornadoes everywhere, but it remained a rich principality. No town in Dunvalos Reach let its people go homeless or hungry. Mountain towns were smaller, less populated, but Cenith still couldn't see an excuse for this.

The narrow road twisted like a serpent, up and down low hills, passing old, rundown shops and houses, then those of better quality. By the time they reached the base of Castle Hill, the street had widened and the continuous rows of buildings had broken up into individual residences with fences, gates, and gardens. Cenith felt like he climbed out of a snake pit into the sunshine, except the worst viper still lay before him.

Four guards stood at attention outside the closed castle gates. The thick, iron banded double doors looked like they'd stop an army. So did the guards. All wore green and gold tabards over heavy armour. Sword hilts stuck out of scabbards belted at their sides and each carried a wicked looking halberd. The guards at the city gates weren't armed and armoured like this.

Soldiers these days only wore full plate on the front lines with Tai-Keth, though Cenith's border guard with the West Downs kept theirs at the ready, just in case some of the clans decided on a different option than trading.

Daric stepped his horse close to one of the guards. "Lord Cenith to see Lord Saulth."

"Yes, Your Excellency." He bowed to Cenith, stepped to a hole in the wall near his post, and reached inside.

It took a second or two for Cenith to realize the guard spoke to Daric. His councillor preferred his old honorific of 'sir' to the one now entitled him.

A bell sounded behind the gates. A few moments later, another guard peered over the battlement above them.

"Lord Cenith has arrived!" the first guard called.

The man above waved and disappeared. Shortly after, a metallic rattle heralded extensive groaning of metal on metal. A series of thumps followed and one of the heavy wooden doors creaked open.

Another soldier appeared, attired to match the ones outside the door. "This way. Lord Saulth is expecting you."

He stepped back, allowing Cenith and his party to enter, two by two. When the last of his men had cleared the gate, the guards closed it and lowered the portcullis. More soldiers decorated the ramparts at regular, and frequent, intervals along the curtain wall.

Across a spacious outer ward stood the Keep of Bredun, an impressive stone structure four stories high. It was clearly built for defence, with little adornment added over the centuries. The entire castle looked like it could withstand almost anything. At first sight, the thought of walking into that fortress made Cenith a little nervous, though he knew even Saulth wouldn't dare imprison them for fear of reprisal from the other lords. Even so, why would Saulth lock himself inside? They weren't at war and locked gates wouldn't stop a tornado.

"Paranoid?"

"Apparently," Daric said. "From a long line of paranoids. Though I must admit your own keep is built to withstand a long, concerted attack."

Cenith's home in Tiras seemed very far away. "From what I've read, the original lords trusted each other about as much as I trust Saulth." Which was why the kingdom had been split in the first place, to put an end to the squabbling.

Keev led the way to the steps up to the door, the banner playing in the wind. More of Saulth's guards stood at attention on either side. Daric ordered the dismount, instructing four of the men to stay with the horses. The rest accompanied him and Cenith through two more thick doors.

A stone staircase, wide enough for four men to walk abreast, commanded the right side of the room. Logs crackled in a fireplace occupying a large portion of the opposite wall. High, coloured glass windows let in the afternoon sun, lighting up ivory painted walls and broad oak ceiling beams darkened by years of smoke. Tables and chairs of tasteful design lined the remaining wall space. Subtle opulence…a relief compared to Maegden's Hall.

Close to the far end of the room, a raised dais, fronted by a semi-circular carpet, held a large, intricately carved, oak chair with bright gold padding on the back, arms, and seat. Saulth reclined there, looking like the king he wanted to be. A dozen guards protected the inside of the hall; two flanking the door, eight along the walls, and one on either side of the dais. At least these weren't in full armour, though their halberds appeared just as deadly as those outside.

Cenith and his men walked toward the dais, the thud of their boots on the oak floor echoing in the rafters. He stopped at the edge of the finely woven green and gold carpet.

Rymon, looking older than Cenith remembered, waited at Saulth's left elbow, Meric to his right. Beside Meric stood a girl of average height, her dark hair the exact shade as Saulth's and Meric's. She looked down at him over Saulth's hawk nose. Iridia. If she'd been the victim of the attack, she didn't appear affected by the experience.

Cenith's heart beat faster, not because the girl attracted him, but because his worst fear had come true. She looked too much like her father. A further search showed Iridia to be the only female in the Hall, no sign of the woman Saulth had married two days earlier. Cenith returned his gaze to his wife-to-be. She flashed him a predatory smile. His mouth dried up. Any words that might have come out stuck in his throat.

Saulth motioned to another guard nearby and spoke to him behind his hand. Rymon's eyes widened and he leaned down. A gesture from Saulth cut off whatever the councillor had wanted to say. The guard passed his weapon to another, and disappeared through a doorway near the back of the staircase.

Cenith watched him go. *What is Saulth up to now?*

* * * *

She lay on her bed, staring at her open door. The pain in her back and bottom had lessened, but she didn't move for fear of making it worse. She only wanted to watch the pretty *wo-mans* and listen to the *mans* make noise. She didn't touch anything. Why did *he* hurt her so bad this time? Was it because of that man? The one who wanted to hurt her? Two more mans came and tried to stop him. That had never happened before.

Her pretty dress came apart. Two of the *mans* tried to hurt each other and then disappeared. Another *gard* with red on his face dragged her back to her room and did something so the door wouldn't open. She had no choice but to sit in the dark with Baybee, repeating the events in her head until she fell asleep. Then *he* had come. *Him*, his *gards*, and the man who walked funny. *He* had hurt her more than *he* ever had before. A darkness blocked the light and she tried to turn her head to see better. The hurts on her back and shoulders pulled and she cried out.

"Don't move, child." It was a *wo-man's* voice. It reminded her of Rani.

The *wo-man* crouched down beside her and held a candle close to her back. She sucked in a breath. "Lacus! C'mere! Ya need t' see this!"

Another darkness showed at the door and a man came in.

"Look at her back," the *wo-man* said.

"Talueth's mercy!"

Still another shadow darkened the door. "What are you doing here? Get out! His lordship wants her."

She recognized that voice. The *gard* who usually came with *him* and held her while *he* hurt her. "No hurt," she whimpered. Her throat was so dry. "Puh...puh-leece."

Rani told her she should always say *puh-leece* when she wanted something. The chances were better she'd get it. It never worked with *him* or *his* guards. She always tried though, just in case. It didn't work this time either. The *gard* yanked her to her feet, sending more pain across her back and bottom, bringing tears to her eyes.

"Please, sir! At least let me put a dress on her."

The *wo-man* helped her into her other dress, the big one, not the one with the pretty cloth on it. That one was broken. When the *wo-man* lifted her arms to put them in the dress, her hurts burned. She couldn't keep the tears from coming. The hurt was too much.

The *gard* grabbed her arm again, hurting her more. Everything blurred. She stumbled after him, trying to keep up. Everywhere hurt, hurt, hurt! Her scream echoed in the hall. She cried and pleaded. He paid no attention.

What had she done? She'd stayed in her room; she'd not gone anywhere, not been bad. Why did he hurt her? "No! No bad! No bad! No hurt! *Puh-leece*!"

* * * *

Cenith stood several feet from the dais, Daric beside him. His councillor found the words he couldn't.

"Lord Cenith is here to keep his end of the agreement. Do you keep yours?"

Saulth sat quiet a moment, his dark eyes drilling into Daric's. The Calleni never flinched, met him gaze for gaze. The Lord of Bredun turned his stare to Cenith, who stood straighter and forced himself to appear relaxed, determined not to back down one inch. Saulth sneered, then nodded once.

"When is the wedding to take place?" Daric asked. "A day or two would give us sufficient time to negotiate the bride price."

Saulth made no effort to respond. Despite his reservations about Iridia, Cenith hoped everything could be done and over with soon. He didn't care what she brought with her into the marriage. If he had to spend any length of time in this castle, he'd have no nerves left.

A girl's cries split the tense silence. Cenith jumped, his eyes darting first to the door the guard had gone through then back to the dais. Saulth sat forward, anticipation lending a darker gleam to his eye.

The soldier appeared a moment later, dragging a young girl by the arm, a child by the look of her. Jet black, tousled hair surrounded a too pale face before spilling to her waist, half covering an old, stained, linen dress that was too big for her. She kicked and screamed, pulling on the guard's fingers, trying to dig her bare feet into the wood floor, desperate to escape his grip.

"No! No bad! No bad!" the girl cried, her eyes wet with fear. "No hurt! *Puh-leece*!"

Why does she talk like that? Cenith glanced at Daric. His narrowed eyes and rigid stance displayed what he thought of the girl's treatment. Daric's fingers played with the hilt of the dagger at his belt. His soldiers reached for their weapons. Cenith set a restraining hand on Daric's arm and signalled caution to the men.

Another man hurried out the same door, dressed in the multicoloured robes of a priest of the eight deities. The guard threw the girl at Cenith's feet. She shrank against his right leg then jerked away.

The soldier pointed a gloved finger at her. "Don't move!" An older man than most of the guards Cenith had seen, under the Bredun patch on his shoulder he wore four gold wheat sheaf pins signifying him as Saulth's guard-commander. His seamed and pockmarked face reminded Cenith of the cracked mud of a dried up stream. The man turned his back on Cenith and the girl, resuming his position near Saulth.

"What's going on?" Cenith demanded.

Saulth smiled ice. "You asked when the wedding is to take place? It is now. Brother Dayfid, if you please."

The priest scurried toward Cenith, his fear as palpable as the girl's. He raised his arms in shaky benediction.

Cenith removed his hand from Daric's arm, fighting the urge to draw his sword. "What are you doing? This isn't your daughter!" He could see no likeness to Saulth in her face.

Iridia's, Rymon's, and Meric's expressions mirrored the shock running through Cenith.

Saulth glanced at his councillor. "Rymon? Is she of my blood?"

Rymon's mouth opened and closed twice before any words came out. "She…she is Saulth's daughter, born of his blood. I witnessed the birth."

"*What*?" Iridia's shrill voice pierced the air. "That clay-brained mammet is my *sister*?"

One look from Saulth and her mouth snapped shut. Meric stood slack-jawed, too stunned to speak. The priest hadn't moved, his arms still raised, looking to his lord for direction.

"Get on with it, Dayfid," Saulth said.

"This was not the agreement." Daric's voice rumbled through the hall. He no longer had his hand on his dagger, it now rested on the hilt of the sword slung over his back. "You dare to marry off your lack-wit daughter to my lord?"

Saulth's guard-commander took a step forward and pointed his halberd at Daric. The other guards followed suit. The rattle of weapons echoed through the rafters. A quiet sob came from near Cenith's feet. He glanced at the girl huddled on the floor, her eyes darting from him to Daric, to the guards, to Saulth. She blinked and squinted, as if the light were too bright.

"Relax, Tajik." Saulth waved the guard-commander back and all the soldiers lifted their halberds. "He is only showing off. He would not be so foolish as to attack us here."

Cenith wasn't so sure. He hadn't seen Daric in battle, but he'd heard his father's stories. "I was to marry Iridia. What are you trying to pull? This girl is no more than a child!"

"My Lord! You can't! Please!" Rymon cried.

"Shut up! Tajik, show Lord Cenith that she is of age."

A few brief strides brought the guard-commander to the girl. He reached down and grabbed the front of her dress. One good pull tore the shoddy material to her waist. She was definitely of an age to marry.

The girl must have frozen with fear; she made no attempt to cover herself. A red line stood out against the white skin of her right breast. It cut across her nipple and disappeared into the remains of her bodice. Before Cenith could get a look at what it might be, Saulth spoke again.

"She will be sixteen this Eighth Month."

Cenith scowled. Saulth could have just said that in the first place, instead of embarrassing the poor girl.

"The marriage document stated you are to marry my daughter. It did not say which one." A sly smile spread across Saulth's face like a cave viper uncoiling to strike.

"We thought you only had one," Daric growled.

Saulth ignored him. "All that is required is the gods' blessing to make it legal." He sat back and waved a lazy hand at the priest. "Brother Dayfid, if you please. I'm sure Lord Cenith would like to leave and find someplace to enjoy his bride."

The laughter of the guards did nothing to ease the situation.

The priest's raised arms shook. "M…Maegden, Father of us all…"

"Skip that part!" Saulth bellowed. "Just the blessing."

Brother Dayfid, his voice trembling more than his arms, intoned the favours of the gods. Cenith's hands curled involuntarily into fists and he forced them open. He'd just become used to the idea of marrying Iridia, and now this? It had to be a nightmare.

Daric's hand remained on the hilt of his sword. Cenith shook his head and he lowered it, though it hovered near the dagger.

"Just one good throw…" Daric said, his voice too low for anyone else to hear.

Cenith shook his head again. The priest finished his listing of the gods' blessings. Saulth waved him away and he almost ran to the rear door without a backward glance.

"The wedding is over. Take your bride and leave. I care not where you celebrate." Saulth signalled his soldiers, who once again pointed their weapons at Cenith's party.

Given no other choice, Cenith reached for the girl's hand. She shrank away from him. The guards' laughter increased. Blue eyes too large for her thin face, blinked continuously.

Daric moved around behind her and scooped her into his arms. She kicked, squirmed, and hit, but her feeble efforts had no effect on the Calleni.

"No hurt! No bad! No hurt!" Her cries degenerated into sobs. *"Hurt! Hurt!"*

"I'm not going to hurt you. Calm down!" Daric's words only made the girl struggle harder.

Cenith signalled his men and led them out of the Hall. Laughter, and one shrill voice, followed them out.

"He was supposed to be mine!"

Chapter Nine

Cenith led his men back to the city gates, travelling as fast as he dared down the crowded street. The clatter of hoof beats on cobblestones pounded along with the suppressed anger in his heart, merging with the calls of merchants and the rattle of cart wheels.

Once outside the city, he gave in to that anger and urged his horse into a full gallop. He rode hard for a few minutes, then remembered Daric had the girl and slowed to a canter. An hour later Daric passed him and signalled to stop. The Calleni led them into a nearby copse of trees, and a small clearing nestled within.

Cenith almost fell off his horse. "That dung-born, hell-hated, varlet! Goat-loving son of a succubus!" He ran out of pacing room and had to turn around. "Pox-ridden, half-faced, lying, cheating, carrion-eating pole cat! May Talueth shrivel his tarse next time he wants to futter his wife!"

"Have you finished?" Daric's droll tone cut Cenith's tirade like a Calleni wrist dagger through silk.

Cenith took a deep breath and scrubbed his hair. "He'd planned this right from the start. No wonder he didn't look upset at the council meeting."

"It does appear that way." Daric glanced over his shoulder where the soldiers sat their horses. "Jolin, you and Varth find some wood. Ead, take my blankets. Lay one on the ground near the fire pit." Still holding the now quiet girl, he slid out of the saddle, graceful as a mountain cat.

Appear that way? What had Cenith missed?

Daric laid the girl on the blanket, on her stomach, and covered her with another. She must have passed out. "As soon as there's enough wood, I want a fire started," he said to Ead. "Send someone to find water. If I remember correctly, there's a stream not far to the west."

"Yes, sir."

Daric's voice maintained his usual calm, but the look on his face put prairie storm clouds to shame. "If Shival doesn't take that blackguard's soul soon, I'll do it for her." He crouched by the girl's side, looking as if he intended to remain there. "Regardless of what you choose to do with her, My Lord, she's not going back to that snake pit."

Cenith frowned and joined him. What he chose to do? He had a choice somewhere? Daric picked up a matted lock of hair and rubbed it between his fingers. Reddish brown flakes coated them.

"Dried blood?" Cenith asked.

Daric nodded. "It's all through her hair, particularly from the shoulders down. I noticed it while we were riding. Too much for the one cut on her breast. There's also these." He held up one of the girl's wrists. Partially healed red wounds encircled it, stark against her pale skin.

The Calleni pulled the blanket down to the girl's waist. Fresh red streaks stained the pale blue linen covering her back. Daric slid his dagger from its sheath and cut through the shoulders and sides of the ruined dress. Once he'd replaced his dagger, he gently peeled the material back. Cenith sucked in a breath.

Long swollen wounds, blending one into another, covered her back. The cuts had begun to scab over, though some of the deeper ones had reopened. Purple and black bruises marred what the whip hadn't.

"What I said doesn't even come close to what that evil bastard truly is." White hot fury burned Cenith's blood, darkened his vision. "How could *anyone* do that to their own daughter!"

"This is one of those rare moments I wish my people believed in a hell. One so deep, dark, and horrific, souls like Saulth's would never find their way out." For Daric to utter those words, he had to be at least as angry as Cenith. Probably more.

"I pray with all my heart that Shival has reserved a special place in Char for that bastard." Cenith forced his fists open.

Daric touched a calloused finger to one of the wounds. "These cuts are at least three days old, possibly four."

"Is there anything we can do?"

Daric nodded. "Whoever tended her has done a good job. I see no sign of infection."

The soldiers returned with the wood and in a short time Ead had warm water for Daric. He washed the blood from the girl's back before applying a salve from his field kit. They had to remove the dress completely to take care of the wounds on her buttocks, thighs, and breast.

Daric then treated her wrists. The men kept their backs turned, giving her a shred of privacy.

Ead, the smallest of the soldiers, offered one of his shirts. Cenith helped Daric put it on her. Through it all, the girl never woke, never made a sound.

The clearing had been used as a campsite in the past. A ring of rocks enclosed a small hole for the fire. Two grey, weather-beaten logs provided seating. Cenith sat on one, resting his head in his hands. The girl slept two feet away, her face toward the fire. The girl. His wife.
I wonder what her name is?

Daric's deep voice murmured in the background. He'd suggested spending the night here to allow the girl time to recover from whatever kept her from waking up. He gave orders to the men, but it wasn't until he told two of the soldiers to re-saddle his horse that Cenith decided he should pay attention. He looked up just as Daric swung himself into Nightwind's seat. The Calleni had removed his leather jerkin and reversed the saddle blanket. No sign of which principality he owed allegiance showed anywhere on him or his horse.

"Going somewhere?"

Daric brought the big bay stallion closer. "There's more to this than the eye can see."

"You said something like that earlier." It appeared as if Saulth had planned this all along. Daric gave the impression he didn't think so. Why?

Cenith thought back to the times he'd met with Saulth, in the meeting, his apartment, and the castle. He played the whole ugly scene over in his mind. Iridia looking down her nose at him....the shocked look on her face when Saulth made his announcement. *'He was supposed to be mine!'*

Cenith jumped to his feet, careful not to step on the girl. "Saulth wouldn't have told Iridia about the wedding if he'd planned it!"
Daric nodded.

"He only decided to do this recently." Cenith's heart sank. "You don't suppose he beat the girl because of me? As a warning? Or revenge?"

Daric leaned down. "No. This is not your sin. It's Saulth's. The look on Rymon's face said Saulth hadn't discussed this with him. It was a quick, ill-thought decision. More important, Rymon begged him not to do it." He sat up. "As I said, there's more here than is apparent."

"What are you going to do?"

"Go back to Valda and see if I can find someone willing to talk. He can't have kept the girl completely secret. Perhaps a little gold will loosen some tongues."

Cenith reached into a pocket sewn on the inside of his armoured jerkin. He tossed a small pouch to Daric. "Here's more. Use what you need."

"Thank you."

Cenith stepped back and Daric walked his stallion out of the meadow. A few moments later, hoof beats drummed into the distance.

* * * *

Daric tied his purchases to the back of the saddle. He'd caught the shopkeeper just as he closed his doors. A few coins of the right colour persuaded him to stay open longer. The little man was generous with more than his time; Daric now knew the name and location of the tavern that would best suit his needs.

Half an hour later, he stood outside the Waddling Duck, an establishment frequented by those who worked in the castle. The inn sat in a quiet district, about halfway between the castle and where the river docks lay under a foot of water.

Friendly light escaped the open door, accompanied by the laughter and chatter of the patrons. Someone played a quiet tune on a lute. Daric took a deep breath and stepped inside. All conversation stopped. The musician hit a sour note that faded painfully into the sudden silence.

Daric scanned the room before heading to an empty table in the far right corner. Surrounded on three sides by walls and the fireplace, it suited him just fine. Taking the bench against the wall, he removed his great sword and set it within easy reach. He signalled to the barmaid. Every eye watched him order an ale and a plate of food.

He'd expected the scrutiny. The inn looked similar to many Daric had seen before. He could be in Ys, Edara, Bel-Shea in the neighbouring country of Cambrel, anywhere in Callenia or Syrth. The climate and decor changed, the faces changed, but the atmosphere didn't. Especially after he'd walked in.

Daric's food arrived accompanied by a pretty smile from the young barmaid. Two men sat at a table nearby. Neither had spoken to the other since he'd sat down, just sipped their beer and eyed him sideways. Daric nodded to one, a portly fellow with a smattering of brown-grey hair and a nose that suggested he spent far too much time in the Waddling Duck. "Evening, friend."

"Evenin'," the man said, making a show of looking him over. Both he and his companion wore simple homespun tunics, shirts, and trousers…like everyone else in the room. "Stayin' long?"

"Long enough to sample the ale and food, and perhaps engage in some pleasant conversation." Daric kept his voice calm and quiet.

"You Calleni?" Red-Nose's companion asked, a tall man with more hair than his friend, though very little of the original dark brown showed through the grey.

"I'm surprised you guessed that. Not many of my people come to Ardael. You must be a well travelled man." Everyone in the tavern, perhaps twenty in all, hunched over their drinks and watched the exchange…while pretending not to.

The tall man puffed out his chest at the compliment. "I've been t' Cambrel, there's more o' yer people there. Ya must 'ave been 'ere for a while. Don't 'ave much of an accent."

"Twenty-two years." *Have that many years really passed?* It seemed only yesterday he'd saved Ifan's life and became his man. Only this morning since he'd fallen in love with Elessa. And when did Kian grow up?

Red-Nose sat back from his ale, a haughty look on his doughy face. "Exile? Or choice?"

"Choice."

"Woman or work?"

Daric smiled, a small one meant to reassure. "Both."

Red-Nose slapped the table and guffawed, almost spilling his drink. "I knew it! Only a woman could keep a wanderin' Calleni tied t' one place for twenty-two years."

The tension in the room eased and the patrons resumed their drinking and conversations. The lute player continued his tunes, keeping the music quiet and light. Red-Nose seemed an important man here. Daric had seen it before. If he accepted a stranger, the rest would as well. Daric sipped his ale and leaned back, almost closing his eyes. Snippets of conversation wafted on a cool evening breeze blowing in occasionally from the open door. "People are starvin'…" "Why doesn't his lordship…" "Home's gone, land's too wet t' grow anythin'…" "Saulth's gotta 'elp 'em…"

Folks aren't too happy around here. I wonder why Saulth isn't doing something?

Daric's food appeared, an entire roast chicken stuffed with vegetables, nuts, and herbs. Warm bread and a pot of butter were brought a moment later. He dug into his meal with relish; breakfast was too long ago.

Red-Nose let him eat half his meal. "Ya said pleasant conversation. How pleasant?"

Daric wiped his fingers on the small towel provided for that purpose. He dug into a pocket, pulled out several coins, two of them gold, and laid them quietly on the table. Red-Nose's eyes lit up, as did those of his companion.

"I'm hoping it'll be quite pleasant." Daric tucked into his dinner while the two men stared at the coins.

"Mind if we join ya?" the tall man asked.

Daric, his mouth full, gestured for them to sit. Both took a seat across from him and Red-Nose ordered more ale, for himself, his friend, and Daric.

"Name's Feth, this 'ere's Cheal."

Daric nodded to each and swallowed his food. "Daric."

Feth chuckled. "Should 'ave known. What other Calleni would stick around a country colder than 'is own?"

A leg of chicken stopped halfway to Daric's mouth. "You've heard of me?"

Both men laughed. "Who 'asn't heard of Ifan's tame desert cat?" Cheal said. "Though I suppose ya belong t' Cenith now." He shook his head. "Sad news that. Ifan was a good man."

Feth leaned close. "Truth tell, we'd liefer 'ave Cenith for a lord than the one we got. The man's mad." He crossed his dark eyes briefly.

Daric almost laughed at the ridiculous look. He finished his dinner in relative silence. When the dishes were removed and the meal paid for, Feth ordered more ale.

Lifting his full tankard, Feth said, "To pleasant conversation." Three pewter mugs clinked. "What is it ya be wishin' t' discuss?"

Daric leaned back against the wall, next to his great sword. Feth's eyes darted to the hilt sticking out of the scabbard, then to the coins on the table.

"A girl at the castle."

Cheal snickered. "Lookin' for some entertainment?"

Feth elbowed him in the ribs and the tall man shut up. "Which girl?"

Daric folded his arms across his chest. "The one who was married off to Lord Cenith this afternoon."

Feth narrowed his eyes and lowered his voice, "Thought it might be that one. 'Tis death to speak o' 'er."

"Would it matter? Now that she's gone?"

"Might."

Daric pulled out five more coins, all gold. He laid them out, one by one, in front of him.

Cheal glanced around the room then leaned forward. "What would ya like t' know?"

"Ya don't know nothin'!" Feth said.

"What'd ya go and say that for!" Cheal sat back, his lower lip set in a pout.

Feth stabbed his finger at Daric, though he looked at Cheal. "Ya see that sword? Ya've 'eard the stories. He finds out yer lyin', and you'll be sliced up faster than Mavy's pigs come butcherin' time." He rested his arms on the table. "Idiot."

Cheal's eyes widened, the only indication Feth had frightened him. He folded his arms and huffed.

Feth leaned toward Daric again, his fingers not far from the coins. "For a price, we can take ya t' th' man what knows."

Daric shook his head. "Bring him here." He had no idea where these men might take him. They didn't really trust him, but then, he didn't trust them either. Meeting the man elsewhere not only put Daric at risk, it put the informant in possible danger as well. Men sitting openly in a tavern were less conspicuous than those sneaking around looking for a secret place to talk. Daric had discovered over the years that hiding in plain sight could be far safer than using covert means.

He pushed two gold coins across the table. “More if what he has to say proves to be what I want.”

Feth nodded and the coins disappeared. “His name’s Aden. His wife looked after th’ girl for a time.”

Cheal snorted. “A short time.”

Feth poked him again then called for the barmaid, a young woman with dark brown hair and eyes. He whispered in her ear. She glanced at Daric and nodded. Feth smacked her rump as she left. She let out a squeal and flashed him a scathing look.

“Aden’s ‘er uncle,” Cheal said.

After a shorter time than Daric would have thought, Aden arrived on the arm of a young man who bore a striking resemblance to the barmaid. The old man himself looked to be on death’s door. He wore a long sleeved, ivory linen shirt and walnut brown trousers made of light wool, both stained and worn. Parchment-thin skin hung on a skeletal, high cheekboned face. Watery blue eyes watched him warily from under bushy white eyebrows. The barmaid sat him down beside Feth.

Word travelled fast. Daric hoped not too fast. While they’d waited for the old man, the patrons in the room had almost doubled…which both worried Daric and reassured him. More people meant more noise, easier to keep their conversation private. Despite the increased crowd however, chatter was kept to a minimum as everyone kept an eye on Daric and the old man, waiting for Aden to speak.

Daric glanced around the room. “Can everyone be trusted not to repeat what they hear?”

Feth turned, his eyes scanning faces. “Most work either in th’ kitchens or th’ stables. I’m th’ stable master and ‘ave known each o’ them for years. I’d be inclined t’ say ‘yes’, but ya never know.” He looked at the coins on the table, then at Daric, and grinned. “A little gold can buy much. Just as a precaution though…” He crooked a finger at a man sitting nearby, one of average height and features who appeared to be about the same age as Feth. “Gebron, go watch th’ door for guards.”

Gebron nodded and, taking his ale with him, moved to the table nearest the door.

"Rani," Aden said, snapping Daric's attention to the old man. "That's the girl's name?"

The old man shook his head. "Rani was my wife. She was 'ired by Councillor Rymon t' look after the girl. She was four at th' time, the girl that is. She'd 'ad others, but none was allowed t' look after 'er for more 'n a few months before a new one was 'ired."

Strange. Why bother with so many nursemaids?

Aden took a sip of ale and continued, "Lord Saulth gave orders that th' girl was to be kept in a storeroom near the kitchen. Taught nothin', 'cept what she needed t' know t' stay clean and 'ealthy. No one was t' talk to 'er, or teach 'er anythin'."

Daric raised an eyebrow. "An odd command. Why would he do that?"

"The reason for it was lost when th' midwives who attended 'er birth died. They'd been threatened wi' death, like the others who looked after 'er, and took what they 'eard and witnessed to their graves." A rattling cough shook Aden's thin body. He took another drink before he could continue. "Wouldn't even talk on their deathbeds for fear o' revenge against their families. I'm only tellin' ya this, ya understand, 'cause I don't care if they come after me, not any more. Rani's gone, and Shival already 'as 'er hand on my soul. Someone 'as to know."

"Can you tell me the girl's name?"

Aden shook his head. "She 'as no name. Lord Saulth refused t' give 'er one. No one was brave enough to disobey 'im. One 'o th' guards outside th' room where she was born 'eard 'im say she 'ad t' earn it." Bony shoulders pushed up his worn shirt when he shrugged. "Don't know what she's supposed t' do. Don't know why he'd go t' all that trouble o' keepin' 'er like he did, then marry 'er off sudden like that."

Word did get around fast. Daric had expected the kitchen staff to know, but not Aden. Perhaps whoever fetched him had talked. The young man who had brought him still stood near, leaning on the chimney. Maybe he was the one. "Tell me about Rani."

The old man's eyes grew moist. "Prettiest thing ya'd ever want t' lay eyes on. Twenty years younger 'n me when we wed. Don't know what she saw in this bag 'o bones, but I thanked Talueth for every day we 'ad together.

"Loved children, my Rani did. Talueth didn't bless us wi' any o' our own. Guess she thought me havin' Rani was enough. Rani leapt at the chance t' look after th' girl." A wistful smile crossed the man's face. "She was brave, my Rani. Fell for the girl right off. Saw somethin' in 'er. She was four years old, the girl that is. Wild little thing, almost like an animal. Hit and bit t' get attention. A neglected child will do that sometimes, y'know? Well, Rani put an end t' that. None 'o th' others what came before 'er would teach 'er much o' anythin'; too afraid. Didn't even know 'ow to use th' chamber pot."

Aden picked up his empty tankard. Daric signalled for another. A crowd had gathered around their table. All pretence of 'minding their own business' had ended. Sometime during the conversation the lute player had put down his instrument and now stood on the edge of the crowd. The ale appeared quickly, along with a kiss to the old man's brow from the barmaid.

"I used to be good at drawin', once upon a time, and Rani asked me to make a picture book for th' girl, so she could teach 'er t' read some o' th' words she'd bin learnin', know what they looked like." Aden waved a crooked, bony finger at him. "Don't let 'er lack 'o words fool ya, she's a smart one. The kitchen staff there now can tell ya that."

Several men in the crowd nodded in agreement. One stepped forward, portly, with dark blonde, greying, hair and a receding hairline revealing a wide forehead creased with worry lines. His top lip made up for the lack of hair on his head. A thick moustache drooped well past the corners of his mouth. "I can attest t' that. Name's Lacus. I'm th' chief cook. I've other things t' tell ya, when Aden's done."

Aden nodded, then kept on nodding. Daric hoped he wasn't falling asleep. The old man sat up with a snort and looked around. "Yes, yes."

"You were talking about Rani?" Daric prompted.

"Rani." Aden wiped a tear from his eye. "Loved that woman. She taught the girl t' read th' words in th' book, simple words wi' simple pictures, but it showed she could be taught. Rani trained 'er t' use th' chamber pot, 'ow to wash 'erself properly instead o' lettin' others do it for 'er, how to brush 'er hair. She even made 'er a doll."

The man called Lacus nodded. "She still 'as it. Carries it wi' 'er everywhere." He looked at the floor. "At least, she did until today."

A murmur ran through the crowd, then some shuffling. Seated in the corner, and surrounded by people, Daric couldn't see what was up. The disturbance died down and Aden continued.

"Five months Rani looked after 'er. Then came th' day 'is Lordship found out what she was doin'. Dragged 'er out o' th' girl's room and out th' kitchen door." Aden's lower lip trembled. "He…he…"

The old man put his face in his hands and cried, unable to continue. Feth put his arm around him and patted his shoulder.

Lacus picked up the tale. "I was twenty-nine when it 'appened, supervisin' th' cleanup after dinner. His Lordship took Rani out back 'o th' kitchen and slit 'er throat. Did it 'imself, then took off 'is belt and beat the girl. I can still hear 'er cries from that day, though he's beaten 'er many times since." Lacus twisted a green felt cap in his hands. "There were no more nannies after that. She cried for Rani for a long time. Most days she was locked in 'er room, sittin' in the dark, cryin' her eyes out. It was 'ard, so 'ard. We watched over 'er, but we didn't dare touch 'er or teach 'er anythin'. Ya understand, don't ya? We didn't dare."

Daric nodded. These were ordinary people leading simple lives under the shadow of a demon lord.

"When she got older, we stopped lockin' th' door, but Lord Saulth would beat 'er whenever she left 'er room durin' th' day," Lacus said. "She learned to wander th' 'alls at night, when everyone was sleepin', learned how t' avoid th' guards. Lord Saulth let her do that, so long as she didn't wander far. Don't know why 'e changed 'is mind 'bout that. Th' library became 'er favourite place. Th' day 'e murdered Rani, 'is Lordship took 'er book away, but smart little thing that she is, she found it in th' library."

Daric stared at a puddle the sweat on his tankard made. Light from the candles in the wall sconces flickered in the wet ring. He'd expected something to come out about the girl, but not in his wildest dreams could he have imagined this.

Aden stopped crying and wiped his eyes with his shirtsleeves. Feth still patted his shoulder. Cheal tried to get him to drink a bit of ale.

"Thank you, all of you. This will help us a great deal." Daric sat forward.

"There's still somethin' I need t' say." Lacus looked around the room. "We's all friends 'ere." The others nodded. Still, he leaned closer and spoke almost in a whisper, "The girl's bin touched by th' gods. There's no doubt o' it." He stood straight, his cap still clutched in his hands.

Daric frowned. "What do you mean?"

"Ya know she'd been beaten?" Lacus kept blinking his eyes, torturing his cap.

"We discovered that. Whoever looked after her wounds did a very good job."

"M' wife did, thank you, Yer Excellency," Lacus said. "He beat 'er 'ard this time. He's never taken a whip to 'er before, always a belt, but she snuck out o' 'er room the night o' 'is weddin'. A guard tried t' rape 'er. Ya saw th' body by th' gate?"

Daric nodded.

"Another guard tried t' stop 'im. They fought and t' other guard died. Lord Saulth beat 'er 'cause 'e says she caused it and 'e lost two guards and had t' whip another o'er it."

Daric put his hand up. "You said this was the night of his wedding?"

"Yes, Yer Excellency. Tho' 'e didn't beat 'er until yesterday."

"*Yesterday?* That's impossible! Those wounds are at least three days old."

"That's what I mean by touched by th' gods. M' wife went in just before Guard-Commander Tajik dragged 'er off. The girl's wounds are healin' far faster than they should. We talked about it after Tajik took 'er. None 'o us can ever remember 'er bein' sick. Not child's pox, not a fever, not so much as a cold. Touched by th' gods. That's th' only explanation."

An incredulous murmur rippled through the crowd.

"Rani said that, more than once," Aden said. "Favoured by th' gods."

The whole concept was ridiculous, but Daric was always one to follow his intuition, and it told him these people wouldn't lie, not about this. *Yesterday?*

"Let me through, please!" A scrawny lad, who looked like a younger version of Lacus, pushed his way through the crowd. He handed a cloth bag to the chief cook, who placed it on the table, avoiding wet spots.

"Take it," Lacus said. "Tis all she owns in this world."

Daric opened the bag and pulled out a well-loved rag doll, a cloth covered picture book with worn pages, and a bone handled hair brush with some of its bristles missing.

"The book! She still 'as it!" Aden cried.

Lacus had said that, but Aden was crying at the time. Daric held the book out to him. He took it with trembling hands. First running his finger tips over the plain, frayed cover, he opened it, looking at each drawing as if it were an old friend. The man did have a remarkable talent.

"Somethin' else ya might want t' know," Lacus said. "I was th' one charged t' bring food t' th' girl's mother. Saulth kept 'er locked in a room on th' third floor. Poor thing didn't want t' be 'ere, but Lord Saulth 'as no 'eart."

"Her mother wasn't Saulth's wife?"

Lacus shook his head. "Brought 'er 'ere in th' dead o' night, kickin' and fightin' th' whole way. Her name was Islara."

Daric jerked upright. "Calleni?"

Lacus nodded, then leaned closer again. "Th' first couple weeks she was 'ere, she screamed th' entire time 'e laid wi' 'er, and cried for hours after. Somethin' strange was goin' on in that room." He touched both his eyes, his nose, and then his mouth, with his index finger. Everyone Daric could see repeated the motion. "But I couldn't find out nothin'."

Daric had heard about three of Saulth's mistresses, but not this one. "What happened to her?"

"The same guard what told us about th' girl 'avin' no name said the birthin' didn't go well. He 'ad th' chore o' helpin' remove th' body." Once more he led the patrons through the motions of the ward against evil. "Lord Saulth ordered 'er cut open t' save th' child. Not so's she could be fixed up agin', mind, just sliced 'er right open, then ranted about it not bein' a boy."

"Niafanna protect us." Daric had seen horrific things over the years, heard about plenty of others. He'd done more than a few. This one ranked near the bottom of the dung heap.

"Guard's comin'!" cried a voice from near the door.

Aden shoved the book back at Daric. "They mustn't get it! They mustn't!"

Daric put the book, brush and doll back in the bag and tucked it down by his feet. The crowd returned to their seats and picked up conversations as if they'd never stopped.

A man in a green and gold uniform stuck his head in the door. "All's well?"

The barkeep wiped the counter as he nodded to the guard, who grunted acknowledgement before continuing his rounds. Daric stood; he had more than he came for. He gave Aden two gold coins and told Feth and Cheal to keep whatever was left on the table.

They both grinned. "If yer ever in need o' more pleasant conversation, ya know where t' come," Feth said.

As Daric made his way to the door, amid friendly farewells, Lacus appeared at his elbow. "What will 'appen to 'er?"

"You've given me much to think about. We'd thought her a lack-wit. I'll be honest, I can't speak for my lord, but he's a kind-hearted man, and no matter what, she'll be cared for."

Lacus smiled, as did those around him. "Thank you, Yer Excellency, it's all we can ask."

Daric tossed several more coins on the bar. "Drinks are on me."

The people cheered; the bartender saluted him. Lacus beamed, and said, "If ya ever need anythin' while in Valda, come 'ere. We'll get it for ya."

Daric nodded and left to retrieve his horse from the livery.

* * * *

Rymon stood in the doorway to the girl's room. Her doll, bed, and few belongings were gone. Two barrels sat in the corner that used to hold her chamber pot. This was now space that could be used for something else.

After Cenith left, Saulth spent much of the next hour soothing Iridia's ruffled feathers then retired to the library to pour over the scroll yet again. Rymon had sat waiting in the chair by the fire, trying to figure out why his lord had given the girl to Cenith. Saulth would tell him, though it would be in his own good time.

Another hour must have passed while his lord stared at the scroll. "I said yesterday she was not the Jada-Drau. I have been saying it for almost sixteen years. If she had any kind of power, she would have used it to save herself. I thought you would be happy, Rymon. After all, I did not kill her. It is over. Time to concentrate on the true Jada-Drau."

Rymon closed his eyes. Saulth's tone had put an end to anything he might have said. Dinner had tasted like ash, the wine like sour vinegar. He had come to the girl's room in the hopes of finding something to ease his soul.

Think positively, you old fool. Even if Cenith risked angering the council and set the girl aside, he'd ensure she had a safe home. He had a heart as big as his mountains. *And if she is the Jada-Drau? Perhaps it is best that kind of power is out of Saulth's hands.*

Rymon opened his eyes. He still saw the girl hanging from the sausage hook, blood running down her back and legs. Saulth had gone mad. There could be no denying it now. Rymon would stick by him though, not only was he too old to do anything else, someone needed to put a restraining hand on Saulth's anger.

"Looks funny, don't it, Yer Excellency."

Rymon looked behind him. A boy about fifteen stood there, one of the scullery workers, finishing late.

"Bein' empty and all. Feels like she should still be there."

"Yes, it does." Rymon turned to go.

"Even funnier 'bout 'er back."

Rymon halted. "Her back? In what way?"

The boy shrugged. "I 'eard Lacus and t' others talkin' earlier, after Guard-Commander Tajik took 'er. They said there was somethin' funny 'bout 'er back. It looked better than it should. More 'ealed."

Rymon's heart almost stopped. The boy stepped back, fear crossing his young face. Rymon reached into a pocket and pulled out a silver coin. He showed it to the boy, whose eyes lit up like Talueth's Spring Festival fires.

"Did they say anything else?"

The boy nodded, his eyes on the coin. "They sat 'round the table and talked about 'ow she'd never bin sick, like they only jus' realized it. 'Touched by th' gods', they said."

Rymon's world spun. "Not sick? Ever?"

The boy shook his head. Rymon pressed the coin into the lad's hand. He grinned, then took off into the kitchen and out the back door. Rymon made his way to the library, deep in thought.

If I tell Saulth, he will send Tajik out after them and who knows what kind of violence might ensue. If I stay quiet, the girl is safe with Cenith. No more beatings and neglect. But Saulth is my lord, I am obligated to pass on what I have learned. The familiar tap-tap of his cane helped soothe his anguish.

Perhaps if I tell him, he will go easier on the girl. He would teach her what she needs to know to save the country. He followed that line of thought a little further. *If I don't tell him, Cenith will keep the girl, with no knowledge of what she is or the role she has to play to protect Ardael. I could be putting my country in grave danger.*

All the way down the hall, up the stairs and down another hall, Rymon guessed and second guessed himself as to where his loyalties and sense of justice truly lay until he finally arrived at a decision…his country came first. Saulth was blowing out the last candle when a breathless Rymon opened the library door.

"My Lord, she is the Jada-Drau!"

"Do not anger me, Rymon. I am in no mood for this."

Flickering firelight brought eerie shadows to life while Rymon told him what the boy had said. Saulth strode to the scroll table.

"Light a candle and bring it here." Saulth ran his finger down the scroll to the second section. "'One sign shall be love in the face of adversity, another shall be unnatural vigour'." He slammed the table, upsetting the candle. Rymon caught it before it could do any damage. "Unnatural vigour! It's not strength, its healing! How could I have missed it? I have read this scroll a thousand times and more!"

Rymon knew. Saulth had anticipated a male Jada–Drau to have instant access to tangible power when he came of age, not a quiet manifestation from a tiny girl. The isolation Saulth ordered had prevented anyone from noticing. He wouldn't see it that way, though. 'Love in the face of adversity.' *Her doll?* It was the only affection she had since her last nursemaid.

Saulth strode to the door. "Send for Guard-Commander Tajik. Now!" he said to the guard.

The Lord of Bredun paced the length of the library until Tajik arrived. "Bring the girl back, unharmed," he said. "It should be easy to get her away from Cenith. He will probably pay you to take her."

"My Lord?" Tajik's leather face crinkled in confusion.

Saulth grabbed the front of his tabard. "Just bring her back! Now!" He pushed Tajik toward the door. The guard-commander ran from the room.

Chapter Ten

Stew had been made and eaten while four of the Dunvalos Reach guards stood watch on the edges of the copse, out of sight. Jolin, Varth, and Trey shared the log opposite Cenith. The rest sat on the ground. The soldiers made a show of repairing equipment, sharpening knives or swords, and pretending not to stare at the sleeping girl. Cenith sat on the log, his chin in his hand, thinking while trying not to think.

All I wanted was justice. Instead Saulth is let off for attempted theft, and possibly the murder of my father. He sticks me with an idiot daughter he doesn't want, makes a fool of me in front of my men… Cenith didn't even want to think about what his council would have to say. Any child he fathered on the girl would be under scrutiny for signs of idiocy—if she let him near enough to get her with child. If he had no sons, it would be disaster for Dunvalos Reach. Cenith sighed, trying once again not to think.

When the last of the sun's rays disappeared behind the trees, the night insects began their chirps and whirs. A breeze wafted through, adding the rustle of leaves to the cadence of the crickets and cicadas. It also caught sparks from the fire and Cenith had to watch they didn't land on the girl.

He had to stop thinking of her that way. She was his wife, though hardly the girl of his dreams. *Why is it I can imagine terrible things, but what really happens is ten times worse?*

If Daric were here, he'd have chuckled at that. Before he left, the Calleni had hinted at a choice. Could he put the girl aside and find someone else? The Lord Council might not be pleased, but then, Cenith had been tricked. That might count for something. The girl was a lack-wit; that might count for more.

A groan sounded from the blankets near his feet. The girl sat up, rubbed her eyes, then stared at the trees as if she'd never seen one. When she caught sight of the soldiers, she scrambled backwards into Cenith.

"It's all right, no one is going to hurt you." *Foolish girl.*

She looked up at him and leapt to her feet, or tried to. They tangled in the blankets and she fell backwards over the log. Crying out in pain, she tried to roll away from him, but the twisted blankets prevented it. She lay on her back, kicking her legs, tears of pain in her rabbit eyes.

"No hurt," she whimpered. "No bad."

Disgusted, Cenith untangled the blankets from her feet. "No hurt," he said, hoping she'd understand her own words. "No hurt. Now keep still a moment." He finished freeing her feet.

She sat up, casting him and the soldiers a wary glance. "No hurt?" Tears of pain glistened in her wide eyes.

Cenith shook his head. "No hurt." He held his hand out to her. "Come, sit. No hurt."

She didn't move. He took one of the blankets and folded it over several times, placing it on the log. He patted the thick cushion and held his hand out again. "No hurt. Sit."

She rolled to her feet, careful of her wounds. Hesitant, she looked at him, the blanket, and the soldiers, most with their weapons still out.

"I want you all to tell her 'no hurt'," Cenith said.

A chorus of the words echoed in the clearing. None of the men laughed, each wore a respectful, serious expression. The weapons disappeared into sheaths and behind the other log. *Bless them!* Cenith patted the blanket again then slid over, giving her plenty of room. The girl took a step, and looked down at her feet. She lifted one foot, then the other. Curiosity replaced fear on her face.

What in Shival's hells is she doing?

After repeating the motion several times, she looked at her arms. The sleeves of the shirt fell past her fingertips and the bottom hung below her knees. "Dress?"

"Shirt." Cenith patted the blanket again.

"Sh…Sh-irt?"

"Shirt," he repeated. *How could she not know a shirt?* He took a deep, quiet breath, trying to keep his patience.

"Sh-irt. Shirt." The girl looked around the campsite. "Dress?"

Cenith picked up the ruined dress. She reached for it without moving her feet. He kept it far enough away that she couldn't touch it and patted the blanket again. His men watched, silent but intent.

"Sit first. Then dress," he said.

The girl frowned, but took a careful step closer to the log. "No hurt?"

Cenith shook his head again. "No hurt."

She stepped over the log and sat on the blanket, seeming ready to run.

Cenith gave her the dress. "I'm sorry. It's too ripped to wear."

The girl had to push the sleeves off her hands in order to take it. She stared at the remains of the dress, stroking it like she would a cat. "R…ript?"

He sighed. "Sort of." *What am I going to do? I can't even talk to her!* "Varth, would you get up, slowly, and bring her some stew? She must be hungry."

Varth stood, and the girl started, dropping the dress.

"No hurt," Cenith said. "Food."

"F-food?"

"Yes, food."

Varth approached them from Cenith's side. He'd brought a cup of water as well and Cenith gave that to her first. She sniffed it then drained the cup.

"Water," she said, licking her lips.

He took the cup and passed her the stew. She sniffed it as well before picking up the spoon, then scooped the food into her mouth as if she hadn't eaten in a week. She gripped the utensil in her fist, like a small child.

Cenith still thought her eyes too big for her delicate features. She looked more fey than beautiful, like a mountain pixie from the stories he'd read as a boy. The dark circles under her eyes didn't help, nor did the bluish tinge to her lips. Her looks might improve once she washed and brushed her hair, and recovered more from her wounds. A little bit of sun wouldn't hurt either. All in all, though, her face was a damn sight better than her sister's, she looked nothing like Saulth.

When she finished eating, she set the bowl on the log, wiped her mouth on a sleeve, and burped. Table manners would have to sit high on the list of things she needed to learn. Provided she could be taught any more than she already knew.

"What's your name?" he asked.

Her brow wrinkled.

"Your name. I'm Cenith. Cenith." He touched his chest.

"Cen-ith?" The frown deepened. "Man." She pointed at Varth. "Man." Then at Trey. "Man." She aimed her finger at him. "Man."

"Well, yes, I am a man, but my name is Cenith."

"Cen-ith." She gave him a dubious look then turned her attention to her feet. She lifted first one foot, then the other, studying the grass under each one. Patting the blanket, she said, "Blan-ket."

"Close enough."

The girl bent over, and gasped. Her wounds must have pulled.

"Don't hurt yourself," Cenith said. "You don't want to reopen those cuts."

She touched the blanket again. "Blan-ket." Then patted the ground with her foot, repeating the procedure when Cenith couldn't figure out what she wanted.

It took a moment for him to clue in. "Oh. Grass. It's grass." *Where has she been that she's never seen grass?*

"Gr-ass." She said the word twice more.

The breeze strengthened, lifting the edges of her tangled hair. She gasped, looking around, holding her hands out as if she were blind.

"What are you doing?"

She touched her cheeks then held her hands out again.

"Tis the wind, m'lord," Jolin said, pointing at the sky. "She acts like she's never felt it afore."

"I'll bet Saulth kept her locked away somewhere." That would explain her death-like skin and her fascination with the grass under her feet. "Wind. It's wind."

She repeated the word three times, then, excited about something, pointed to the edge of the clearing where the horses stood. "Teree! Teree! Horz! Ohhh! Horz!"

"Yes, those are trees and horses." Cenith stressed the proper pronunciation. "Jolin, can you tell me how she knows trees and horses, but doesn't know wind or grass?"

The young soldier shrugged. "Maybe she's seen 'em from a window."

An odd look crossed her face. "Nesses." She stood, scanning the campsite, then looked at Cenith. "Nesses?"

"I don't know what you want," he said. "Jolin?"

"Sorry, m'lord. Can't help ye there." The others muttered their apologies.

All the soldiers with him were young and unmarried. Cenith didn't like taking men from their families for what might be weeks at a time without a good reason. These men probably didn't know any more than he did about what to do.

"If ye don't mind my sayin' it, m'lord," Jolin said, his backwoods accent still thick despite three years in the guard. "The lass don't look like a lack-wit t' me. My older brother took a fall as a babe, ain't been right since. Can't talk, can't look after himself. His eyes are dull, don't have that spark o' life hers do. Can't say what ails her though."

Do I dare hope?

The girl's expression changed to one of horror and she let out a shriek, "*Baybee!*"

Cenith winced. Her voice had been quiet until now.

She sat down hard on the blanket, her face twisting in pain. "Baybee! Book! Baybee!"

Tears welled in her eyes then escaped to run down her cheeks. She hugged herself, saying the words over and over. Cenith touched her shoulder in an attempt to comfort her.

She jerked away. "No hurt!"

He ran the offending hand through his hair in frustration. "All right, no touching. No hurt." *Daric! Where are you?*

Varth sat up straight, cocking his head. "I hear hoof beats, My Lord."

With the girl crying beside him, it took Cenith a moment longer to hear them. *Maegden, let it be Daric!*

Ead, on sentry duty, appeared at the east side of the clearing. "Riders, My Lord."

"We hear them. Go back and see who it is, but stay hidden in case it isn't Daric. He should be riding alone."

Ead nodded and vanished into the darkness.

"The fire needs more wood, m'lord," Jolin said, "but I don't want t' frighten the lass. She's upset enough."

"Just go slow. If she makes any move, I'll try to reassure her. Provided she'll let me."

The girl proved to be too upset too lost in her grief over whatever 'baybee' and' book' were, to notice Jolin. Maybe she meant a real book. It would explain how she knew about trees and horses, but then maybe she mangled the word like she did others.

Jolin had just finished adding the wood when the hoof beats stopped. A few moments later, Ead re-entered the clearing, mounted riders behind him. Cloaked, with their hoods pulled down, Cenith couldn't tell who they were. The horses' tack bore no insignia or colours. The lead rider held a sword to Ead's back.

Jolin dove for the sword he'd hidden behind the log. Steel slid from sheaths and his men formed a wall between him and the riders. Cenith stood and drew his own blade. The girl stopped crying and shrank away from him, her eyes on the mounted men.

"Sorry, My Lord," Ead said. "They almost ran over me coming in here."

"Stop there," the rider said to Ead. "Spotted your fire. Thought we'd visit for a bit."

The girl shrieked. "No hurt! No hurt!"

She fell off the log in her haste, crying out in pain when she landed on her back. Cenith grabbed her arm and pulled her to her feet. The lead rider slid back the hood of his cloak. The others copied him.

"Tajik," Cenith spat. The girl must have recognized his voice. "What do you want?"

"The girl."

Cenith frowned. "Why? What's Saulth pulling now?"

"Let's just say…a mistake has been made. My lord had a bad day yesterday and chose to take it out on you. He regrets his actions and would like to make amends." Tajik grinned like a sick weasel. "He's willing to exchange this one for Iridia, as originally planned."

The girl tried to peel Cenith's fingers off her arm.

"No hurt," Cenith said to her. "I won't let them hurt you. No hurt."

She stopped picking at his fingers but still tried to keep her distance.

Cenith turned back to Tajik. "Why does Saulth want her? So he can beat her again? Hasn't had enough of torturing her?"

Tajik's grin disappeared and his eyes hardened. "She's an idiot, stupid as a cow. No kind of wife for a Lord."

"Perhaps not, but she doesn't deserve to be beaten like that either."

"You know nothing." Tajik turned his sneer from Cenith to the soldiers guarding him and the girl. He grinned again. "Where's your pet Calleni? Off futtering a goat?"

The laughter of the Bredun men brought Cenith's sentries into the clearing, raising their number to twelve. The guard-commander's soldiers looked hard, cold, all older and more experienced than his own men, but Tajik's were outnumbered two to one. Cenith doubted it would've mattered if the odds were reversed; each of his soldiers had been trained by Daric. A good thing, considering keeping hold of the girl hampered him. He didn't dare let go in case she ran. She'd have no chance of surviving in the wild on her own.

"Something you might want to know," Tajik said. "She's bastard born, by product of time spent with one of Lord Saulth's mistresses. As I said, no wife for a lord."

Cenith let him wait while he pretended to think. *Daric! Hurry up!* "She grows on a person. I think I'll keep her."

"Just hand her over and we'll be on our way," Tajik said, pressing his sword harder into Ead's back.

Ead winced, but kept quiet. Tajik gave his men a signal and they pulled their weapons. Cenith opened his mouth to give the order to attack.

"You'll be on your way now, with your men or without them." Daric, on foot, materialized near the Bredun soldiers, his great sword in hand.

Ead dove forward. Tajik snarled and slashed, catching the back of Ead's shoulder. The Bredun soldier nearest Daric lifted his weapon. Daric's sword sang and the man fell backwards off his horse, sliced across his chest.

Tajik wheeled his mount, but Daric had already closed the distance, swinging his sword at the guard-commander. Tajik threw himself back to avoid the blow and lost his balance. He toppled over, his right foot caught in the stirrup. Eyes showing white, Tajik's horse bolted, dragging him with it.

Daric's swing shifted and another guard's sword flew into the clearing, a hand still attached. The man screamed and clutched his arm to his chest. Daric signalled his men to surround the remaining Bredun guards, who lowered their weapons.

"When you catch up to Tajik," Daric said, "tell him the girl is staying with us, if for no other reason than Saulth wants her back. Now take your wounded and go."

The senior guard ordered two of his men to put the man with the chest wound on his horse. Both injured men were led out of the clearing.

"Well, that was good timing," Cenith said, still not believing his luck.

"Not really. Forgive me, My Lord, but I saw this lot leaving Valda and followed them. I waited in the bushes to see how you'd handle it."

So much for luck. "So…how did I do?"

A wry smile slid up one side of Daric's face. "Quite well. You did just fine."

"I'm so glad."

Daric chuckled. "Jolin, take Trey and Madin. Ensure our 'guests' have left." He strode to where Ead sat on the ground, his hand on his left shoulder. "Varth, my kit, please. Nightwind is just inside those trees." He pointed to where he'd appeared. "Everyone else, circle Lord Cenith in case they decide to return."

The soldiers scrambled to carry out their orders. Cenith found himself surrounded. Sometime during the brief conflict, the girl had stopped struggling. She stared at the Bredun guard's sword, and the hand still holding it.

Cenith pulled her close enough to block her view. "No hurt. No one will hurt you."

Eyes blue as a mountain tarn in summer bored into his. Jolin was right, intelligence lived there. "No hurt."

Not a plea for mercy, was it a thank you? Had he finally convinced her he had no intention of hurting her? She tugged on the hand still holding her arm. Cenith let go. She rubbed the spot and tried to see past him without coming close enough to touch. He didn't let her. She dropped her gaze to her hands, then tugged on one. When it didn't come off, she frowned.

"Would someone please get rid of that hand?" Cenith said, stepping in front of her again when she tried to have another look.

"Aye, m'lord," said a quiet voice behind him. Keev.

Varth appeared with Nightwind in tow.

"Look, a horse," Cenith said.

The girl turned to where he pointed. "Horz!"

"Give Daric his kit, I'll look after Nightwind." Soldiers broke the circle to allow Cenith to take Daric's horse from Varth as he passed by. Varth gave him a nod and carried on. The girl cooed in delight when Cenith showed her how to pat Nightwind. She touched the horse, hesitant, brushing just the tips of her fingers down his neck. Nightwind shook his head and she jumped back, but moved close again when the horse quieted. Cenith glanced back at the clearing; the grisly object, and the sword it still clutched, was gone.

Ead had his jerkin and shirt off so Daric could tend the wound. It didn't appear too bad, though Cenith couldn't get a good look. Another coo drew his attention back to the girl. She touched Nightwind again. When the horse didn't react, she set her hand on his neck as Cenith had done and patted him once, then again. A little smile briefly showed itself. Varth returned and offered to hold Nightwind's head while she stroked and patted the horse's mane and neck. Daric finished with Ead and came toward them. Jolin had returned with word that Tajik's men had left, and now helped Ead back into his clothes.

"No hurt! No hurt!" the girl cried, when she saw Daric.

"No hurt," Cenith said. "Daric won't hurt you. No hurt."

She calmed, though her eyes still darted from Cenith to Daric.

"No hurt?"

"No hurt. Honest. Pet the horse." He gave Nightwind a couple of strokes on the neck. She did the same, though kept a wary eye on Daric.

"How's Ead?" Cenith asked.

"A small puncture wound in the middle of his back. The one on his shoulder is worse, but not bad enough to hold us up. It's bandaged and will be fine for a couple hours until I can take the time to stitch it. I used part of her dress to hold the bandage. Not much left of it now." Daric nodded at the girl. "I see you're making progress." He moved around to the opposite side of Nightwind to stow his kit.

"Jolin thinks she's not as dumb as she appears, and I have to agree." Cenith removed his hand from the horse so the girl could pet all of Nightwind's neck. She didn't smile now, but still made the odd sound of delight. "Did you find out anything in Valda?"

"Plenty. And Jolin's right, she isn't a lack-wit, but the story's complicated and I don't want to tell it here. Tajik could send others after us." Daric finished with his saddlebag. "Varth, tell the others to pack up. We're leaving."

"Yes, sir." The young soldier strode off, issuing orders.

"You didn't happen to find out her name, did you?" Cenith asked.

Daric took over Nightwind's reins. "Sort of. She doesn't have one."

"How can she not have one?" Everyone had a name.

"Saulth never gave her one. Said she had to earn it or some such nonsense. I'll explain later. I also bought her a couple dresses, but it might take some time to get her into one of them. She doesn't seem bothered by the night air, so if we just wrap her in a blanket it should suffice until we stop." Daric rubbed Nightwind's nose and the horse whickered, startling the girl, though she didn't remove her hand from his neck. "Oh, and here's your pouch, I only used a few coins." He reached into a pocket in his jerkin.

"Good thinking," Cenith said, taking the money. "How are we going to get her onto a horse? She doesn't seem to like being touched."

The same odd look that had crossed the girl's face earlier made a reappearance. "Nesses." She stepped away from Nightwind and scanned the campsite, then turned back to Cenith. "Nesses?"

"She said that before Tajik came. Any idea what she wants?"

Daric watched the girl a moment over Nightwind's back, then chuckled. "I've seen that look on my daughters' faces many times. She's looking for a privy. I'm going to make a wild guess and say 'nesses' is her word for 'necessary'. Just a guess, mind."

Cenith's cheeks warmed. "What do we do? We don't have a chamber pot, never mind a privy."

Daric shrugged. "She's your wife. Take her into the trees and show her how it's done."

Now Cenith's cheeks blazed. "I can't do that! I…she's…I don't know how!"

Daric's chuckle turned into a deep laugh.

"Nesses," the girl said, the look on her face turning desperate. "Puh-leece?"

"How to show her, I mean!" *Damned Calleni is enjoying this!*

Daric came around to their side of Nightwind, a smirk firmly in place. The girl backed away from him.

"No hurt, My Lady." Daric's smirk turned into a smile. He gave a bow to her first, then Cenith, a twinkle in his dark brown eyes. "With your permission, My Lord, and if My Lady will let me, I'll undertake the chore. It won't be the first time I've shown a girl how to piss in the woods. I've had that honour with each of my daughters."

"Yes! Please! You have my permission," Cenith said, relief, and a convenient breeze, cooling his face.

Daric took a careful step closer to the girl and bowed to her again. "Nesses," he said, holding his hand out toward the woods.

She looked at Daric, the woods, then back to him, her expression more than a little dubious. "Teree," she said, as if anyone should know.

Daric straightened. "Nesses in trees. Come." He walked past her several steps then turned toward her. "Nesses in trees. Come."

He held his hand out to her. The girl looked at Cenith, who nodded, and back to Daric. She took hesitant steps until she caught up to him, though she didn't take his hand. Daric led her into the woods. Everything was packed up, except for Daric's blankets, and the fire put out before they returned, the Calleni in the lead. The girl no longer appeared distressed. He must have had some success touching her because the sleeves of the shirt were rolled up to her elbows.

"How did it go?" Cenith asked, not that he wanted any details.

"Not well until we found a log with a hole in it. Things progressed rapidly after that." Daric's mouth twitched in ill-concealed humour.

"Now there's the small chore of getting her on a horse," Cenith sighed.

"Might I suggest she ride with you? If you plan on keeping her, she needs to become accustomed to you, not me," Daric said.

That hint again, that he might not be stuck in this marriage. For some reason, there didn't seem to be such a rush to find a way out, nor was this the time to discuss it.

Jolin brought Cenith his horse and he settled himself into Windwalker's saddle. "See if she'll let you put her behind me."

"Ohhh!" The girl pointed at him, excited about something. "Man! Horz! Man! Teree!" Then the look of horror returned. Her shriek pierced the night air. "Baybee! No! No! *Baybee!*"

She sank to her knees looking like her world had ended. Tears glistened, then fell in two streams down her face.

And things were going so well. "Daric? Any idea what this is about?"

"I think I can help." Daric opened another of Nightwind's saddle bags, rummaged in it a moment, then pulled out an old rag doll. He walked over to Cenith before letting her see it.

"*Baybee!*" she cried, joy, mixed with relief, altering her features. She went to Daric as quickly as her wounds would allow, then held her hands out to receive the doll. "Baybee." She seemed to have two levels to her voice; soft, quiet as a dove, and an ear-shattering shriek.

Instead of letting her have the doll, Daric set it behind Cenith. "You have to sit here first. You." He pointed at the girl. "Horse." He patted the saddle. "Then Baybee."

Confusion replaced joy. Cenith thought she might start crying again. "Horz? Baybee?"

Daric nodded. "Horse. Then you can have Baybee."

He passed the doll to Cenith, who felt like an idiot holding the worn toy. He glanced over at the soldiers. Every eye watched them, but, once again, they had the grace not to laugh, though a few looked like they struggled, particularly Jolin, who still held Windwalker's bridle.

"I have to touch you," Daric told the girl. He moved around behind her and put his hands on her waist. "Hurt?"

She gave several quick nods. "Hurt! Baybee?"

Daric let go. "Horse first. This is going to be interesting." He retrieved his blankets from the log. Folding one, he laid it across the back of Cenith's saddle. The other he gave to Cenith, who now held blanket and doll.

"Sir? What if I let her use me as a step stool?" Jolin suggested. "She can't weigh much."

"Excellent idea," Daric said.

Varth took over holding Windwalker. Jolin stood close to the horse and crouched down, bent over, hands on the ground. Daric held his hand out to the girl. She blinked her eyes, but made no move.

"Horse first. Then Baybee," Daric said, his voice firm, but quiet. "Take my hand, or no Baybee."

She stepped toward him and put a shaking hand in his, her small white one engulfed by his darker one. Daric helped her climb onto Jolin's back, then put one of her hands on the horse to steady her. He moved her feet to Jolin's broad shoulders and the soldier slowly stood until her feet came level with the back of the horse. Cenith laid the doll and blanket on the saddle in front of him and took her left hand. She flinched, but didn't pull away.

Daric helped her sit behind Cenith and covered her shoulders with the blanket, making sure it wouldn't slip off. He showed her how to hold onto Cenith's belt, telling her she'd be hurt if she let go. Finally, he gave her the doll, wedging it between her and Cenith so it wouldn't fall.

"Take her around the clearing a few times," he said.

When she had the hang of it, Daric mounted and signalled the men into riding formation.

"We're going to have to ride for a couple of hours at least," Daric said to Cenith. "We can't move quickly in case she falls off. She'll be sore enough as it is. Might I also suggest you think of a name for her while we ride?" He mounted Nightwind.

"Me!"

"You are her husband."

Daric signalled Trey and Warin, who would be their scouts, to head out, then led the rest of the party out of the clearing. Cenith pulled in behind him.

A name? Every female name he'd ever heard vanished from his memory. He let Windwalker follow Nightwind while he tried to recover them.

At this late hour, they should be wrapping themselves in blankets and falling sleep. Cenith stifled a yawn. He barely felt the girl behind him or where her child-like hands gripped his belt. It had been a long, eventful day and the night showed little promise of improvement.

* * * *

Rymon shook his head. Things had gone from worrisome to desperate to disaster, all in the matter of a few hours. Tajik stood at attention at the base of Saulth's dais, if that could be called 'at attention'. The man could barely stand. His cloak hung in tatters, his usually pristine uniform torn and filthy. Tajik bore numerous scratches, visible on his face and through the rips in his clothing. He shifted uncomfortably off his injured foot.

"I apologize, My Lord. I should have taken more men. I didn't think Lord Cenith would actually consider keeping the girl," Tajik said.

Saulth drummed his fingers on the broad arm of the chair. "Neither did I. I had no idea he could be so spiteful. He is just a runny nosed kid."

Who was trained by Daric, Rymon sighed to himself. A fact Saulth had a tendency to forget, or ignore.

"He may be a runny nosed kid, My Lord," Tajik said, "but he was about to give the command to attack when Daric showed up."

Saulth stopped drumming his fingers. "That Calleni is becoming a serious liability. Tajik, I want Buckam brought to me before you see to your injuries."

Tajik executed a stiff bow and hobbled out of the Lord's Hall.

"Buckam, My Lord?" *What possible use could he be right now?* "He will be laid up with his wounds for at least ten days. The healer is already concerned about infection."

"I do not care if he is on his deathbed!" Saulth spat. "He will present himself or leave my service."

Rymon waited in silence until Buckam appeared, leaning heavily on another guard's arm. He wore uniform trousers, but no tunic or jerkin. The blood stained bandages covering his wounds lay in a snug band beneath the thin fabric of his white shirt. Curls of blonde hair, darkened with sweat, clung to his forehead and neck.

"My Lord," he said in a strained voice, "I await your orders."

Saulth sat back in his chair, a triumphant smile on his face. "Do you wish to redeem yourself?"

"Yes, My Lord." The boy struggled to stand straight. "I wish to prove I am worthy to be one of your guard."

"I want you to take a horse and ride to Tiras. Stay ahead of Cenith. It should not be too difficult, he is hampered by the girl."

Buckam's flushed face paled. "Ride...My Lord?" He gulped.

Saulth shrugged. "I only lashed your back, not your ass. You should not have too much trouble sitting a horse. Once you are in Tiras, I want you to find your way to Cenith's study and retrieve a piece of parchment. It should be easy to find, it looks similar to the ones in my library. I need the girl back as well. When you have both, then you may return."

Rymon's shoulders sagged. Saulth delivered Buckam a death sentence. The guards assigned to looking after the girl were all chosen for their stealth and ability to remain quiet for long periods of time. In full health, Buckam stood a chance of succeeding. Bearing deep whip wounds, however, he had no hope of performing as needed. Provided he even made it to Tiras alive.

Saulth leaned forward, his dark eyes drilling into Buckam's blue ones. "You must get there before Cenith arrives, is that understood?"

Buckam slumped against the guard, who struggled to hold him upright. "I will do as you ask, My Lord." His voice came out more like a croak.

"Excellent." Saulth reclined once more. "Succeed and you will earn yourself not only a redemption but a promotion as well. Do not wear your uniform or even carry it with you. Wear only the clothing of a common man. Ensure there is no indication you are one of my guards on either yourself or your horse. If you get caught, you do not work for me. Understand?"

Buckam nodded.

"Take whatever you feel you will need to accomplish your mission," Saulth continued. "Tell the stable master you are to have Hawkwing. He is fast and has a smooth gait. Take the Old West Road so you do not run into Cenith. You must leave as soon as you are ready."

"I understand. Thank you, My Lord. I will not fail you," Buckam said. Hope deserted his eyes. The guard almost carried him from the room.

When they'd gone, Rymon dared voice his thoughts. "He will be dead before he even reaches the pass."

"I am sure he will be." Saulth looked pleased with himself.

Rymon's tongue thickened. "My…My Lord?"

Saulth chuckled. "Daric will be looking for another attempt at both the parchment and the girl. We will give him one. Do you really think Daric would be foolish enough to follow the main road?" He rested his elbows on the arms of the chair and tapped his fingers together. "He will find Buckam, probably dead."

"And when Daric finds him, the girl will recognize him. Daric's suspicion will be proven and he will relax his guard," Rymon finished. *Why do I have misgivings about this?*

"That is the plan. Meanwhile, Rymon, I want you to pay a visit to Snake."

For a moment, Rymon thought his heart had stopped. "Snake? That murderous cutthroat?"

"We have an understanding, Snake and I. He does the odd job for me and I turn a blind eye to some of his more…lucrative…dealings." The light in Saulth's eye showed Rymon depths of hell he'd never wanted to see. He had known nothing of this arrangement. What else was Saulth keeping from him?

"Have him send a band of his jolly fellows to Tiras," Saulth continued. "I should have sent Snake in the first place. I want them to get the parchment and the girl, and bring both to me. I do not care how they do it."

Snake! Just the thought of the man turned Rymon's bowels liquid.

"Tell Snake I will pay one hundred gold for the girl and the same for the parchment. If they kill Daric while they are at it, I will double it."

Saulth raised a finger. "However, they are not to kill Cenith. I want to see the look on that boy's face when I show him what his wife really is and the power that could have been his. Not to mention avoiding all-out civil war. I am not ready for that yet."

The death of a councillor…well, these things happened. The murder of a lord, however, wouldn't be overlooked by the other lords. Rymon's blood turned colder than Frost, the hell where Saulth's heart seemed to have taken up residence. The bottom fell out of his stomach and his knees shook. For the first time in his life, Rymon felt truly grateful for the cane.

How could he have come up with that plan so quickly? We had both expected Tajik to succeed!

"Assuming the girl is returned, My Lord," Rymon said, fighting to keep control of his body. "How can you be sure she will obey you?"

Saulth laughed. The echo of it bounced off the rafters and slammed into Rymon's ears. "She is afraid of me. She will do anything to ensure I do not beat her again. And once I start teaching her what she needs to know to fulfill her role, I will reward her for her efforts. She will be so grateful she will both fear and love me. How can I fail?"

Chapter Eleven

Cenith ran a hand through his hair, trying to absorb Daric's tale. His wife sat on one of his blankets beside him, her doll clutched to her chest, another blanket around her shoulders. She watched a moth flit overhead. Cenith told her the word for it and she had to say it three times. *My wife. Will I ever get used to the idea? Or her?*

"Knowing why she's like this makes it at least a little easier to take," he said to Daric. "It also makes me hate that goat-turd more than I already do."

The Calleni had taken back his blankets and now lounged on one nearby. "If that's possible."

Quiet 'oohs' and 'ahhhs' of wonder escaped the girl's lips from time to time. A cricket would chirp, or an owl call to its mate, and she'd tilt her head, a puzzled look on her face. She'd only made half the journey before she slid off the horse, unconscious. Jolin, riding close behind them, had saved her from falling to the ground. She rode the rest of the way sleeping in the crook of Cenith's arm. If she'd been awake, he doubted she'd have allowed the close contact.

Such a brave little thing. The only hint he'd had of her pain was the occasional little whimper or quiet cry if Windwalker stumbled. She'd slept while Daric filled him in on what he'd learned and had woken up moments before, cautious, but not in fear. She even allowed Cenith to sit closer.

Though smaller than the other copse, this one also had a well-used fire pit. Nonetheless, Daric had forbidden its use in case Saulth sent more men after them. With the night air milder than what they were used to this time of year in the mountains, they didn't need one. Cenith ensured the girl had a blanket around her, though, her tiny feet tucked in.

"What is she, Daric? It's been less than two days since Saulth beat her and yet the wounds look like it's been twice that long."

Daric shook his head. "I can't even make a guess. It's not just her quick healing that has me concerned. It's her health in general."

"She doesn't look healthy, that's for sure," Cenith said. With her ashen skin, dark circles under her eyes and blue tinge to her lips, she looked fair game for Shival. She didn't act it though.

"Her confinement to the storeroom explains her pale skin," the Calleni said. "The dark circles and bluish tinge are a direct result of blood loss from the beating. No, it's not a lack of health I'm concerned about. She's too healthy for the life she's been forced to live."

Too healthy? Despite her appearance, the girl's eyes shone bright and if not for her wounds, Cenith felt sure she'd be chasing the moth she watched.

"What do ye mean, sir?" Jolin asked, the only one of the guards not abed, except for those on watch.

Daric's eyes took on the dark, faraway look they sometimes had when he dredged up memories best forgotten. It took him a moment to answer. "I've seen men who've spent far less time out of the sun than she has. Once strong, their legs were bent, twisted; they were always in pain. She should be malformed and sickly."

"If ye don't mind me askin', sir. Where did ye see these men?" Jolin's piercing green eyes held those of his former guard-commander, now snapped back from the past. Cenith swore his soldiers spent more time prying stories out of Daric than they did in weapons practice.

The two locked gazes for the span of three score heartbeats before Daric chuckled. "A misspent youth."

Jolin's look said he wanted more than that.

Daric drew his long legs up and rested his arms on his knees before he continued. "I've told you my mother was a whore and that she passed into Niafanna's arms long ago."

Jolin nodded.

"I didn't tell you the manner of her death." Daric stared at a spot on the ground.

Jolin barely breathed. The only sound came from the girl, who now had two moths to watch.

"I was eleven years old," Daric said, after a few tense moments had dragged by. "I'd spent the afternoon scrounging the back alleys of the better neighbourhoods of Baharet for any scraps of food the inn owners had thrown out. That was my job when Mother was busy entertaining a 'customer'.

"When I returned home, I found her lying in a pool of blood. The floor of our home wasn't straight and her blood had run in a red river to the wall, then down to a rat's hole in the other wall. I can see it even now. I thought it odd at the time that blood could flow like that and yet still be splattered everywhere; the bed, the wall, all over the floor. I tried to shake her awake, even though I knew she was dead."

"Oh!"

Cenith turned to the girl, who pointed at the edge of the clearing. He squinted, but could see nothing in the darkness. "Shhh. Daric's talking." He touched her hand. She snatched it away.

"I'd seen the man when he first came," Daric continued. "He stared at me as if I'd crawled out of a hole. While the authorities took what was left of my mother away, I burned his face into my memory. I didn't know the man's name and even though I gave the city guards his description, they said they could do nothing without a name." Daric grunted. "Didn't know then that the guards wouldn't waste their time on a whore's murderer."

Daric stretched his right leg out straight. He'd injured it long ago in a distant war and the wound still bothered him from time to time. "Much happened over the next fourteen years, some I've told you, some I won't, no matter how much you annoy me."

The corner of Jolin's mouth twitched up, but he kept his gaze solidly on Daric. "Interestin', and I'm sorry about yer Ma, but it don't tell me where ye saw those sick men."

The girl cooed again and struggled to her feet, the blanket sliding from her shoulders. *If her wounds hurt, why doesn't she just stay put?* She picked her way to the edge of the clearing, to the spot she'd pointed to, Daric's tale delayed while they all watched her.

"Nesses?" Daric asked.

The girl shook her head, then started to bend over. She winced and changed her mind, sitting on the dew damp grass instead, wincing again when she rested her weight on her bottom. She held out her hand. A rabbit hopped out of the bushes. Too small to have been long away from its mother, it wriggled its nose and moved close enough to sniff the girl's hand. She made little noises of delight when it touched her, more when the rabbit let her stroke its ears, which Cenith found odd.

"Rabbit," Cenith said. She repeated the word three times. *Why does she do that? Did Rani tell her to?* Until the girl learned to talk properly, there were a lot of questions that would have to wait their answers.

Daric stared at her, an intense look on his face.

"What's the matter?" Cenith asked.

"How many times has a wild rabbit come up to you and let you pet it?"

It didn't take long for Cenith to respond. "Never."

"Jolin?"

"Not once that I recall, sir. Would make catchin' 'em for stew a lot easier if they did."

"Wish I knew who she really is," Daric said.

"You don't think she's Saulth's daughter?" Cenith wouldn't put it past Saulth to foist a scullery lad's get on him.

"It isn't her sire I question. Rymon wouldn't have lied, he's not the type," Daric said. "It's her mother. There are those among my people who have…special abilities, gifts from Niafanna, especially amongst the nobility. Some can predict the future, others can tell when a sandstorm or unexpected rainfall will happen. I knew a man who could find water with a forked stick. Every time." Daric nodded his head in the girl's direction. "There are even those who have an uncanny talent with animals, both wild and tame. But I've never heard of someone with more than one ability or of anyone who can heal as fast as she does."

A curious girl raised in strange circumstances. *Just what is Saulth up to? Of what possible use is a girl with no knowledge or experience of the world, who can heal quickly and pet wild animals?* Perhaps that's why Saulth dumped her on him; she didn't have what he wanted. Which led to the question 'What does Saulth want?' Then right back to 'What is Saulth up to?' A never-ending circle. More important, why did he give her away, then want her back?

The three of them sat lost in their thoughts, watching the girl pet the rabbit, doll in one arm, until Cenith stifled a yawn. "We should try to get some sleep."

He wished the girl would settle down but she showed no sign of sleepiness. Pain, yes. Tired, no. The rabbit decided it had had enough attention and hopped back into the bushes.

She studied the ground for a few minutes, then touched it with the tips of her fingers. "Hurt."

"If you hurt," Cenith said, "then come and sit here on the blanket. It's more comfortable."

She stood, careful of her wounds, and looked up at the night sky. "Stars."

Cenith had told her that word. Then she gasped. "Oooh!"

The moon had travelled far enough that it now shone through the trees. She pointed at it, almost jumping in excitement, and looked to Cenith for the word. He couldn't help but smile. His smile grew when she returned it.

"Moon," he said.

"Ohhhh! Moon!" Twice more she repeated the word, gazing at the orb, reaching for it as if she wanted to grab it from the sky.

"Ahem." Jolin brought Cenith's attention back to him. "Beggin' yer pardon, sir," he said, speaking to Daric. "Ye never did answer my question."

Scowling, Daric stretched himself out on his blanket and leaned on one arm. "I was hoping you'd forget about it."

"Who? Me, sir?" Jolin grinned. "I believe fourteen years had passed since yer Ma was killed and ye were tellin' us about those sick men ye saw."

"Think I'm too old to remember where I left off in my story, Jolin?" Daric's voice rumbled through the clearing.

Jolin's grin never wavered. "Nay, sir. My Ma didn't raise me t' be stupid. Jus' wanted t' make sure ye kin answer my question sometime afore mornin'."

Daric laughed. "All right, for the sake of sleep, I'll be brief. I finally ran across the bastard that took my mother from me. He turned out to be a prominent merchant from Parth. I hired on as a guard on one of his trips to Baharet. I'd built a reputation by then and merchants were eager to part with their coin for my services. Though I charged the camel-dung double, he paid it gladly. It was easy getting close enough to kill him. I made a mistake, though. I was too eager."

"Got caught?" Jolin asked, his grin gone.

Daric nodded. "When the other mercenaries heard my story, they said it was deserved. His personal guards didn't see it that way. Spent almost two months in Baharet's worst prison."

"I knew it!" Varth leapt up. Ead joined him, careful of his recently stitched wound. They startled the girl and Cenith went to her.

Jolin groaned. The other 'sleeping' soldiers sat up, some looking pleased, others not. The four on duty ran into the clearing.

"No hurt," Cenith said to the girl. She calmed and he indicated they should sit on the blanket again. She followed him, keeping an eye on Ead and Varth, but remained standing.

"Do I want to know what this is about?" Daric's scowl deepened. He sat up.

"Ead and Varth said ye'd been in prison, the scars on yer back proved it. I said no, ye were too honest. Yer morals wouldna' let ye do anythin' t' deserve it." Jolin shook his head. "I was so sure."

"Funny thing about morals. I didn't have, nor want, any until I got out of that prison." Daric's eyes twinkled, giving lie to the stern expression on his face. "I gather the bet didn't remain between the three of you?"

"Nay, sir. We were runnin' half 'n half. Not jus' us, ye understand. The entire keep guard."

Varth hunkered down beside Jolin, his grin wider than his friend's previous one. "Is that where you got the scars, then, sir?"

Ead joined Varth and Jolin, though he remained standing.

"It is. And where I saw the sick men. Many died in the time I was there, some from illness, some from wounds. I was damned lucky to get out when I did. Niafanna and Cillain both watched over me and I thank them every day."

"Speaking of, you haven't done your night prayers," Cenith said.

"Niafanna and Cillain understand when circumstances prevent it," Daric said. "Now we really should get some sleep. Varth, you, Yanis, Trey, and Madin can take the next shift."

"Sir? How did ye git out?" Jolin asked. Neither Varth nor Ead had left his side. A strange friendship. Nobles' sons, Ead and Varth had grown up together. Jolin's simple home lay so far back in the mountains, his family almost lived in the West Downs.

"As I said, luck." Daric picked up a small piece of worn bark and tossed it into the cold fire pit. "Another merchant in the city, a rival to the one who'd killed my mother, paid for my freedom. Said I'd done him a favour, though I had to work for him for three years without wages to pay him back."

"Still must have been worth it, to kill the man who murdered your mother," Varth said.

"Let me tell you something about revenge." Daric lost the gleam in his eye. "I spent fourteen years thinking of ways to kill that wretch when I finally did find him. And I had no doubt I would one day. When the time came, I gave him what he gave my mother, and more. Sitting in that stinking hell-hole for two months made me realize it had accomplished nothing."

Varth frowned, as did some of the others. "What do you mean, sir? You got your revenge."

"I did. He took not only my mother's life, but a good portion of mine as well. I can't tell you what my life would have been like if I hadn't sought revenge. Ten years were spent working under one master or another just so I'd have the strength and knowledge to do what I felt I had to." Daric fixed each of them with his gaze. "Four more building a reputation I'd rather not have. And when all was done, it did nothing to bring my mother back. That bastard stole another two months and would have had my entire life if the merchant hadn't bought my freedom. Violence feeds violence and I am a shining example."

Daric lay down and rolled over, putting an end to the tale. Varth stood and motioned to the other guards now on watch. All four disappeared into the trees.

"Nesses?"

"She's your wife," Daric said.

Cenith groaned, but held out his hand. "Come on, then."

Hesitant, she took it. A small breakthrough, but a significant one, and Cenith took care not to hold her hand too tight. She let him lead her into the trees, her doll still clutched in one arm. Her bare feet took tiny careful steps. They would have to stop in a village before they reached the mountains; she needed shoes.

Cenith had no desire to spend the rest of the night searching for a suitable log. Once well inside the trees, he dug a hole in the soft dirt with his heel and pointed to it. "Nesses. And please be quick about it, I'm tired." He turned around.

Several long moments later, she appeared at his side. Moonlight highlighted a wet spot in the hole. Cenith kicked dirt over it and offered her his hand again. She took it right away, and gave him another smile.

Once back at the blankets, he lay down and patted the spot beside him. "Sleep now."

"Food. Puh-leece?"

Cenith groaned again and sat up.

"I'll git somethin' for her if ye'd like, m'lord."

"Thank you, Jolin. I'd appreciate it." He looked up at the girl. "Sit, then food."

She sat beside him. Jolin brought cheese and bread, careful to come up on Cenith's side. The soldier let him give it to her. Once she had the food, she dug into it with great relish. Cenith lay down again.

"Food," he said. "Then sleep."

She stopped eating long enough to say, "No sleep."

"Yes, sleep." Cenith's eyes closed by themselves. He ignored her repeat of 'no sleep'.

* * * *

The world lurched while Buckam tried to stay mounted on Hawkwing. He clung to the palfrey's mane, the reins clutched in his fists. Buckam's back burned fire. Sweat trickled down his face despite the cool morning air.

He'd passed a few small villages during the night and stopped to rest and water the horse once. Buckam hadn't dared dismount. He'd needed help getting on the horse in the first place and knew he'd never make it back into the saddle himself.

Another village blurred by. The few inhabitants stared at him as if he were a ghost. *Which I might well be in a few hours.* Hawkwing slowed to a walk, ambling down the empty road as if on a morning stroll. Buckam lay across his neck too sick and too tired to force the gelding to move any faster. The smell of sweaty horse added to the nausea brewing in his gut. He hadn't eaten since the beating. *Just as well. I would have lost it by now.*

Caden, wherever Shival sent you, I hope she sends me to the same place. I need to see a friendly face. But would Caden want to see him? *He's dead because of me. Caden, with his easy smile and quick wit. My friend! Can you ever forgive me?*

Trees passed, some in pink and white bloom. The road flowed by, grey and brown. Colours swirled together and his father rode beside him, tall and proud. A captain in Saulth's guard, he'd only wanted Buckam to follow him, to protect and honour their lord, as he'd done, and his father before him. A wasting sickness had stolen him away three years earlier. Yet now he rode beside Buckam, astride his black destrier, a smile on his face, the wind in his hair.

What would you think of our lord now, Father? He has gone mad! Taxes are doubled. He spends more time staring at that old scroll than he does seeing to the needs of the principality. He treats that poor girl worse than an animal. How can I respect someone like that? His father shook his head, a sad expression on his noble face. *Will you be waiting for me, Father? Will I be allowed to sit at Maegden's side with you? Are you proud of me? I am still loyal to Bredun. I am!*

Buckam was sure his father didn't sit in one of the hells; he'd been brave, honourable, and kind. Despair washed over him. *Shival will never allow me to be with you. I caused this. I am responsible for that girl's pain, and Caden's death.*

His back screamed agony. The swirl of colours settled into one. Black. Shades of black. With white spots. *Hot, so hot*. He needed to swim in the pond near his home with his friends. With Caden. *Caden? But I didn't meet Caden until I joined the guard.*

A pale shape blocked out the black. Something warm and wet touched his face. A gust of horse breath blew up his nose. *Hawkwing.* He looked up into the horse's face. *When did I fall off?* Something tugged on his hand. He still held one of the reins.

Water. I need water. The canteen hung on the saddle. Buckam had to get to his feet. *I can pull myself up with the reins.* He rolled onto his stomach. It didn't ease the pain any. Long grass tickled his nose. The rich dark earth, damp from dew, filled his nostrils. If he didn't get up soon, that dirt would cover him. *I have to stand or I will die. I have to…*

* * * *

She hugged Baybee and watched the moon until it disappeared behind the *terees*. The round light had a *wuhd*. Moon. It was a nice *wuhd*. So much had happened since the *gard* took her from her room, so many things she didn't have *wuhds* for; but she'd learned new *wuhds* too and that was good.

These *mans* weren't like *him* or *his gards*. These ones kept saying they wouldn't hurt her. So far, they hadn't, not even the really big man. Not since he'd picked her up. Her back and bottom hurt, but it wasn't these mans who'd done that. They gave her food and water and taught her new *wuhds*. She had to be careful, though, they might change their minds.

Their nesses were strange, but that didn't really matter, not so long as there was something she could use. They let her pet a *horz*, and that was nice. So was the *rab-bit*. She smiled at the new *wuhd*. She had even got to sit on a *horz*, like the man in the cloth pit-chur. It would've been nicer if it hadn't hurt so much.

She shifted, careful she didn't hurt herself more. Her hurts weren't as bad as before, but if she sat for too long, they got worse.

All the *mans* she could see were asleep except one. He used a piece of wood to play in the grey and white stuff that looked the same as the stuff where the fire was, near her room. If there was someplace to make *pit-churs*, and if she didn't hurt so much, she'd show him what the stuff was supposed to be used for.

She turned her attention to the man sleeping beside her. He looked so much like the man in the *pit-chur* in the Book Room, more than he did. Much more. Cen-ith, he said while pointing to himself. He was a man. Ones like him were *mans*. Ones like Rani were *wo-mans*. Yet, Rani was Rani, and Rani was a *wo-man*. Could he be a man and Cen-ith too? Was there a *wuhd* for her? A *wuhd* all her own? That would be nice.

The man who was awake looked nice too. His hair was darker than the man sleeping beside her, the same colour as hers. He talked different, but he had a nice smile. This one had let her step on him so she could sit on the *horz* and get Baybee. She hugged Baybee hard; she'd missed her so much and thought she'd never see her again. It was nice of the big man to find her, even though he looked mean sometimes. The Book was nowhere to be seen, though, and that made her sad.

She sighed. Outside was so much more than she'd imagined, so big it was hard to take it all in. The *terees* were different than the one in her Book and from each other. So many *terees*, all over the place. The noises, the smells, the tickle of the green stuff on her feet—grass, another new *wuhd*—those were all different. Outside was strange, big, and nice.

What wasn't nice was the hurt she felt when she touched what lay under the grass. She couldn't feel it when she sat on the *blan-ket* or on the *horz*, only when she touched the grass. This was a big hurt, an old one, but no less hurting because it was old. She'd tried to tell the man Cen-ith that it hurt, but she didn't know the right *wuhds*. She hoped she could learn them, then she'd tell him.

It had been so strange when *his gards* had come. She'd been afraid they would take her to *him*. Many *wuhds* were said that she didn't know, but she didn't need *wuhds* to know the *mans* were angry. Their faces and the feeling in the air told her that. These mans didn't let the *gards* hurt her. Strange. Stranger still when that *gard's* hand came off. She'd tried and tried to take hers off, but it wouldn't come.

She looked up at the stars. That was a nice *wuhd* too. She frowned. The stars weren't as bright anymore. The big light was coming! She was supposed to be in her room! Where was her room? She tried to stand, but her hurts stopped her and she cried out. The man with the dark hair stopped playing in the white and grey stuff and came close to her.

The man sleeping beside her slept no longer. "Shhh," he said, taking her hand. He spoke *wuhds* to the man with dark hair and more to the big man, who was awake now too.

"Room!" She had to find her Room or *he* would come and hurt her more. She couldn't take any more hurt! "No hurt! Room!"

"No, no hurt. No room. Sleep." The man Cen-ith patted the *blan-ket*. "Sleep."

She hurt so bad her eyes watered and she let the man Cen-ith pull her down beside him. He lay next her and put the *blan-ket* over her. She settled so she lay mostly on her stomach and the hurt in her back eased. Maybe she didn't have to go back to her room.

"No Room?" The thought frightened her, and yet, if she didn't have to go back to her Room, did that mean *he* wouldn't hurt her anymore? "No hurt?"

The man Cen-ith smiled. "No room. No hurt."

He took his hand away. Maybe these *mans* would always be nice to her. She'd like that. She reached over and touched his hand, wondering if he'd mind if she did. It was hard, rough, and smelled like the *horz*, but warm. She'd not touched a person since Rani went away. It felt nice. *Mans* touched *wo-mans* without hurting, she knew that from the times she watched them in the Big Room, the same as just before *he* hurt her this time. The man Cen-ith's smile grew and he closed his hand around hers, more gentle than she thought a man could be.

An odd feeling rushed into her chest and she had to think about it. She remembered a feeling like that from long and long ago, when Rani was still with her. It was a good feeling. One she missed. The man Cen-ith's kind eyes and nice smile followed her into her dreams.

Chapter Twelve

Cenith glanced down at the girl sleeping in the crook of his arm, her doll clutched tight against her. Waking her had proved difficult, but they had to move on. They also needed to find a sheltered stream so she could have a bath and change into one of the dresses Daric had purchased.

The girl had allowed Daric and Jolin to help her on Windwalker, the same as the night before. Though she fussed at sitting sideways in front of Cenith instead of behind, she soon fell asleep again. Daric covered her with a blanket to keep her delicate skin protected from the afternoon sun.

Jolin had stayed awake the rest of the night and half the morning keeping an eye on her. When Cenith asked him why, he said he was concerned she'd wander off. Cenith had watched Jolin over the past few months. Backwoods born he might be, but he showed a talent and initiative Cenith needed in his guard. He reminded himself to talk to Daric about giving Jolin a promotion when they reached Tiras. Perhaps his own squad.

Varth and Trey scouted ahead while Daric kept close to Cenith. Everyone else had spread out behind, watching their rear, the most likely place for trouble to arrive. Except for Jolin, who slept in the saddle. Ead rode beside him in case he fell off, though Jolin insisted he'd done this many times.

Daric suggested they follow the Old West Road, hoping to avoid trouble. They'd left the flooded Asha River behind and now followed a northwest path through sodden fields of green, skirting the villages. Daric feared Saulth's men would force the villagers to help them recover the girl. For the same reason, they'd sleep in one of the copses littering the landscape instead of the way stations or inns. One of the sentries had heard a single horse gallop by late the night before, but nothing since.

The girl murmured and shifted slightly before settling once more.

You need a name. "Daric, I give up."

His councillor lifted an eyebrow.

"Every name I come up with just doesn't seem to fit her. How about a Calleni name? What about her mother's name? Islara, wasn't it?"

Daric nodded. "A common Calleni name. Too common for an uncommon girl."

"What about your mother's? Would you mind if we used it?"

"Her name was Gurtha."

Gurtha. She looked less like a 'Gurtha' than any of the names Cenith had come up with. "Would you be offended if we didn't use it?"

Daric chuckled. "My mother hated her name. I wouldn't be offended."

They drew closer to yet another copse of trees, mostly silver maple. Cenith ran more names through his mind. His mother's name, Zyree, was Syrthian. It didn't suit the girl either.

"There was a girl who lived near us," Daric said, a different kind of lost look in his eyes. "When we were six, I asked her to marry me. She said she couldn't because another boy in the neighbourhood had already asked." Another chuckle rumbled in his throat. "Broke my heart. Had the sweetest face, and hair just as fine and silky as this one."

Fine and silky? Cenith fingered a lock sticking out of the blanket. He supposed it did feel fine and silky, underneath the dirt and bloody mats. "What was her name?"

"Tyrsa."

"Tyrsa. That's a pretty name." One that suited her. "Tyrsa of Tiras. Sounds almost poetic. We'll see how she likes it when she wakes."

Varth and Trey entered the copse of silver maple. Moments later, Trey thundered back toward them. The remaining guards surrounded Daric and Cenith, their weapons already out. Jolin showed no sign of sleep.

"My Lord! Sir!" Trey said, reining in his horse. "We found a man lying by the road."

"Is he alive?" Daric asked.

"Yes, but he's not in good shape. He's feverish and the back of his shirt shows fresh blood stains."

"Take Madin, Fallan, and Yanis," Daric said. "Scour those trees. This could be an ambush."

"Yes, sir!" The soldiers named followed Trey back up the road at full gallop.

"Do ye want me t' go too, sir?" Jolin looked hurt.

"No, I want you here in case the ambush comes from another direction."

Mollified, Jolin scanned the low ridges to the left and right of them. Ead watched behind.

Cenith glanced again at the sleeping girl. If Saulth's men were lying in wait, how far would he go to protect her? Could he justify the loss of some of his men? All of them? Even Daric? Would he go so far as to die defending her?

She shifted again. Perhaps her wounds were bothering her. Her eyes fluttered open and he found himself sinking in their blue depths.

"Rani," she murmured, then closed her eyes and snuggled closer.

The answer to his questions hit him like a rock in the back of the head. *Yes.* An answer which only brought more questions. Particularly 'why'. Daric said he wouldn't give her up, if for no other reason than Saulth wanted her. For Cenith, it was more that. He'd already made his decision to protect her before Daric had appeared.

What was there about the girl that made him do that? He didn't love her, though now that he knew more about her, the possibility did exist. She brought out a side of him he never knew he had. Was this how fathers felt about daughters? Or perhaps it was the male in him wanting to protect a helpless female. Noble, but even that didn't feel quite right.

Varth rode back to them at an easy canter. "No sign of anyone in the woods, sir. The man is still unconscious. Looks like some villager or farmer. We did find his horse though; at least, I assume it's his."

Daric glanced at the sky. The sun had worked its way past dinnertime. "Her day will start soon. This is as a good a place as any to stop for a rest."

Cenith welcomed that idea, his arm ached from holding the girl. *Tyrsa. Her name is Tyrsa.*

Yanis had found a large clearing deep in the copse. A small stream ran nearby. Varth and Jolin set up camp while Trey and Madin carried the sick man in. Daric took Tyrsa from Cenith and laid her on a blanket. She never stirred.

With Trey's help, Daric removed the man's light wool shirt. "We're going to have to risk a fire. I need clean water to dress these wounds. Another flogging victim. Coincidence?"

Daric's tone said otherwise. Cenith crouched beside him, flexing his stiff arm. The 'man' looked more like a boy, his thin face flushed and tight with fever. His back had fewer cuts than the girl's, but they appeared far worse. "Do you think he has a chance?"

"It depends on him. On how badly he wants to live. I hope he does recover, at least long enough to answer some questions."

The guards took advantage of the fire and cooked a hot meal while Daric, with Trey's assistance, cleaned the man's wounds. He also ordered Jolin to sleep until dinnertime. When both cleaning and eating were done, Yanis and Barit extinguished the fire.

Full dark arrived before the girl woke. Cenith took her some food and sat with her, wondering how he should approach the subject of her name.

When she'd finished eating and had two cups of water, he pointed to himself and said, "Cenith. Cenith."

She frowned, but said his name, better than she had before. Cenith pointed at Daric, Trey, and Jolin, saying each of their names and making her repeat them.

Now for the interesting part. He pointed at her. "Tyrsa. Your name is Tyrsa."

Her face screwed up in puzzlement and Cenith struggled not to laugh. She pointed at him. "Cenith." Then at Daric, Trey, and Jolin, saying each of their names again. She pointed at herself. "Tyrsa?"

Cenith nodded. "Tyrsa."

She smiled, and her eyes lit up. "Tyrsa. Tyrsa." She stood, careful of her wounds, and walked over to Jolin. She pointed at him. "Jolin." Then herself again. "Tyrsa."

Jolin laughed and gave her a bow. "Lady Tyrsa."

She approached Varth and the soldiers not on watch, repeating the performance. Daric and Trey were last. When they'd each said her name, she looked down at the injured man and lost her smile.

She pointed at one of the wounds on his back. "Hurt."

"Yes, he's hurt," Daric said, applying more salve to a deep cut on the man's shoulder blade.

Tyrsa knelt, keeping her back straight, and looked at the man's face. She almost fell over trying to back away. "No hurt! No hurt!"

She ran to Cenith, who had jumped to his feet when she cried out. He took her hand and pulled her to him.

"He can't hurt you. No hurt," he said, stoking her matted hair. She huddled against him, quivering.

"That answers one of my questions," Daric said. "He's definitely one of Saulth's men. Jolin, search his belongings."

"Aye, sir." Jolin returned a few moments later leading a pretty, cream coloured palfrey. Certainly not the type of horse a commoner could afford.

Jolin wore a grim expression. "He didn't have much with him. Some food, a half full canteen, and a change o' clothes. Nothin' outta th' ordinary, except his horse. I remember this one." He patted the horse's nose. "A handler had him out for some exercise while Lord Cenith was…um…bein' married. Ead and I had a discussion on how much he'd cost."

"Why would Saulth send a sick and wounded man to do a job six healthy ones couldn't?" Cenith asked.

"You have echoed my thoughts." Daric finished with the salve and stood. "Lacus said Saulth whipped one of his guards the same day he beat the girl. Chances are excellent this is him."

Cenith gritted his teeth. "Are we now supposed to think Saulth's plan failed and not look for any more pursuers? How stupid does he think I am to fall for an obvious ruse like this!"

Daric finished packing up his kit and joined Cenith. "Quite, I'd say, which could be to our benefit. I assume Saulth figured he'd be dead when we found him." Daric glanced back at the unconscious man. "We should try to get some sleep. I'd like to leave in a few hours."

"What do we do with him?" Cenith had no objections to just leaving him there. "I suppose we could drop him off in the next village."

"If you don't mind, I'd rather bring him with us. There are questions I'm hoping he can answer. We can build a litter and tie it behind his horse. A rough ride, but we can't sit here waiting for Saulth to make his next move."

Cenith nodded, still stroking Tyrsa's hair. Somewhere in the back of his mind, past the Bredun guard, the shock of his speedy wedding, and the entire fiasco at the Lord's meeting, he was surprised she let him stay so close.

* * * *

Cenith wanted sleep, but Tyrsa needed a bath more. He and Daric took her to the stream Yanis had found. Her doll had to come too. The butterflies that had plagued him in Edara made a sudden reappearance.

"Are you sure you won't help her bathe, Daric? I know you've done the duty for your daughters."

"That I can't do. As her husband, you're the only man who has the right to see her naked. It was only acceptable for me last night because I acted as healer." Daric turned his back, holding one of her new dresses and a blanket to wrap her in. "You're on your own. I'll keep watch."

"Thanks," Cenith said dryly.

Tyrsa stood at the edge of the stream, her eyes fixed on the burbling water. "Ohhh!"

Cenith handed her the soap. "I hope you know what to do with this."

She took it, then looked from the soap to him, the stream, and back to him. "Bath?"

"Bath." Thank Maegden she knew what he wanted. Maybe he could join Daric while she did the deed.

Tyrsa looked around her. "Bath?"

Cenith pointed at the stream. "Water. Bath."

She frowned. "Bath?"

He nodded. She stuck her foot in, then pulled it out. "Brrr!"

"Yes, it's cold, but it's all we have." He pointed at the stream again. "Bath. And could you please hurry?"

A snigger came from Daric's direction. "I doubt she's ever seen moving water," he said. "You may have to join her."

"Join her! She…she's…"

"Your wife." Daric's snigger turned into a chuckle. "You don't seem to have any problem getting naked in a whorehouse."

"That's different." *Don't have to get naked to do this.* Grumbling, Cenith sat on a nearby rock, pulled off his boots, then rolled up his trouser legs. He stepped into the water. Tyrsa gave him a dubious look, set her doll against the rock, and took his offered hand.

Taking small, careful steps, she entered the stream. "Hurt! Brrr!"

The stones covering the stream bed were small and rounder than most of those found in the mountains. The water, though warmer than the glacial rivers Cenith knew, was still cold. Tyrsa wouldn't be used to either.

"I really hate to say this, but you're going to have to remove the shirt." Cenith pointed at the only article of clothing she wore.

Tyrsa let go of his hand to give him the soap, then pulled the shirt over her head, wincing when she stretched her back. Cenith passed her the soap took the shirt and tossed it on the bank, trying not to look at her. She picked her way closer to him and tugged on his jerkin.

"Bath," she said, her voice firm.

"Not me. You." Cenith forced his eyes to stay focused on hers.

Another chuckle sounded from the bank.

"Bath," she said again.

"No." Cenith pointed at the water. "Your bath. Now."

Tyrsa frowned and stepped away from him. The frown changed to a look of surprise when she lost her footing. Cenith grabbed her arm as she went down. Light though she was, she weighed enough to pull him off balance. He shifted his foot to compensate, but found loose rock instead. She hit the water just before he did. Tyrsa cried out in pain. Cenith cursed as he landed on his left hip while trying to keep her from hitting too hard.

Daric appeared at the edge of the stream, without the blanket and dress. "Is she all right?"

"I don't know." Cenith stood, ignoring the blossoming pain and his dripping clothes.

Cenith switched his grip from Tyrsa's arm to her hand and helped her up, not sure if the drops on her face were water or tears. She shook from pain or cold, maybe both. He led her to the edge of the stream and held her close while Daric checked her back amid sniffles and 'hurts'.

"It doesn't look like she's reopened any wounds." After a few moments, Daric said, "As a matter of fact, these seem to be much better than they were last night. Even the bruises have faded significantly. Quite a difference from our friend back at the camp." He strode several steps away from the stream, no longer a healer. "I suppose you should have taken your clothes off after all."

Daric chuckled. Cenith grimaced. Tyrsa shivered.

"Frost and Char!" Cenith pushed her away, making sure she had her footing, and pointed his finger at her. By some miracle, she still held the soap. "Don't move!"

Her eyes widened, but she stayed put. Cenith strode out of the stream and removed his clothes. He entered the water faster than he'd left it and sat down when he reached her side. Tyrsa blinked, staring at his manhood until it disappeared into the water. Cenith's cheeks warmed.

He held out his hand. "Sit. Bath. Now."

Tyrsa took his hand and sat, letting out another 'Brrr!" She rubbed the soap over herself.

Cenith tried hard not to look—and failed. In the starlight, her pale skin resembled fresh milk. The wound on her breast stood out like a dark ribbon. She lifted one arm to wash underneath, then the other. Her breasts weren't as large as they'd first appeared in Saulth's hall; they only looked it on her small body, sitting high on her chest like two perfect moons.

Tyrsa washed quickly, her teeth chattering. Her hair took longer. When she leaned back to rinse away the soap, her breasts thrust toward the sky, the heat in Cenith's loins warred with the cold of the stream over what size his manhood should be.

"If you don't finish soon," he grumbled, "my tarse is going to shrivel into nothing, despite the view you're giving me."

Deep laughter echoed in the trees and Cenith's cheeks burned anew. *His hearing is too damn good!*

Tyrsa sat up and handed him the soap, shaking like an autumn leaf in a stiff breeze. Cenith made short work of his bath and stood, offering her his hand. The girl stared at his manhood again, a puzzled look on her face. He pulled her to her feet and led her out of the water. The blanket and her dress sat on the rock.

Cenith set the soap on the grass, wrapped her in the blanket, and tossed the dress over Daric's shoulder. "Hold this."

Tyrsa's teeth chattered while she huddled on the rock, a pathetic, thin waif, while Cenith put his wet clothes back on. He took the dress from Daric and gave it to her. She stared at it, her puzzled look back again.

"This is yours, for you," he said.

"D…dress?" she asked through rattling teeth.

"Yes, a dress, for you."

"Ohhh!" Her eyes shone. Cenith hoped it meant she was happy and not coming down with something. Then he remembered Daric said she'd never been sick.

Cenith helped Tyrsa into the dress. If he could get a few more pounds on her, she'd look more appealing. When finished, Tyrsa brushed the dark blue velvet lightly with the tips of her fingers, then with firmer strokes, making little noises of pleasure. Daric had made a reasonable guess. Though big everywhere else, the dress fit her chest.

"Let's get her back to the fire. She's almost frozen solid," Cenith said.

Daric joined them, picking up the soap, shirt, and wet blanket. Tyrsa already had Baybee, showing the doll her new dress. She let Cenith hold her hand while she tried to keep the bottom of the gown from dragging, without letting go of the doll.

Thank Maegden that's over with!

* * * *

Not for the first time on this trip, Cenith wished he were home. He yawned. The past two days had been spent in the saddle or trying to sleep. The Bredun guard drifted in and out of consciousness, lying on his stomach on the crude litter. Daric's medicines kept the fever from climbing too high, but delirium still addled the guard's brain. Nothing he said made any sense.

Tyrsa rode behind Cenith when awake, in front of him when she wasn't. Not only her back hurt now, but the inside of her legs as well. Daric gave him a liniment to rub into muscles unused to riding a horse. Applying it the first time proved another source of embarrassment for Cenith, though only the strong, bitter smell of the ointment bothered Tyrsa. Now they were both used to it.

Cenith worked hard on improving Tyrsa's pronunciation of the words she knew. When Daric brought out her book one morning in an effort to keep her awake as long as possible, she spent over two hours showing it to everyone, avoiding the Bredun guard. She kept well clear of him.

Tyrsa had spent most of the morning sitting behind Cenith, hidden under a blanket, tugging on his shirt sleeve when she wanted to know the word for something. Every now and then she came out with a string of words that made no sense whatsoever, and others that were painfully obvious in origin. She now slept curled up in his arms.

"We've spent all this time teaching her new words," he said to Daric. "How do we unteach some of those old ones?"

'It's burnt,' and 'No, not like that,' didn't bother him, but at breakfast, when she told Jolin that his 'motha musta futter a mool' he almost choked on the food in his mouth. Fortunately Jolin had a good sense of humour.

Daric shrugged, but didn't take his eyes off the swirling storm clouds surrounding them. "I'd recommend leaving that up to Elessa. She has an amazing talent teaching children what they should and shouldn't say."

"Doesn't it involve a wide piece of wood?" Cenith remembered she'd had it specially made for Kian after he spent an afternoon in the guards' barracks. "I don't think it would be a good idea to punish Tyrsa that way. She's been hurt more than enough."

"The wood is for the boys more than the girls. Leave it to Elessa. I'll make sure she knows about Tyrsa's past."

Thick rain drops spattered the road, creating small craters in the dust. Cenith tucked the blanket closer around Tyrsa's face, pushing back a lock of her hair. Daric was right. Once brushed, her hair shone, corn silk soft, each strand as delicate as the most expensive thread. Despite the fine texture, she had a lot of hair, which made brushing the mats out a chore, especially with her worn out brush. She'd refused any help.

Cenith glanced at the sky. The clouds had taken on a sickly green hue to the northwest and a green, bordering on black, to the northeast. Much too reminiscent of the storms they'd dodged on the way to Edara.

"I don't like the look of this," Daric said. "Ead, tell Madin and Yanis to watch for a place to hole up. We might be in for some nasty weather."

"Yes, sir." Ead kicked his black stallion into a gallop to catch up to those in the lead.

The rain increased. So did the clouds, roiling and churning above them. The wind picked up, whipping old leaves, dirt, and rain in their faces. Cenith hunched over Tyrsa, protecting her from the coming storm. A roar, like Canyon Falls, rumbled into existence.

"A tornado!" Jolin pointed to the northeast. A long funnel snaked out of the black clouds, less than a mile from them, churning up a spray of dirt and debris.

"There's another!" Trey pointed to one approaching from the northwest. Two miles separated the storms.

Ead galloped back toward them. "There's no buildings we can shelter in, My Lord! Sir!" He had to shout to make himself heard above the storms. "But Madin says the road crosses a small ravine with only a little water in it a few minutes from here."

"That'll have to do," Daric said.

"Maegden's balls!" Varth pointed due east. "There's a third!"

Cenith held Tyrsa close to him. The wind whipped his hair while the rising dust stung his cheeks. Three tornadoes stood out against the darkening sky and looked like they had every intention of converging right where they stood.

Hampered by Tyrsa and the Bredun soldier, they couldn't move as fast as Cenith wished. It seemed an eternity before they reached a small stone bridge crossing a narrow, shallow, ravine about ten feet deep. A few inches of muddy water ran in a steady trickle along the bottom. Tyrsa woke when Daric took her from Cenith, her wide eyes staring in every direction. Cenith slid off his horse, then took her in his arms before setting her on her feet. Branches, dust, and small rocks pelted them. He couldn't protect her while guiding her down the steep bank of the ravine and she cried out when a stone hit her back.

"Take the bridles, packs, and saddle bags off the horses!" Even Daric had to shout now. "Keep hold of them, especially the bag with my kit. Turn the horses loose in that field!" He indicated one just behind them.

Soldiers hauled packs and bags off the horses while Daric untied the Bredun guard from the litter and laid him as far down the incline of the ravine as he could, sheltering him with his own body. Cenith did the same for Tyrsa.

"Talueth protect us!" Varth cried. "All three are headed straight for us!" The guards almost fell into the ravine.

"Keep your head down!" Daric said.

"Baybee?" Tyrsa struggled out from under Cenith and tried to stand up. She no longer held her doll.

"No! Stay with me! It's too dangerous!" Cenith pulled on her arm, but she dug her heels in.

"Baybee!" Her hair whipped around her head, trying to fly in all directions at once. "*Baybee!*" Her shriek almost drowned out the screaming tornadoes.

Cenith pulled harder, forcing Tyrsa to her knees. "Get down! Hurt!" He pushed her to the ground, covering her.

"Baybee?"

He held her tight. A maelstrom of screaming wind ripped words from throats. Daric lay beside him. His mouth moved, but Cenith couldn't hear him; yet several yards away, he heard Varth say, "I see the doll! It's on the road! I'll get it!"

"Varth! No!" Jolin tried to grab his friend and missed.

Varth ran onto the road in a crouch, the wind whipping his reddish-brown hair so it stood on end. He grabbed the doll and turned to run back. The force of the converging winds almost blew him off his feet. He dove for the side of the ravine just as a rock, hurtling through the air, caught him on the side of his head. He collapsed in a heap in front of Jolin. Trey helped him pull Varth to safety.

The rain turned hard, pelting them with hail. Cenith wished he knew how Varth fared, but he didn't dare look. He kept Tyrsa sheltered with his body while covering his head with his arms. Dust and dirt stung his eyes; clogged his nose. The wind pulled at him, forcing him to dig the toes of his boots into the wet earth. The trickle of water in the ditch grew into a small stream and soaked his legs.

Tyrsa wriggled under him.

"Stay down! Hurt! Hurt!" He had to make her understand.

"No hurt! No hurt!" She cried and begged, repeating the words over and over, turning them into a chant.

The wind tore at Cenith's clothes, showered him with dirt and stones, then blew them away again. Hail slammed into his back, arms, and legs. Water rose to his hips, his waist. A horse screamed. The sound travelled over his head, then faded into the howl of the storms thundering above him. Cenith felt the wind try to lift him off the ground. He twined long grasses around his fist, forcing himself back down.

Tyrsa's chant blended with the roaring filling his ears, drowning out thought and reason, leaving behind only the need to survive.

And then silence, cold and still as a burial cave, broken only by Tyrsa's chant, reduced now to a whimper.

Chapter Thirteen

Silence pounded in Daric's ears. He shook his head, sending out a spray of wet dirt. The man beneath him groaned. Other moans and grunts of pain sounded all around him. Cenith pushed himself off Tyrsa.

"No hurt. No hurt," she said, her voice a quiet sob.

Daric stood. Rising water rushed by his thighs. "Out of the ravine! Now!"

Men struggled to their feet, slogging out of the mud and water. Ead and Jolin hauled Varth onto the road and laid him on his back. Daric carried the Bredun guard up the bank and set him down beside Varth, both men unconscious. The litter had disappeared.

Once the soldiers had a moment to recover, they began to inventory their injuries. Jolin sat wearily on the bank, trying to stem the blood flowing from the ragged cut on his right cheek, while Ead, kneeling beside the still unconscious Varth, appeared to be in shock. Many of the men rubbed sore spots. Daric understood; he'd suffered just as much under the pelting they'd taken from rocks and hail, but they could take no time to rest.

"Madin, find my kit. Yanis, Dathan, Fallan, Keev, Warin, retrieve the horses. Jayce, Trey, gather up the packs and check our supplies."

Daric crouched beside Varth. Blood covered the left side of the soldier's head. "Has he been conscious at all?"

"Nay, sir." Jolin looked exhausted. "Will he be a' right?"

"I don't know. I've seen plenty of head injuries over the years. Sometimes men recover with no ill effects. Some die, taking weeks to do it. Others fall somewhere in between." Daric pushed Varth's brown hair away from the wound, the reddish highlights now hidden by mud and dirt. A three inch long cut stretched from his temple to above his ear. Stitches would be needed to close it.

Daric undid his jerkin, tore a piece off the bottom of his shirt, and gave it to Ead. The soldier needed something to do. "Take some water from a canteen. Clean his face and around the wound, but don't touch it. I can't do anything else until Madin locates my supplies. Jolin, take Barit and find something to burn. I need hot water."

"Aye, sir."

"Daric!" Cenith's voice came from the ravine. "Help!"

"Get out of the ravine! The water's rising fast!"

"Can't! Tyrsa's stuck!"

Daric strode to the edge of the ravine. Tyrsa's arms were stretched up, and into, the bank, buried past the elbows. Water covered her to her chest, but she looked more surprised than hurt or upset. Daric slid down the steep incline, bracing himself so he didn't slip too far into the water. The stream had developed a strong current.

"How did she manage that?"

"I don't know! How do we get her out?"

Cenith had dug away some of the dirt around her left arm, but he needed help before the water rose too high. Anchoring his feet in the muck, Daric positioned himself so he could pull on Tyrsa's right arm while preventing her from being swept away by the rising water once they'd freed her. She cried out when Daric pulled too hard.

"I tried that already," Cenith said, scraping more mud away from her arms.

"We're going to have to dig her out." Daric scooped a few inches of soft earth away before he hit solid ground.

"How could she have done this?" Cenith asked, working on her left arm. "The ground looks like it opened up enough to let her arms in, then closed around them."

"I have no answer." Daric drew his dagger. Tyrsa struggled, panic in her eyes. The rushing water now reached her chin.

"No hurt! Puh-leece!"

"I won't hurt you. No hurt. I have to get this dirt away." Daric chipped and dug, Cenith imitating him on the other side.

Water flowed into the holes he and Cenith created, helping wash away the dirt. It also covered Tyrsa's mouth, forcing her to tilt her head back. Dirty brown water covered her arms and prevented Daric from seeing clearly. He shoved his dagger back into his belt, concerned he might hurt her, and resumed using his fingers. Tyrsa now had to breathe through her nose.

Daric tried pulling again. A sucking noise preceded a 'shlurp', and her arm came free, followed a few moments later by the other. Cenith lifted Tyrsa out of the water enough so she could breathe. She coughed and gulped in air.

"Hold her," Cenith said to Daric, and climbed up the bank. He reached down and helped Tyrsa onto the road, the heavy, wet velvet of her dress dragging behind her.

Daric moved to follow them, and couldn't. "By Cillain's blood!"

"What is it?" Cenith asked.

"My boot's stuck in the mud." Daric twisted his right foot back and forth in the hope it would loosen.

"Do you need help?"

"I'm not sure." Daric wriggled his foot again, then pulled hard.

His foot came out; the boot didn't.

"Damn." Daric couldn't worry about it now; water swirled around his chest, the strong current almost dragging his legs out from under him. He had to get out. Scrambling up the bank, he stopped long enough to ensure Cenith and Tyrsa were all right before joining Madin. The soldier stood beside Varth, holding the field kit.

"Those were good boots too," Daric grumbled, taking the other one off so he could walk without limping.

Jolin and Barit crossed the bridge, back to their side of the ravine. Barit dragged the remains of the litter, while Jolin had an armload of small branches.

"This is all we could find, sir," Jolin said. "We spotted another copse on a hill up ahead, but wi' th' wounded, it'll be a two hour trip."

"Hopefully this will be enough wood." Daric crouched once more beside Varth. "You might as well start the fire right here. Barit, collect the canteens, the water in the ravine is too dirty and too dangerous to go near." Branches and other detritus rushed along with the current.

"Baybee?"

Daric looked back at Cenith and Tyrsa. The girl shivered hard, blinking in what would be bright light to her.

"Don't worry about Baybee right now," Cenith said. He tried to hold her, but she leaned away from him.

"Baybee." Her lower lip trembled. Tears watered her eyes.

Ead strode past Daric, the doll in his hands. "Here's your thrice damned doll! I hope you're happy now!" He threw it at Tyrsa.

"Ead!" Daric covered the distance in three strides.

Cenith stared up at the guard in mute shock.

Tyrsa grabbed the doll, hugged it to her, and scuttled away from him. "No hurt. No hurt," she whimpered.

"If it hadn't been for her and that doll, Varth wouldn't be lying there unconscious!" Ead cried, taking another step toward Tyrsa.

Cenith, his jaw set in anger, stood, reaching down for the girl. She cringed and crawled backwards away from him.

Daric left her to Cenith. "Varth chose to go on his own," he said, taking hold of Ead's arm. "No one ordered him. No one asked."

"If she hadn't said anything, he wouldn't have gone for it!" Ead's eyes filled with tears. He blinked them back.

Jolin appeared at Ead's side. "Tis not th' lass's fault. She doesn't understand."

"Then she has no business being married to Lord Cenith!" Ead spat.

"That may be," Daric said, keeping his voice calm, yet firm, "but until Lord Cenith decides otherwise, she is his wife, and that makes her your lady. What you have done is disrespectful and in some places would be considered treason."

Ead's mouth dropped open. "Treason? But she's…"

"Your lord's *wife*." Daric tightened his grip. "Now, are you going to drop it?"

Ead's jaw clenched and he stood straight. "Yes, sir. May I return to Varth, sir?"

Daric nodded and let Ead go, keeping an eye on him until he sat beside Varth, his head in his hands.

"Don't pay no attention t' him, m'lord," Jolin said to Cenith, who had given up trying to get close to Tyrsa. "He's jus' upset."

"Maybe he's right," Cenith said, his anger gone. "Look at her."

Tyrsa sat huddled on the road, hugging her doll tight against her, her feet tucked into her wet and muddy dress. She stared at one spot, rocking back and forth, her eyes wide with fear. "No hurt. No hurt."

"Don't give up on her, m'lord. There's somethin' special 'bout her."

"A little backwoods intuition?" Daric asked.

"Perhaps, sir, but if she wasn't special, then why does Lord Saulth want her back so bad?"

Jolin had a point. Cenith nodded his agreement.

"If ye don't mind, m'lord, sir, I'll go check on th' water."

Daric dismissed Jolin. Cenith looked at Tyrsa and sighed. "What am I going to do with her, Daric? Jolin's right in that there's something special about her. We can't let Saulth have her back. But do I want to be married to her?" He shrugged. "I don't know." Cenith turned his gaze back to him. "You said something about me choosing to keep her. You think there might be a way out of this marriage?"

"I do." Daric indicated they should sit. A rock, or a large chunk of hail, had caught him behind the knee. He needed rest as much as any of them. "You haven't yet taken your rights as a husband..."

"I can't do that to her! She'd have no idea what was happening, not to mention she won't let me touch her. I don't know if she'll ever let any man touch her now, especially that way."

Daric held his hand up. "I'm not suggesting you should. What I mean is, she's still a maid. You could go before the Council and explain what has happened. They all thought you were supposed to marry Iridia. I'm sure they'd understand if you chose to put Tyrsa aside, particularly if you didn't tell them she's not a lack-wit. We could find someone in Dunvalos Reach who would be willing to take her in. Perhaps in a few years she might be ready to court a man."

Cenith rested his chin on his knee and watched Tyrsa a moment. She'd stopped talking, but not rocking back and forth. "I'd made some breakthroughs with her, Daric. She smiles sometimes. She not only let me hold her hand, she reached out the other night and touched mine. Riding in my arms doesn't bother her the way it did. And now this. I feel like I'm back at the beginning."

He lifted his head and met Daric's gaze. "Nevertheless, I don't want to give up yet. She's special; and not just her healing. She makes me feel like I never have before. It's not love, I know that feeling. It's..." His brow furrowed. "...I don't know. I can't find the words for it."

Cenith's grey eyes looked to Daric for an answer. He didn't have one. His own feelings for the girl were perfectly explainable. Tyrsa brought out the father in him. He wanted to ensure her safety and at least a measure of happiness; two things she wouldn't have if they returned her to Saulth. "Keep trying to regain her confidence. She might surprise you. The water must be hot by now, and I have to clean Varth's wound as well as check on the Bredun lad. Not to mention the cut on Jolin's cheek."

Cenith nodded and stood. "I'll see what I can do."

This was a lot to put on Cenith's young shoulders. Only a scant few years out of childhood, Ifan's son had to deal with his father's untimely death, the responsibilities of a lordship, an unexpected, and strange, new wife, and the threat of Saulth's plans, all in the space of a few months. Cenith held up well for someone raised in the quiet, laid-back atmosphere of mountain life. Daric just hoped his lord could continue to do so.

Daric ran a hand through his short-cropped hair. Numerous bumps and bruises made themselves known, but there was nothing he could do about those. He stood, pain erupting everywhere.

Ead still sat beside Varth. Daric would have to speak to him again in private. He'd seen no hint of how Ead felt about Tyrsa before this, and Daric sincerely hoped it was only a reaction to Varth's injury. They had enough problems. Tension amongst them would only make matters worse.

* * * *

Cenith crouched near Tyrsa. His back and legs hurt, but he couldn't give up. "No hurt," he said for what must be the fiftieth time. "I'm not going to hurt you. I promise. Please. Just take my hand."

He reached out to her again. She blinked, then loosened her hold on her doll.

"No hurt. I promise."

"No…no hurt?" Tyrsa shook from the cold.

So much wet mud and detritus clung to her ruined dress, he could hardly tell what colour it should be. Cenith would gladly buy her another, if she'd only take his hand.

"No hurt Baybee?"

Cenith smiled. "No one will hurt Baybee. You're getting better, aren't you. That's three whole words you put together." Not including the strings of nonsense and kitchen tripe she came out with from time to time.

"Three wuhds?"

"Words. Say it right. I know you can." Cenith wished she'd take his hand, his arm hurt from holding it out for so long.

"Words." Tyrsa said it slowly, but correct this time. She held out a hesitant hand.

Cenith had to duck walk to get close enough to take it. He could have kissed that hand, if it wasn't coated in mud. Without letting go, he sat beside her.

"No hurt, Tyrsa. I'm not going to hurt you. Not ever." He put his arm around her. She shivered, but didn't pull away.

"I found an almost dry blanket, m'lord." Jolin's voice came from behind them.

Tyrsa jumped.

"Jolin won't hurt you either, will you, Jolin."

The guard smiled, despite the cut on his face. "No hurt, m'lady. Just a blanket."

Cenith took the offered item. "Thank you. How's Varth?" He wrapped Tyrsa in the blanket and held her close to him, trying to warm her thin body.

Jolin's smile faded. "He still hasn't come 'round, m'lord. Councillor Daric's done as much as he kin. Varth's in Talueth's care now." He touched his fingers to his lips then held his hand over his heart in the mountain people's wish for good luck.

"Hurt?" Tyrsa pointed at Jolin's cheek.

"Only a little, m'lady." His smile returned and he bowed.

"When can Daric see to that wound?" Cenith asked.

"He says soon. He's carin' for th' Bredun man. A couple o' his wounds have opened agin'. When he's done with me, he wants us t' pack up and go t' the copse up ahead." Jolin nodded in the direction of the bridge. "Says we kin rest there."

Cenith nodded. Rest sounded like a wonderful idea. A hot bath, clean clothes, and hotter food sounded just as good, though he doubted Daric would allow another fire.

"How many horses have been recovered?"

"Ten, m'lord, and th' Bredun palfrey. Dathan found Warin's horse wi' a piece o' wood in its side. Had to put th' poor thing out o' its misery. Brought the tack back with him, though. Warin says he kin ride wi'

Yanis." Jolin picked at some drying blood under the cut. "Nightwind's still missin', as are Varth's and Fallan's mounts."

"Probably won't find them now," Cenith said. The horses were all well trained; an expensive loss.

"I told Councillor Daric he could have my horse. I kin ride wi' Ead. Might be a good idea if someone rode wi' him, anyway. Keep his head on straight, if ye know what I mean, m'lord."

"I do. When Daric starts work on your cut, have someone bring me Windwalker. It might take some coercion to get Tyrsa back on him." Cenith sincerely hoped it wouldn't take much. He rubbed his tired eyes, his patience wearing thin.

"Aye, m'lord. Oh, Keana must've talked sweet to Aja. None o' the wine bottles broke."

Cenith nodded. That was the least of their concerns. "Thanks for the blanket, Jolin. You should go see if Daric can take you."

"Aye, m'lord, and yer welcome." Jolin bowed to them both before leaving.

Tyrsa had stopped shivering, though her feet must still be cold; she kept them curled up inside her dress. She reached down and touched the rough road they sat on, then looked up at him. "Hurt," she said, her dirty face serious. She patted the ground. "Hurt." Then she held her hands out in front of her, the same way as when they were trapped in the ravine. "No hurt."

"I'm glad you don't hurt. I was worried about your arms." Cenith hoped that was what she meant.

Tyrsa pushed out with her arms, as if trying to touch something. "No hurt."

"I don't know what you mean. What doesn't hurt?"

She touched the ground again. "Word?"

"Ground. That's the ground," Cenith said.

"Ground." Tyrsa patted the dirt. "Ground hurt."

Ground hurt? What in the hells is that supposed to mean?

She put her arms out again. "Ground no hurt."

"Ground hurt. Ground no hurt. I wish I knew what you were getting at."

"My Lord?"

Trey held Cenith's horse. Windwalker didn't look too much the worse for wear. The same couldn't be said for Trey. It was difficult to tell where the natural brown of his hair met the dirt and mud covering his face. Cenith removed his arm from around Tyrsa and took her hand. He stood, bringing her with him. Her blanket slipped, hanging off one shoulder.

"We have to ride now." He patted Windwalker's saddle.

"Horz?"

"Horse. Say it right, Tyrsa."

"Horse. Horse." She shivered again, but couldn't wrap the blanket around herself, not with Baybee in one hand and him holding the other. Cenith fixed it for her.

"Would you like me to perform Jolin's duty of playing stepping stool, My Lord?" Trey asked.

"Not if you're too sore." They would have to find another way to get her up. Cenith didn't know the condition of her wounds and he didn't dare risk hurting her.

Trey shrugged. "I'm all right, My Lord. It's my legs that got hit the most. My back's good and she doesn't weigh much. Jolin says he hardly knows she's there."

"Thank you. I'd appreciate it." Cenith prayed to Maegden and Talueth both that the girl would cooperate. She did, insisting she sit in front of him rather than behind. That surprised him, she usually only allowed it when she wanted to sleep. He wrapped the blanket around her and guided his horse toward Daric.

A whinny sounded from over a rise behind them. Nightwind trotted up, looking as if he'd just returned from a morning walk.

"Where did you come from?" Trey asked, surprise widening his normally sleepy eyes.

The horse whickered and tossed its head.

"Horse!" Tyrsa said, reaching out to Nightwind. The horse came to her and blew softly when she touched his nose.

Cenith pointed to himself. "Cenith." Then her. "Tyrsa."

She repeated the names, a puzzled look on her dirty face.

He pointed to Daric's horse. "Nightwind."

"Ohhh! Night…wind." Tyrsa patted the neck of the horse she rode. "Word?"

"Name. The word is horse. The name is Windwalker."

"Name? Wind…walker?"

"Yes." Cenith had Trey take Nightwind to Daric, and guided Windwalker to where the councillor stood finishing with the cut on Jolin's face. Tyrsa repeated the horses' names three times.

"Glad to see no simple tornado could do you in," Daric said to his horse. He packed up his kit and asked Trey to move his saddlebags from Jolin's horse to Nightwind.

Once seated in the saddle, Trey and Warin lifted the Bredun guard up behind Daric and tied the man's hands together in front of him. They did the same with Varth, tying him to Ead. Cenith took a last look around for anything left behind. The little fire was out, though not much of it remained.

Daric signalled for Jayce and Dathan to take the lead and they crossed the bridge in search of someplace to rest.

* * * *

Tyrsa sat on a blanket and picked another piece of dirt off the back of her hand. *Tyrsa.* That was a nice word. *Name.* Cenith said it was a name, and it was *her* name. A word, a name all her own. She hugged Baybee tight. Dirt fell off her too. That made her sad. She pulled some off, trying to make Baybee better again.

The new dress, the green one, was too dirty to wear, so she wore the blue one. That had made Tyrsa sad too. She liked both her new dresses. They were warm and soft, like the cloth that covered the wall she could see through.

This Outside was strange and strange. There was wind, which could be felt but not seen. Water, hard and soft, that fell all around her and moved fast instead of staying in one place where it belonged; and using pieces of trees instead of cloths for the *nesses* was very strange.
So much had happened since the *gard* had taken her from her room. All the time there was new things, some good, some bad. So much. She was tired, but she had to sort everything out before she went to sleep.
The big wind and falling water had been scary, but not like when she thought Baybee was lost again. The man Ead had found Baybee. He didn't look happy about giving her back. He'd been angry and that was

scary too. She was afraid he'd hurt her. Cenith had said many words for a long time until she felt safe again.

Cenith slept beside her. They all slept, except the ones hiding in the trees...and the ground. The ground didn't sleep. The ground hurt, she could feel its pain whenever she touched it. She had to keep her feet in her dress so she didn't touch it unless she wanted to. The hurt was more than her own hurts. It was too much hurt.

Tyrsa had tried to tell Cenith of the hurt, but she didn't have the words. She told the wind to stop hurting her and Cenith and the other *mans*…man…men who were nice to her. She had to beg and plead and ask the ground to help her. The ground did, even though it hurt it more. It had taken her arms; it was the only way. And then the wind stopped, and that was scary too because the ground couldn't let go.

She reached down and touched the ground. It still hurt, but not as much as before, and during, the big wind. Tyrsa tucked her hand back into the folds of her dress. The stars and moon couldn't be seen. Everything was dark, yet not quite as dark as her room. New smells crowded her nose. There were noises all around, noises she didn't know. The wind made noise too. It was now a noise she knew. It spoke through the trees, though it didn't blow hard anymore.

It said the hurt in the ground had to be stopped. Bad things would happen if it wasn't. The wind moaned and sighed about all the bad things. It didn't use words like the men did. Even so, she didn't understand most of what the wind talked about. One thing she did understand. She was the one who had to stop it. Too bad the wind didn't tell her how, or why, though that might be part of what she didn't understand.

Tyrsa shivered. The bad wind had made her cold inside and out. She lay down beside Cenith. He was always warm and didn't seem to mind her taking his warmth. She cuddled close to him, like she used to with Rani. He opened his eyes and smiled. She liked his smile. Tyrsa smiled back. He put his arm around her and tucked the blankets in close. It felt strange to be touched like that, but nice too.

She closed her eyes and wished she could tell Cenith about the bad things the wind told her; he might know what it meant. The wind talked to her, loud and then soft, until she fell asleep.

Chapter Fourteen

Cenith jerked awake. Trey's quiet voice penetrated the fog dulling his brain.

"My Lord, I'm sorry to wake you, but Councillor Daric needs you."

"Tell him I'll be there in a moment," Cenith said, surprised the words made it past his thick tongue.

Tyrsa's black hair, matted with mud, spread across his arm and onto his chest. She'd never slept this close to him. His heart surged with…something. Relief? Probably.

Cenith slid his numb arm out from under her. Tyrsa didn't stir. He sat up, keeping his groans to a minimum. Every part of his body that had been struck by stones or hail screamed at him, adding to the pain in his hip from when he fell in the stream. Feeling rushed back into his arm, bringing more discomfort. Rubbing helped; unfortunately he couldn't rub the pain out of his bruises and bumps.

He glanced at the sky. Midmorning and not a sign of the clouds that had caused so much trouble yesterday. The sun hadn't moved past the trees enough to shine on Tyrsa, but Cenith covered her anyway. Her eyesight was adjusting, but her skin would suffer in direct sunlight.

Once he could stand, Cenith made his way to Daric, who crouched beside the Bredun guard. Trey pressed a cup of hot tea in his hand and he mumbled a thank you, surprised Daric had allowed a fire. Nearby, Ead wiped Varth's brow while Jolin dribbled a few drops of water into the unconscious man's mouth. Cenith sent a silent prayer to Talueth for Varth's recovery. The rest of the guards, except for those on patrol, kept themselves busy with the odd jobs that always needed attention.

"What's the problem?" he asked.

Daric stood and motioned him to the edge of the clearing. "Our friend is awake. He knows who we are, spotted the horses' tack. I wanted to wait for you before questioning him."

Cenith nodded. The butterflies chose that moment to reappear, flitting in his empty stomach. He hadn't missed them.

They returned to the wounded man. Daric crouched facing him while Cenith took a place at his head. The guard still lay on his stomach, his hands tied behind his bare back. Though he had fewer wounds than Tyrsa, they were far worse than hers. Each long stripe rose from his skin, red ridges of angry flesh. Half of them still showed the yellow-green of pus. Tyrsa's should heal to fine lines, these wouldn't.

"Now then," Daric said, his voice hard enough to send shivers down Cenith's spine. "You can answer my questions truthfully, or I can hurt you. We'll start with your name."

The Bredun guard's eyes widened. "Buckam, My Lord."

Daric shook his head. "I'm not a lord."

"Sir?"

"That will suffice. We're off to a good start, Buckam. Let's keep going, shall we? Who did this to you?" Daric, his features hard enough to cut stone, had yet to blink. His eyes bored into those of the guard.

The answer took a moment to come, as if he had to think about it. "B…bandits."

"Bandits." Daric's expression never changed, but Buckam could look him in the eye no longer. "Bandits who didn't take your horse, fine as he is. I might as well tell you now, Buckam. We know you're one of Saulth's men."

Buckam closed his eyes and let out a slow breath through his nose. He almost sounded relieved.

"Let's try that question again, shall we? Who did this to you?"

"Lord Saulth, sir. But I deserved it." Buckam tried to swallow, then licked his parched lips instead.

"Would you like some water, Buckam?" Daric reached out his hand. Trey put a canteen in it. He shook it, the sloshing sound quite audible. He pulled a cloth from one of his pockets.

Buckam licked his lips again and twisted his hands, testing the knots. "Yes, sir. Please, sir."

Daric poured a small amount of water onto the cloth, then held it close to Buckam's mouth. "Why did you deserve it?"

"I…" Buckam swallowed. "I was negligent in my duty, sir."

Daric raised an eyebrow. Amazing, how much reaction one facial expression could cause.

"I was assigned to watch the girl, sir," Buckam said, as fast as his dry mouth would allow. "She wasn't supposed to come out of her room until the kitchen staff left. I spent the time with my girl instead of watching her."

"Very good, Buckam. You've earned yourself a little water." Daric let him suck the cloth dry. That small an amount couldn't have eased his thirst much. "Did Saulth have guards watching her all the time?"

"No, sir. Only at night, when she liked to wander. We told him where she went and what she did, and to ensure she didn't go where she wasn't supposed to."

Daric poured more water on the cloth. "What did she do, when she wandered at night?"

"She went to the kitchen to eat and play in the ashes of the fireplace. Sometimes the kitchen staff prepared a bath for her. Then she'd go to the library and look...at books."

Cenith glanced at Daric, who returned it. He'd caught the hesitation as well. Daric didn't give Buckam any water.

"Where did she go the night you were negligent?"

Buckam waited a moment before answering. "That was the night of Lord Saulth's wedding. She went to the balcony…to watch the dancing. She knew she wasn't allowed there. She knew it!"

Cenith clenched his jaw. Daric cautioned him to silence.

"And if you'd been watching her, she wouldn't have gone?" Daric asked, holding the wet cloth close to Buckam's face.

The guard's eyes never left the cloth. "I do not know. Probably. She did not know we were watching. If she did go, I was to tell Guard-Commander Tajik and he would look after the problem."

"How? By beating her?" Daric squeezed the cloth enough to release two drops, right in front of the guard's nose.

Buckam watched each drop fall. They splashed into the dirt. Cenith's own mouth felt dry. He took a sip of his tea.

"N…no, sir! Only Lord Saulth was allowed to do that!" Buckam closed his eyes a moment. "We were only to watch and report. That was all. I swear it!"

Daric let him have more water. "Why?"

Buckam blinked his eyes. "Sir? I…I do not know what you mean."

Daric raised his eyebrow again. "Don't you? Don't you think it a little odd that he'd keep his daughter in a storeroom? Beat her when she tried to have contact with other people?"

"His…his *daughter*?" Buckam's voice came out a dry squeak.

"Are you telling me you had no idea she's Saulth's daughter?" Daric's eyes narrowed.

Buckam couldn't answer fast enough. "No sir! None of us, sir! We were never told who she is. I swear it!" Sweat beaded on his brow, dripped into his hair, onto the ground.

Daric wet the cloth again and squeezed out a few more drops, just in front of Buckam's nose. "Then you have no idea why Saulth treated her the way he did."

"No, sir! We could not even guess why he did what he did to her. I swear it! Please, My Lord…sir!" Buckam leaned closer to the cloth.

Daric moved it away and swung it back and forth. "What else did the girl do in the library besides look at books?"

Buckam's eyes followed the movement of the cloth. "She looked at books, sir, for the pictures. That's all."

Daric handed the cloth to Trey, who replaced it with a knife. "Don't take me for a fool, Buckam. You were doing so well too."

The guard's eyes almost popped out of his head. Daric touched the point of the knife to one of the infected wounds, pushing just hard enough to break the skin. Green pus oozed out. Keeping the knife out of Buckam's sight, Daric massaged the spot with the tips of his fingers, forcing more pus from the wound.

Buckam twisted and squirmed, trying to get away from Daric. "It hurts! Stop! Please!"

"Then stop moving. What else did the girl do?" Daric pressed on the wound again. More pus escaped, this time mixed with blood.

Cenith's gut churned. He set the tea aside.

"The scroll! Please! Stop! She looked at the scroll!" Tears formed in Buckam's eyes, trickled across the bridge of his nose to fall on the ground.

"Scroll?" Daric shifted his gaze from Buckam to his lord.

"Coincidence?" Cenith mouthed the word.

The Calleni shook his head and returned his attention to the guard. "What scroll?"

"There…there is a scroll that sits under glass on a table in the library. It is old, very old…in four pieces. Lord Saulth takes extra care with it, but he lets the girl look at it. He…" Buckam swallowed. His eyes darted back and forth from Daric to Trey, who still held the cloth. "He wanted to know whenever she looked at it. She…she would touch it sometimes, trace the words. Lord Saulth wanted to know exactly what she did each time."

"What does the scroll say?" Daric touched the knife to another pustule.

"I do not know. I cannot read it. I swear!" Sweat and tears both watered the ground.

The knife eased off without breaking the skin. "How were you able to watch the girl without her knowing it?"

Buckam closed his eyes and clenched his teeth. Daric pressed down on the pustule. The young guard's eyes flew open. "Tunnels! There are tunnels in the walls!"

Tunnels? I wonder if we have any? Father never said anything. Cenith wondered if Daric knew.

Daric picked another part of Buckam's back to place his knife tip. "What were your orders? Why were you sent out in your condition?"

"To redeem myself. I was to get a piece of parchment from Lord Cenith's study. I was told it would look like the pieces of the scroll."

Cenith didn't think Buckam could have looked more miserable, but he managed it.

"And?" The knife pressed against the wound. Buckam cried out and tried again to twist away. Pus welled up around the point.

Cenith glanced over at Tyrsa, a much better sight than the mess on Buckam's back. The girl hadn't moved; he put it down to sleeping next to a noisy kitchen all her life. Some of the soldiers stood nearby watching the performance, every face grim and angry.

"I…I was to bring back the girl as well." More tears fell. "I am sorry about the girl. So sorry she was whipped because of me." Buckam sucked in a shuddering breath. "He…Lord Saulth…made me watch while he beat her. He just kept hitting her. He would not stop!"

Daric passed the knife to Trey and untied Buckam's arms. The young man sobbed and let them fall to his side. Once he regained control of himself, he asked, "Is…is she still alive, sir?" His voice trembled.

"She's alive, and doing better than you are," Daric said, taking the knife back from Trey.

Buckam's eyes widened with fear. "Are you..going to kill me?"

"Why would I do that? You answered my questions. Your death would serve no purpose." Daric's voice remained frighteningly calm.

"There are a couple of places on your back that need my attention. If I don't get the infection under control you'll die and it won't be my doing, but your lord's."

In one instant, Buckam changed from a snivelling child to an angry man. "If you are so concerned about my health, *sir*, then why did you torture me?" He brought his hands up level with his chest and clenched his fists. Cenith stood and reached for his sword, then remembered he'd taken it off to go to sleep. His dagger lay beside the sword. The soldiers moved to draw their weapons.

Daric signalled them to stop and took the canteen from Trey. He held it close to Buckam's face. "Would you like more water? Drink all you want."

Buckam didn't take it, though he looked like he wanted to.

"I didn't add to the mess on your back," Daric said, with a sigh. "I only cleared some pus from the wounds. The torture was all in your mind. All I had to do was set it up with the water. You did the rest. Now, do you want a drink?"

Cenith would have laughed, but the look of horror on Buckam's face put a stop to it. What would he have done in the same situation? He liked to think he could've held out. Cenith sincerely hoped he never had to be put in that position.

"Sit up, son. Have some water. You need it." Daric helped Buckam sit and gave him the canteen. The fight disappeared from Buckam as fast as it had come. His hand shook while he gulped, draining the canteen.

Daric ordered Buckam to lie down and he resumed cleaning the wounds. The guard clenched his teeth and made not a sound.

* * * *

Cenith lay on his back beside Tyrsa, his head resting on his arms, having no desire to watch Daric take care of Buckam's wounds. He should be hungry, dinner last night had been light and long ago. The butterflies had fled, but after watching Daric play with a man's mind, not to mention the wounds, food just didn't seem appealing.

Daric had a shadowed past. He'd told many tales, but too few for the years that had passed before he met Cenith's father. The ease with which he'd extracted the information from Buckam was frightening. When he thought about it, though, Buckam was young, probably younger than Cenith himself. What would have happened if Saulth had sent an older, more experienced man? *It would have been ugly. Extremely ugly.* Cenith had no doubt Daric would still have extracted the information he wanted.

He yawned. Cenith's bumps and bruises had kept him from falling asleep for a long time, but too much had happened for him to go back to sleep. Not that he should, otherwise he wouldn't sleep tonight. Perhaps he should wake Tyrsa. She'd never get on a normal schedule if she slept most of the day. He turned on his side, and looked into wide open blue eyes.

Words fled. They must have joined the cowardly butterflies.

"Sun?" Tyrsa's quiet voice brought the words back.

"What about the sun?"

She blinked and squinted. The sun had travelled far enough that it shone on most of her body. Cenith stood up, blocking the bright light, and helped her to her feet. He used the blanket to form a hood around her face and led her to the other side of the clearing, into the shade. She sat on a stump close to Varth—and Ead—but the size of the clearing limited the places that were out of direct sunlight. Tyrsa kept a wary eye on Ead.

Cenith crouched in front of her. "Are you hungry?"

"Food?" Tyrsa turned her attention to him.

"Do you want some food?" He stressed each word carefully. "You say 'yes, I would like some food, please'."

"Food. Pleece?" She sat, patient, innocent, guileless. How could Ead possibly blame her for Varth's injury?

"Tyrsa, say the words. 'Yes, I would like some food, please."

"Yes. Food. Pleece?"

Cenith sighed and stood. "Maybe that's too many words at once. All right. Food it is."

Jayce had something brewing in a pot over the small fire. The enticing smell of cinnamon travelled on a wayward breeze straight to Cenith's nose. Maybe he was hungry after all.

"What's in the pot?" Cenith asked.

Jayce scratched his crooked nose. "Porridge, m'lord." He shared Jolin's backwoods ancestry as well as his black hair, though his eyes were dark brown, not Jolin's intense green. "Should be ready in a few minutes."

Both their stomachs would have to wait. Cenith wandered over to Daric. Buckam's wounds were cleaned and salved, and the man slept.

"He passed out not long after I started," Daric said, putting the last of his kit away. "I'd hoped to get a cup of willow bark tea into him, but this is for the best, I suppose. Easier to work on him."

"That's why he was so quiet," Cenith commented. "I just thought he was trying to be brave."

"He was, until he passed out."

"I don't suppose you have any idea what that scroll says."

Daric stood. "Not a clue. I'd have to have a really good look at it, but unless it's written in Calleni, Cambrellan, or Syrthian, I won't be able to understand it."

Ah, well. It had been a small hope. "I thought you knew Tai-Kethian too."

"I do, but the horse-lords don't have a written language."

"Get away from him!" Ead's voice rang through the clearing. Startled birds flew from nearby trees.

Cenith ran back to Tyrsa. Daric beat him and positioned himself between the girl and Ead. Tyrsa backed up until she hit the stump, sitting hard when she lost her balance. Cenith put his hands on her shoulders to steady her.

"No hurt, Tyrsa," he said, leaning down close to her ear. "No one will hurt you."

She didn't try to run like she usually did when upset. Instead of frightened, she looked more shocked and disoriented.

"Explain yourself," Daric said to Ead, his voice hard as rock.

"I just went into the woods to relieve myself and when I come back, she's touching him! Right on his wound!" Ead twisted to face Jolin, who still crouched beside Varth. "And you let her!"

"She didn't hurt him, Ead," Jolin said, more worried than angry at Ead's words. "She barely touched him."

"You're on sentry duty as of right now," Daric said, his anger showing only in his eyes and a tightening of his neck muscles. "Relieve Fallan. You're off duty when I say you are. Understood?"

"But, sir, she…"

"Understood?" Daric's tone left no room for anything other than strict obedience.

Ead squared his shoulders. "Yes…sir." He formally saluted Daric, fist to chest, bowed to Cenith, and strode away, anger screaming in every step.

Cenith released his breath, slowly. Something would have to be done about Ead, but how do you punish a man for fearing his friend might die? A tornado was a difficult thing to blame a death on, intangible and fleeting. Cenith could see now how Ead would find Tyrsa an easy target.

"I'm sorry, m'lord, sir. He's jus' worried 'bout Varth."

"Don't make excuses for him, Jolin." Daric crouched beside Varth and gently probed the wound. "We're all worried, but we don't take it out on each other."

Jolin sat on the other side of Varth. "How is he, sir? Honestly. I need t' know."

"As far as the wound goes, very good. It's healing nicely. As for what's happening underneath, it's anybody's guess."

Jolin's shoulders sagged. He nodded. "I was hopin', maybe…" He shrugged.

"Hoping what?" Cenith asked.

"Nothin', m'lord. 'Tis silly."

"Silly thoughts have saved lives and won wars." Daric stopped his prodding and sat back on his heels.

"I jus' thought, since m'lady is so good at healin' herself, maybe she was tryin' t' heal Varth too." He looked at the ground and ran a nervous hand through his hair. "Like I said, silly."

"It's not silly," Cenith said. "It's a nice thought. I just wish it was true."

A shiver ran through Tyrsa. Cenith drew her to her feet and held her close. She shivered again. With no hesitation, she leaned into him. At least she trusted him again, and that meant much.

"Did she say anything when she touched Varth?" Cenith asked.

"She said 'hurt' a couple o' times, like she was askin' permission to touch him. I didn't think it would matter." Jolin's eyes lifted to his. "I thought Ead had calmed down 'bout her. I'm sorry, m'lord. Maybe I shouldn't have let her."

"I doubt she'd have hurt him," Daric said, rising to his feet. "She seems to be sensitive about wounds. Perhaps she can't understand why we don't heal the way she does. Or maybe it's because she's been hurt so much in her life."

Jolin stood. He looked at Tyrsa first, then Cenith and Daric. "If I ever git the chance, I'm askin' permission, m'lord, sir, kin I run my sword through Saulth's gizzard?"

Cenith opened his mouth to say 'no', he wanted that honour for himself, but Daric spoke first.

"I'd like to say yes, but I'm afraid a soldier killing a lord would create more trouble than Saulth's death would solve."

Jolin grimaced. "I suppose, sir. I guess I'll have t' settle for killin' him in my dreams."

Cenith looked down at the dark head resting against him. Tyrsa still trembled. *As will we all.*

* * * *

Daric scanned the patchwork fields of long grasses, searching for any movement contrary to the wind. He'd ordered a day of rest yesterday. The tornadoes had strained everyone's nerves to the edge, and they all needed to be alert for the rest of the journey. The clearing they'd chosen had no place for a proper bath, but everyone cleaned up as much as possible.

Cenith, with Tyrsa asleep in front of him, rode behind to allow Ead to travel beside Daric, Varth tied to his back. Jolin had offered to carry Buckam, which pleased Daric; it left him free in case of trouble, and to think. He had to find a way to convince Ead that Tyrsa wasn't to blame for Varth's condition, but the young soldier put up a brick wall, with no door, whenever Daric attempted to discuss it. A more pressing problem weighed on Daric's mind; Bredun's lord and what he'd do next.

Deep in his bones, Daric knew Saulth had intended for them to uncover the truth about Buckam. The horse was a subtle hint, not one everyone would have caught. Not that it really mattered. Saulth would make another attempt at retrieving Tyrsa. The only questions were where and when. If it were up to Daric, he'd wait until they reached the mountains where a small number of men with bows could wipe them out in a matter of moments.

Sneaking past the guard station at the pass would be simple enough. He'd mentioned the fact to Ifan on more than one occasion, but with all of Ardael at peace, there was no real need. Now the need was all too real. If Saulth had sent someone, any counter measure Daric could take would come too late. Once home, he'd speak to Cenith. *If* they arrived home.

Daric had spent most of the morning studying the passing terrain, coming up with, and discarding, possible places Bredun soldiers might lie in wait. Attempting to figure out what Saulth would do was like trying to get inside the mind of a sick badger. Both were unpredictable and vicious.

And where does the scroll fit into all this? Daric had seen the piece in Tiras many times; it had hung on the study wall since long before he'd arrived at the keep, but he'd never bothered to study it hard enough to try to make out words.

Somehow, Tyrsa and the scroll were linked. They had to find out what their piece of scroll said. It might give a clue as to the contents of the rest of it, and why Saulth wanted Tyrsa looking at the scroll even though she didn't have an icicle's chance in a sandstorm of reading it.

"Any possibility of getting some water?"

Daric's head snapped to the left. Varth still rested against Ead's back, but his hazel eyes gazed back at him, clear and focused.

"Varth! You're awake!" Ead reined in his horse, then fumbled with the knots at Varth's wrists.

"Why are my hands tied? And why am I not on my own horse? Not that I mind." Varth shrugged, then winced.

Daric called a halt and sent Fallan to bring back the scouts. Ead finished with the ropes, tossed them to the ground, then slid off the horse, forcing Varth to sit up straight. He continued falling backwards. Daric caught him just before he went over.

"Whoa!" Varth leaned forward again, grabbing hold of the saddle horn. "I feel like I've had an extended evening at Silk's Tavern, headache and all."

Ead helped Varth off the horse while Daric dismounted and dug out his kit.

"Lay him down in that flat area there, near the fence," Daric instructed. "Warin, help Jolin. I want Buckam over there as well. Trey, take Lady Tyrsa so Lord Cenith can dismount. I suggest you stay here," he said to Cenith. "In case we're attacked, there's more room to maneuver. I'll leave the bulk of the guard with you." Cenith nodded.

Daric strode to a rise near an old rail fence. Most of the low lying land around this part of the road lay under a thin sheet of water, despite the sun. "Everyone keep your eyes open, those ridges might appear small to eyes accustomed to the mountains, but a smart man could hide an army in there." Daric indicated the series of low ridges to the west leading up to the steep mountains of the Dunvalos Range.

Dathan and Ead helped Varth to the rise. Ead had tucked a blanket under one arm and lay it down for his friend. Jolin had done the same for Buckam and the two rested several feet apart. Buckam groaned and rolled onto his side, facing away from Varth. Jolin left him and joined Ead. Daric sent Dathan back with the rest of the guard.

"What happened? The last thing I remember we were riding into a storm." Varth laid his arm across his eyes, then removed it and poked at the wound above his ear. "How did I get this?"

"Ead can fill you in later," Daric said, crouching by his side. "I gather you have a headache."

"Yes, sir. One large enough to knock a bear to the ground." Varth put his arm over his eyes again, blocking out the sun.

"Anything else not quite right?" Daric pulled a small oilskin bag from his kit.

"I feel like my stomach wants to turn inside out. I'm hungry, but I don't think I dare eat."

Daric put the bag back and took out another. "No willow bark then. I'm going to give you some ginger to chew on. It should help the nausea." He cut a slice half the width of his little finger off the end of the thick root and gave it to Varth. "What's the last thing you remember?"

Varth took a nibble, making a face at the pungent taste. "I remember the clouds, and rain. Nothing after that."

"You don't remember the tornadoes?" Ead asked, his eyes widening in surprise.

Varth stopped chewing. "Tornadoes! What tornadoes?"

Ead and Jolin both looked at Daric, worry creasing Ead's brow. Jolin's intense eyes were the only sign he showed of his concern.

"I've seen this before." Daric cut off two more chunks of ginger root. "Sometimes the man recovered his missing memory, sometimes he didn't. Fortunately, you only seem to have lost a few minutes. Here's more ginger root. Save it for later if you need it." He left the three friends and squatted in front of Buckam.

Daric set the back of his hand against the young man's flushed skin. The fever had gone down, but not enough. He pulled out his jar of salve and the bag containing the willow bark. Mostly honey, the thick salve fought infection like no other medication he knew.

Buckam stared somewhere past him. Daric didn't think he'd seen a more dejected man. He removed the canteen from his belt. "Drink this."

Daric helped Buckam to sit. The guard drained the canteen then tried to lie down again.

"I need your shirt off so I can tend your wounds." He helped Buckam out of the shirt, then had him lie on his stomach.

Buckam's movements were listless, wooden, his eyes dull. Daric poked the worst places on the young guard's back; Buckam made no sound during the painful procedure. The redness had receded and he could see no sign of pus. Daric spread another layer of salve over his back, hoping it would take care of any lingering infection; not enough remained to fight another round.

Daric replaced the jar and opened the bag of willow bark, removing a small piece. "Chew this, it'll help the pain and fever." He'd initially made tea with it and dribbled it into Buckam's mouth, but they couldn't risk a fire, or the time.

Buckam lay like a slug, ignoring the bark.

"Are you going to take it?" Daric asked.

"Why not just kill me?" Buckam sounded like he wanted Shival to come for him.

"I've taken the lives of many men, all for a reason. There's no reason to take yours. Chew the bark."

"I have failed my lord. I have failed as a man. Just slit my throat and be done with it."

Daric lowered his arm and sat back on his heels. "What makes you think you failed as a man?"

"I gave in…and you did not even torture me." Buckam's fists clenched and he squeezed his eyes shut. "I am a weakling and a failure. I deserve to die."

Daric sighed. "How old are you, Buckam? Fifteen? Sixteen?"

Buckam opened his eyes. "I have seen seventeen summers, sir." He sounded indignant.

"Seventeen." *I think I was that age once.* "I've extracted information from men two and three times your age, hardened mercenaries as well as experienced soldiers. They all gave me the information I needed. Some sooner than others." Daric shrugged. "Some lived, some didn't, but they all gave in. I'm good at what I do, Buckam, though it's not a skill I'm proud of. It's simply necessary. Berating yourself for the inevitable is a waste of time."

"I am weak." Buckam clenched his jaw.

"You are young." *And stubborn.* "As to your other personal flaw, you didn't fail your lord, Buckam. He failed you."

Buckam frowned. "What do you mean?"

"I asked you yesterday why Saulth sent you out wounded. You said it was so you could redeem yourself."

"That is right." Buckam's frown turned to puzzlement.

"What were your exact orders?"

"I was to dress in ordinary clothes and go to Tiras Keep. I had to get ahead of Lord Cenith…"

Daric held his hand up. "Why did you take the Old West Road? It's longer than the main one."

"Lord Saulth said you would be on the Bredun Road and to take the Old West Road to avoid you." Buckam shifted so he lay more on his right side.

"One more question. Why did Saulth give you the palfrey?"

Buckam's puzzled look changed back to a frown. "He said Hawkwing was fast and had a smooth gait. He would be easier to ride."

"You may not agree with what I'm going to tell you," Daric said, "but indulge me. First of all, Lord Cenith and I have been expecting an attempt at the girl. Sticking to the Bredun Main Road would have meant we'd be forced to pass through the larger towns and villages, where Saulth had access to more people to stop us. Here, the villages are small, few, and off the road, the land more open. Saulth could still send a large force after us, but we'd at least have some warning, and these ridges and copses offer good places to hide. Saulth knew we had to take this road." Daric shifted so he could sit and stretch out his right leg. The old wound in his thigh had stiffened again. "Second, if Saulth really wanted you to redeem yourself, there had to have been at least some chance of success. In your condition, you were doomed to failure. He knew you wouldn't make it."

Buckam opened his mouth to protest.

"Hear me out." Daric held up his hand again. "Third, Saulth gave you that horse specifically. Not because he has a smooth gait, but because he's a nobleman's horse too expensive for a commoner to own. Why have you dress as a common citizen and then give you a mount none but a rich man could afford?"

Buckam's mouth dropped open.

"The girl confirmed our suspicions. She recognized you. Saulth intended for us to find you, dead from your wounds. We were supposed to think you were the second attempt and stop looking for one." Daric leaned closer. "You weren't supposed to have survived to talk to us."

"That is not true!" Buckam struggled to a sitting position. "Lord Saulth would never do that! I was ordered to keep secret that I served him. He would not tell me that if he expected me to die!" Yet, something glimmered in Buckam's eyes that spoke of doubt. The seed had been planted.

Daric just had to sit back and see what grew. He stood and picked up his kit. "I said you might not agree with what I had to say. Just think about it. You don't appear to be a stupid man, merely a young one. Your entire life lies before you. It's up to you what you do with it."

"Councillor Daric!" Jolin called. "Ye need t' hear this!"

Daric pressed the bark into Buckam's hand and moved from one patient back to the other. "What's the problem?"

"Varth says he dreamt while he was unconscious." Jolin's grin threatened to split his face. A confused Ead stared at Varth as if he'd never seen him before.

Daric had never heard of an unconscious man dreaming; he'd been out cold on several occasions and didn't remember having a dream. It didn't mean it couldn't happen though.

"Tell him, Varth," Jolin prompted.

"There was just one dream, but it seemed to last forever." Varth still shaded his eyes. The headache must be painful. Unfortunately, Daric couldn't do anything about it until his stomach settled down. "I was walking in a forest," Varth said, his voice almost wistful. "A full mountain forest, not the sad excuses they've got here. It was night, with no moon and no path. I was lost and kept getting turned around. I passed the same stump over and over. I remember being afraid and calling for Ead and Jolin. No one answered, and there was no sound. No birds, no wind. Just the forest, the trees, and the same stump."

Varth raised his arm enough to allow him to look at Daric. "Then it changed. The moon came out and lit a narrow path. I followed it around a bend. Lady Tyrsa stood in an open clearing, holding her doll, lit by moonlight. She glowed, sir, like a…a beacon, or something. When I got close to her, she reached out and pointed to my head, to where the wound is. She said 'Hurt', and then touched me. There was a blinding flash of light, and…that's all I remember."

"Ye see, sir? I was right!" Jolin jumped to his feet, unable to contain himself. "She healed him! If Ead hadn't chased her away, maybe she could've healed him completely!"

Ead still looked confused, and maybe a little embarrassed.

"It's just coincidence, Jolin," Daric said. It couldn't be anything else. "Nobody but the gods can heal with a touch. Some would say it's blasphemy to say otherwise."

Jolin lost his enthusiasm.

"I'm not saying I'm one of them, mind. It would be a wonderful thing if it were true." It could also be a bad thing, for Lady Tyrsa. "I want this kept between us, is that clear? At least until we've something else to go on besides an injured man's fevered dreams."

"But, sir…"

Daric cut Jolin off with a gesture. Superstition ran rampant in the mountains, and Daric hated to interfere with a man's beliefs, but Jolin had to understand that more lay at stake here than wishful thinking. "I need you three to consider Lady Tyrsa. If, by some miracle she can heal others, and it's made public knowledge, people will line up by the thousands, clamouring for her to heal them. I doubt you two noticed, but after that incident she was not well. She couldn't stop shivering and wouldn't eat until nightfall. I'd put it down to being upset with Ead, but if this is true, and I'm not saying it is, you might be putting more than just her privacy at stake."

Daric made the three of them swear to silence before he ordered them all back on the road.

Chapter Fifteen

Cenith paused at the top of the ridge and looked back. Past the rolling scrubland, Bredun's soggy fields stretched in an endless expanse to the east. He tucked the blanket tighter around Tyrsa. Rain bothered her. Over the last two days, she'd spent most of the time hiding from it.

"If any more rain falls, Saulth might want to consider changing to rice as a crop," Daric said, coming up beside him.

"I don't care what he does, as long as he stays away from us."

Five days had passed since the tornadoes, eight since the marriage. For the past two, the rain had hardly quit. They only stopped to rest the horses, sleeping in the saddle. Tyrsa fussed sometimes, and Cenith did what he could to keep her as dry as possible, but they were all uncomfortable and just had to cope with it.

Daric checked both hers and Buckam's wounds when they rested. Tyrsa's dry scabs had almost fallen off and she didn't seem bothered by them much anymore. Daric's ministrations had finally beaten the infection in Buckam's stubborn cuts, though the Bredun guard didn't enjoy the continuous riding. He shared Jolin's horse; the amiable mountain man didn't mind one way or the other. The rest of the soldiers had made their distrust of Buckam obvious.

Varth's stomach had eased enough to allow him to chew the willow bark, though between him and Buckam, that was now gone, along with the last of the salve. Other than a lingering headache, and the missing memories, Varth showed no effect from his experience. The cut had closed to a thin line and Daric said the stitches could be taken out, which brought up the question of why Varth had healed so fast.

Cenith pulled back the blanket from Tyrsa's face, shielding her from the rain with his body. She slept, peaceful and innocent. Daric had told him about Varth's dream, and Jolin's conviction that it was really Tyrsa who'd healed whatever kept Varth unconscious.

Ead still had reservations over it, but it didn't take much to convince Varth. The two shared a horse and Cenith didn't think it would be long before he changed Ead's mind.

"I know you don't believe Tyrsa's responsible for Varth's recovery," he said to Daric. "And it's possible Varth woke up simply because he was ready, but how do you explain his injury? It's just like Tyrsa's wounds."

Daric sighed. "I'll be honest, I can't. However, I'm reluctant to jump to the conclusion that Tyrsa has the ability to not only heal herself, but others as well. It may be that Varth simply has a remarkable constitution. Call me stubborn, but I need more evidence."

"It could explain why Saulth wants her back so bad." Cenith wanted to believe Tyrsa could heal with a touch; an easy step to take after watching her own wounds.

"If he knew about her healing, why would he give her up in the first place? If she can heal others…" Daric held up a cautionary finger, "…and I'm not saying she can, Saulth could use her to make himself far more money than grain and wine bring in."

Good point. "Which means Saulth didn't know about her healing. Which leads to another question we've asked a hundred times…why does he want her back? What happened to make him change his mind? I refuse to believe he's found his heart and guilt is driving him."

"Those are questions that we can't answer, and I, for one, have no desire to return to Valda to ask him."

Another good point. Cenith replaced the blanket and urged Windwalker forward. The guard station lay less than an hour away. Rest, hot food, and a measure of safety seemed almost a dream.

The expected attack hadn't come. Yet. Cenith doubted there'd be one this close to the station. They'd decided to stay for several days to dry out and rest up; the trip through the mountains could prove treacherous, and not just from avalanches.

The Old West Road had faded to nothing more than a rough path near a long abandoned outpost. They followed it off the ridge and into a forested vale, the floor thick with bushes of various varieties. After curving through the dell, the path lay straight north to the guard station. Lightning ripped across the sky, followed by a rolling boom of thunder. Tyrsa jumped in Cenith's arms. She pushed the blanket back from her face and sat up straight.

"That was thunder," Cenith said. "It's only noise, nothing to be afraid of."

"Thunder?" she repeated, her blue eyes wide with fright. She shivered and leaned into him, soaking wet despite the two blankets wrapped around her.

"We're almost to the guard station. It'll be warm there and we can all get some proper sleep."

"Sleep. Tyrsa sleep. Cenith sleep?"

"Yes, and Daric, Jolin, Varth…all of us." Cenith guided Windwalker around a deep hole.

"Cenith sleep Tyrsa?"

Startled, he pushed her away enough to look at her. "Did you understand what I said? You couldn't have." Was that worry in her eyes? Worry that he wouldn't be with her? His heart warmed at the thought. "Yes, I," he pointed to himself, "will sleep with you." He touched her nose.

Tyrsa's face scrunched up in puzzlement. "I? No I. Cenith." She set her hand against his chest, then hers. "No you. Tyrsa."

Cenith laughed. The concept of 'I' and 'you' were proving a difficult challenge. He'd tried yesterday, with dismal results.

Another fork of lightning lit up the sky.

"Oh! Hurt!" She hid her face.

"No hurt, Tyrsa. Lightning. It's just lightning, and it's too far away. No hurt."

"Hurt!"

A long roll of deep thunder reverberated across the plains.

"Hurt!" Tyrsa cried, covering her ears.

"No hurt, Tyrsa. Shhhh. No hurt." Cenith held her close to him, trusting Windwalker to follow Nightwind. "It's thunder, remember? Thunder can't hurt you."

A twang sounded behind and to his left, followed by a grunt.

"Get down!" Daric cried.

Cenith tightened his grip on Tyrsa and swung his leg over the saddle, preparing to slide off. Another twang, and his left shoulder erupted in pain. Daric wheeled Nightwind to Cenith's left, protecting him and Tyrsa with his body.

The twang of another bow pierced the air. Horses screamed; men cursed. Still holding Tyrsa, Cenith slid off Windwalker. Daric joined him and took both sets of reins. Using the horses for cover, they made for the thick bushes on the right side of the path. Cenith laid Tyrsa on the ground, keeping between her and whoever fired the arrows. Setting himself against the pain, he pulled the arrow out so he could remove his cloak. The bushes rustled behind him and Cenith rolled over, his dagger at the ready. Daric lay nearby with his belt knife already out.

"It's jus' me m'lord, sir." Jolin's face appeared from behind a birch. He crouched low.

"Where's Buckam?" Cenith asked, sliding his sword out of its scabbard. He tucked the dagger in its sheath.

Jolin pointed back over his shoulder. "I cut the ropes when Warin was hit and dragged him to a bush jus' over there." He pointed east. "Ead and Varth are nearby, so's Trey and Jayce. Can't say for anyone else."

"Did someone pull Warin to safety?"

"No need, m'lord. Warin's dead. No doubt." An arrow thunked into the birch. Jolin ducked down further.

"Aja's blasted luck!" Cenith gripped his sword hilt, wishing he could plunge it into Saulth. "I thought we'd be safe until we entered the mountains."

"I'm not sure this is Lord Saulth's doin'," the backwoods mountain man said.

"Jolin's right." Daric lay on his side near Cenith's feet. "Whoever is shooting at us isn't very good. If these were Saulth's men, more of us would have been hit initially. Speaking of, how's your arm?"

Cenith rotated it. It hurt, but he could deal with it. "My leathers took the brunt of it. I'll be fine for now."

"Baybee?"

"Not now, Tyrsa. Keep down. Hurt!" Cenith pushed her head closer to the ground. "We'll find Baybee later. Hurt! Do you understand?"

"Hurt? Baybee hurt?" Her voice quivered with fear.

"No, Baybee isn't hurt. But you will be if you don't keep down."

"Jolin," Daric said. "Tell Ead and Varth to circle back the way we came and check the forest on the left side of the path. See who else you can find and come back here. Tell everyone where Lord Cenith is and to announce themselves before they approach him."

"Aye, sir." Jolin crawled on his elbows back into the bushes.

He returned a few moments later with Jayce, Dathan, and Trey. "Ead and Varth took Fallan, Madin, and Yanis with them."

Daric nodded, then turned to Cenith. "You'll be all right here by yourself?"

"Yes." Cenith patted his sword. "We'll be fine. Go ruin those men's plans."

Daric followed Jolin's example and crawled further into the bushes, the soldiers behind him. Cenith lay almost on top of Tyrsa, listening for anyone who might come close to them. His shoulder stung, but he forced himself to concentrate on what he heard.

Long moments dragged by. The rich scent of damp earth and moldy leaves filled his nostrils. Tyrsa quivered underneath him, but kept quiet. No birds could be heard, though a horse whinnied somewhere to the south. A man's cry echoed in the trees. Cenith prayed it wasn't one of his; losing Warin was bad enough.

A twig snapped to his right. He readied his sword while he waited for whoever was in the bushes to identify himself. No sound came. Something brushed the wet bushes nearby.

Cenith rolled off Tyrsa and brought his sword up, slashing at waist level. The intruder jumped back, unharmed. Cenith leapt to his feet. He prayed to Aja that Daric and his men were keeping the other attackers busy, especially the archers. The man, dressed in a ragged assortment of clothing, backed up against a birch. He looked more like a hungry farmer than a bandit.

Armed with only an old short sword, rusty and dented, the man charged. Cenith dodged, trapping the bandit's sword arm against him. He thrust, skewering him in the gut. The man grunted, his eyes opening wide. Cenith heaved upwards on the sword. Blood dribbled from the man's mouth and his weapon dropped to the ground. Life left his eyes. Cenith used his foot to push the man off his sword. He ducked down again, thankful the archers hadn't seen him.

"Tyrsa…" She wasn't where he'd left her. "Tyrsa!"

"Baybee?" Her voice came from the road.

Cenith duck-walked toward the edge of the brush, taking cover behind a beech tree. Tyrsa stood in clear view, searching for her doll. Warin lay not five feet from her, a crude arrow through his neck, but she paid him no attention. Several more arrows stuck in the ground nearby. A feathered shaft sprouted at her feet. She ignored that too. A cruel laugh sounded from the other side of the road and another bolt landed near her. More laughter followed it.

He's playing with her! Which explained why the archer hadn't shot at him.

Tyrsa didn't know she stood in danger's path. The arrows came from between two shrub enshrouded birches on the opposite side of the road. This archer was at least competent at short range, possibly the one who had killed Warin. Cenith had to get Tyrsa off the road, but how, without getting hit himself?

"Baybee?" Tyrsa wandered closer to the archer's side of the road.

"Tyrsa, no!"

An arrow hit the tree just above Cenith's head. He ducked lower and scanned the ground nearby, praying the doll lay somewhere close. There was no sign of it, leaving him with only one choice.

"Tyrsa! Baybee's here! I have Baybee!" He hated lying, but he had to get her off the road.

"Baybee?" Tyrsa walked toward him, smiling with joy.

A whistle sounded from the opposite side of the road and an arrow hit the dress where it dragged on the road. It pulled when she tried to move. A puzzled look crossed Tyrsa's face. She twisted to see what had stopped her from walking.

Ten feet separated her from Cenith. Who knew how long the man would play with Tyrsa before he killed her. Or worse, captured her. Cenith searched the ground at his feet. He dug out a small rock and tested its weight.

Keeping low, he threw it to his right, into the bushes. An arrow followed it and Cenith ran toward Tyrsa. He picked her up, tearing the dress where the arrow had pinned it, then dove for cover.

Something hit him in the back. Tyrsa cried out, though Cenith tried not to land on her.

"Hurt! Hurt!" Tears filled her eyes.

"I'm sorry, Tyrsa, I'm sorry. I had to get you off the road. You were in danger!"

Cenith rolled to the side. Searing pain erupted, darkening his vision. He took a few short breaths to gain control. Reaching behind, he felt an arrow protruding from just below his ribs.

* * * *

Keeping his back against the tree, Daric slid far enough around to allow him a good view of the man creeping away from him. Not wearing boots allowed him the advantage of moving in relative silence. In this weather, it led to cold feet, not to mention the muck oozing between his toes, but those he could ignore. The sound of rain falling on leaves and bushes also helped mask noise.

Daric shifted his sword to his left hand and pulled one of his wrist knives. Holding the point between two fingers, he threw it. The man grunted and pitched forward. Keeping careful watch, Daric retrieved his dagger from the man's neck. He rolled the bandit onto his back. Bulging brown eyes in a weathered face stared accusations his mouth tried to voice. A quick movement of the knife slit the man's throat. Daric cocked his head, listening.

Jolin and the other men with him had spread out on the west side of the road, the side the arrows came from. Just before Daric ducked into the forest, Keev and Barit, today's scouts, rode into view. Daric filled them in and instructed them to stay east of the road and look for more trouble.

The trill of a desert partridge echoed from the south; one of his men, since the bird didn't live this far north. Daric headed in that direction.

"Tyrsa, no!"

Cenith!

The echo reverberated through the trees, making it difficult for Daric to locate Cenith. He had to trust that his lord stayed close to where he'd left him. Daric switched direction and, keeping low to the ground, headed back to the road. A cry from Tyrsa verified the location.

A patch of dark blue against green bushes alerted Daric to something that shouldn't be there. Hidden behind a cover of tall shrubs and birch, a bandit, armed with a short bow, waited for a target. Daric scanned the road, just visible through the trees. Not a horse could be seen. Warin lay in a heap near the center. Tyrsa's blankets rested not far away. He could see no sign of Cenith or Tyrsa. He hoped that meant his lord and lady were safe.

Regardless, the bandit had to go. Several yards lay between them; too far to get an accurate throw with his knife. Two maples stood close together, fifteen feet behind the man. If Daric could make his way there while remaining unseen, he had a much better chance.

Daric backed away and moved deeper into the forest. When he judged himself directly behind the maples, he crept forward, knife in his right hand, sword in the left.

A desert partridge call sounded from his right, close by. Daric ducked behind an alder. Trey's head popped up from some soap berry shrubs. Daric waved him down and pointed to the archer. The bandit had heard the call and, bow ready, scanned the area where Trey crouched. Several moments later, he turned his attention back to the road.

Daric signalled to Trey to move south, and indicated he wanted him to make the bird call again. Trey nodded and disappeared. A few long moments later, the call came. The bandit's head whipped in that direction and Daric took the opportunity to move in behind the maple trees.

He waited, then took a cautious look at the bandit. The man had returned his attention to the road. Daric stepped out from behind the trees and threw the knife, straight toward the bandit's heart. The man moved at the last second and the blade bit deep, but to the right of the intended target.

The bandit grunted and swung his bow around. Daric hadn't waited and covered the distance in a few long strides. He wrenched the weapon from the man's hand. Short and lean, the archer was no match for Daric. He shoved the murderer against the tree, heedless of the knife sticking out of his back. The man cried out and raised his hands.

"I surrender!" the bandit said, staring down at Daric's sword, resting hard against his groin.

"How many?" Daric asked.

"How many what?"

Daric pressed harder. The man's eyes almost popped out of his head.

"I'm coming up on your right, sir." Trey's voice came from near the road and he appeared a few moments later, followed by Jolin and Dathan.

"Jolin, take over," Daric indicated his sword and the weapon changed hands. "Dathan, check Lord Cenith, he should be in the bushes straight across from us. Trey, whistle the regroup."

Dathan trotted across the road while Trey's shrill tune recalled the men.

Daric gripped the knife sticking out of the bandit's back. "How many?"

"Jus' me," the bandit said, not taking his eyes off the sword. "I works alone."

"Trey, see if Dathan needs assistance."

"Yes, sir."

Daric yanked out the knife. The archer bit off a cry of pain. He grabbed the man's left hand, held it up against the tree, and pinned it there with the knife. Daric took a measure of satisfaction in the man's scream. It rang through the forest, a warning to any bandit who yet lived. The thief squirmed in agony, his eyes travelling up to his hand, then down to the sword.

"Sir!" Trey ran back across the road. "Lord Cenith's been hit in the back with an arrow!"

Daric's stomach dropped to his knees. "Is he still alive?"

"Yes, sir, and talking, but he's in a lot of pain. Dathan wants to know if he should pull the arrow out or wait for you."

"Where exactly is it?"

"Lower back, right side," Trey answered.

"Wait for me. Hopefully we can make it to the station and tend him there."

Trey nodded and ran back across the road. The others appeared in ones and twos. Keev and Barit first, followed by Ead, Varth, Jayce, Madin, Fallan, and Yanis.

"Men, I want to know how many bandits each of you killed."

"Three, sir!" Jolin said with a grin.

As the soldiers called out the tally, Daric totalled them up in his head, adding the four he'd killed. "I get twenty three. With you that makes twenty four. That's a little more than one."

Daric slid his other wrist dagger from its sheath and touched it to the man's nose. Sweat ran down the bandit's cheeks into his ragged black beard. “I’m going to ask the question once more. I want a truthful answer. How…many?”

“That’s all! Jus’ twenty four! I’m tellin’ the truth! I swear it!” The man looked cross-eyed at the dagger indenting the end of his bulbous nose.

Trey made a reappearance. “Lord Cenith says not to worry about him, just do what you have to. He also said this one shot arrows around Lady Tyrsa, playing with her.”

The man’s eyes scooted from the dagger to the sword to Daric. “Didn’t mean nothin’! Was just playin!”

“Isn’t that funny?” Daric said, grinning. “That’s just what I’m doing.”

The man tried to cringe away from him.

Daric’s grin faded. “You’ve greatly inconvenienced my day. You killed one of my men and put an arrow in my lord’s back, not to mention tormenting his wife.”

“His…his wife? That stupid kid?” The bandit realized his mistake, but the knowledge came too late. The whites of his eyes displayed his fear.

“That stupid kid is a lot smarter than you.” Daric motioned Jolin away and slipped his dagger back into its sheath. He took his time wiggling the knife out of the man’s hand, ignoring the cries of pain. The bandit slumped to the ground. Daric passed the knife to Jayce and picked the man up, holding him sideways.

“I know you’re lying, but I don’t have time for this.” Daric mustered his strength and slammed him against the tree. An audible snap preceded the man’s scream, and he hung limp. Daric tossed the body to one side.

Jolin’s eyes widened. “Think he’s still alive, sir? Shouldn’t we finish him off?”

Daric retrieved his dagger from Jayce and cleaned it on the wet grass. “I hope he is. He can spend the rest of his short life reflecting on the error of his ways.” With a broken back, the man would be no threat.

“I wonder if he told th’ truth.” Jolin passed Daric his sword.

“As I said, I sincerely doubt it. However, we could spend the next month searching for them and not find a thing. We have more pressing concerns.”

Daric sheathed his sword, motioned to the men, and strode across the road. Cenith lay on his left side, his head on Dathan's lap. Tyrsa huddled against a tree. She had her arms wrapped around her knees while she rocked back and forth, her wide eyes staring at nothing.

"Jayce, Fallan, Madin, Yanis, Keev, go find the horses."

'Yes, sirs' mingled with 'aye, sirs', and the named soldiers vanished into the trees.

Daric knelt by Cenith's side to examine the wound. The leathers hadn't stopped much of the arrow this time. The entire head lay buried in the young lord's back, though Daric couldn't tell if the arrow had hit the kidney. He prayed it hadn't.

"I can't get Tyrsa to come to me," Cenith said, his teeth clenched against the pain. "We were attacked. I killed the man, but Tyrsa went onto the road to look for her doll. I had to lie to her, tell her I'd found Baybee, to get her to come back. I think I hurt her when I dove for cover. Now she won't come near me."

"Guess that answers my question, sir, 'bout the number o' bandits," Jolin said, pointing to the body. "Shall I go look for the doll?"

Daric nodded and leaned back. The arrow had to come out. Cenith couldn't travel like this, not even the short distance remaining to the station. If it hadn't hit the kidney, riding a horse could easily shift it, making matters worse. Daric broke off the fletching and, with Trey and Dathan's help, sliced through Cenith's padded leather jerkin, so he could slide it off the arrow. He removed the wool tunic and shirt underneath the same way, exposing the wound.

"Hold his shoulders," Daric told Trey. "Careful of that other wound." It would need stitches as well, but it could wait. He tore off a large piece of Cenith's shirt, folded it into a compress, and passed it to Dathan.

Daric wrapped his hand around the shaft and gave one hard pull. Cenith sucked in a breath, then let out a long groan. Dathan quickly pressed the cloth against the wound. Daric glanced at Tyrsa. The girl appeared in shock. She needed blankets, something to keep her warm.

"Varth, Lord Cenith's cloak must be around here somewhere. See if you can find it and put it around Lady Tyrsa."

Varth nodded, and motioned to Ead to join him in the search.

"As soon as some of the horses come back, we're going to need blankets for them both," Daric said, taking over for Dathan, keeping pressure on the wound. "Barit, go take that arrow out of Warin. We'll have to put him on a horse. I'm not leaving him here."

"Yes, sir."

"Is anyone else hurt?" Daric asked.

"A few cuts, but nothing serious," Trey said. "That man was the only one we could find with a bow."

"Got the doll, sir. It was tangled in th' blankets." Jolin crouched by Daric's side. "She ain't in good shape though. Looks like one o' th' horses stepped on her. Stuffin's comin' out her side. I poked it back in, but it'll need stitchin'."

"Take a strip off Cenith's shirt and tie it around the hole. Maybe one of the women at the station can fix it." Daric peeled back the cloth on Cenith's back, blood welled up and he reapplied the pressure. *Too much blood.*

"And, um…one other thing, sir." Jolin looked more than a little sheepish. "I've lost Buckam. He's not where I left him."

"It doesn't matter. We got what we needed from him." Daric didn't think the Bredun guard could travel too far. They hadn't passed any villages or inhabited farmsteads in over two days. In this weather, his fever could easily come back.

Water dripped from leaves. Birds called to one another once more. Daric looked up at the grey sky. Sometime during the altercation it had stopped raining. *Niafanna, Cillain, hear me. Please let us make it to the station.*

* * * *

Daric led the party out of the vale on Windwalker, an unconscious Cenith tied to him. Once Tyrsa had her doll, she recovered from most of her shock, though she remained subdued and jumped at any noise. She said 'hurt' several times and pointed to Cenith's back, but wouldn't go near him. Jolin offered to let her ride with him and, to everyone's surprise, she accepted.

All but three of the horses had been located. Jayce and Yanis lost their mounts to arrows. Neither had been killed initially and both were found farther up the road, one on its knees coughing up blood, the other down completely. They had to be destroyed. Jayce rode Buckam's palfrey while Yanis shared Keev's horse. Nightwind had gone missing again, though Daric wouldn't put it past the horse to show up when least expected. That one was a survivor, so long as the remaining bandits, or Buckam, hadn't taken him.

Dathan rode behind Trey, leading Shadowgait who carried a blanket shrouded Warin across his back. Fallon sat behind Madin, while Varth and Ead shared a horse. Jayce and Barit were the only ones who rode alone, Barit in front, while Jayce watched their backs.

Keev and Barit had ridden by the concealed bandits with no knowledge they were there. The band must have spotted them earlier and set up the ambush. It said much for the desperate way of things that they would attack fourteen well-armed soldiers.

Jolin moved up beside Daric. "M'lady's shiverin' hard, sir, but there's no dry blankets."

Tyrsa huddled under Cenith's cloak, sad and forlorn.

"There's nothing I can do," Daric said. "We're travelling as fast as we dare."

Jolin nodded and dropped behind.

Not far out of the vale, Barit galloped back. "There's a man standing over the next rise, sir! I think it's Buckam. Looks like he's got Nightwind."

Now there was a surprise. Not the horse, the man. Perhaps Daric's words had made some sense to Buckam after all.

The Bredun guard stood still until they reached him. He handed Daric Nightwind's reins. "Your Excellency, I am sorry I could not help in the attack. Not only am I not fit, but I have no weapon. One thing I could do was go after your horse. He led me a merry chase, but finally took pity on my poor soul."

Buckam fell to his knees, disregarding the mud, his words coming out in a rush. "I have thought long on your words, Councillor Daric, and I have come to the conclusion that you are right. My lord has gone mad. He has forsaken not only his people and his lands, but honour as well. I cannot serve such a man. I beg you, please allow me to serve Lord Cenith. I am not as big and strong as the rest of you, but I am quick and quiet when I need to be."

Daric raised his eyebrow.

Buckam's words came out faster. "I know you cannot trust me, nor do I expect you to. I will serve in his stable, in his kitchen, wherever you choose. I will work hard to earn your trust."

Noble words, but this could easily be another trick. "I can't speak for my lord, who is unconscious at the moment, but I'll relay your words to him when his condition improves."

Buckam bowed his head. "It is the best I can expect."

"Do you think yourself capable of riding alone?"

Buckam nodded.

Daric aimed a thumb over his shoulder. "Jayce rides your horse behind us. Nightwind's gait is not a smooth one. Wait for him, then trade horses. When that's done, ride up here with me."

"Yes, sir!" Buckam struggled to his feet, bowing as Daric and Cenith passed by.

Jolin moved his horse back up beside Daric. "That was a surprise, sir."

Daric nodded. "If I read him right, a pleasant one."

Rather than the frown Daric expected, Jolin grinned. "You trust him, then?"

"No, not yet. I'd like think he's sincere, but we'll have to wait and see what the future holds. He'll have to prove himself, and still be watched. If a man can turn once…" He shrugged.

The rest of the journey passed in silence. The smoke from the station's chimneys greeted them first, rising friendly and warm against the darker clouds. When they were spotted, several guards rode out to meet them.

"Councillor Daric! What happened?" Aleyn asked, concern creasing the man's brow. "We'd expected you from the east."

"A long story, one better told after a hot meal and some rest. Lord Cenith is injured. Send someone ahead to prepare the room for him and his wife. Make sure there are medical supplies at hand. I'm almost out."

Aleyn's concerned look changed to one of surprise. "His *wife*?"

Jolin moved up beside them and pushed the cloak away from Tyrsa's face. She'd fallen asleep, huddled against his chest.

"She's not the only one who looks in need of a bath and hot food," Aleyn said. He turned to one of his men and relayed Daric's orders. The man took off at a gallop.

Aleyn signalled half the remaining men to guard their rear, then swung his horse next to Daric. "We received no word of the marriage by rider or bird, sir."

"It all happened rather suddenly," Daric said, urging Windwalker forward. "We're tired, chilled, and hungry, not to mention injured." His toes stung with cold and small cuts from walking through the brush barefoot. Where he'd find boots to fit him until he got home, he had no idea. "Would you mind if the explanations waited until we feel human again?"

"Of course not, sir." Aleyn kicked his horse and he moved to the front, leading them to warmth, food, and safety.

Daric thought about all that had happened since the last time they'd visited the station. Not in his worst dreams could he have imagined what had lain before them. He looked to the mountains, and the pass they had to traverse. *What lies in wait up there?* Only Cillain knew, but they needed to rest and heal before they had half a chance of facing it.

Chapter Sixteen

Daric sat by Cenith's bedside, arms crossed, his heart sick. A hard thing, watching your lord die and knowing you could do nothing. Harder than when Ifan was swept away by a ton of snow not fifty yards behind him. That had been quick, over in mere moments.

I shouldn't have left him alone. There'd been no reason not to; competent and quick with the sword, Cenith should have been well able to take care of himself. They'd faced an unknown number of bandits; Daric needed all his men in the fight. He'd thought Cenith safe, but he hadn't factored in the girl.

Isn't hindsight a wonderful thing? A knock interrupted his thoughts. "Enter."

Jolin stuck his head in the door. "How's he doin', sir? We're all worried."

Daric motioned him in. "Close the door."

Jolin stood at the end of the bed. *How to tell him?* It hadn't been easy telling Cenith about his father. This would be at least as difficult.

"I've done everything I can." Daric ran a hand through his hair and leaned forward, resting his elbows on his knees. He kept his gaze on Cenith, the dark circles under his eyes, the blue tinged lips—signs of a man dying from loss of blood. For some strange reason, it was easier than watching the dawning grief on Jolin's face.

"He'll be a' right, though…won't he?"

The hope in Jolin's voice punched Daric in the gut. He shook his head. "The arrow only nicked the kidney, but by the time we got him back here, his stomach was hard from internal bleeding. He never regained consciousness. A few hours…that's all. There's nothing I can do."

Jolin fell to his knees. "Why? Shival, *why*?" Tears fell unashamed from the young soldier's eyes. "Not him! For th' love o' Maegden," Jolin sobbed. "Take *me* instead!"

Daric stood and put his hand on Jolin's shoulder. "I'll tell the others. Stay here as long as you like."

Men handled grief in different ways. Some, like Jolin, displayed theirs openly, others slipped away to mourn in private. The women broke down, consoled by husbands trying to deal with their own sorrow. Daric sought his comfort in the stable and Nightwind's quiet affection. The horse seemed to understand his dark moods.

Like a long time acquaintance, grief had trod in Daric's shadow all his life. Friends came, friends went; the reason Daric had tended to avoid close relationships in his early life. When Ifan died, he mourned and moved on. Though he missed Cenith's father, death was nothing new. *Then why does this one hurt so much?* Perhaps, the older one grew the more important friends became…even young ones. Ifan had been more lord than friend, Cenith more son than lord. It could be that Cenith reminded him of Kian. To lose a son would be at least as painful as this.

"Sir?" Aleyn appeared at the stable door. "Sorry to disturb you, but My Lady wants to see Lord Cenith. She's…causing problems."

Daric heard Tyrsa's voice as soon as he left the stable. For such a small thing she could attain remarkable volume.

"No! No! Tyrsa sleep! Cenith sleep! Cenith sleep Tyrsa!"

Of necessity, he had to leave Tyrsa's story to Jolin, who reported on her reactions while Daric worked on Cenith. Waking up to so many strange faces had been traumatic; getting her into a bath and clean clothes, even more so. She refused to let go of Baybee through the entire experience.

Daric entered Aleyn's home. Tyrsa cowered in the corner of the common room, repeating her rant, the muddy doll clutched tightly to her chest. Her face alternated between fear, anger, and confusion. Mareta, Aleyn's wife, tried to coax her out.

"Let me see what I can do," he said.

Mareta joined her husband by the fire. "The poor little thing. How can we explain about his lordship?"

Daric shook his head. "Death is difficult enough for us to comprehend. Trying to make her understand will be impossible. I don't think we should even try." He crouched in front of Tyrsa. "No Cenith, Tyrsa. No Cenith. Do you want food?"

"No food! Cenith! Cenith sleep…"

"No Cenith, Tyrsa," Daric said, interrupting her rant. "Do you understand? No Cenith." He pointed to her doll. "Baybee is hurt. Look."

Daric tried to touch the doll. Tyrsa attacked him, hitting, kicking, screaming, a desert cat gone insane.

"No Baybee hurt!" she cried. "No Baybee hurt! Cenith hurt! Cenith! Cenith!"

She couldn't harm him, though she forced Daric to cover his face with his arms. Someone came up behind him.

"Stay back! Let her get it out," Daric said.

Tyrsa flailed and hit, her words turning into incoherent wails. Finally, she collapsed in a heap, her sobs sending shudders through her small body. Daric gathered her into his arms and rocked her.

"Shhh, now. It's all right. You know he's hurt, don't you. Shhhh." Daric wished he could do something…*anything*…to bring Cenith back, if only for her. He'd gladly take his place, if Niafanna would just allow it.

Tyrsa's sobs turned to sniffles, interrupted every now and then by a hiccup. Daric shook his head over how quickly she'd become attached to Cenith. Growing up essentially in isolation, Daric thought it would have taken much longer to trust a stranger, let alone fourteen of them.

"Sir?" Jolin stood behind him. "Kin I take her t' see Lord Cenith?"

"I'm not sure that's a good idea," Daric said, stroking Tyrsa's hair, still damp from her bath.

"I…I think she needs to." Jolin's green eyes were rimmed with red.

"Jolin…"

"Please, sir. I think she'll understand if she sees him. It might help her."

Mountain intuition? Jolin seemed to have it in full measure. More likely it had to do with Varth's dream. The pair of them held firmly to the conviction that Tyrsa had healed Varth. The entire idea fell into the realm of the ridiculous, not to mention impossible; but could he take the chance, however miniscule, that it wasn't?

Daric nodded. He released Tyrsa and stood. "Come with us. We'll go see Cenith." He helped her to her feet.

She couldn't have understood all the words, but she calmed considerably.

Jolin held his hand out, a sad smile on his face. Tyrsa took it, her other arm choking Baybee and attempting to hold up the simple green dress the women had given her. He led her up the narrow, wooden stairs, quiet and respectful. Daric followed, waving Aleyn and his family back.

Varth, Ead, Trey…they were all there, leaning against the walls, sitting in the two chairs or on the floor in front of the fireplace. Jolin wasn't the only one with red eyes.

At Daric's questioning look, Varth said, "We couldn't leave him to go to Shival alone, sir. We're sending prayers, telling Her how kind and good he is, that he's worthy of Maegden's Hall."

Ten solemn men nodded their agreement.

"Where's Buckam?" The Bredun man had taken the news exceptionally hard.

"In the barracks. He's not one of us," Ead said.

Jolin added, "Not yet."

"Oh." Almost a whisper, Tyrsa's one word spoke a library. She knew. There it was, plain on her face, the pain…the sadness. How could she know? Daric closed the door, shot the bolt home, and leaned against it. Whatever happened, for good or ill, this was an important moment.

* * * *

Cenith lay on his stomach, his eyes closed like he was asleep. Except he wasn't. The man who had been so nice to her looked bad. His face was the colour of the white-grey stuff she used to draw *pit-churs*. Tyrsa could feel his hurt, she didn't need to touch him. That bothered her. So did the woman sitting beside him on the bed, stroking his hair.

She wore a strange black dress. It fit tight, like she wasn't wearing a dress. Much of her chest showed. The ends of the long sleeves looked like they'd been torn over and over. Tyrsa couldn't see her feet, the bottom of her dress just blended into the floor. Her hair, the same colour as the dress, floated around her as if moved by wind, but no wind blew in the room.

The woman smiled, though she didn't mean it. She wanted to take Cenith, like she'd wanted to take Varth. Tyrsa stopped her from taking Varth, but it had hurt, more than when *he* hurt her. Much more, but in a different way. This hurt went deep inside her. It burned, worse than when the candle burned, worse than when she'd tried to touch the fire long and long ago. It was bad.

Jolin led her to Cenith's side. Close. Too close! She pulled her hand out of his and backed away. "No hurt. No hurt!"

The woman's smile twisted on one side. She made a noise like the cats did when she patted them. "You are afraid. If you touch him, the pain will be worse than last time. A lot worse. You know it. That is why you are afraid." The woman didn't speak in words, her mouth didn't move. "You will not save this one. I know what you are now."

Behind her, Jolin spoke words, words she didn't know.

"Would you like to know what he is saying? I can make it so you will know all the words that have ever been, or ever will be. Would you like that?" The woman ran her finger down Cenith's cheek. "He belongs to me now, but in exchange I can give you much. All you have to do is worship me."

Tyrsa didn't know 'exchange', 'worship' or many of the other words. "No hurt Cenith. Tyrsa hurt…" What was the word Cenith used? She understood now what it meant. "…you." Then she realized she hadn't spoken those words, she'd said them in her head, but the woman understood them anyway.

Jolin spoke again.

The woman laughed. "You cannot hurt me. You are a product of the old gods. They have not ruled here in centuries. My brothers and sisters and I defeated them long ago. You can do…nothing." With that word, her yellow eyes lit up like two candles. She waved her hand in the air, then rested it on Cenith's head.

That made Tyrsa angry, but it also made her afraid. Somewhere inside her, hidden away, lay what she needed to make this woman go away, never to come back. Buried deep, too deep for Tyrsa to touch on her own, it first appeared when she told the big winds to go away. It left, but came again when she touched Varth's hurt. She'd only wanted to show she hurt because Varth was hurt. She didn't like him being hurt. He was nice. Now the thing sat inside her, always there, but hard to touch. The woman laughed again. It made Tyrsa shiver like the big winds had. Jolin said more words.

"I shall show you my power, that I am stronger than you." She waved her hand, but in a different way, and Tyrsa knew Jolin's words.

"I'm here, m'lady. We're all here. No one will hurt ye," he said.

Tyrsa turned to him. He smiled, a better one than he had before. This man was very nice, and…and… The woman put a word in her head. *Brave.* That was it. He was brave, and kind. Like Cenith. She wanted…needed…to tell him about the bad woman.

"Wo-man." Fear made her insides feel strange. She could understand Jolin's words, but she couldn't speak them back. "Wo-man hurt Cenith." Tyrsa pointed to the woman on the bed.

Jolin looked like he didn't understand. "What woman? There's no woman there, m'lady." He couldn't see her.

The woman laughed louder. "If you want to have full use of all the words, little insect, you must worship me." She used the sharp end of her finger to make a red line on Cenith's cheek. "You decide. Words, or no words. Either way, this one is mine."

Tyrsa let go of Jolin's hand. It would be wonderful to learn all the words in the Book Room. So many words. She could talk to people. She could tell them how the ground hurt, that it needed to be fixed.

"Yes, wonderful. Words are a power in their own right," the woman said. "You could do so much. And he is only one man. There are so many more." The woman lifted her arm, her hand pointing to each of the men. "You could have any of them, all of them if you wanted. Especially that one." She pointed to Jolin. "He's handsome, strong, brave, and…yes…I thought so, he fancies himself in love with you." Her laughter deepened. It sounded very bad.

Love. What was love? An image of Rani flashed before Tyrsa's eyes. Rani, and the warmth she felt when the woman held her, so long and long ago. Was that love?

"You will know all about love and why Rani did not come back. Just worship me and you will know. Words, or no words. The decision is yours."

Words, all the words she wanted. She could have words without the woman, but it would be long and long before she learned them. The words…oh! The words! Their wondrous sounds and meanings!

"All yours, to play with, to speak, over and over." The woman leaned down and put her mouth near Cenith's. Something white, not quite there, came out of Cenith's mouth. She was taking him away. His warmth. His kindness. His smile.

"No! No words! Cenith!" Tyrsa threw back the covers and tore the cloths off his back. Baybee fell to the floor. She hesitated only a moment, bracing for the pain, then put her hands on Cenith's hurt. Fire burned through her hands, her arms, to her back. His pain! Her pain! The hurts *he'd* given her came back, and more. They burned with Cenith's hurt, in her lower back; with Varth's hurt, in her head; with all the hurts she ever had…the beatings, her falls, when she first tried to touch fire…all of it. All at once.

Tyrsa shrieked, but didn't lift her hands from Cenith's back. The bad woman jerked away from Cenith and the white stuff went back inside him. Her face twisted, like *his* did when *he* got angry with her. Tyrsa feared she'd beat her, like *he* did.

She whimpered. The pain! It was too much, but she couldn't let go. She couldn't! Deep inside her, the…something…that lay hidden flared up. It gave her strength, it gave her hope, and a promise. A white light covered Tyrsa's hands. It spread like spilled water up Cenith's back to his head, where the woman's hand rested.

It touched the woman and she screamed, her face moving, twisting like Tyrsa's fireplace pictures when she smeared them with her fingers. The woman stood, her whole body shifting the same as her face. She faded, her scream faded, and she disappeared into the floor.

Still, the fire burned in Tyrsa, hot, raging. She sucked in air. It wouldn't come. The words the woman showed her faded too. Tyrsa fought the fire within, struggled to keep the words. *Brave! Brave! Brave! Love! Love! Love!* She repeated them over and over, following them into the dark.

* * * *

"Keep back!" Daric left his post by the door and pulled Jolin away from Tyrsa just before he touched her. The girl stood rigid, her hands on Cenith's wound. A strange white glow covered her hands and Cenith's upper body. Tyrsa's screams ripped into his head, his heart. "Varth! No one comes in! Is that clear?" He had to shout to make himself heard over the cacophony.

"Yes, sir!" In three strides, Varth reached the door taking up Daric's former position.

"She's in pain! 'Tis too much!" Jolin's fear lent him unnatural strength.

Daric mustered every ounce of his own considerable muscle to hold him back. "You wanted her to do this, Jolin!"

"It wasn't like this with Varth!" he sobbed. "I didn't think it would kill her!"

"Maybe it is and maybe it isn't!" Daric gripped Jolin's shoulders, made the young man look at him, not the girl. There'd be bruises, but he couldn't allow him to touch Tyrsa. "Do you know what she's doing?" He shook Jolin. "Do you? Maybe this is what she has to do to save him, and maybe it's all for ill, but now that she's started, do…not…stop her. Understand?"

Jolin took a couple of shuddering breaths, then nodded. Daric relaxed his grip. Ten other faces stared at the girl, horror replacing the grief that had commanded them only moments before.

Someone pounded on the door. "It's all right!" Varth said. "We don't need you!"

Tyrsa's scream ended abruptly and the glow faded. She fell backwards, stiff as a tree trunk. Jolin leapt past Daric, just catching the girl before she hit the floor. He cradled her now limp body in his arms, touching his fingers to the translucent skin at the base of her throat.

"She's alive, sir. She's still alive!" Tears flowed freely down his cheeks.

Daric left Tyrsa to Jolin and crouched beside Cenith. His fingers found a steady pulse, still weak, but not the flutter it had been. The dark shadows under his eyes, the blue shading his lips, faded. His colour hadn't returned, but that would come in time. Daric stood to check the wound itself. Though not yet healed, it had closed and wouldn't require stitches. He turned Cenith on his side and pressed gentle fingers to his stomach. He shook his head.

"Sir? He's…she…didn't help?" Varth's voice shook with unrestrained emotion.

"This is impossible," Daric said, unable to believe his eyes, what every ounce of healing skill he possessed screamed couldn't be true.

"Is the wound healed?" Barit asked.

Daric shook his head again, trying to find words to explain something that couldn't have happened. He could feel the fear, the disappointment behind him. "No, not completely, but she fixed the worst of it. Not only is he not bleeding anymore, she…" This is what Daric found so difficult to believe. "His gut was filled with blood. Now, it's normal again. He should be dead. Cenith was too close to death for anyone to save him."

The shoulder wound had closed over completely. Daric hadn't bothered stitching it, there hadn't seemed any point. Now Cenith would bear a less than attractive scar. He turned on his heel and crouched beside Jolin and the girl. The incredible, wonderful, *frightening* girl. "Who are you? What are you?"

Jolin's face broke into a slow, wide grin, his cheeks glistening in the candlelight. "She's m'lady, sir. She's m'lord's wife. She couldn't let him die."

"Then she should rest beside him." Daric lifted Tyrsa from Jolin's arms and carried her to the opposite side of the bed.

Trey hustled to get there first and pulled the blankets back. Daric laid her gently beside Cenith and tucked her in. He placed a fresh bandage over Cenith's wound and covered him as well. Jolin picked Baybee up from the floor and headed for Tyrsa's side of the bed.

Daric grasped his arm. "Not yet." He took the doll. "Barit, fetch me a needle and thread."

While Barit retrieved the items from the kit by the bed, Jayce leapt out of his chair and leaned against the fireplace, letting Daric sit down. Ead stood by the window, his mouth agape, staring at Tyrsa. Varth left the door to go to him, his steps silent. He set a comforting hand on his friend's shoulder. No one spoke. All of them seemed afraid to breathe, to shatter the moment.

Daric unwound the cloth from around the doll, each move as careful as if she lived and breathed. To Tyrsa, she did. He set her on his lap while he threaded the needle, then turned her on her side. With tiny, careful stitches, he closed the rent seam.

The past ten days had been hard on Baybee. Dirt masked the green of her dress, darkened the pale material used for her body. Too much of the yellow yarn that adorned her head had disappeared completely. One button eye hung askew. Daric fixed it. The other looked recently mended and he wondered who'd had the courage to fix the doll of a girl they were supposed to ignore.

Daric enjoyed the work. This patient didn't squirm or scream in pain, so he took his time. The men watched, their expressions intent.

"Didn't know ye were trained as a seamstress, sir."

Jolin's dry humour shattered the silence. Varth broke first, his chuckle gaining momentum until it became a full blown laugh. Trey followed, then Barit hard on his heels. In seconds, the room rocked with laughter; a far distant cry from the grief that had engulfed it only moments earlier.

Daric struggled to maintain his composure. Laughter filled the room, brightening the dingy corners, chasing the last of the darkness away. Surely those downstairs must think they'd gone mad. He glanced back at his two charges, asleep on the bed. Neither stirred, though their chests rose and fell in the rhythm of life. The laughter faded, some into fresh tears, now of happiness, others into grins and smiles.

"Say what you will." Daric put a final stitch to Baybee's eye. "Just remember who'll be playing seamstress the next time you find yourselves on the wrong end of a sword."

Laughter began anew, Jolin's the heartiest. Interesting that he now stood at Tyrsa's side. Daric had a feeling that in the unlikely event Cenith decided to set Tyrsa aside as his wife, she wouldn't go far. He tied off the thread and passed the needle to Barit, who'd waited at his side to stow it away. Daric held the doll before him.

"You need a bath, young lady," he said.

"Ain't you afraid she'll fall apart, sir?" Jayce asked.

"She might. We'll give her to the women. They might know what to do." Daric stood.

"Sir?" Jolin moved away from the bed, blocking Daric's path to the door, his face serious once more.

"We should leave. They both need rest," Daric said.

Jolin squared his shoulders and looked him straight in the eye. "You swore th' three o' us t' secrecy, 'bout Varth's injury. Fact is, sir, we'd already discussed it 'mongst ourselves afore Varth ever woke up."

Nods and murmurs of agreement filled the room.

"While we sat here, afore you came up, we talked 'bout a lot o' things, and, one thing we decided, if m'lady could do what we hoped she could, we wanted t' form a new regiment, a small one."

Daric's eyebrow rose.

"A regiment dedicated t' protectin' our lady. We won't abandon Lord Cenith, we will hold to our oath to honour and protect him always. But m'lady is special. I knew it even afore she healed Varth. She's a stranger t' our ways, and will need people she knows around her. We wish t' be those people, t' honour and protect her. T' help her."

"You were right, sir, when you said that people would take advantage of her power," Varth said. "We won't let that happen."

A personal guard for a lord's wife. Unheard of in Ardael, though Daric had seen it in other parts of the world. Noble idea. Noble men.

"It's not my decision," he said. "It'll be up to Lord Cenith, when he recovers." When, not if. Daric couldn't stop the grin.

"It'll be a company o' twelve," Jolin said, matching his grin.

"Twelve? There are only eleven of you."

"No, sir." Jolin shook his head once. "There's twelve. Warin's here. We can't see him, but we kin feel him. He liked m'lady too. I know he'll watch over her, Frost, Char or no."

Ead came out of his trance. "I request to be the first to bend the knee to her, sir. I'm ashamed of the way I behaved. The rest of my life won't be long enough to make it up to her."

Daric didn't know what to say. A short time ago, his heart had been dead, now it burst with life and pride. He gripped Jolin's shoulder. The young man beamed with conviction. A quick glance around the room showed they all did. Daric had no doubt each of them would willingly lay down their lives for a pixie of a girl with black, corn silk hair and large blue eyes.

"I'll put it before Lord Cenith, when he's well enough to receive it. For now, we should let them rest."

Ead stepped forward. "May Varth and I sit with them? To make sure all remains well."

Daric nodded and in a few moments shifts were assigned. As the remainder of the soldiers left the room, Daric studied the two on the bed, especially the girl.

Jolin called you special. You are that. But what else are you? What else are you capable of? Somehow, he had to find out what that scroll contained.

Chapter Seventeen

Cenith felt the pain first, deep in his back. It took a moment for him to remember why he hurt. Bandits. They'd been ambushed in the forest, but now he lay in a bed. They'd made it to the station. Relief washed over him and he opened his eyes.

Bright, afternoon light illuminated Daric sitting in a chair beside the bed, his deep brown eyes fixed on him. Cenith opened his mouth to speak but could only manage a hoarse croak. He struggled to sit up. It took longer than it should have and required Daric's assistance.

Daric picked up a pewter cup off the bedside table and poured a small measure of water into it. "Sip this."

The water tasted damn good. Cenith licked his still dry lips and tried again. "How long have I been asleep?" He sounded less like a bullfrog in heat.

Daric poured more water, waiting until Cenith had drained that as well before he spoke. "You should have gone to Shival's judgement three days ago."

"Three…" Cenith's voice cracked, "…*days*?" Daric gave him more water. "I should be dead? I didn't think I was hurt that bad. Thank you, I owe you my life."

Daric shook his head. "Not me, her."

He pointed to Cenith's left. Tyrsa slept on her back, with her head turned toward him, her hair flowing over the pillows like a dark sea. The blankets, pulled up past her chest, didn't quite hide the forest green nightgown she wore.

Cenith whipped his head back to Daric. "Tyrsa? Did she…do what she did to Varth?"

Daric nodded. "Did you have a dream?"

Cenith frowned. "Not that I recall. The last thing I remember, I was lying on the ground in the forest in a lot of pain. You were working on me."

Daric sat back and rested his hands on the thin arms of the wooden chair. "The arrow nicked your kidney enough to leak blood into your belly. I couldn't stop it. All my instincts, all logic, say you shouldn't be sitting here talking to me. If not for Tyrsa's little performance, you'd be over the back of a horse, on your way to Tiras to join your mother in the burial cave."

Performance? "Did you see what she did?"

Daric nodded. "The men too."

"You were all in here?" It must have been crowded.

"They were keeping vigil, praying for you. Jolin insisted that Tyrsa needed to see you. At first, she was afraid. I think it hurt her when she touched Varth and that's why she acted so peculiar afterward."

Hurt her? No wonder she'd been scared.

"She stared, not at you, but at a spot on the bed beside you. We watched her face change from fear to anger to puzzlement, and a host of other emotions." Daric leaned forward again. "This is the interesting part." He shrugged. "One of them anyway. She said 'woman hurt Cenith'. There was no woman in the room."

Fingers from the grave touched him; their ethereal caress stroked shivers up Cenith's spine. "Do…do you think she saw Shival?"

Daric shrugged again. "After what I witnessed, I'm willing to believe almost anything."

Cenith looked at Tyrsa again. *So small, so innocent. She knows nothing of the gods.*

"After that, her face took on first a wistful look, then fear, then determination. She ripped the covers and bandages off you and put her hands on your wound. She said 'No, no words' and then your name."

"No…words? Not no hurt?"

"She said 'no words'." Daric leaned back again and folded his arms across his broad chest.

"Strange."

"Not so strange as what happened next," Daric said. "Her hands glowed white, then it spread to you. She screamed, but that doesn't describe half the pain she must have felt. I swear I've never heard anyone scream that loud, for that long." By his own admission, Daric had tortured a lot of men. For him to say that meant a great deal. "I have no idea how long she touched you, it seemed an eternity. She finally passed out and we laid her here, beside you. She's been asleep ever since."

It took a moment for Cenith to find words. "She did all that. For me?"

"Something you need to understand. Tyrsa not only stopped the bleeding, she removed the blood that had pooled in your belly, as well as replaced what you'd lost. No healer or physician could ever dream of such a thing." Daric stared at him, making Cenith feel awkward, then shook his head. "I still can't believe you're here, sitting up and talking to me. Your heart had almost stopped beating. Tyrsa brought you back from the brink of death and that might be why it hurt so much, and why she hasn't regained consciousness."

Cenith reached over and touched Tyrsa's face. For once, her alabaster skin didn't feel cold. "Do you think she went too far? That she won't recover?"

"I can't say. I pray she does."

Barit opened the door and stuck his head in, his grin wider than the Kalemi River. "May I tell the men Lord Cenith is awake, sir?"

Daric raised an eyebrow, but couldn't keep a smile from lifting the corner of his mouth. "You may, but no one is allowed to visit until I say so, understood?"

"Yes, sir!" Barit ducked out, then back in. "Welcome back, My Lord!" The door closed.

"Uh, thank you."

Daric chuckled, his low rumble matching the one in Cenith's belly.

"Any chance of getting something to eat?" Cenith asked.

"Some broth to start. We'll see how you do with that." Daric stood and opened the door. He spoke quietly to someone out of sight.

"Aye, sir. Is m'lady awake too?"

Jolin.

"No, she isn't." Daric closed the door.

Cenith could almost feel Jolin's disappointment through the wood. A ruckus sounded outside the single window—cheers, whoops, and hollers. He exchanged glances with Daric, who strode to the window and looked out.

"What's all that about?" Cenith asked.

"The rest of the guard are out there. Aleyn is there…looks like most of the men from the station as well. Their wives, children." He looked at Cenith, a genuine smile adding more creases to his face. "I'd say they're pleased you're awake and on the road to recovery."

A warmth filled Cenith's chest. "I…I don't know what to say. I don't deserve this."

"Of course you do. You're not only their lord, you're a kind and decent man. They see, and hear, what's happening in Bredun and count their blessings." Daric waved acknowledgement to those below. The cheers broke out anew. "I see Buckam's out there as well."

"Buckam!"

Daric sat once more, resting his long legs, and bare feet, on the end of the bed. He folded his arms. "There are some things we need to discuss, if you're up to it."

Before Cenith could answer, a knock sounded at the door.

Daric answered it, stepping back to admit a beaming Jolin bearing a cloth covered tray.

"I'd be out there too, m'lord, but I was gittin' yer dinner."

"Thank them for me, would you, Jolin? Tell them they've warmed my heart."

"I'll do that, m'lord." Jolin looked at Tyrsa before heading for Cenith's side of the bed.

Daric moved the water jug and cup, making room for the tray on the bedside table. Jolin removed the cloth, revealing a deep bowl of steaming broth, beef by the smell of it. He set a teapot, two pottery mugs, two small wooden spoons, and a little pot of honey on the table before transferring the tray to Cenith's lap.

"When do ye think m'lady will wake, sir?" Jolin asked.

Daric shrugged. "This is well past my area of expertise. Come to think of it, it's past anyone's. She wakes up, when she wakes up. Her breathing is steady, as is her heartbeat. We'll just have to wait."

Jolin poured tea from the pot, adding a dollop of honey and placed it on the tray. "Enjoy yer meal, m'lord."

"Thank you." Cenith wished it was a large steak, swimming in gravy, and a mug of dark ale.

Daric dismissed the guard. He poured himself a cup of tea and sat down.

Cenith picked up the bowl, blew the steam away, then sipped some broth. "You said we had some things to discuss?"

"Finish that first."

The broth tasted rich and delicious. It went down quickly. Cenith picked up the mug of aromatic tea, allowing Daric to take the tray and set it back on the table. "I'm assuming you still wish to keep Tyrsa's healing quiet. What did you tell everyone about my miraculous recovery?"

"First, that all the noise was Tyrsa upset at your condition. The rest, that it was their prayers and the will of the gods." Daric shrugged. "Fortunately your people are a superstitious lot. They seem to have accepted it."

Good enough. "What's first on your list?" Cenith raised the mug to his lips.

"Buckam. He's offered his allegiance to you."

Cenith lowered the mug. "Why would he do that? He seemed so loyal to Saulth."

"I think he may have seen the error of his lord's ways. That, or he's trying something sneaky." Daric set his empty mug on the table and leaned forward, resting his elbows on his knees.

"I'm leery about trusting him." Cenith ventured a sip of the tea. It tasted just as good as it smelled.

"As am I. His back is healing, though far slower than you two. He's been quiet and helpful, finding odd jobs to do around the station."

"What do you mean, you two?"

Daric looked at the floor a moment before answering. "You knew Varth's wound was healing faster than it should, after Tyrsa had touched it."

Cenith nodded, taking another drink of tea.

"So is yours. It looks about a week old. I never got around to stitching your shoulder wound. It's not a pretty scar."

Cenith moved his left arm enough to see it. Thick and jagged, it resembled a pink lightning bolt. It didn't hurt, not even when he poked it. He added up the days in his head, nine since Jolin received the cut on his face, three since the attack. Daric hadn't removed the soldier's stitches yet. Cenith scratched the scar on his shoulder, resisting the temptation to shake his head. *This is just too weird.* His gaze moved to his sleeping wife. "She transfers her quick healing to the one she touches?"

"It looks that way. I don't know if she can heal a wound as bad as yours completely, or if she just takes the person out of danger and lets them heal on their own, albeit at a faster rate. Who knows how far she would've gone if she hadn't passed out?"

"If I'm healing so fast, why didn't I wake up sooner?"

Daric shrugged. "Possibly because it took almost as much out of you as it did her. Perhaps because you were so close to death. I can only guess. I find the whole thing difficult to believe, yet I can't doubt what I've seen with my own eyes."

Cenith had wished it could be true, though he could never have asked her to heal him, especially knowing the pain it caused her. Nonetheless, he was grateful. *Grateful.* That word just didn't say how he felt. No words could. Time to move on to a more comfortable subject.

"So, what do we do with Buckam? Have him ride with us?" Cenith drained his mug and held it out for more.

Daric poured the last of the tea into it, along with some honey, and Cenith took another drink.

"That's my thought. Let him prove himself under a watchful eye. He suggested the kitchen. Start him there." Daric sat back. "Next item."

He explained Jolin's idea of a special regiment assigned to protect Tyrsa. Saulth wanted her back. Cenith would do whatever he could to prevent that, and not just to spite the man, though that was his original intention. Jolin said it, Tyrsa was special. Who knew what else she could do? Char would freeze over and Frost burn to a crisp before Cenith would let Saulth have her back.

Then there was Tyrsa herself. She'd lived an unimaginable life. How lonely she must have been, wandering Saulth's halls at night, afraid she might do something wrong and he'd beat her again. Even if he did end up setting her aside, he couldn't let her fall into Saulth's hands. She deserved so much more. Cenith could understand the men's desire to protect her. She brought out that side of him in full force. "A guard, all her own. It's a difficult idea to argue with."

"It is." Daric leaned back, tilting the chair.

"There's only one problem I can see," Cenith said.

The Calleni lifted his eyebrow.

"What are we going to call them?"

Daric chuckled. "A problem that can be solved another day. You need rest." He stood and closed the heavy drapes, darkening the room.

"One of the guards will be outside your door at all times. Just call if you need anything."

Daric left and Cenith slid down under the covers. He rolled toward Tyrsa. The wound pulled, forcing him to shift until the pain went away. She hadn't moved. How can I ever thank you? He reached over and cupped her cheek.

"Please wake up soon," he whispered. "Please."

* * * *

Bright moonlight lent an ethereal cast to Tyrsa's features. Cenith lay on his side, watching her, unable to sleep. Two more days had passed. He grew restless and worried she'd never wake up. The women came to wash her and change her nightgown. Daric dribbled water and broth into her, but she looked thinner every day. Cenith feared she'd simply waste away.

Daric had let him up for short periods, though Cenith didn't go far from Tyrsa's side. His food now consisted of tasty stews and hearty soups, served with warm bread. He'd tried holding a bowl up to Tyrsa's nose, hoping the aroma would wake her. He gently shook her, stroked her hair, her cheek. Nothing worked. Her skin felt cooler. Was that a good sign? Or not?

"Please wake up, Tyrsa. I want to show you my home. I want you to meet Kian, my best friend and Daric's son. You'll like him, he's a good man."

Cenith sat up and gathered her into his arms. The shallow spot at the base of her throat pulsed with a strong heartbeat, his only hope that she might still recover. He kissed her cool forehead, then her cheek. His lips slid to hers. He pretended she kissed him in return.

Tyrsa gasped, and her eyes flew open. Cenith's head jerked back. "You're awake!" He crushed her to him, though she tried to push him away. "It's all right. Everything will be all right now." He kissed the top of her head. "No hurt."

She gave up her struggle, as if just realizing who he was, and hugged him. He returned it.

"Cenith?"

He let her go enough to look at her face. "I'm here, Tyrsa."

"No hurt?" Her voice was a whisper in the darkness. She must be parched.

"No hurt. Thanks to you." Holding her in one arm, Cenith reached behind him for a cup of water and held it for her while she drank.

When she finished, he poured her another, then lit the candle on the bedside table. "I was worried, so afraid you'd die," he said, taking the cup from her and gathering her to him again.

Tyrsa touched her lips, then his, a quizzical expression on her face.

"Kiss. That was a kiss. And so is this." He kissed her forehead.

"Kiss?"

"Yes, and this…" Cenith kissed her cheek, "…and this." He moved to her lips again, a quick kiss, to get her used to the idea.

"Oh!" Tyrsa touched her lips when he pulled back.

Cenith quit smiling long enough to kiss her again. Tyrsa took his head in her hands and pulled him down, lightly brushing his forehead with her soft lips. "Kiss." A quick sweep along his cheek. "Kiss." A feather touch to his lips.

She let him go. "Kiss?" Her quizzical expression returned.

"It's what men and women do to show they care for one another. But you're supposed to move your lips." Cenith kissed her again. "You'll learn, and it's going to be fun teaching you."

Tyrsa looked past him, to the dark window. "Oh!"

She slid off him, onto the floor, and kept going, landing in a heap.

"You're not strong enough yet," Cenith said. He threw back the covers and stood. "I probably shouldn't do this."

He bent down and picked her up. A twinge in his back told him he was right. He ignored it and took her to the window.

Tyrsa patted the glass. "Word?"

"Window."

She gave a little gasp of wonder. "Ohh. Window." Tyrsa touched the glass, the frame, repeating the word twice more. Her expression changed when her stomach rumbled. "Food?"

Cenith laughed.

A knock came at the door. "My Lord? Is everything a' right?"

Cenith turned his back to the window. "Everything is wonderful!"

The door opened to reveal Jayce's dark head. Cenith silently thanked Maegden that Tyrsa's nightgown hung down enough to cover him. "Tell Councillor Daric my lady is awake and hungry."

Jayce's broad face broke into a wide grin. "Yes, m'lord!" He disappeared behind the closing door.

While they waited for Daric, Cenith told Tyrsa more words… the drapes, the table, the fireplace. She had to know the name for everything, her pixie face beaming, until his back complained to the point where he couldn't ignore it. He sat in the chair by the fireplace, the coals glowing a comforting red, Tyrsa on his lap. He kissed her. She smiled and kissed him back.

Daric didn't bother knocking before entering. He strode to the chair and crouched down, wearing only his leather pants. The bruises on his back and arms had faded to purple and yellow, highlighting the white of the old lash scars, along with the plentiful collection of others he'd gained over the years. Jayce followed, carrying a tray, which he set on the bedside table.

"Jayce, light some candles," Daric said. He reached out, almost touching Tyrsa's face. "No hurt. I won't hurt you."

Tyrsa smiled. "Daric no hurt Tyrsa."

Daric's surprise mirrored Cenith's.

"That's four words you put together," Cenith said, not to mention she no longer seemed leery of Daric.

Tyrsa leaned over and kissed Daric on the lips. Jayce's laugh joined Cenith's at the look on the Calleni's face.

"Just how long has she been awake?" Daric asked, the corner of his mouth twitching.

"Long enough for Lord Cenith t' teach her how t' kiss, sir," Jayce said, his grin growing wider.

"That's how I woke her," Cenith said. "I hadn't expected it to work, I just…" His cheeks burned as Daric's grin matched the guard's. "Well, she is my wife!"

Daric's laugh drowned out Jayce's. "Now you just have to teach her who she can kiss and who she can't."

Jayce finished lighting the candles and Daric checked Tyrsa over before allowing her to have some broth, the same as Cenith had when he first awoke.

While she sipped it, Daric turned to Cenith. "You didn't pick her up, did you?"

"She fell when she climbed out of bed. I couldn't leave her there on the floor."

Daric scowled. Tyrsa finished the broth and held the bowl out for more. While Jayce ran the errand, Daric lifted her off Cenith's lap and set her in the other chair, then checked Cenith's wound.

"It looks all right, but don't pick her up again for a while." Daric stood and rummaged in the wardrobe. "You might want to get into some pants," he said, handing Cenith a pair.

Cenith rose from the chair. Daric tried to stifle a laugh and failed. One look at Tyrsa explained why. She sat staring at his manhood, the same way she had when they'd bathed. Cenith blushed and made short work of pulling on the pants.

More broth arrived, and, while Tyrsa downed that, Cenith tried to explain that she could kiss Daric on the cheek, but not on the lips. He wasn't sure she understood.

"Oh! Baybee!" Tyrsa stood on wobbly legs, looking around the room.

Daric picked her up and set her back in the chair. "Not yet. You're still too weak."

Jayce retrieved the doll from her pillow. They all watched her reaction to the miracle the women had performed. Tyrsa stared, transfixed.

Baybee looked like a new doll. She wore a dress made of a dark blue material with tiny white flowers stitched with care, a white apron over top. All her hair had been replaced with fine, bright yellow yarn, arranged to hang down like Tyrsa's own. Her pale blue button eyes matched each other. How they managed to fix her body, Cenith couldn't even guess. The material looked brand new, yet, this was Baybee, right down to the yarn smile.

Tyrsa sat, just staring, for so long Cenith and Daric exchanged worried glances.

"Baybee." She whispered the word and hugged the doll gently to her chest. Then she smiled. A bigger one Cenith didn't think he'd ever seen. The look in her large, blue eyes was all the thank you they needed.

The news of Tyrsa's recovery travelled fast. Jolin poked his head in, then Varth and Ead, followed by Dathan and Fallan, until Daric growled at them to wait until morning. He waved Jayce out as well before ordering Cenith and Tyrsa to get more sleep, then closed the door behind him. Cenith couldn't even think of sleep, he'd done little else for the better part of five days.

He took Tyrsa back onto his lap and taught her more about kissing. She learned quickly, and he realized he could never set her aside. For good or ill, no matter what she really was, Cenith wanted her for his wife. Teaching her to kiss was enjoyable, showing her the rest of what being a wife meant would be more so, but that would have to wait until they reached home.

* * * *

Sixth Month had arrived before Daric judged Cenith fit for travel. Other than weight loss, which the women strived to correct, Tyrsa showed no ill effects from the healing experience. She spent the days growing acquainted with the people at the station; a slow process, until she discovered the children. They fascinated her, and, once she became used to their boisterous ways, she liked spending time with them, provided they didn't try to touch Baybee.

Her cheeks bloomed with more exposure to the sun, making her look less like she belonged in a burial cave. Though Daric restricted her time outside, still concerned about too much sun at once, Tyrsa discovered plenty to fascinate her, particularly the flowers.

Buttercups, daisies, violets, and many others blossomed in colourful profusion. She spent much of her time outside picking, smelling, and mauling flowers. The softest and most fragrant became her favourites. When Jolin showed her how to put them in her hair, she tied and twisted them all through her silken locks. Tyrsa insisted Baybee wear them as well, though Cenith put his foot down when she tried to adorn him.

The guards had started calling themselves the Lady's Companions. Whenever Tyrsa spent time outside, the guards were there, lounging nearby, ostensibly resting from their journey, but ever watchful. The guards had buried Warin with full honours in the little graveyard near the station. Cenith wasn't conscious at the time, but paid his respects when Daric allowed him.

They left the station in bright sunshine, ten days before summer solstice. Tyrsa wore a dark green cloak and a blue dress, both altered from clothing the women at the station no longer wore. Three other dresses were packed with Cenith's clothes; the four bottles of wine he'd carried distributed elsewhere to make room. Of the twenty four they'd started with, twenty had survived, the others lost in the attack. Remarkable, given the circumstances.

Tyrsa spent all her riding time in front of Cenith, pointing at each new wonder, wanting to know the words. To her great delight, she discovered new flowers; trilliums, snow lilies, and most particularly, a tiny purple and white flower Jolin called a fairy orchid. Mountain lore claimed the fairies used them for pillows. Bright, soft, and delightfully fragrant, this new flower outshone all the others. Every time she saw one, she had to have it, to the point where the guard stopped calling her Lady Tyrsa. She was now Lady Orchid.

Two days travel found them close to where Cenith's father had died; two long, strained days, with everyone keeping their eyes and ears open for trouble. Most times the only voice breaking the silence was Tyrsa's. She'd picked up a remarkable number of words while playing with the children, though she still had trouble grasping some intangible concepts, like sharing. What was hers was hers and that was that, especially when it came to Baybee.

"Cenith, look! Robin!"

It sat on a branch on the top of a skinny pine tree growing out of an outcrop below them. Cenith had to look down to see the bird.

"That's *a* robin, yes. *A* robin," Cenith stressed. Another concept that troubled Tyrsa.

He held his hands in front of her, letting her hold the mountain pony's reins, and showed her one finger. "A finger." He raised another. "Two fingers."

Tyrsa shook her head. "One finger. Two fingers."

"It means the same thing. "A" is one."

Tyrsa shook her head. "One finger. Two fingers."

Cenith sighed. "Stubborn wench."

Jayce appeared around a bend in the path in front of him, on foot since the trail was now too narrow to allow a horse to turn around. He spoke to Daric, three horses ahead of Cenith, then trotted back.

Cenith glanced up at the southern face of the mountain looming over them; Shadow Mountain, the same one that had witnessed his father's death. Snow still clung to shallow gullies in its steep side while wispy clouds hid its white crown like a shroud. Daric dismounted, hugging the rock face until Jolin and Dathan passed by.

"The place where your father died is just around the curve," Daric said. "Jayce says he thinks he can make out what looks like a horse's leg sticking up from the pile of snow below."

Cenith nodded, not eager to have a look for himself. Nothing had been found when they'd passed this way less than two months ago, but when spring arrived in the mountains, it came with a vengeance. The warm sun worked at a quick pace.

"When we get to Tiras, I'll send a party back to dig him and the others out and we can finally put him to rest." Daric's shadowed face reflected Cenith's ongoing grief. They both needed to see Ifan laid beside his wife in the burial cave.

Daric told Jolin and Dathan to switch ponies with him so he could ride in front of Cenith. Once the rearranging was completed, Daric mounted Dathan's pony and he carried on round the bend. Cenith tried to keep his eyes on Daric's back, but they treacherously slid downwards to the hill of snow below.

The sheer precipice dropped straight before sloping away to a deep gorge. Chunks of snow, some the size of large boulders, half buried the broken pine trees littering the slope. Blessedly, Cenith could see nothing resembling a horse's leg. Jayce must have leaned over the edge to see it.

Tyrsa wriggled out of Cenith's arms and reached out to touch the rock face. "Oh!" She snatched her hand back.

"What is it?" Cenith stopped the pony, glad of something to take his mind off what lay below them.

"This." She touched the rock again, but only with the tips of her fingers. "I feel…I don't know word. It's bad, but not bad."

"How can it be bad and not bad?"

Tyrsa shrugged. "I don't know. Something is there. It is…sad?"

Teaching Tyrsa emotions had been another interesting experience. The guards had joined in, making complete fools of themselves while demonstrating happy, sad, angry, and so on. It had resulted in an afternoon of laughter and good companionship…an afternoon Cenith wouldn't soon forget.

"Rock sad? That doesn't make sense."

"Not rock. Something…in rock. It is angry too." Tyrsa sat back, shivering.

"I wish I knew if you were saying the right words."

"Words right. Something is there."

"The words *are* right. Even so, there's nothing we can do. It's rock, and there's no caves near here." Cenith urged the pony onward. Then he had to explain 'cave'.

Daric twisted in the saddle, looking back at them, one eyebrow raised. When they caught up, Cenith said, "I'll explain later. It's…difficult."

The councillor nodded and they moved forward. Not long after, they passed the unmanned keep that watched over the upper end of the pass. In a few days, twenty guards would call it home. Saulth may have already made his move, but Cenith couldn't take the chance. Nightfall found them in a large cabin perched in the middle of a peaceful alpine meadow. They arrived without incident and Jayce, with some help from Madin, had stew cooking over a hot fire in no time.

Cenith's bed, wide enough for two, sat in the loft at the top of a narrow staircase. Everyone else would have to share the floor, but at least they could all sleep inside.

While the stew cooked, Fallan and Keev chopped wood to replace what they would use. Others tended the horses and equipment. Daric and Cenith sat in front of the fire in the only chairs available, Tyrsa on Cenith's lap. Neither could make sense of what she'd felt in the rock.

"I wonder if it's lingering emotion from when your father and the others died. Who knows what she's capable of detecting?" Daric said, stretching his bare feet out to the fire.

The women at the station had made him and Tyrsa felt shoes. Though warm, they weren't waterproof. Both pairs sat by the fire; Daric's drying out from walking in snow and mud, Tyrsa's because she didn't like wearing them indoors. She wore them outside because then she couldn't feel the ground hurt. Another mystery.

"That doesn't explain what she feels in the ground," Cenith said.

"True. Did the rock feel the same as the ground does?" Daric asked Tyrsa.

She shook her head. "It is…not same as ground."

"Different, the word is different, remember?" Cenith gave her a little squeeze.

Tyrsa smiled. "Different. Many words, hard to…remember?"

Cenith chuckled. "Yes, remember."

"Maybe it's lingering emotion then," Daric said. "There are many stories of places haunted by those who have died violently."

Daric's words sent a chill through Cenith, dampening his mood. He sincerely hoped Shival had allowed Ifan to go to Maegden's Hall rather than force him to hang around a frozen precipice. Perhaps giving his father a proper burial would set things right.

The next two days passed much as the first two had. No ambush, nor did they see a single other person until they came down from the High Road the night before they reached Tiras. Steep and treacherous, the road to Eagle's Nest Pass was a seldom used one, but it was faster than taking Black Crow.

They stayed in a small village, guests of the innkeeper. Tradition stated the lord and his retinue stayed for free, though it was common practice to leave coins under the pillows, ostensibly for the woman who cleaned the room. That woman usually turned out to be the innkeeper's wife.

Despite the tension, Cenith enjoyed the ride. Spring had arrived in a riot of colour as flowers, shrubs, and trees hurried to make use of the short growing season.

Tiras Keep came into view before the town did, part of it built right into the mountain, watching over the town in the broad river valley below. Blue and white banners snapped in the wind, waving a welcome. Neither Cenith nor Daric could figure out why there'd been no attack, though they'd refused to let that thought dampen their spirits.

As they rode alongside the swollen Avlone River, Jolin broke into a song. The others joined in.

Dunvalos Reach, my heart, my home,
Thy mountains touch the sky,
Thy crystal waters run
In sparkling streams and waterfalls,
That glisten in the sun.

Tyrsa looked back at Cenith. "Sing?"

"Yes, they're singing. They're glad to be home."

"Children sing. I like sing."

"Singing," Cenith laughed and joined in the next verse.

The snow had left the valley a few weeks earlier, allowing farmers to prepare the soil. They waved a greeting before resuming the task at hand. A deer ventured into an empty field, prompting an immediate reaction from Tyrsa. It bounded away a few moments later. She watched the spot where it had disappeared until they turned a bend in the road. As they drew closer to the town, they spotted children scouring meadows for the first four–leaf clover. The one who found it would have good luck for the rest of the year.

All seven verses of the song had been sung by the time they reached the gates. Unlike the gaily painted wood and limestone houses in Valda and Edara, the buildings in Tiras were made of grey and black stone, a plentiful material. People added their own little touches, some with planters or bright awnings, others with different coloured rocks decorating the outside walls and steps. The bright dresses and outfits of the men and women more than made up for the drab buildings. Old horseshoes or dried out sprigs of mistletoe, entwined with ropes of garlic, hung above almost every door, a ward against evil. Cenith hadn't seen anything like them in Edara or Valda and realized it must be just a mountain custom.

The guards greeted them with warm smiles and heartfelt salutes. The wide, cobbled streets were clean, with no starving families sitting on the sides. Some of the girls from Silk's Tavern and Brothel hung out upper windows, laughing and waving. The Companions whistled, hooted, and blew them kisses. The local Story Teller sat on the edge of the fountain in the center of town, surrounded by children eager to hear yet another tale of the Old Ones. It was good to be home.

People cheered them a welcome, many pointing to Tyrsa. Cenith could imagine the thoughts running through their minds, especially since he'd chosen not to mention her in the messages he'd sent from the station about his delay. She huddled against him, hiding her face. Too many strange people.

"It's all right, Tyrsa, no one's going to hurt you. This is your new home."

"Home?"

"It's where we're going to live, you and I." He pointed to the keep, at the top of the winding road. "Up there."

She peered out from under the blanket.

Home. Finally! Now Cenith could keep Tyrsa safe, teach her what she needed to know to be a lord's wife, and perhaps find out what connection she had to the scrap of parchment laying in the treasure room.

Chapter Eighteen

The first thing Cenith did upon entering the keep's Great Hall was stand back, sheltering Tyrsa from the advancing hoard. The first thing Daric did was kiss his wife, while the products of their love swarmed around them. Five sons and four daughters, including two sets of twins, clamoured for his attention.

Kian, four months older than Cenith, had learned long ago to wait until the rush died down before greeting his father. He joined Cenith by the main doors, raising an eyebrow when he spotted Tyrsa. A younger version of Daric, he bore every inch of his father's height and the promise of his girth when he finished filling out. Kian bowed low to him, then to Tyrsa, who hid behind Cenith, huddled in her cloak.

"Welcome home, My Lord." Kian's dark eyes danced with amusement.

"Stop that nonsense, or I'll be forced to jump on your back and strangle you," Cenith said, embracing his friend.

Kian laughed. "Are you going to introduce me to your companion? Or shall I just nudge you out of the way and show her around myself?"

"I'm not that much smaller than you, you over-grown mountain goat, and I'll have you know this is my wife you're trying to abscond with."

Both Kian's eyebrows shot up. Cenith picked up the grin Kian dropped when his jaw hit the floor, pleased he'd decided not to send word on ahead about Tyrsa.

"How in Shival's hells did that happen?" Kian asked.

"Rather suddenly."

"Isn't she a little young?"

Cenith shrugged. "She's almost sixteen. Wasn't your mother the same age when she married your father?"

"Uh, yeah."

Cenith turned to Tyrsa, who had backed up against the wall, and took her hand. "It's all right, Kian won't hurt you. He's Daric's son."

Cenith had spent another interesting evening explaining sons and daughters, mothers and fathers, and husbands and wives to Tyrsa—in between kisses. He'd also made it plain that Saulth was her father and he shouldn't have treated her the way he had. She'd taken the news quietly, with no comment, making it difficult for him to be sure she understood.

"Why would she think I'd hurt her?" Kian's wounded look reflected no hint of humour.

"A long story, and not her fault. Tyrsa, I'd like you to meet Kian. He's my friend."

"It's nice to meet you, My Lady." Kian gave her another bow, and a gentle smile to accompany it.

"Now you say 'It is nice to meet you, Kian'," Cenith said to Tyrsa, pulling her up beside him.

Her cloak fell open, revealing Baybee hugged tight to her chest, prompting another quizzical look from Kian.

"Later. Say it back to him, Tyrsa."

"It is nice to meet you, Kian," she said, though she didn't sound like she meant it, her eyes darting from Kian to the hoard.

Kian's smile warred with a frown of curiosity. "Welcome to Tiras Keep. I hope you like it here. We do."

"Anything exciting happen while we were gone?" Cenith asked, wishing to change the subject.

"The mines are all open for the season, except one. A little hitch with some rotted timbers. It's being fixed as we speak. Goats and sheep having been giving birth all over the place, with more on the way. The milk cows have already dropped their calves." Kian scratched his chin. "There were three more avalanches, but the only victim was an old cabin no one uses. Black Crow Pass is open and the first caravans arrived two days ago. For around here, I suppose that's exciting."

Higher than Eagle's Nest, the snow left Black Crow Pass later and arrived sooner, but the wide roads allowed carts and wagons access to the mountain towns and villages. It also lay farther north, near the border with Amita, and would have added several days to their journey.

Cenith glanced at Daric. He had the five year old twins in each arm while Mina and Nani, his two youngest daughters, hugged his hips. Elessa held baby Rade, less than a year old. By Elessa's quick peeks at Tyrsa, Cenith assumed Daric was telling her at least part of the story. The hoard paid rapt attention to what he said. Cenith and Daric had agreed ahead of time that everyone should keep their distance until Tyrsa adjusted to her new home.

"Avina and Jennica aren't going to be happy. They both had an eye on you," Kian said, barely restraining his grin.

Cenith sighed. "I've told them a dozen times they're like sisters to me. I care for them both, but not that way." Daric's oldest daughters, the two next down the line from Kian, appeared less than pleased. Avina, the older, frowned her indignation. Jennica blinked back tears.

"I think they both hoped you'd change your mind."

Cenith couldn't worry about that now; it wasn't as if he'd had a choice. "You haven't seen any strangers around, have you? Anyone acting suspicious?"

"Only old Gavril. He's been sober for almost two weeks. That's strange." Kian grinned again. Gavril did odd jobs around the stables, just enough to buy him more ale.

"I'm serious. Tyrsa may be in danger."

Kian lost his grin. "No, I haven't seen, or heard anyone mention, a stranger in the keep. Perhaps Ors should increase the watch."

"Your father already thought of that. In the meantime, we're both in dire need of a bath and a hot meal." Cenith rubbed the sparse stubble on his chin. "Not to mention a shave."

Kian's grin came back. "That won't take long."

Cenith would have hit him, but didn't want Tyrsa to take it the wrong way. He settled for a glower that set Kian to laughing again.

"Baths are already being prepared and dinner will be served as soon as you two are ready. Where's your lady's baggage?" Kian asked.

"She doesn't have much, and that's in my saddlebag." At Kian's questioning look, Cenith said, "Later. Trust me, this will take a while. When Tyrsa's asleep, I'll send for you. Once she's out, an avalanche could fall beside her and she wouldn't wake up. We can talk then."

Cenith scanned the smiling faces waiting to greet him, all nobles who lived in the castle; Zev, the Master of the Treasury, Hollis, Master of the Horse, Ors, the new Guard-Commander now that Daric was Councillor, and the others who helped run castle, city, and principality. All faces he'd known for years, and every one of them would have a report for him.

The hall looked the same too. The dual fireplaces on opposite walls stood ready to light should the weather require it. The tapestries, paintings, and statues sat in their appropriate places. Not a thing looked out of order.

He sighed to himself. *Let's hope it stays that way.*

* * * *

Cenith sat in the study, looking over the orders arranging for the overseer of the Amita mine. The council meeting in Edara seemed an eternity ago. Daric perched in a chair across from him, sorting parchments.

The whole process had quickly become a boring ritual. He signed the document, melted a blob of red wax at the bottom, and pressed his signet ring to it. Cenith leaned back and rubbed his eyes.

Tyrsa had taken far longer to fall asleep than he'd wished, making his time with Kian, and sleep, that much later. He'd had to ease his wife's fears about her new home and the people who inhabited it. Cenith reassured her several times that she could go wherever she wished and no one would punish her for setting foot in the wrong place.

Daric's wife had helped Tyrsa with her bath and putting her few belongings away, getting the girl used to being around her. Daric had filled Elessa in on all the details when they were alone. Cenith hoped Elessa could assist in Tyrsa's education, particularly in matters he didn't feel comfortable with. Dinner had been eaten in Cenith's rooms due to Tyrsa's lack of table manners, one of the problems where he needed Elessa's assistance.

Once in bed, Cenith had fallen asleep quickly, but it seemed only moments before Laron, his valet, had woken them to start the day. After breakfast, Elessa took Tyrsa to be measured for clothes and shoes suitable for the Lady of Dunvalos Reach, as well as supplying her with other things she'd need. The keep children had been instructed not to approach her, letting Tyrsa make the first move.

Cenith spent the morning signing documents Kian left for him, reading reports, and catching up on recent events. Ors was ostensibly in charge while Cenith and Daric were away, but he didn't feel comfortable handling the administrative duties. Cenith had left that responsibility to

Kian. Some might think Daric's son too young for the job. Fact was, Kian had a better head for those things than Cenith himself, and with Ors as Daric's replacement for Guard-Commander, Cenith had no qualms about leaving Tiras in their hands. Everything sat in neat piles according to priority. So far, Cenith could find nothing amiss.

Despite the work waiting for him, it felt good to be home again. The comfortable old furniture in the study brought back memories of his father, sitting in this very chair, signing papers, meeting with dignitaries, the local dukes, and officials from Ardael and lands west and south of the mountains. Cenith always knew he'd occupy this chair one day, just not so soon.

Some distant ancestor had panelled over the stone walls with oak; expensive, but it added a warmth and intimacy to the room Cenith had always loved. Long before Cenith's birth, Ifan had commissioned a painting of his wife. It decorated the wall behind him, joined by a recent painting of his father. Two colourful tapestries, both depicting hunting scenes, hung on the walls to the left, while a stone fireplace, flanked by bookshelves, warmed the room on the right. The space between the tapestries had, until recently, been the home of the scrap of parchment. The empty spot stood out like a black bear in a snow drift.

The first item Cenith had taken care of that morning was the hardest—a letter to Warin's parents. At least one of the Companions would have visited to relay the bad news in person, but he wanted them to know how he felt about the young man and that Warin would be missed by more than his family.

Daric passed him another parchment, the orders moving his contingent of men to the Chance River in Kalkor.

Cenith sighed. "One thousand men. I wish the lords would take into account the population of a principality before randomly choosing a number. If you want to fully man the garrison at Black Crow Pass, as well as put more men in Eagle's Nest, not to mention doubling the guard here, the only place we can take them from is the border with the West Downs. It'll cut our strength there by a third." Most of the clans were trading partners, but any sign of weakness would be an invitation for them to band together and invade.

"There's a way to make it look like nothing has changed," Daric said. "Take them from all across the border, with instructions to those remaining to keep the same number of campfires lit every night. No one will be the wiser. In the meantime, we can send men out to garner more recruits."

"Have I ever told you, you're worth your weight in gold and more?" *A lot more.*

A crooked smile creased the Calleni's face. "From time to time."

"Well, it isn't enough."

Arrangements were made to put twenty men in the old station at the head of Eagle's Nest Pass. The garrison would need repair, but supplies and men for labour could be sent after the soldiers arrived. They could camp out if they had to. An additional thirty soldiers would be sent to the garrison in Black Crow Pass, another thirty to augment the station at the foot of Eagle's Nest Pass. The barracks would be crowded, and more supplies would have to be sent, but Cenith, Daric, and Ors felt the extra security a precaution they couldn't ignore. All three units would leave the next day.

Daric slipped another document in front of him. This one confirmed the Lady's Companions as an official regiment, with Jolin as captain. The young man knew nothing of his promotion and Cenith couldn't wait to see the look on his face when he made the announcement. From regular soldier to captain would raise more than a few eyebrows, but Jolin deserved it. Trey would be first lieutenant and Jayce second, for they were the two Tyrsa seemed most comfortable with after Jolin. Both were competent and responsible, and Cenith had no qualms about either of them.

Despite the nice thought about Warin watching over Tyrsa, a twelfth Companion would have to be selected. An odd number would be considered unlucky. *I wonder if Kian would be interested?* Probably not. Daric had other plans for him, following in his shoes as councillor if Cenith read it right. A banquet was planned three days hence to celebrate Cenith and Tyrsa's marriage. It would be the perfect time to announce the regiment and promotions.

"I've taken the liberty of talking to Ors about moving all the Companions to the barracks on the first floor," Daric said. "It would be easier for them to protect Tyrsa if they weren't scattered all over the keep and courtyard barracks. He agreed and has ordered the move to take place this afternoon."

Cenith nodded and Daric placed the parchment with the orders in front of him. Another signature, another blob of wax.

"Is that the last one?" Cenith asked.

Daric rifled through a pile of parchments. "Looks like it. I'll send Kian to get the piece of scroll and tell Elessa we need Tyrsa." Daric opened the door and spoke to one of the guards before taking his seat again.

"How's Buckam making out in the kitchen?" Cenith asked.

Daric chuckled. "I let him have the morning off, but he should be scrubbing pots and pans by now. I've left instructions with Jarven to work him hard, but fair, and to watch for signs his wounds aren't bothering him, not to mention treachery."

Cenith tipped the chair back and rested his feet on the corner of the desk. He steepled his fingers and tapped them against his lips. "I'm torn on this one. Some strange instinct says 'trust him', but my common sense says if a man will turn once, he'll turn again." Instinct spoke louder than common sense. He shook his head to quiet it. "We'll just have to wait and see, I suppose."

Kian arrived before Tyrsa did. Cenith set the fragment, still in its glass and wood frame, on his desk. Yellowed with age, the sides were dark and frayed, yet the faded ink showed clearly. The narrow parchment held only a few lines of script, and the top and bottom edges had been roughly torn. The top had a tiny spur near the right edge with part of a word on it.

The fragment had hung on the study wall of the four-hundred-year-old keep for as long as anyone could remember. According to the tale, Cenith's ancestor, the builder of the keep, found it during construction. Whatever its origin, whatever it said, Saulth wanted it.

The door opened and Tyrsa came in with Elessa. When she saw Cenith, her face lit up. She ran to him, hugging him tight. He bent down to give her a kiss on the cheek.

"I hold Rade," she said, giving him a big smile, making the whole room seem brighter.

Tyrsa clutched Baybee tight against her. Perhaps if Elessa let her hold Rade more, she'd give up the doll. Cenith could only hope; the looks the staff and the nobles who resided in the castle gave them were embarrassing. Better yet if he could give her a baby of her own.

"I have something I want you to see," Cenith said. Taking her hand, he led her to the table. Elessa, Daric, and Kian joined them.

"Oh! This…" Tyrsa touched the glass. "I see this, in...the...Book Room. It is…different, and the same." Elessa must have been instructing her on words. Tyrsa had trouble with 'the'.

"Do you know what the words say?" Daric asked.

Tyrsa shook her head. "Many words are different. Some same...the same." She traced the words with her finger. "This one has no picture."

Cenith took out a clean piece of parchment and a stick of soft lead. He'd woken up one morning at the station to discover Tyrsa on her knees by the fireplace, drawing pictures in the ash she'd spread out over the hearth, her hands and nightgown covered in it. He showed her how to use paper and lead instead.

"Can you draw the picture?" Cenith put the parchment and lead in front of the empty chair and asked her to sit. He took Baybee from her and set the doll on the upper corner of the desk, out of the way.

Daric moved his chair around to the side of the desk, then dragged over the two stuffed chairs from near the fireplace. He placed them opposite Tyrsa, giving Cenith one, Elessa the other. Kian pulled over a plain wooden one from the corner near the door and sat across from his father.

In the top left corner of the parchment, Tyrsa drew a circle. The left side she turned into a crescent moon. The right became a stylized sun with wavy rays. When she finished, Daric touched a meaty finger to the edge of the drawing.

"The words might be an ancient form of Calleni. This is an old symbol for Niafanna and Cillain; the goddess of the moon and the sun god."

"There's more." Cursive script, like that on the fragment, flowed onto the parchment. Tyrsa wrote nine lines, slow and careful, before stopping. "This is one. There are four."

Cenith glanced at Daric. The councillor's eyes were riveted on what Tyrsa had written.

"Buckam's scroll?" Cenith asked.

Daric lifted his head long enough to answer. "That's my guess."

Tyrsa took her time tearing off what she'd written, placed it above Cenith's fragment, leaving a gap, and continued. Amazing, for a girl who couldn't read and, until recently, knew only a handful of words.

Her face held a tiny smile and a look of total rapture while she wrote unknown words from a past long forgotten. When she finished, Cenith leaned over to see what she'd done.

The last line had part of a word missing, near the right edge, and she'd smeared a couple of letters of the part that was there. Tyrsa carefully tore the parchment as she'd done with the first, though she took great care to create a space for the missing part of the word. When done, she placed it on top of Cenith's fragment, and underneath the first one she'd written. The glass and thin wooden frame prevented the two pieces coming together, but they looked like a perfect fit.

"Incredible." Cenith couldn't believe she'd remembered everything, down to how it had been torn. "How often did you look at the scroll? How many times?"

"Many, many times, since long and long ago." Tyrsa's perception of time had suffered with her confinement; something else Cenith would have to work on.

"It…talks to me. No, that's not right." Tyrsa's brow dipped in a frown. "I feel it, like it is mine." She sighed. "That's not right too."

"Either," Cenith corrected. "There are two pieces left?" She nodded. Daric had sent for the midday meal. A knock on the door heralded its arrival. "Have something to eat, then you can do the other two."

"No. I will do this." She held up the remaining scrap of blank parchment. "It is too small."

Cenith took out another sheet from the top right drawer of the desk, and Tyrsa began again. They ate while she wrote. The fourth section was short, but the last portion was much longer, with some parts resembling the structure of a song or poetry. She tore each piece and set them in place, a satisfied look on her face. By the time Tyrsa finished, lunchtime was long past.

"It feels…like one. It is right." She smiled.

Daric moved the pieces so he could have a look. He pointed first to one word on the fifth section, then another. "This is definitely an ancient form of Calleni. These words I know. They've changed little over the years." His eyes fixed on Cenith's. "Cillain and Niafanna. I'm no scholar, but judging by the structure, the fifth section is prayers to them."

Cenith frowned. "Why would Saulth be interested in prayers to your gods? He's always been obvious in his hatred of you and your people."

"If it gave him access to power, I suspect the man would do anything," Daric replied. "He's already done things I wouldn't have guessed at a year ago."

"Can you recognize anything else?"

Kian placed a finger on a word in the first section and another in the fourth. "I know these ones…born and unborn."

Daric nodded. "I caught those as well."

"How can something be born and unborn?" Elessa asked.

Her husband shook his head. "They may not be related to the same thing." Daric scanned the document again. "The only other word I can even make an attempt at is this one." He pointed to a word that appeared in all the sections except theirs. "This says *Jada-Drau. Jaden* is 'choice'. It might be coincidence, but maybe not. It must be important, it's here several times."

Cenith stroked his chin with his thumb. "I wonder what kind of choice it means?"

Daric shrugged. "Who knows? It probably refers to something that occurred centuries ago."

"Then why would Saulth be so interested in it now?" Elessa asked.

"Maybe it tells the way to a hidden treasure." Kian's grin told Cenith his friend meant it only in jest, but anything was possible.

"Does that mean my ancestors worshipped your gods?" Cenith asked.

Daric shrugged.

Cenith rose and moved behind Daric to get a better look at the scroll. "You said this picture is an ancient depiction of Niafanna and Cillain." Daric nodded. "How ancient? Any idea?"

"Quite. It's found on the lintels of crypts so old, the words on the surrounding stone have been rendered unreadable. I'm only guessing… fifteen, possibly even twenty centuries, or more."

Cenith whistled, startling Tyrsa.

"How could a parchment from that time survive? Especially if it was torn into five pieces?" Kian asked.

Daric shrugged. "Any guess would be better than mine. By all rights, this piece should have rotted long ago, particularly if it had been found in the ground as the story claims. In the desert, it would last longer, but would still be in rougher shape than this one."

"Regardless of how or why the thing survived," Elessa said, "dinner is waiting, as are the children. Not to mention the fact that Tyrsa has had nothing since breakfast." She stood, Daric and Kian following suit. "You can mull over this after we eat."

"And I should get some sleep," Kian added. "I'm on duty tonight."

Daric shot him a glare. "You could have said something. You didn't have to stay here."

"And miss all the fun?" Kian's grin returned with every bit of his irrepressible humour. "Besides, I had everything arranged for Cenith last night so I could sleep in this morning. Avina helped me."

Daric just shook his head while Elessa tried to hide a smile.

"Have our part of the scroll put back under lock and key," Cenith said. "As a matter of fact, put it all there." Daric nodded his agreement. Cenith pulled Tyrsa to her feet and kissed her hand. "Thank you. I don't know what use it'll be, but you have answered one question for us."

Tyrsa gave him a quizzical look. Kian raised an eyebrow.

"We know for sure she's linked to the scroll," Cenith said. "Now all we need to do is find someone who can read it. He's out there, somewhere. Saulth had to have learned from someone. He knows what his portions say. Otherwise, why would he want ours so bad?"

* * * *

Artan ducked his head, concentrating on the broom he held, his nerves tauter than a bowstring. He kept his movements slow, purposeful, as if tired and bored. The two Dunvalos Reach guards standing at attention outside a thick oak door paid him no mind; nor did the one striding up the hall. He held something in his hand. Artan looked without appearing to, just as Snake had taught him. Parchments; and what looked like a wooden frame. The new guard, a remarkably large, dark haired man, nodded his head and one of the others pulled a set of keys from his belt. This man appeared too young to be Daric. *There's two that size? Must be his son. I'd hate to run into them together.*

The guard unlocked the door and, without a word, opened it for the newcomer. The big man had to duck to enter. A few moments later, he came out, nodded at the two guarding the door, and returned in the direction he'd come. Artan worked his way toward the back stairs leading to the first level, trying not to smile. Snake would be pleased. One of the objects the guard had carried looked suspiciously like the parchment they'd come for. The object of their search had disappeared from the place Saulth told them it sat, precipitating a covert hunt.

Artan had found the room three days ago and tagged it as the treasure room. What else would be guarded like that? *Except there were only two guards before today…not four.* One other problem he'd identified—the parchment's location lay on the same floor as, and close to, the officers' quarters. Complete silence would be mandatory.

Once Cenith returned home, Artan had come here after every guard change. His perseverance paid off. If what the guard had put in the room wasn't the parchment, it still had to be in there. Maybe this would finally earn him his assassin name.

Two years Artan had been with Snake's company. Two years of handling the dirty and boring jobs; cleaning, polishing, and boot-licking. Too young for action, just right for spying, he had one of those faces that could fit in anywhere, and Snake took advantage of it every time he could.

Artan resisted the urge to whistle while he worked. He'd stolen a rough wool tunic and trousers belonging to a stable worker. They were now so covered in food and other stains there could be no telling where they'd started out. He pretended to be a lowly drudge, and his manner had to match the disguise. Once out of sight of the treasure room, Artan kept up the pretence for the soldiers who now stood at the servant stairs. Until today, there were no guards there. A concern to discuss with Snake.

Dinnertime provided the ideal opportunity for Artan to lose himself in the hustle and bustle. If you looked busy, people rarely tried to give you something else to do. Artan strode purposefully through the large kitchen, dodging workers like he'd done it all his life. He slipped out a small door at the back of the crowded, hectic room. In Valda, he'd be in the rear courtyard. Here, the back portion of the first floor of the castle had been extended into the mountain. Tunnels led to massive storage areas, more like caves than rooms, and could hold supplies enough for a years-long siege. Here, also, could be found the entrance to the unused dungeon; a perfect hiding place for their company.

Torches lit the hallway for several yards in both directions, the smoke wafting upwards and away. Now that he'd left the warm kitchen, his breath copied the smoke. Keeping things cold here wouldn't be a problem. Somewhere above fresh air vented in, but Artan hadn't discovered its source, though he'd found an underground stream flowing behind the storage rooms. Whoever built the keep had taken the time and trouble to ensure food and water in time of war—odd for a country that had always been at peace. Perhaps it had to do with their border with the West Downs. No matter. It only made the assassins' job that much easier.

Artan set down the broom, picked up a spare torch, lit it, and carried on to the left until he reached a small, wooden door. One of his first jobs upon finding it was to oil out the squeak. It opened quietly at his touch and he headed down the narrow stone stairs, closing the door behind him.

Disguising the assassins as guards on a caravan had proved simple enough, as had Artan's insinuating himself into the keep. The others stayed in various inns around Tiras until he found the way in; the stream meant to provide water during a siege. Removing the rusted gate at the exit proved no problem and the rest of the company slipped in unnoticed, albeit somewhat wet and extremely cold. Every one of them had muttered curses and complaints about the frigid water and how long it took to warm up afterwards. Artan wondered if Lord Cenith even knew the stream existed.

Half way down the stairs, Artan removed his shoes and extinguished the torch. He tiptoed the rest of the way, careful of where he placed his feet. He'd almost reached the bottom when he stepped on a loose stone and had to bite his tongue against the sharp pain. It didn't help. Stone grated on rock, not much, yet too much. Artan almost groaned.

"Better, lad." Snake's voice echoed off damp stone walls. Weapons rattled. "You almost made it."

Artan had expected Snake to say something, but he jumped anyway, then sighed. He'd tried so hard to be quiet. He slipped his shoes back on, kicked the offending stone down the remainder of the stairs, and entered the room. Nine men, all dressed in black, pointed various pieces of lethal metal at him. Once confirmed he was one of their own, the weapons disappeared into sheaths and clothing, except Ice's. He liked to hang onto to his pair of narrow, foot-and-a-half knives longer than necessary. Sometimes he just sat, like now, caressing them.

That one frightened Artan to the core. The assassin had been given the name Ice because of his cold, pale eyes—they matched his heart. He'd seen him use his razor sharp long knives to slice a man's head off. The body had taken several seconds to drop. Artan guessed the fellow hadn't realized he was dead.

Snake sat on his lean haunches facing a small fireplace, the only heat in the room. He held his hands out to its meager comfort. Dry wood was hard to come by; dry anything for that matter. "You bringing me good news?"

Artan crouched near him. "I am. I saw a guard put what looked like our item in the treasure room."

Snake grunted. "Figured they'd want to look at it pretty quick. Shival was watching us this day."

Shival had nothing to do with it. It was all me! No sense arguing with Snake, though.

The grizzled assassin turned his back on the fire and motioned everyone into a circle. "We do this tonight. Two hours past midnight. I've had enough of this damp, cold stone. Listen close. I'm not going to repeat myself.

"First, the scrap of parchment. Ice, take Sting and Artan. You two..." he indicated the older assassins, "...take out the guards on the treasure room."

"A warning," Artan interrupted. "There's four there now."

Snake's dark grey eyes flashed. "Why?"

Artan shrugged. "Don't know, but they've doubled the guards everywhere today and have posted them on the servant stairs."

"Maegden's balls!" Snake spat into the center of the circle. "Well, it won't change much. Just take longer." He grunted. "If we run into trouble, we might have to think about a diversion. Leave that to me if we do. If everyone works quick and quiet, we won't need it. Artan, your job is to grab the scroll and get out through the stream with the supplies. Meet us at the cave."

Artan's heart sank. *No action. Again!*

Snake turned his attention to the other assassins. Ice's eyes glinted when he and Sting were given the job of killing Daric.

"If you repel down from the roof you won't have to deal with the guards in the hall, "Artan explained. He'd scouted out the route days ago. "Take the servant stairs. There should be two guards at each level. Go straight to the fourth floor. Cenith's rooms are to the left, but that's not where you're going.

"There's a small door to the right of the stairs," Artan continued. "The entrance to Cenith's rooms is around a corner, so the guards won't see you. The door leads to a tower with stairs to another floor and a window that opens onto the roof. I've never seen anyone in there. Watch for the guards on the parapets. There's only one per side, so you should be able to avoid being seen. Though they may have been doubled as well.

"Daric's rooms are on the third floor. The two windows just before the second balcony lead to his bedroom." Artan drew a diagram in the dirt on the floor with his finger. "There's plenty of room to stand on the grillwork outside the window. You should have no problem using the glass cutters to remove the lock."

Both men nodded. If they thought that part of their task more than a little dangerous, they didn't show it.

"Blade, you and Slash will repel down to Cenith's bedroom windows on the fourth floor," Snake said. "His is the large balcony in the middle and you want the two windows to the right." He glanced at Artan, who confirmed the location with a nod. "The rest of us will clear the guards on Cenith's floor and take care of any other unforeseen problems. When you hear us enter the sitting room, come through and take Cenith out. Now remember, you're not to kill him. Four hundred gold will set us up nicely for a long time. That's too much to risk Saulth's wrath."

When Artan finished explaining the escape route to the back of the keep, Snake said, "The path from the rear of the keep to the road is steep and dangerous, and we'll have to do a bit of climbing, but if we're quick and quiet, we should have a couple hours before the dead guards are discovered." He sniffed and wiped his nose on his sleeve. "Our standard rules apply. Take out only who you have to in order to get the job done. No free kills. Not even for Saulth. We've contracted for taking the parchment and the girl. Daric is our only paid kill. Understood?"

"Clear," Blade said, his voice raspy from an old throat wound.

Snake's gaze scanned his men, resting on none. "Questions?"

Silence, and a couple shaking heads, were the only response.

"Then that's it. Get some rest." Snake turned back to the fire and tossed on more wood.

Artan had not only found their way into the keep, kept them hidden, scouted out the routes the assassins would take to accomplish their tasks, and located the parchment, on one of his outside excursions he'd found a convenient cave not far from where the stream exited the mountain. It lay behind a boulder near the road to Eagle's Nest Pass. A perfect place to meet up and hide out for a couple of days if necessary. He didn't even get a thank you. Somehow, his small percentage, large as it would be, seemed less and less worth the trouble.

"Artan," Snake looked back at him, a gleam in his eye. "You did good. Get some food, say your prayers to Shival, and sleep. You'll need it."

He couldn't have agreed more.

Chapter Nineteen

Daric folded his arms behind his head, the pillows supporting him, watching Elessa slip her pale blue linen nightgown over her head. After eight pregnancies, producing ten children, her hips and waist had spread, though less than many other women in the keep. He glanced down at his stomach; despite training with the men, he'd thickened there as well. Elessa's breasts didn't sit as high as they once had, but she was still a fine looking woman and had welcomed him home in right proper fashion the previous night. He couldn't keep the smile from his face.

"Someone had taught Tyrsa to say 'please'," she said, sitting at the lace decorated table displaying an array of her possessions. She picked up her brush and began the nightly ritual on her walnut brown hair. "You'd think they'd teach her 'thank you' as well."

"I don't think she's had much to be thankful for in a long time."

"I suppose she hasn't." Elessa sighed. "Regardless, we worked on that today, as well as 'body noises that are best kept silent'."

Daric chuckled.

She tugged on a stubborn knot before adding, "Between selecting materials, getting her measured, and all that business with the scroll, that was all we had time for. Tomorrow we work on utensils and how to use them. Spoons and fingers are not enough. Couldn't the women at the station have helped with that?"

"She's their lady, not to mention peculiar to start with. They were more than a little in awe of her. I doubt they saw it as their place to correct her behaviour. Especially when it came to 'words that should not be said'." Daric loved Elessa's quiet laugh and he smiled to hear it now. "Think you'll be able to turn her into a proper lady?"

Elessa finished brushing and swept her long, thick hair back. Deft fingers fashioned a braid in quick order. "Given time, I can teach her anything. She's a smart girl. It's her stubborn streak that has me concerned...among other things."

She stood and Daric pulled back the covers for her before resuming his reclined position. He knew his wife well enough to know it wasn't Tyrsa's stubbornness that overly worried her. "What other things?"

Elessa waited until she'd settled herself, sitting up, the covers pulled to her waist before she answered. "The two of them together for starters."

"It was unexpected. Not just the marriage, but her as well. There's not much that can be done now. It doesn't look like Cenith's planning on setting her aside."

"That's not what I mean."

Daric raised an eyebrow. She gave him a look that let him know 'obtuse' was the order of his day.

Elessa waved her hand in the general direction of Cenith's rooms, one floor up. "When they're together, they look more like an older brother escorting his little sister than husband and wife. There's well over a foot difference in their height."

Daric still couldn't see what direction this was headed in. "What difference does that make? There's a foot between us. What's a few more inches?"

"A lot when you're the size she is." Elessa folded her arms across her stomach. "You were right when you said Cenith isn't planning on setting her aside. A blind man can see he's fallen for her and that means he's going to want to take her as his wife fully."

"I'm sure he'll be careful, if that's what you're worried about."

She gave him that look again. "It doesn't matter how careful Cenith is, he's going to get her pregnant. He has to if he wants an heir. Despite having you and Kian around to make him feel otherwise, he's a tall, strong man, with every chance of fathering a big child. From what you said happened to her own mother, Tyrsa giving birth to Cenith's baby could turn into a nightmare."

Daric lost his good humour. "You got me there. I hadn't thought of that." Elessa almost spit her babies out.

"Men tend not to." She pulled her braid out from behind her back and tugged on the end, a habit she had when worried. "Cenith is as bad a romantic as his father. I wouldn't put it past him to not marry again, just like Ifan. Look at the trouble that almost caused."

Ifan's older brother had been killed in a hunting accident, leaving him an only child. After Cenith, the next in line for the lordship was a second cousin with a penchant for drink and gambling, an older man, no better than Meric. If Cenith had died…

Elessa tugged on her braid again. Daric slid down and motioned her into his arms. She snuggled up to him and rested her head in the hollow of his shoulder; she fit perfectly.

"There's not a lot we can do, love," he said, "except be more careful if she has to be cut open. Garun is an excellent physician. If there's a way to do it, he'll either already know, or find a way. Her healing ability might also help with that."

"It might, but I hesitate to count on it. I doubt she can heal from death."

Daric suppressed a shudder. Now that would be frightening. Elessa rolled over far enough to blow out the candle on the table beside her before snuggling into him again. Her warm breath tickled the hairs on his chest. It had been a late night and a long day. Now that she'd aired her concerns, she'd fall asleep soon.

He, on the other hand, had too much running through his mind. Tyrsa's myriad abilities not only confused him, he found them worrisome as well—both the ones he knew about, and the ones he didn't. He wasn't so naïve as to believe he'd seen them all. The girl herself had no idea what she could do. Another frightening thought.

Besides her healing, the wind and the ground talked to her. The three of them had spent an evening at the station discussing those subjects; a difficult chore given her limited vocabulary. All she could tell them was that bad things were coming; that the ground didn't cause the tornadoes that had threatened them, but had instead helped her stop them, even though it hurt to do it. *How can ground hurt? How can it, or the wind, talk?*

Something had caused the floods, the tidal waves, the tornadoes…but what? And how could it be stopped? How do you stop nature? Daric didn't have a clue, but apparently it was up to Tyrsa to do it and the scroll probably contained the information they needed. They had to find out what it said. Which brought his thoughts around to Saulth.

That man knows exactly what it says. But if Tyrsa was needed to stop all this, why did he give her away to Cenith? Did he want the country in ruins? Was there a way to turn it to his advantage and take over as a single ruler? He'd made no secret that he wished one lord over all the others and Daric had no illusions about Saulth wanting anyone but himself. Problem was, Bredun suffered just as much as the other principalities. For that matter, the only one that had felt little effect was Dunvalos Reach itself.

Did Saulth send Tyrsa here to cause trouble? Or find the solution? But then, why does he want her back? There were too many questions with no answers. *Could this be a ruse?* Was Tyrsa just playing a role to get inside the castle? That thought didn't sit right with him. The girl would have to be a master in acting to put up with the lashing and all she'd gone through since then. Even the best actress in the world couldn't fake the healing he'd personally seen. No, Tyrsa couldn't be shamming.

That turned his thoughts to the whole incident when she healed Cenith. Tyrsa had insisted a bad woman had wanted to take Cenith away. Had she really seen Shival? That had shaken Daric to the roots of his very soul. Cillain and Niafanna were the only gods he believed in. He wouldn't press his beliefs on others and quite enjoyed his discussions with Cenith on the subject, but Ardael's gods and goddesses simply didn't exist for him; until Tyrsa healed Cenith.

The woman had told Tyrsa she knew what she was and that she could do nothing to stop her; but Tyrsa had stopped her. One thing Daric knew for sure. He had to find someone who could read the scroll, and that meant contemplating something he hadn't done in a long, long time.

A pounding at the door jerked him from his thoughts. Elessa cried out and sat up.

"Councillor Daric!" a guard cried. "There's trouble in Lord Cenith's room! Lady Tyrsa is screaming!"

* * * *

Cenith removed his light wool tunic and linen shirt, hanging them on a peg on the back of his door. Laron would take care of them in the morning. That reminded him that Tyrsa would need a personal maid to help her dress and do her hair. For now she wore the simple dresses the women at the station had given her, but the current fashion called for more elaborate outfits. Elessa should have some ideas on who would be appropriate, someone with a mine full of patience.

He sat in the chair by the fire, kicking off his boots before taking a sip of the Cambrel red he'd poured for himself. Tyrsa decided she didn't like wine. Perhaps if he watered it down she might change her mind.

Cenith had sent his wife to change into a nightgown, though he had every intention of removing it soon. He also asked that she leave Baybee in the bedroom; he wanted her undivided attention.

They'd been married for over a month. Tyrsa responded well to his kisses and liked sitting on his lap, her head resting on his shoulder. Most evenings during his recovery were spent just that way. Some nights, restraining himself had taken every scrap of willpower he could muster. Cenith had no idea how she'd react to what he had planned and the thick stone walls of the keep would allow a measure of privacy unavailable in the house at the station.

Tyrsa exited their bedroom wearing a dark blue silk gown with a low cut neckline and ivory lace trim on the sleeves and hem. She found the whole idea of wearing clothes to bed a novelty. Especially since Cenith usually wore nothing.

"That's pretty. Is it new?"

"Yes," Tyrsa said, her smile as bright as her eyes. "Elessa made it from her daughter's."

Cenith doubted she meant that as it sounded. "You mean from a gown that had belonged to one of her daughters?"

"Yes. That's what I said." Tyrsa sat on his lap, shifting to find a comfortable spot, then laid her head on his shoulder. "You're not wearing a shirt."

"I don't need one tonight."

Cenith put both his arms around her, all too aware of the thin material separating him from her. Memories of their first bath together, of rubbing liniment into her thighs, and all the times she lay beside him on the journey and at the station, flickered through his mind. At first, he hadn't wanted to look, or touch. Now it was all he thought about. He stroked her back in ever-widening circles, conscious of the thin ridges of her scars. He wondered if they would ever fade completely. His hand dropped lower, to her bottom.

"That's good," she said, closing her eyes.

He'd have to be careful or she'd fall asleep. Cenith slid his hand to the nape of her neck and undid the tie of the nightgown. Lifting her chin, he kissed her, then lowered his hand, brushing her breast.

"Oh!" Tyrsa sat up, looking down at her chest. "That was…different."

Cenith struggled to keep his grin down to a smile. "Did you like that?"

"I…I don't know."

"Then let me do it again." Keeping his touch gentle, he rubbed his thumb over her nipple.

Tyrsa gasped. He lifted his thumb and she leaned forward, as if seeking him.

"Well? Do you want to me to do it again?"

"Yes."

"It's better this way," Cenith said, slipping the nightgown over her shoulders and down to her waist.

Her pretty breasts waited, begging for his touch, his kiss. He obliged them. Tyrsa moaned as he paid attention to first one, then the other. She wriggled on his lap, increasing his discomfort, but he had to go slow, each step a test.

Cenith moved his kisses to her lips, caressing her soft skin, enveloping her in his desire. She leaned into him, her unsure, hesitant hands stroking his chest, his arms. He deepened his kiss, sweet and hot, until she pulled back, breathless.

"I…I don't…" The look on her face, sultry, yet innocent and confused, stirred his passion all the more.

"Do you remember when I told you about husbands and wives?" he asked, fighting not to ravish her there on the spot.

"That they live together? And have children?" Tyrsa's sweet breath teased him, adding fuel to the flame.

"And that I'd show you how that was done?"

"Yes."

Cenith kissed her again, devouring her delicious lips, made fuller by passion. "I'm going to show you tonight. Do you want a baby like Rade? One who lives and breathes as we do?"

"Baybee..."

"Is very nice, but not the same as Rade. You know that. I can give you a real baby, one that'll hug and kiss you, like I do." Well, not quite the same, but there was no point in delving into that subject. It could wait.

Cenith kissed her again, touching, caressing. He pushed her gown down further, allowing him to stoke the soft skin of her bottom. She trembled, her breath coming in short gasps.

"I...I feel different," she said, her words a mere whisper.

"Where?" Cenith let her sit up, worried he'd overwhelmed her.

Tyrsa laid her hand across her lower belly and Cenith smiled.

"It's natural for you to feel that after what we just did. It means you want us to share our bodies."

A little frown wrinkled her brow. "Share our bodies? How do we do that?"

"I'm going to show you. Stand up."

Tyrsa slid off his lap, her gown pooling at her feet. "Oh!"

"Don't worry about your nightgown. You won't need it," Cenith said.

He picked her up and took her into the bedroom. Setting her on her feet, he undid the laces on his trousers and removed them along with his small breeches. As expected, her eyes dropped immediately to the swollen result of their foreplay.

"Oh! It's bigger than before."

"Don't be afraid, it's supposed to do that." Feeling self conscious, Cenith pulled back the covers, lifted her on the bed and indicated she should slide over enough to let him in.

"I don't have that," she said, touching herself.

"Women don't. That's what makes me a man." Cenith brought the blankets up to their waists and cuddled close to her, resuming his kisses and caress. He reached under the blanket and cupped her womanhood. "And this is what makes you a woman."

Keeping his hand there, he stroked and teased, eliciting more gasps and moans. Tyrsa might not know what to do, but her body did, writhing and wriggling, seeking his touch when he dared remove it. She had to be close to her peak, close to experiencing the best part of life, and that excited him more.

Without warning, Tyrsa pushed him away. "No! Too much touch! Too much feel!" She thrashed off the covers and rolled to the far end of the bed.

Cenith clenched his teeth, forcing himself to remain calm. He sat up. "It's all right, Tyrsa. You're supposed to feel that way. You'll get used to it, just as you got used to me holding and kissing you. Did it hurt?"

Tyrsa knelt on the edge of the bed, her chest heaving. She shook her head.

"Did you like it? Even a little?"

She nodded, shook her head, then nodded again.

"Which is it? It can't be both. Come," Cenith held out his hand, "I'll hold you while we talk." Hesitant, she returned to his arms. He held her close, careful of where he put his hands. "If you want a baby, then we have to do this. Tell me what you didn't like." When she didn't respond, he said, "Think about the words, Tyrsa. You know them. Tell me."

"I was afraid. I felt like…like I was going to fall."

He lifted her chin, forcing her to look at him. "Like you were at the edge of a cliff? One push and you'd go over?"

She nodded.

"If you'd let yourself fall, you would have felt something so wonderful, I can't even tell you. There are no words for it. It's something you have to feel for yourself. There's no danger, Tyrsa, only a wonderful feeling." Cenith risked a caress, then a stroke. She shuddered, but didn't pull away.

He shifted so he lay more on his side. "I'll tell you what. I'll show you what you have to do to make me fall off the cliff. Then you'll see there's no harm."

Tyrsa nodded. Cenith laid her down, kissed her, then showed her where and how to touch him. He only let her play for a few minutes; he already trod too close to the edge of the cliff.

Settling himself on top of her, he kissed and nuzzled, stroked and caressed, bringing her close to the point where she'd panicked.

"I have to tell you this," he said between kisses, "it'll hurt a little, but only because it's your first time. Then it won't hurt anymore. It's only a little hurt, do you understand?"

Once again she nodded, her eyes widening with fear.

It's now or never! Cenith entered her. She gasped. One careful thrust, and he tore her maidenhood. The gasp turned into a cry. He kissed her and murmured reassurances until she calmed.

Cenith tried to hold back. She was so small, and the last thing he wanted was to hurt her, but he found himself lost in the passion, the desire to leap off that cliff and fall into its heavenly depths. Her cry didn't sound like one of pain, so he spread his wings, bent his knees, and dove off the precipice. The fall proved to be everything he'd expected, and more.

Tyrsa writhed and squirmed beneath him, making the plunge that much more glorious. An eternity later he landed, panting for breath. Tyrsa thrashed under him, her cries turning to screams.

Cenith rolled off, afraid he'd hurt her. His fear multiplied into terror. Tyrsa's normally bright blue eyes blazed an unearthly violet. She arched her back, shrieking in agony. Her belly, covered in sweat from their lovemaking, glowed with a bright, white light, growing, spreading, enveloping her.

Tyrsa dove off the bed and rolled on the floor, as if trying to extinguish the light. Cenith yanked a blanket off the bed and covered her, then ran to the sitting room door.

The door rattled. Someone on the other side pounded on it. Cenith shot back the bolt. The two worried faces outside weren't Companions. "Get Daric! Now!"

Cenith ran back to Tyrsa. She'd thrown off the blanket, kicking her legs, flailing her arms. He knelt beside her, covered her once more, and took her glowing body into his arms, restraining her. *What in all Shival's hells is going on!*

* * * *

Daric pulled his pants on and grabbed his sword. Elessa threw on her dressing gown.

"Where do you think you're going?" he asked, opening the door.

"If it's what I think it is, you're going to need me more than that sword."

Daric blocked the exit. "And if it's what I think it is, you'll turn right around, gather the children in our rooms and barricade the door. Understood?"

She nodded. Daric signalled the guards to follow. Making sure he didn't outdistance his wife, he moved as fast as he dared, keeping an eye out for trouble. The guards on the stairs and in the hall stood at attention. Everything appeared normal.

When they reached Cenith's rooms, silence, and three guards, greeted them.

"Intruders?" Daric asked.

"No, sir. We don't know what the problem is." One of the soldiers opened the door for them. "My Lady stopped screaming a few minutes after we sent for you," he said, then stood back to allow them entry. "They're in the bedroom."

Daric ushered Elessa in first. It looked like she'd been right. Tyrsa's nightgown lay in a puddle near one of the stuffed chairs.

"Daric?" Cenith sounded frightened.

Elessa reached them first. "Talueth!" It sounded like it wasn't what she'd expected either.

Daric leaned his sword against the arm of a chair, moved to the bedroom door, and looked over his wife's head. Cenith sat on the floor, Tyrsa cradled in his arms. She glowed through the blanket covering her. There could be no other word for it. A soft, white light enveloped her from head to toe. She lay in Cenith's arms as if asleep, except her eyes were open. Daric blinked, not believing what he saw. Violet! Her eyes had turned violet.

A quick glance at the bed confirmed his suspicions on one matter. "I gather you've made her your wife in truth," he said, careful to keep any hint of accusation out of his voice. How could he blame him?

"I tried not to hurt her. I was so careful." Cenith's voice sounded calmer than it should, which worried Daric. His young lord appeared to be in shock, yet, somehow he'd managed to put on a pair of pants. On Elessa's behalf, Daric silently thanked him for that.

Elessa crouched down opposite Cenith. "I don't think this happened because you hurt her. This is something else entirely." She rested her hand against Tyrsa's forehead. "She's cold as ice. Let's get her into the other room by the fire. And into her nightgown."

Once that was done, Cenith sat in one of the chairs. Daric lifted Tyrsa onto his lap while Elessa covered her with the blanket. She still acted as if she slept, except for the wide open, eerie coloured eyes. Daric sent the guards assigned to his room back to their post, added more wood to the fire, then leaned against the warm stone.

"What did I do? What can I do to stop it?" Cenith asked, showing some of the emotion Daric expected.

"I don't know. We haven't a clue who, or what, she really is," Daric said. "She's already displayed abilities she shouldn't have. This might be a reaction to losing her maidenhood. Bear in mind, however, it's only a guess."

Cenith looked up at him, hope flared briefly in his eyes, and died just as quick. "If this happens every time we…" He looked back at Tyrsa. "I'm not sure it matters. I think I hurt her. She probably won't let me touch her again."

Elessa sat in the other chair. "That's a worry that can wait until tomorrow."

Tyrsa sat up, almost bumping heads with Cenith. She breathed deep and the glow faded, though the odd colour in her eyes remained.

"Tyrsa! Are you all right?" Cenith tried to hug her, but she squirmed out of his grip and off his lap.

She stared at the fire, her eyes darting from the flame to the hearth. Cenith moved to stand, but Daric waved him back. Tyrsa fell to her knees on the hearth and scooped out the cooler ash at the edges of the fire. She spread it out, just as she had at the guard station.

Daric stepped back, then slid behind Cenith's chair to give Tyrsa more room.

"No! Ya burn it! Idiot!" Tyrsa said, smoothing out the layer of ash.

"Paper," Cenith said. "She needs paper." Leaping out of his chair, he strode to the small writing table sitting to the right of the balcony doors.

Daric reached him just before he pulled the drawer open. He took his lord by the shoulders and directed him back to the chair. "No. Let her do this. I don't think we should disturb her."

At the top middle of the hearth, Tyrsa drew an exact replica of the symbol she'd drawn on the scroll, the ancient sign for Cillain and Niafanna. "Don't stop! Ya got wax in yer ears."

Below it she drew a full sun with rays, Maegden's symbol. Under those, but at the left edge of the hearth, Tyrsa drew a thin line with a small circle at the bottom and a wavy line passing through the circle. "Kep stirrin'. Ya ruin it."

"What is that?" Daric asked.

"A threaded needle," Elessa explained. "It's a little used symbol for Talueth."

Working from left to right, Tyrsa drew a pair of dice, a stalk of wheat, and a spear—the signs representing Aja, Keana, and Siyon. Tyrsa kept up her litany of kitchen talk.

"This isn't what she usually drew, back at the station," Cenith said. "She only copied the things in her book."

"I have no explanation for you," Daric said.

Soon, the last three symbols of the gods joined the others—three short wavy lines, one under the other, representing Tailis, god of water, a flame for Ordan, and a heart for Shival.

Once done, Tyrsa fell silent, staring at the heart she'd drawn. She crouched, quiet and solemn, for several minutes, then stabbed her finger at the heart, startling all three of them.

"Bad! Hurt!" she said, her tone angry, accusing. "No hurt!"

"She's remembering when I was dying?" Cenith asked Daric, keeping his voice low.

"Possibly. Hard to say."

Tyrsa moved back to the left of the hearth, careful not to disturb what she'd drawn. In the upper corner, she spread more ash, then drew a cup, tilted on its side, with a drop falling. She shifted again, to the far right this time, to draw a tree, though not like the ones she'd drawn before. Instead of a fat, bushy one, this tree stood tall and thin, like a mountain pine.

"Any idea what those mean?" Daric asked.

Both Cenith and Elessa shook their heads. Elessa leaned forward and rubbed her forehead, a sure sign she was overtired. Tyrsa sat back, a satisfied look on her face. She folded her arms across her stomach and slowly rocked back and forth on the balls of her feet.

After several minutes, Cenith asked, "Can I offer you some wine?" He didn't take his eyes off Tyrsa.

Daric and Elessa shared a meaningful glance. It was clear Cenith was in shock. Elessa shook her head, declining their lord's offer.

"No," Daric said. "But I think you need some." He poured Cenith a glass and pressed it into his hand. It went down quick and he poured another. "You might want to sip that one."

Daric turned to his wife. "Why don't you go to bed, love? Who knows how long she's going to sit there? One of us might as well get some sleep."

Elessa nodded and Daric helped her to her feet. He kissed her at the door and instructed one of the guards to escort her back to her room. She didn't argue, which only proved how tired she was. Before he went to bed himself, he'd have to remember to tell the guards not to disturb them until she woke. Daric sat in the chair next to Cenith, with little to do except wait to see what Tyrsa would do next.

Chapter Twenty

"You haven't finished those pots yet? I swear your arms are made of straw and your brains of horse dung, lordling," Buckam muttered, imitating Jarven's high-pitched voice. "Your pissant rank means nothing here, whelp. You're just another piece of offal, a dog what needs a beatin'."

The kitchen's chief cook sounded like he had no balls; until it came to dishing out abuse. The man didn't need to hit, the edge of his tongue could slice the head off an iron statue. Buckam had lost track of the number of insults he'd endured that day. Jarven had a way of making you feel like you'd started life as a slug and had only progressed further down.

Buckam stood in the scullery, a small, stuffy room off the main kitchen that smelled of wet wood and the leftovers of whatever had been served that day. Every once in a while the yeasty smell of rising bread wafted in, reminding Buckam that his dinner had been a while ago.

He leaned into a pot half as tall as him so he could reach the burnt mess stuck to the bottom. *I am…or rather was…a nobleman's son! What do I know about cleaning pots?* Jarven just told him to do it, not how. *I should have kept quiet about working in the kitchen, stuck to the stable. At least I know how to clean up after a horse.*

Buckam scrubbed more water into the mess. Using a heavy metal spoon, he scraped burnt potato off, then scooped the result into a wooden bucket sitting on the floor beside him. One of the kitchen girls told him the scrapings went to feed the pigs out back of the stables, which surprised Buckam. He didn't think anything living would want to touch that, let alone eat it, and he stood at the top of the list.

Thank Maegden this is the last one. It must be well after midnight. Due to their long journey, they'd let him sleep in late and he hadn't started his new duties until an hour before noon. He made up for the lost time now and ached in places he didn't realize he had muscles.

Everyone else had gone. Before Jarven left, he shocked Buckam by telling him he could leave the pots to soak overnight and get up early to finish. He'd refused the offer. This was one task he wouldn't avoid, not even if given permission. How could he prove himself if he appeared lazy? One thing this day had shown him—a new respect for those who worked in kitchens. Everybody hustled to produce meals on time. With an entire keep to feed, it was a lot of food. Buckam had never thought about where his meals came from or who prepared them. They just arrived on time, piping hot.

Buckam stuck his head back in the pot, ignoring the ache and pulled wounds in his back. According to Councillor Daric, they were healed, but if Buckam overdid it, he paid for it. *It is my own fault. If I had not shirked my duty in Bredun I would not be here.* But then, he wouldn't have found out the truth about Saulth, either.

In the time spent with the Dunvalos Reach men, both on the road and at the station, he'd learned in quick order that matters were different here in the relations between the guards and their lord. An open honesty and trust existed that couldn't even be considered in Bredun; the kind of faith Buckam had seen in his father's eyes, though he realized now that trust had only gone one way.

Buckam scooped out another burnt mass of potato, his thoughts drifting back to the vision he'd had of his father during what he'd come to call his 'hell ride'. The sad look on his face when Buckam thought of all that Saulth had done in recent years, he now took as his father's permission to leave an unfit lord for one he could trust and honour. Buckam would prove himself, even if it took twenty years of scrubbing pots to do it.

Wood scraping on stone sounded from the back of the main kitchen. Jarven said sometimes the guards came down for a late meal, but they'd come to the main door, not the small one leading to the storage rooms. Buckam quietly set the pot on its bottom and froze, his instincts on alert. He blew out the single candle and flattened himself against the back wall. Whoever came trod silent. Silhouettes of three men, all dressed in black, slid by the long fireplace on the far wall of the kitchen. *Assassins!*

Saulth wanted the girl, Lady Tyrsa, back again. It had to be Saulth who sent these men. After what his former lord had done to her, Buckam couldn't allow it.

He held his breath until they disappeared, then tiptoed to the scullery door. No one in sight. Buckam slipped a butcher knife out of its rack and peered around the corner of the main door just in time to see the last of the men vanish up the servant stairs. An instant later, two bodies slid down those same stairs. Dunvalos Reach guards. Neither moved. Buckam wondered if Cenith's keep had secret tunnels like Valda. They'd come in handy now.

The small wooden door scraped again. Too far from the scullery, Buckam ducked out the main door and under the stairs, making himself as small as possible in the shadows created by the single lit wall sconce. With only a kitchen knife, he could do nothing else.

Something dripped. He held his breath. A dark pool formed on the floor beside him. It glistened in the flickering candlelight. Blood. Buckam looked up at the source. One of the dead guard's arms lay stretched out not two stairs above him. Drops, black in the darkness, fell from motionless fingers.

Two more assassins appeared and crept up the stairs. When they were no longer in sight, Buckam ran for the main keep doors and the guards he knew would be there.

* ***

"You sure took long enough with that girl," Varth said to Jolin as they climbed the keep steps, crinkling his nose. Ead followed, a grimace on his face.

Jolin laughed and winked at Kian, who opened one of the doors for them. "What kin I say? She likes me."

Daric had given the Companions three days off to rest from the journey. Jolin figured he'd need the other two to recover from this one.

"I'm jealous," Daric's son said. "Wish I could have joined you instead of being stuck here." He scowled. "Now that Lord Cenith is an old married man, I need a new wenching partner."

"Jus' for yer information, I prefer my time wi' the ladies one on one."

The other three guards laughed and Kian pushed him through the door, closing it behind them.

"Now if you want some real fun," Ead said, leading the way to his quarters. "You're welcome to join Varth and me for the rest of the night. Or are you too tired now?"

Jolin resisted the urge to roll his eyes. One drunken night had been enough to make him decide he only wanted girls. "Between movin' all my stuff t' th' new room, entertain' Tafya, an' countin' in th' late hour, I'm definitely too tired. Sorry." He didn't like hurting their feelings; at least this offered a diplomatic way out. Fortunately, they didn't ask often, preferring their privacy.

I wonder how many o' the guard actually know 'bout these two? Or their parents for that matter. As third son of a noble, Varth might have more freedom, but Ead was the eldest. His parents would expect an heir. *Could present a tad of a problem.* Not that it mattered to Jolin. They were his friends and the evening spent gambling and sporting at Silk's Tavern had gone far too fast.

"Guess this is g'night, then," Jolin said, unfastening the top hooks of his jerkin.

Footsteps pounded down the hall behind them.

"Jolin!"

Jolin pulled his weapon and spun just as Buckam, dressed in stained tunic and trousers and holding a butcher knife, skidded to a stop mere inches before skewering himself on the three swords pointed at him. His blonde hair stuck up in all directions, matted with some sort of mess.

"There are intruders in the castle!" Buckam managed to gasp out. "I was working late and I saw them come from the storerooms behind the kitchens!" He looked down at the knife he held and dropped it on the carpet. "It was the only thing I could grab!"

"How many?" Jolin asked, glad he'd had a couple hours exercise to wear off what he'd drunk. He lowered his sword and motioned the others to do the same.

Buckam stood at attention, as if reporting to his guard-commander. With his filthy clothes and matted hair, he presented a less than respectable sight. "I saw five, but there might be more. All dressed in black with only their eyes showing."

"Assassins!" *That's why we weren't attacked on th' road!* "Where'd they go?"

"Up the servant stairs. They have already killed at least two guards there."

"Take the knife. Go back t' th' kitchen and stay there. Keep hidden. If ye see anyone else, tell someone soon as ye kin!" Once Buckam had the knife, Jolin pushed the young man back in the direction he'd come.

"What if he's lying?" Ead asked, his blue eyes flashing.

"What if he ain't? Kin we take that chance?"

"You're trusting him!" Ead looked ready to go after Buckam, not the intruders.

"No, I'm trustin' my instincts. Varth, tell Kian t' get Councillor Daric and send someone for the Guard-Commander. Ead, help me wake the Companions!" Jolin grabbed Ead's sleeve and pulled him along.

Aja had rolled his dice in their favour. That very afternoon Ors had interrupted the Companions' rest day and ordered them to move inside the keep. Jolin and Ead, joined shortly by Varth, ran down the corridor, pounding on doors. "Companions! To me! Intruders! To m'lady's room!"

Kian passed them, heading for the main staircase at the end of the hall. Trusting the men to follow, Jolin ran after him, alerting the guards stationed at each level, instructing them to remain at their posts and keep alert. At the top of the stairs, he turned. Ten Companions stood ready along with a dozen other guards who'd woken at the call, none officers. They were all armed, but dressed only in what had been at hand.

"Companions, with me. We have assassins in th' keep! Everyone else, search t' other floors by th' servant stairs!" Confusion showed on the other guards' faces, but Jolin had no time to explain. "Jus' do it!"

To the Companions, Jolin said, "Go quiet, now. We don't know what t' expect."

They moved quick and silent through the halls to Cenith's rooms. Jolin held a finger to his lips to hush the guards outside the door. Keeping his voice low, he said, "There's intruders in the keep. Any sign o' trouble?"

"Yes, but not with intruders." The guard, an older man named Jemry, frowned his confusion. "Lady Tyrsa was screaming and we sent for Councillor Daric. Been quiet for a while now."

"You four go check th' back stairs. We kin look after m'lord and lady," Jolin said.

"Nope." Jemry shook his head. "We don't leave until an officer says otherwise."

Jolin blinked. "No, o' course ye don't. Shouldn't have asked." *Shouldn't o' let orderin' those other guards go t' my head, neither.*

He knocked, then opened the door and motioned the Companions to follow. This was the first time he'd been in Lord Cenith's suite. The sitting room was spacious but held little in the way of furniture. An oak writing table, with matching chair, sat in one corner. Bookshelves flanked the large stone fireplace while more took up space on the other walls. Two wide balcony doors were dressed in deep blue velvet curtains held back with silver–coloured braided cord. Colourful tapestries depicting hunting scenes helped keep the room warm. The carpets were of an expensive weave and tastefully done in blues, greens, and gold.

For some reason, Jolin had expected the lord of the principality to have rooms that were more ostentatious, but then realized that both Lord Cenith and his father were down to earth, sensible men, unlike many of the lords in the lowlands.

Lord Cenith and Councillor Daric sat in a pair of large, overstuffed chairs near a fire now reduced to glowing coals. They both wore only a pair of pants. Daric's great sword rested close at hand; he must have expected some kind of trouble. Lady Tyrsa crouched by the hearth, dressed in a blue nightgown stained with ashes, rocking back and forth, staring at something drawn there. She wore a fey look Jolin had never seen.

Daric turned to the Companions, setting a finger to his lips. He frowned when he took in their various states of dress, and their drawn weapons. Jolin hunkered down between him and Lord Cenith. A blanket lay crumpled on the floor in front of him. He only briefly wondered why.

"Buckam spotted five intruders in th' kitchen. Assassins, sir," Jolin said in a low voice. "They headed up th' servant stairs, at least two dead. Guard-Commander Ors has been alerted. Hope ye don't mind, I've set some o' the guards searchin' th' floors. I also sent Kian to fetch ye. Thought ye'd be in yer rooms."

"You did right." Daric stood and picked up his sword. To Lord Cenith he said, "We were wondering why we weren't attacked. Now we know. I suggest you stay here, My Lord. She needs all the protection she can get, and who knows what she'll do next."

Lord Cenith nodded, staring at his wife. He looked lost.

"You're in charge here, Jolin. Disperse the men," Daric said. "Six here, four in the bedroom. If these are assassins, keep as quiet…"

"Twelve."

They all looked at Lady Tyrsa, who stared at Jolin, her eyes fixed on his. They were the colour of violets on a bright summer's day, not the blue they should be. Some would have made the sign against evil. Jolin didn't. Like the pixies, fairies, and tree spirits of the mountains, she wasn't evil. She just was, regardless of what had happened to her eyes.

"I need twelve."

"Twelve what, m'lady?" Jolin asked, since her gaze stayed firmly on him.

"Companions." Lady Tyrsa continued to rock back and forth, her arms folded across her stomach.

"We kin pick another tomorrow, m'lady." This was hardly the time for that.

"No. Buckam. Buckam's heart is true." She turned back to the hearth and what had been drawn there.

"Buckam, m'lady?" Jolin looked to Daric, who shrugged. *But she's always avoided him!* Mutters from around the room showed the others' disapproval.

"Don't argue with her. Not now. It's been an odd night," the councillor said. "And don't leave them."

"Don't intend to, sir." Jolin rose to his feet, directing four of the men into the bedroom.

Lady Tyrsa stood, stretched, and yawned. When she opened her eyes, they were blue once more. Lord Cenith leapt to his feet. He looked like he wanted to run to her, but remained hesitant, though only a scant few feet separated them. She smiled as if nothing had happened, walked toward him, and pushed him back in the chair. Sitting on his lap, she kissed him, then laid her head on his shoulder and closed her eyes.

"Tyrsa? Are you all right?" Lord Cenith asked, trying to see her face without disturbing her.

No answer. From where Jolin stood, she appeared to already be asleep.

"As I said, it's been an odd night." Daric headed for the door.

Just before he reached it, it opened, admitting Kian, his expression blacker than Jolin had ever seen it. He tossed Daric his padded uniform tunic. "We definitely have intruders, Father. At least two cut the glass around the locks on your bedroom windows. They killed the guards and knocked Mother out. She'll have a bruise, but she's fine and says not to worry, just do what you have to and be careful."

Daric's eyes flashed, his features hardened, but he let Kian finish his report.

"It's obvious they're after you too. I gathered the rest of the family in your rooms. The assassins already know you're not there, so I'm hoping they'll decide there's no point in coming back. I've put Valin and Taro on guard, with strict instructions to lock the door, stay inside the rooms, and don't go looking for trouble. Avina and Jennica are also armed."

Jolin had helped with Valin and Taro's training. The fourteen-year old twins showed talent, and a recklessness Daric and Kian didn't, but were hardly ready for skilled assassins. Though Daric insisted the girls have defence training, they wouldn't be much better.

"Good thinking. Counting those two and the five Buckam saw, we're facing at least seven, probably more. Jolin, keep alert. They might try the same window trick in here." Daric waved Kian to follow. To the guards outside, he said, "You're with us."

Keev closed the door quietly behind them.

"M'lord, I suggest we blow the candles out. Keep as still as possible," Jolin said.

Lord Cenith only nodded, stared into the fire, and held his wife. The Companions took over and in moments only the coals lit the room. Jolin motioned Barit, Yanis, Dathan, and Fallan to flank the double doors of the balcony and draw the heavy drapes. Keev and Trey he set at the hall door. In the bedroom, he had Varth and Ead take a window, while he shared the one on the right with Jayce. Madin, the only one with a crossbow, stood against the far wall, ready to take out whoever might come through the left window. Jolin warned the others not to put themselves in his way.

In the few moments before he ordered the drapes closed, the sparse moonlight allowed Jolin to study the layout of the room. It held a little more furniture than the sitting room. A large four–poster bed sat between two tall windows on the east wall. Three floor–to–ceiling wardrobes covered the opposite wall, while a wooden chest made of various shades of wood nestled against the foot of the bed. An elegant full-length mirror sat near the door to the garderobe.

The moonlight also allowed Jolin to see the dishevelled bed and the stain on the sheet. His heart tightened. Jolin knew Lord Cenith would keep his wife, but somewhere, deep inside, there'd burned a small hope, now extinguished.

Was that the trouble that had brought Daric here? Had Lord Cenith hurt her? He wouldn't have intended it, but that wouldn't explain the change in the colour of her eyes or her odd behaviour. She slept now, peaceful and content, in the arms of her husband. The experience couldn't have upset her that much.

Jolin pinched the bridge of his nose between his fingers, forcing himself to concentrate on the matter at hand. Lady Tyrsa was his responsibility. It didn't matter that she could never be his. He had to keep her safe. For her, for Lord Cenith, and for him.

The sitting room door crashed open.

"My Lord!" It was Guard-Commander Ors.

An instant later, a scraping noise sounded from both bedroom windows. Jolin held his arm up, cautioning the others to let the intruders finish cutting out the locks. The windows swung in, pulling the drapes apart. Jolin dropped his arm. The twang of Madin's bow preceded a thump and a groan.

Jolin stabbed his man clear through the chest, Jayce slashed him just below. The intruder fell forward, his legs tangled in the drapes. Gasping, the doomed man tried to cry out, but only wet gurgling noises came from his cloth-shrouded mouth. He thrashed his legs in a desperate attempt to free them, while his outstretched hands clawed at the carpet. Jolin drew his dagger and slit the assassin's throat. He waited to see if anyone else came through the window, then looked to see how the others fared.

A gust of wind must have blown the curtains around, for Madin's bolt had pinned their man to the drapes, partially concealing him. Varth and Ead had also slashed him across the chest, cutting drapes and assassin. Blood flowed freely from both sword wounds. Wide-eyed, the man poised in the air a brief moment before his weight finished shredding the ruined curtains. Varth finished him off as Jolin had the other intruder, while Ead kept an eye out for anyone following.

Jolin signalled everyone to stand aside. Madin had already reloaded his crossbow. Ors and Keev appeared in the doorway. Jolin waved them back.

A cool wind tossed the torn remnants of the dark blue velvet curtains, but no one else ventured through the windows. Rather than stick his head out to check, Jolin used his sword. The only resistance he met was a loose rope. No one clung to it.

One thing his Da had drilled into his head, if you're going to bother starting a job, might as well finish it. Jolin reached up and grabbed the rope, slicing it off as high as he could without risking his neck, then indicated Ead should to do the same. If any of the other assassins had planned this as an escape route, it would be a long drop to the courtyard. Jolin wiped his blade clean on the assassin he'd helped kill. He signalled the others to move the bodies out of the way, listened for any unusual noise from the windows, then joined the others in the sitting room.

"When I saw no guards outside your door," Ors was saying to Lord Cenith. "I feared the worst."

Jolin set his sword against the back of Lord Cenith's chair and picked up the blanket from the floor. He covered Lady Tyrsa with it. The windows couldn't be closed now and the torn drapes would do little to hold back the cool night air.

Lord Cenith mouthed a thank you. "Daric took the guards with him," he explained to Ors. "I don't hear any signs of battle. How many can there be?"

"Don't let that fool you, My Lord," Ors said, heading for the door. "There's bodies all over the place out there, all ours. The guards outside the treasure room are dead and all the ones on the servant stairs. More are lying in the hallways. I haven't taken the time to check, but I suspect we've lost that parchment."

Jolin retrieved his sword. "Buckam saw five come through th' kitchen, sir. Two more came in Councillor Daric's windows, and with these two…" He aimed his thumb at the bedroom. "…that would be at least nine."

Ors shook his head. "There could easily be twice that many. At least I know you two are safe," he said to Lord Cenith. "And I'm glad you look before you skewer, Keev." The Companion gave him a nod. "I'm going to rouse half the guard in the south barracks. We need more numbers, but I don't want everybody tripping over themselves. With luck, I'll run into Daric." He gave Lord Cenith a quick bow and left.

Both outside barracks held a thousand men each. Even with half the south barracks, it would give them a better chance of pinning the assassins down.

Jolin took a moment to scan what Lady Tyrsa had drawn on the hearth. "Is this important, m'lord?"

"Tyrsa seemed to think so." Lord Cenith shrugged. "We simply don't know."

Jolin didn't recognize the symbol above those of the gods, but he did know the two on the far sides. He pointed to them. "I ain't seen those signs since I left home."

Lord Cenith's head jerked up. "They're the only ones we didn't know." He indicated Jolin should sit in the other chair.

Jolin perched on the edge, resting his arms on his knees. "The cup there, that's for th' pixies, fairies, and brownies, so's they don't make mischief while yer sleepin'."

Lord Cenith frowned. "Pixies, fairies, and brownies? Those are just stories, for children." He looked around at the other men in the room. All but Keev gave him lost looks.

Jolin chuckled to himself. *City boys. Don't know what they think they know.* Keev knew, as did Madin and Jayce. They also came from mountain villages, though not so far as Jolin's home.

"Nay, m'lord. If ye don't leave a bit o' milk or somethin' for them at night, expect trouble. I've seen it. Yer cow will dry up, things will go missin', perfectly good tools will break for no reason…" Jolin shrugged. "Happens all th' time. So, we don't take no chances and we don't have no trouble."

Lord Cenith turned his frown to the hearth. "After what I've seen lately, I'm ready to believe almost anything." He pointed at the symbol on the right. "Other than it being a tree, what does that one mean?"

"It represents th' spirits o' th' forests and mountains, the dryads, naiads, trolls, and such." Jolin scratched the new scar on his cheek.

"Of course it does." Lord Cenith didn't sound convinced. "But why did she draw them?"

That one Jolin couldn't answer. After a few minutes, he stood. He should be back at his post, not gabbing with his lord. "I'll be in t' other room, m'lord, if ye need me."

Lord Cenith nodded, his gaze still on the drawings on the hearth.

* * * *

Trying to keep flat against the wall, Daric scanned the shadowed corridors of the first floor barracks. More than half of the first level of the keep, and all of the second, contained a warren of hallways leading to offices and quarters for the guards, officers, and staff. Searching them all proved frustrating at the least.

"There you are." Ors caught up to him near the main doors. Obviously Daric hadn't succeeded in keeping flat enough.

"I'm surprised to see you alone," Ors said. "I'd expected to find at least Kian with you."

"I thought it would be better to split up. I sent Kian to the north wing of the second floor with two of the guard, two came with me. I lost them both to those bloody throwing stars. At least one of those damned assassins is too good with them." Daric grimaced. "A coward's weapon used by someone too afraid of an honest fight." He waved his hand at a darkened doorway. "It's like chasing shadows. They're there, then gone. Won't face you like a man."

Ors grabbed Daric's right arm and plucked something from the thick padding on the back of his shoulder. "Almost lost you to one too."

Holding the flat center of the weapon between two fingers, the guard-commander passed the star to Daric. Razor sharp edges lined curved waves that could cut into a man with little effort. Both of the guards were hit in the neck, dead in mere moments. Daric had been in the lead when the coward struck from behind. Before he could react, the assassin had done his work and disappeared. He'd wondered why they'd left him alive. The bastard must have thought he'd killed him and hadn't waited around to make sure.

With one toss, Daric sent the star up to stick in the high ceiling. "One less of the thrice blasted things to kill my men."

"Have you been able to take any of them out?" Ors asked.

Daric snarled. "No. As I said, they're bloody cowards."

"Maybe they won't come near you, but they've been doing a spectacular job of slicing up the guard. Two came through Lord Cenith's bedroom windows. The Companions cut them down before they could say hello. At least our lord and lady are safe."

Daric nodded, silently blessing Jolin for his idea. "I'm going to..."

An alarm clanged in the court yard just as one of the main doors flew open. A tousle-haired lad wearing only small breeches gasped out his message. "The stable's on fire!"

"Cillain's blood and balls!" Daric clenched his teeth. Just what they needed.

"It'll clear both outside barracks," Ors said, heading for the doors, Daric right behind. "Only problem is, the guard will be prepared for fighting fire, not assassins. Let me take care of this. I'll get more soldiers for here. You..." He pointed to the wide-eyed boy still standing in the doorway, "...we have assassins in the keep. Go to the stable master and let him know I need some of the men."

The boy turned on his heel and disappeared into the darkness. Daric left Ors to his job and continued the sweep of the first floor, stepping over fallen guards, and scanning the shadows for anything that shouldn't be there.

Ors' voice carried loud and clear. "South Barracks guard! Regiments eleven to twenty! Arms and armour! Assassins in the keep!"

Chapter Twenty-One

...Let yourself fall...something so wonderful... Cenith's words pulled Tyrsa closer to the cliff she pictured in her mind; one she'd seen on the way to Tiras, steep, narrow, and guarded by a mountain. This time, instead of bright sunshine, soft, fluffy clouds lay around her, hiding the sky and what lay below. She stood on tiptoe, her arms spread like the wings of a bird.

Tyrsa's body ached, wanting, *needing* something. Something Cenith could give her. He said there'd be a little hurt, and there had been, gone as quick as it came. He was here, with her, yet he wasn't. She was alone, but she could feel him inside her; so strange, and yet, so right.

The sensation in her belly increased, warming to the point of heat, like the coals of a fire. It didn't feel so good anymore. Maybe she'd waited too long; maybe she should let herself fall now. Tyrsa bent her knees and jumped, pushing herself enough to clear the edge. She didn't go down. Something she couldn't see slammed into her, pinning her to the rock of the mountain looming above.

The heat intensified. It burned. Tyrsa heard someone screaming. *Is that me?* It had to be; she was the only one here. She looked down at her naked body. Her feet didn't touch the ground. Nothing held her against the rock, and yet she couldn't move. Tyrsa tried to kick, to pull herself off. She could do nothing. Worse, she could no longer feel Cenith inside her and that made her feel very alone.

The burning grew, spreading inside and out. It glowed white. She glowed white. Tyrsa watched it spread, up her tummy, down her legs still tucked together from her attempted jump. The glow reached her chest, flowed down her outstretched arms. Somewhere in the distance, the screaming continued.

Child. It is time. A voice sounded in her head. No. Two voices. One a man, the other a woman. They spoke the words together.

Tyrsa tried to talk back to them, but all that came out were more screams.

You have hurt worse than this, the voices said. *You can make the pain go away. You must learn to control it, or it will control you.*

Once again the memory of hurt flooded through her—loneliness, the beatings, Varth's and Cenith's hurts, the fight with the woman who wanted to take Cenith from her. The voices were right; this hurt was less. She stopped screaming. Now she just had to figure out how to stop the hurt.

Concentrate, the voices urged.

That wasn't much help. Maybe trying to control her body would work. Sometimes, after he'd hurt her, she could make the hurt less by concentrating on moving her hands and feet because they didn't hurt. They hurt now, everything did, but it was a place to start.

Tyrsa forced her fingers to curl into fists. They obeyed her and the hurt left them. She squeezed her hands tight together, harder, until her hands shook with effort. The pain fled up her arms to her shoulders, but the glow stayed. She needed to rest. Her arms fell limp, her hands relaxed.

Pain flared anew down her arms and she had to clench her fists once more. The hurt went away again, reluctant, angry at being forced to obey. Tyrsa realized she couldn't stop, she couldn't rest. She held her arms out in front of her and clasped her hands together, pushing the hurt from her head, her neck, and into her chest. Breathing grew difficult. She sucked in air. So tired! But she couldn't quit. Not now. The deeper she breathed, the farther down the pain went until it reached her belly. There it stayed, refusing to move.

Her feet. Maybe she could free her feet. Directing her concentration down, she clasped her hands tighter, willing the pain to leave her toes. As it did, she curled and flexed them, driving the hurt up into her calves, to her knees. Without giving up what she'd won, Tyrsa sucked in three deep breaths and dragged the pain back to her belly, where it had begun. It writhed and twisted, seeking escape. It burned, and hated, and hurt!

Take it out, the voices said. *You can do this.*

Tyrsa unclasped her hands and touched her fingers to her belly. She pushed, and her fingers disappeared inside. Strange that she couldn't feel her hands inside her belly, only the hurt, hot and pulsing. Stranger still, that she could do it at all. Keeping a good hold of the thing she found in her belly, she pulled it out. Still pinned to the rock, she sagged in relief. The thing no longer hurt her, though she could feel its pain, its anger, and its need to be back inside her.

No bigger than the palm of her hand, it looked like a ball, a toy the children at the station played with. She still glowed white, but this glowed red. That didn't feel right. "What is it?"

It is you, child, the voices said. *It is your power…that which makes you what you need to be.*

"Why is it so angry?"

Because you have suffered. You were hurt by one who should have sheltered and protected you. This was not intended. Even to such as us, things can go wrong.

Tyrsa remembered all the lonely times when no one would come when she cried. When she hurt and no one cared. She caressed the ball, like she would a cat. It quivered in her hands, threatening to spread once more. "How can I fix it?"

There is only one cure, and you have been learning it ever since Cenith took you away from Saulth.

Cenith. "He should be here with me."

He is.

One of the clouds in front of her shifted. Tyrsa looked down and saw herself cradled in Cenith's arms. He sat on the floor of their bedroom in the new place. Home, Cenith called it.

This cliff, this mountain, is in your mind. It is interesting that you chose this particular place. Do you recognize it?

"Yes, this is where I touched the rock and it was sad. Why is it sad?"

All will come in its own time. First, you must control your power, for if you let it control you, all is lost.

Tyrsa looked at the cloud again, and Cenith. He was sad and afraid. It made her hurt inside to see him that way. She liked him so much. Much more than the other people she'd met since leaving her room, though they were nice too. Then a word came to her. An important word. One she'd heard when the woman tried to take Cenith from her. She'd forgotten it. *Love.*

Images filled her head; Rani holding her on her lap, humming to her as she fell asleep; the times she held Baybee tight because she needed someone to hold on to in the dark, to know she wasn't alone; the mothers at the station hugging their children, making sure they were safe and warm and had lots to eat; the men who protected Cenith. They'd been upset when they thought the woman was going to take him. Now they wanted to protect her too.

Cenith himself; not letting the guard take her, even though he didn't know her, or anything about her; sheltering her with his body when the bad winds came; holding her hand, smiling; the kisses and the sharing of their bodies. It wasn't just their bodies they shared; somehow, they shared their hearts too.

She knew now that love had many forms. The love she felt for Cenith was the best love of all. Her heart warmed, but there was still the pain she held in her hands.

Tyrsa concentrated once more, transferring her love for Cenith to the angry ball. Another ball drifted out of her chest to blend with the one in her hands; this one bigger and bright white. She caressed them both, joining them into one, soothing them as she'd seen a mother at the station do when her child had cut himself.

The balls melded, one into the other, turning pink, then fading to white as she pushed the hurts into the deepest part of her memory, to remain there, for they could never be truly forgotten. The glowing white light in her hand sang to her. There were no words, only joy. Tyrsa pushed the ball back into her belly where it belonged, the center of her being, all that she was. She felt…complete.

Well done, child. The voices sounded very pleased.

"When can I come down off this rock?" Tyrsa asked, wiggling the toes of her still dangling feet.

Whenever you wish. You have control now.

With a mere thought, Tyrsa drifted down to stand on the narrow path. She looked at the cloud that showed her and Cenith. Daric and Elessa were there now. They moved her to the other room and Cenith held her wrapped in a blanket. He looked so worried, she wanted to hold him and tell him she was all right.

Not yet. There is still much to be learned.

Tyrsa looked at her hands. The glow faded, as did the one around the Tyrsa Cenith held. She watched herself sit up.

"Why are my eyes different there?"

It is a manifestation of your power. The Tyrsa you see in the cloud is a part of that manifestation. She will be with you from now on, a gift from us, to help you when you need it. She is what you should have been, but, once you leave here, she will only exist in your head. She does not have a body of her own.

The Tyrsa in the cloud climbed off Cenith's lap and spread ashes on the hearth.

"She is using my body?" Tyrsa didn't have the words for how strange this all was. "Will I get it back?"

Yes, she is only there to help you. Be patient, child. We will show you. Watch yourself and learn.

Her other self in the cloud made pictures in the ashes, but not the ones Tyrsa usually drew. As the symbols emerged, the voices explained what they were, who they represented. Then came the stories, the beginning, the between times, and the ending, which turned out not to be an ending so much as a number of different possible beginnings.

Tyrsa learned much from the voices. The truth of many things; things that had been long forgotten, others that may or may not happen in the days to come, and the most frightening of all—War. This terrible thing could destroy all she'd come to love. Tyrsa cried and the hurt threatened to return. She forced it back.

"What can I do to stop this?" Tyrsa asked the voices, for she knew it had to be stopped.

We cannot tell you. It is up to you to find a way. The choice, the decision, and what you do with it, is yours. It is why you are, though you are not what you were meant to be. The sadness in the voices made her want to cry again. *You must leave soon. Be warned. You will forget much of what you have learned here.*

That seemed quite unfair. "Why must I forget? Why tell me all this if I can't use it?"

It is too much at once for your true mind to handle. You would go insane, and that would be worse than disaster, for you have the power to save Ardael, or to destroy it. You will remember what you need to, when you need to. It is the only way. The scroll will help you.

The scroll. She knew what it said now. "I will forget it too?"

Yes.

Tyrsa sat on the narrow path, her feet dangling over the side of the cliff, watching herself rock back and forth on the hearth. She could see into the past, the present, and the future, and all the possibilities it held, both wonderful and tragic. Holding out her hand to the cloud, she centered her thoughts on her belly, her power, channelling it.

What are you doing, child? The voices now sounded concerned.

"There's something I need to do. Before I forget."

Making changes here is not a good idea. They do not always work as planned. Some things could turn out far worse than you can imagine. You could alter what is meant to be.

"You said this was my choice, my decision. That means I'll be altering things anyway," Tyrsa argued.

We do not agree with this.

"I understand." She sent a thought to the Tyrsa on the hearth, who looked at Jolin crouched between Cenith and Daric. It bothered her that he loved her as much as Cenith did, for she couldn't return that kind of love to Jolin, even though she liked him very much. Maybe it was a good thing she'd forget. She risked a peek into his future, and smiled. Someone waited for him. She could be content with that.

The two Tyrsas spoke the words together. "Twelve. I need twelve."

"Twelve what, m'lady?" Tyrsa heard Jolin's response through her other ears, the ones in the same room as him.

"Companions."

"We kin pick another tomorrow, m'lady."

"No. Buckam. Buckam's heart is true." It was done.

Tyrsa didn't wait for his response, already much of what she'd learned faded from her memory. She stood and stumbled, far more tired than she thought. It was time to go home.

We hope you have made a wise decision, child. Regardless, know that we watch over you. It is little comfort, we know, but it is all we can offer.

"I understand."

Tyrsa stared down into the depths below her, the clouds, the trees, the piles of snow now visible. She sighed. "I didn't get to fall off Cenith's cliff. He said it would be the most wonderful thing I have ever experienced."

You will, child. Soon. Humour coloured the voices. Love softened them. *Now that you have control, we will not bring you here again.*

Something caressed her left cheek, tender and gentle. A hand, though she couldn't see it. Another touched her other cheek, this one rougher, more firm, yet no less gentle. The loving touch of a mother? A father? The way it was supposed to be?

Tyrsa closed her eyes, enjoying the brief show of affection. When she opened them, she saw Cenith, standing, eager to come to her. Past and future memories, not all her own, whirled together, blurred, then faded to one need—Cenith's arms around her. She pushed him back into the chair, climbed onto his lap, kissed him, and fell asleep.

* * * *

Artan wiped his knife on the dead man's small breeches. He stripped out of his black clothes, hid them under the bed, and rummaged through the clothespress for pants and a shirt. The man lay sprawled on the bed where Artan had dumped him, his dead eyes adding to the shocked look on his face. *That's what you get for your nosiness, idiot.*

The man, a servant Artan assumed, had been standing outside his door, peering down the gloomy hallway. A clash of steel sounded from that direction, distracting him. So much for Snake's wish to be quiet. Artan had wasted no time applying a quick knife thrust under the man's ear. He needed a disguise, and fast. Using a dead guard's uniform was out, too much blood. His cohorts were efficient, but rarely neat.

Ice and Sting had taken out the treasure room guards with throwing knives, quick and quiet, then disappeared on their quest for Daric, leaving Artan to locate the parchment. After a long search, he found it lying flat on a high shelf, covered with other papers. He had to stand on a pile of sacks to reach it. When one of those sacks broke open, he couldn't resist stuffing his pockets with some of the gold glittering through the tear.

Artan had then made his way back to the kitchen to find the room no longer empty. A young man, holding a butcher knife, moved from the middle of the room to somewhere out of sight on the right. He looked a mere kitchen boy, but the way he flipped and played with the knife as he walked showed he knew how to use it.

Artan had no stars and no sword, only his dagger, with no clear line of sight to throw it. He might win the fight. Artan knew he was good, and he had the advantage of surprise. He could walk right up to the man and take him out before he knew what happened. Or, he could wait to see if he came into view again; he'd only need one throw. How lucky did he feel? How long could he wait? Someone else could come at anytime.

He patted the precious lump hidden under his black shirt. His job was to grab the parchment and run for safety. If he blew that, Snake would have his balls on a thong around his neck. Artan decided he couldn't take the chance. The only safe way lay in sneaking out of the keep. He'd crept back up the stairs to the second floor, darting from door to door, hoping to find one unlocked. Instead, he found a man with a terminal case of curiosity.

Artan transferred the stolen gold to the pockets of the dark brown pants, wrapping the coins in cloth to stop them from clinking. The parchment he shoved between his skin and the shirt. He grabbed a long sleeved, woollen tunic from a peg on the wall and put it on. He set his ear against the door. Nothing nearby.

No longer identifiable as an assassin, Artan now had freedom to move, just another stupid servant out where he shouldn't be. Shouts and screams sounded from the direction of the main stairs. He ducked back to the ones he'd come up, once more stepping over the bodies of the guards Ice and Sting had killed. He walked past the kitchen door as if someone might leap out at him.

"I would get out of here if I were you," said a voice from the kitchen. The same young man who'd been there earlier appeared in the doorway. He spoke like a Bredun noble. Odd.

Artan jumped at his words, keeping to his role of frightened servant. "Wha…what's going on? There's dead guards and people fighting everywhere!"

"Assassins. You should leave or lock yourself in somewhere." The boy frowned, taking in his clothing. "What are you doing up this late anyway?"

Artan thought fast. "Visiting. My girl, that is. I could ask the same of you."

"Working late." The lad flipped the knife, catching it by the tip, then balanced it on the end of his finger. "Maybe you should go back to your girl and lock the door. Safer there." He tossed the knife again, catching it by the hilt, and pointed the sharp end at Artan.

Perhaps he'd made the right decision after all. Artan shook his head. "If my father finds out I'm gone, I'm dead anyway, and I think an assassin would do a faster job of it. I'll take my chances."

The kitchen boy laughed. "Well, may Aja roll his dice in your favour."

"Thanks." Artan nodded and almost ran down the corridor.

Once out of sight of the kitchen, he slowed to a walk, keeping his eyes and ears open for trouble. Twice he ducked into an empty room to avoid Dunvalos Reach guards; it was easier than talking his way past them. Artan maneuvered through the hallways until he reached the end of the corridor leading to the main doors. Voices sounded from the direction he needed to go.

Relying on the gloom to keep him hidden, Artan risked a peek around the corner. Two older Dunvalos Reach guards stood not far from the doors. Judging by his size, one of them had to be Daric, very much alive. Either Ice and Sting were dead, or Daric hadn't been in his rooms when they attacked. Artan hoped it was the latter and the two assassins had yet to run across him. He'd hate to lose his share of that two hundred gold.

Judging by his shoulder pins, the other man had be the guard-commander. He couldn't make out what they were saying, but whatever it was, he wished they'd leave and discuss it elsewhere. Daric tossed something in the air. It didn't come down again. Artan jumped as a loud clanging sounded from outside. One of the main doors slammed open, admitting a panic-stricken boy.

"The stable's on fire!"

That must be Snake's diversion.

The boy ran back outside. The guard-commander followed a moment later, while Daric, sword in hand, headed down the corridor, away from Artan. He whispered a thank you to Aja and a prayer to Shival to aid in his escape.

Despite the noise outside, the guard-commander's words came back loud and clear. "South Barracks guard! Regiments eleven to twenty! Arms and armour! Assassins in the keep!"

So much for the diversion. Artan sincerely hoped the others could finish up quickly and get out, though it looked like Daric might be a problem, and not just for Ice and Sting. The big man crept down the hallway, forcing Artan to duck into the shadows as he moved closer to the doors. He had get out fast, the hallway he stood in would soon be filled with armed guards. Artan was sure he could talk his way out, but he'd rather not.

Keeping an eye on Daric, Artan crossed to the other side of the hall, ducking behind an old suit of armour. Now he stood on the same side as the doors. Daric's shape became a shadow briefly outlined by a lit wall sconce. A moment later, he disappeared. Artan strode purposefully to the main doors, and out. A quick walk to the gates and he'd be free of the keep.

A rough hand grabbed his collar and hauled him around. Artan looked up into the biggest nose he'd ever seen. Bulbous and red, with dark hairs begging to escape, it dominated the man's face. Artan's heart leapt against his breastbone. His palms grew sticky with sweat.

I'm caught! But how could he have known?

"Where do you think you're going?" The man twisted his grip and Artan now faced the burning stable. "Fire's this way."

Forced to walk with the man, Artan stumbled his way to the end of a line of people.

"You work here until told otherwise." Big Nose shook him for emphasis, then stomped off to 'recruit' someone else.

An older man ran up behind him and shoved a bucket of water in his hands. Artan stared at it. *I can't stay here! I have to get out!*

"Pass the bucket, you idiot!" The nasal voice came from in front of him.

Artan passed the bucket. *Now what do I do?*

* * * *

Ors stood to the right of the main door to the south barracks. Armed soldiers poured out while he studied the keep and the nearby stable roof, blazing merrily away. *Just how did those bastards get in?* The two assassins the Companions had killed could only have reached the roof from inside. His gaze strayed to the parapets, high above, following the familiar lines, until he spotted an odd configuration that shouldn't be there. Ors squinted and the shape resolved itself into three shadowy figures. From where they stood, it wouldn't be far to toss a torch to the stable roof.

He grabbed the arm of the next guard out the barracks door. "Quin, get two crossbows and extra bolts. Now!"

The young guard returned in moments, giving Ors one of the weapons and a quiver of bolts. In seconds, both were loaded. "Follow me."

They joined the soldiers heading for the keep. "There's three of them up on the walk, between the second and third merlons. I don't see our guards up there." He clenched his teeth. "I have to assume they're dead. I'm guessing these fellows are the ones who started the fire, stopping to admire their work. I doubt they realize their little blaze has lit them up like harvest lanterns."

When Ors judged them close enough, he took aim. "You can have the fellow on the right, the left is mine. See if we can reload fast enough to drop the middle one."

Two bolts shot through the air, both right on target. Two bodies spun with the impact, but by the time Ors and Quin reloaded, the third had vanished.

"Aja's blasted luck!" Ors cleared his throat and spat. "Let's go see what we did." Keeping the crossbows, they ran for the keep doors.

Chapter Twenty-Two

The sudden influx of guard interrupted Daric's sweep, forcing him to direct soldiers to various floors and wings. Finally, he appointed a young lieutenant to take over and headed for the servant stairs to do his hunting alone. Here, away from the fighting, he found two dead guards, one sprawled at the foot of the stairs, the other part way down. He also found silence, until a creak from somewhere above stopped him cold.

Ducking into the last doorway before the stairs, Daric made himself as thin as possible, not an easy job given his size. A shadowy figure in black crept down the stairs, a sword in his hand.

Ten feet separated them. As the assassin's foot touched the bottom step, Daric leapt from the doorway. The man's blade flashed up. The Calleni great sword caught the hilt of the assassin's weapon, ripping it from the man's grip. The sword flew up and over the intruder's head, landing somewhere in the darkness of the staircase.

Daric swung his sword back, trying for the man's knees. His foe eluded him by leaping to an amazing height, tucking in his legs and flipping over both the sword and the body of the guard. He hit the ground running, straight for the kitchen. Daric didn't hesitate to follow. The man was fast, but that didn't matter. *Why is he heading for the kitchen? There's no way out there.* Worse case would be having to search the storage rooms for him.

A clang and a thud brought Daric to a skidding halt in the doorway. In the middle of the kitchen stood Buckam with a pot in his left hand, a butcher knife in his right, and a surprised look on his face. The assassin lay flat on his back, out cold.

"He was not one of ours, sir." Buckam's wide-eyed stare almost made Daric laugh.

"You did great, son." Daric strode into the room and crouched by the unconscious intruder. He removed the cloth hiding the man's features. Buckam had nailed him square on the forehead. "I'm surprised you got him with the pot instead of the knife."

"I am mostly left-handed sir. I was about to put the pot away when I heard him and reacted without thinking." Buckam looped a ring on the handle of the utensil over a hook hanging from the ceiling. The pot clanged against the others beside it. "I do not think anyone will notice the extra dent."

Daric chuckled. "This one might. He's going to have a lovely lump. It's the least he deserves. Any rope around?" He hadn't even dared dream about capturing one of them.

"There might be some binder twine from the flour sacks."

"That'll have to do."

Buckam disappeared into the scullery. While the young man rummaged through drawers, Daric studied the unconscious man; he wasn't pretty. Scars crisscrossed his lean face, contorting his features into a grotesque mask. His once brown hair had turned almost grey, which Daric found surprising given the man's agility; but then, he'd have to be agile to stay alive as long as he had.

"Is this enough?" Buckam dumped a pile of twine of varying lengths and thicknesses near the assassin's head.

"I hope so. We'll strip him down to his small breeches," Daric said. "I don't want him coming up with any surprises."

A complete search of the man's clothes revealed no weapons; which explained why he ran once he'd lost his sword. By tying pieces of thick twine together, Daric came up with enough to truss the fellow up like a goose at Twelfth Month Festival. They put him on the floor of the closest storage room. Daric bolted the door, then jammed one of his many daggers through the mechanism, just to be sure.

"Would you like me to watch for any more, sir?" Buckam asked, once they'd returned to the kitchen.

Tyrsa's words came back to Daric. *Buckam's heart is true.* It appeared she was right. The former Bredun guard had to know who ordered the assassins here and yet twice he'd helped them, not Saulth. Daric shook his head and leaned against the counter, taking the chance for a brief rest. "I don't understand why this one ran here. There's no way out."

"They came from back there." Buckam pointed to the rear door. "But I have only seen storage rooms."

"I'm assuming that's where they hid until they were ready, but they had to have come in some other way." Daric folded his arms across his chest. *But how?* He'd go over every inch of this keep if he had to...later. "Want to prove yourself?" Buckam nodded. "Find a weapon and come with me. There's more of those snakes out there."

Buckam grabbed the large kitchen knife he'd held earlier, a determined look on his face. Despite his youth, he acted like he actually might know how to use it.

"Good enough until you can find something better." Daric pushed himself away from the counter.

"Just a moment, sir." Buckam rooted through the assassins clothing, putting on the long, black shirt. A dark cloth concealed his blonde hair. "It will help hide me in the shadows," he explained.

Daric nodded, then led Buckam back to the servant stairs in time to see Ors and Quin come down them. They both carried crossbows as well as their swords.

Ors explained their limited success. "One died instantly, the other we had to help along. Too bad we missed the third."

"I think Buckam nailed him. He's tucked away in a storage room, nice and tight," Daric said.

Ors' already lined forehead crinkled in surprise. "He's alive?" At Daric's nod, he added, "Well, well. That's an unplanned bonus."

"To my count, that makes four dead, one captured, and Cillain knows how many still skulking around." Daric blew out a slow, exhausted breath. It had been a long, tense night, and morning lay not far away. "You carry on to the third floor, I'm heading for the second. Kian should be somewhere up there."

Ors nodded and led the way up the narrow stairs, stepping around the bodies lying there. Nothing they could do about them right now. Daric and Buckam turned off at the second floor. Daric gave up trying to stay flat against the wall. A few glances behind showed Buckam had great success in disappearing into the shadowy doorways.

Daric's long strides took him quickly down the corridor. The bodies of too many Dunvalos Reach guards littered his path. Blood pooled on the floor and spattered the walls. Two men lay, one across another, in the middle of the hall. He recognized them as the two guards Kian had taken with him. The hairs on Daric's arms and neck stood up. Fear stabbed his heart.

He stepped over them, taking two more strides, then, acting purely on instinct, dodged the blade that cut the air in front of him. A man leapt out of the darkness behind the open door. Dressed all in black and carrying two long knives, he pressed in with a flurry of steel, forcing Daric to retreat. Assassins tended to be lean and of average height. The one before him could easily match Cenith for size.

Daric stepped back to avoid yet another blow, then swung his own sword in a move that should have taken the man's head off. Instead, the assassin bent backwards, his spine as supple as the viper he was, and ducked under the blow. *Another agile asshole!* That was all the thought Daric had time for as the assassin came up inside his guard.

Daric dropped his now useless sword and chopped, bare-handed, at the wrist holding the blade nearest him, blocking a blow to his face. An instant later, he did the same to the other, barely avoiding a thrust that would have disembowelled him. Daric took another step back. He dodged a sideways jab at his chest from the right knife, then pretended to take a hit on his wrist from the one on the left.

The assassin struck for the advantage, but Daric twisted his body, avoiding the blow, and grabbed the intruder's right wrist. He bent his arm so the man now found his own weapon aimed back at him. The assassin tried to thrust with his other blade, but Daric was able to get a grip over the crossguard and force it back far enough to keep it from running him through. Blood welled between his fingers, making the metal slippery.

Daric grappled with all his strength, but the night had been long and tiring and this man proved strong. The soft slide of a foot on carpet dragged his attention behind him, but he didn't dare take his eyes off the assassin in front. *Buckam?* Daric had left him somewhere behind. *What is that boy doing? A little help would be appreciated.* His skin crawled.

He kept his ears on what occurred behind, his eyes on the bold, confident, icy ones of the assassin he fought. Daric shifted his weight to his left leg and hooked his right around the assassin's left, forcing him to the ground. Daric had to use caution and not bring his weight to bear. He'd end up skewering himself as well as his opponent. The assassin had his knife pricking the padding over Daric's stomach, while the one Daric controlled almost touched the man's right breast; an impasse.

The hair on the back of Daric's neck rose and his skin prickled as another half-heard sound from behind alerted him all was not right there. *Buckam! What in Cillain's name are you doing!* Could Tyrsa have been wrong? Could Buckam be readying himself even now to stab him in the back?

Cold fury washed over Daric. *I trusted him! I trusted her!* He cursed himself for an old fool, but there was nothing he could do except wait for the inevitable. His brow broke out in a sweat. *Damn, this bastard is tough!*

Something fell beside them; a black clad body. Daric couldn't take his eyes off the man he fought, but his peripheral vision showed a butcher knife jutting out from under the right ribcage of the man beside him. A hand removed it and a familiar covered head flashed nearby.

Daric drew on every scrap of strength he had left. For an instant, the ice blue eyes of the assassin glanced at the body near them. Now, for the first time, worry creased those eyes. Anchoring one foot, Daric twisted his entire body. The change in tactics was enough to lift his assailant's left side off the ground.

Buckam dove in, stabbed the assassin in the lower back, and disappeared just as quick. Taking advantage of the assassin's shock and sudden weakness, Daric shoved the blade he controlled deep into the man's lung, then sideways until he hit the heart. Blood spurted, coating both Daric and the assassin. Icy eyes glazed, then dulled, and the man collapsed without a sound, leaving Daric holding both weapons.

An instant later, a stabbing pain shot through Daric's right thigh. Without a thought, he slashed back with one of the knives, slicing into the neck of whoever had struck him, adding more blood to that of the assassin Daric had killed. Daric wiped the mess from his eyes with his sleeve. The man who stabbed him was the one Buckam had taken with the butcher knife.

"Sorry I did not get here sooner, sir," Buckam said, crouching by the man he'd wounded. "This one came out of a room behind you. I almost did not catch him in time."

"Thank you, Buckam, I sincerely appreciate that. Hold these." Daric passed him the assassin's long knives. He gritted his teeth and pulled the small knife out of his thigh. "Just one thing…"

"Yes, sir?"

Daric stuck the knife in its owner's blood-covered chest. "Always finish your man."

"Yes, sir. Sorry, sir. I thought he was unconscious. How bad is your wound?" Buckam set the blades aside, taking care how he placed them, and tore several strips off the tunic he wore under the black shirt. "I am afraid these are not terribly clean, sir."

"Better than nothing." Daric leaned against the wall, catching his breath before inspecting the cut. "Fortunately it was a small knife, just hit flesh." He took the offered bandages and tied one securely around his thigh. The cuts on his right hand weren't as bad as he'd thought. Painful, but he could still use his fingers.

While Daric worked on his wounds, Buckam kept staring at the man he'd stabbed. "This your first battle?" Daric asked.

Buckam nodded. Though he didn't look green or vomit the way some men did, he didn't appear comfortable with the idea either.

"Don't let it get to you. I doubt this will be the last time you'll have to skewer someone. Just remember, he was an evil man who killed on a whim. The world's better off without him."

"Yes, sir. I always knew it would happen one day. I guess I am just a little surprised at how easy it was." Buckam picked up the two blades and wiped them clean on the assassin. He then sat cross-legged and laid them across his knees, his fingers caressing, yet not quite touching, the deadly weapons.

"Like them?" Daric asked, winding another bandage around the cut fingers.

"Yes, sir. These are beauties. Whoever made them is a true craftsman." Buckam ran a careful touch along the edge of one. His finger came back with a fine bloody line across it. "They have been well taken care of."

"Keep them." Daric tossed a nod at their dead owner. "He doesn't need them anymore. But I recommend finding someone to teach you how to use those. You could end up taking your own head off."

"I will, sir. Thank you, sir." Buckam's grin lit up his face. "I have been practicing with blades since I was five. I kept playing with the cooking knives, so my father decided the only way to keep me from killing myself was to teach me to use them. I have never seen a pair like these, though." Setting the blades aside once more, he removed the harness the assassin had used to hold them and wiped it clean with part of the man's shirt. He put it on. "Too big, but I think I can alter it."

Daric used the last of the cloth to clean the blood from his face. He blew out a long breath, then laughed. At Buckam's curious look, he said,

"I finally get the opportunity to fight one of the vipers and I'm too tired to do a proper job of it." He sobered and studied the young man in front of him. "Thank you. Again. Keep going, Buckam, and before you know it, you'll have a position here to be envied." *And may Niafanna and Cillain both bless you. Tyrsa, I'm sorry I doubted you.*

Buckam actually blushed. "You are welcome, sir. How many more do you think there are?"

"That's anybody's guess." Daric held out his hand. "Help me up. I doubt we're done."

One good pull had Daric on his feet. The lad proved stronger than he looked. Daric tested his leg; it throbbed, but it would have to do.

"Perhaps not, sir, but you are."

Daric shot him his best training ground glare.

"Done in, I mean, sir." Buckam's words came out in a rush. "Are you sure you can carry on?"

"It's not a matter of can I, but that I have to. Another thing to remember, battles don't end just because you're tired." He wondered where Kian was.

"Yes, sir." Buckam passed Daric his sword.

A few turns in the corridor brought the sounds of battle close. Around the next corner, bodies lay everywhere, including one dressed in black, his head almost removed, sprawled between him and those involved in the fight. Two of them. His eyes focused just in time to see Kian make the mistake Daric had managed to avoid.

"Kian!"

Time slowed, though Daric tried to run faster, leaping over the body that lay between them. His wounded leg almost buckled beneath him. He forced it to hold. Blood pounded in his ears. The assassin dodged Kian's great sword, then stabbed a dagger into his son's sword wrist with his left hand. During Daric's next stride, the killer stepped past Kian's guard. An eternity later, the sword in the intruder's hand appeared, wet with blood, out of Kian's back.

"Kian! No!"

The assassin pushed Kian off his sword, but not in time to use it again. Daric's final stride brought him close enough to deliver a powerful blow, shearing the man's left arm off below the shoulder and lodging the great sword deep in his chest. Daric caught Kian's falling body. He collapsed to the floor, cradling his eldest.

"Kian!" Daric's voice sounded like a whispered croak. *My son! Niafanna, no! Not my son!* His world spun, twisting and turning, funnelling his vision until all he could see was Kian, his little boy with the laughing eyes and a grin that commanded his sweet face.

"Father, I..." Red froth bubbled from Kian's mouth. He swallowed, then coughed. "Mother, I...I'm sorry..."

Blood gushed from the wound in his son's chest. Daric could tell him all the useless things; 'Don't talk', 'It'll be all right', 'Help is coming'. All useless. There was no time. No time to take him to Tyrsa, even if she had the strength to heal him. The light in Kian's beautiful brown eyes dimmed. More blood trickled down his chin. There was only time for..."I love you, son"

"I love you...both." Another cough spilled bright red spittle. Fear flashed briefly in his fading eyes. From somewhere, Kian found the strength to grab Daric's collar. "Don't...don't let her take me, Father!"

"You shall rest with Niafanna. I swear it!"

With a last shuddering gasp, Kian's hand slid from Daric's neck, his arm falling across his ruined chest. He breathed one last long sigh and his sightless eyes rolled back in his head No more breath. No more words. No more laughter. Daric kissed Kian's eyes closed then gently pressed his forehead to his son's. The first tears he'd shed since the death of his mother washed down his cheeks. "Niafanna, Mother of us all, take my boy to your breast."

The children were products of both gods, his and Elessa's, but they'd left it up to each child as to who they worshipped. Barring Rade, who was too young, all had chosen Cillain and Niafanna. Shival should have no right to Kian's soul, and yet, Daric had doubts. Fears. Ardael wasn't his homeland. Other gods held sway here. Tyrsa had proven that.

"Niafanna, Giver of Life, Taker of Life. Protect him, teach him, guide him in his next life." Daric held Kian, whispering prayers over and over. He had to be sure. He had to keep his promise that Shival wouldn't take his son. She had no right to him! He rocked him, tears mingling with the blood on Kian's face. *How can I tell Elessa? Dearest Niafanna! How?*

Daric raised his head and forced his tears to stop. He tried to wipe away the blood but there was just too much. *Elessa can't see him like this. Not like this.*

Where Daric found the strength, he didn't know or question. He heaved the body of his son over his shoulder and limped to the baths, the farthest rooms of the west wing on the first level, a good place to hide him, for now. He wanted no one else to know of Kian's death until he had a chance to break the news to Elessa and their family. Only by sheer luck did he avoid running into anyone alive.

With Kian safely tucked away, he and Buckam continued the search for assassins. Just before dawn, with the castle cleared, they returned to the baths where they stripped and washed Kian's body, Daric repeating the prayers to ensure his son's safe arrival in Niafanna's arms. From somewhere, Buckam produced a litter and a blanket to cover the body. They carried Kian to his quarters, just another victim of a terrible night.

* * * *

Artan passed yet another bucket along the line. Sometime during the night more people had joined his row, completing the line from the well in the center of the large courtyard to the burning stable.

His hands bled and his arms ached, but Artan quickly realized that if he had to be stuck in the keep, standing in a line of anonymous people who were too busy and too tired to talk offered a strange sort of safety.

Another bucket found its way into his hands. Artan gave it to the man in front of him and wiped his brow on his tunic sleeve. He glanced at the sky, and blinked. The sun had risen, illuminating a cloudless sky, though it had not yet cleared the eastern mountains.

"That's it!" a loud voice shouted from somewhere near the stables. "The fire's out!"

Thank Shival! Artan sank to the ground, as did everyone around him. His entire body ached. He hunched over as much as he could and wiped his bleeding palms on his trousers. Artan felt through his clothing, checking the parchment still in its frame. Everything seemed intact, though it had rubbed against his skin, leaving the left side of his stomach raw. He moved it to the right.

"Thank you. All of you, from myself and his Lordship."

The voice came nearer. It was Big Nose, his face and bare arms blackened with smoke. He strode through the crowd like he owned the place, his fists pumping the air as if he'd just won a great battle. "Tables have been set up on the eastern side of the South Barracks. You're all invited to help yourself to breakfast."

A cheer went up from the townsfolk.

You're bloody welcome. Now let me out of here. Artan waited a few minutes to gather what strength he had left before dragging himself to his feet. His stomach growled. Maybe some food would be a good idea. All their supplies waited near the exit to the underground river. He'd have to take the round-about route to retrieve them.

As Artan walked across the compound, two guards came out of the main doors of the keep carrying a body wrapped in a blanket. They took great care and reverence in laying it on the ground next to another corpse. *Looks like the fighting's over inside.* Artan counted fifteen bodies, and more were being brought out. *The assassins must be making their way to the cave with the girl. They may even already be there.*

Another row of bodies lay near the wall of the keep. Artan's heart thudded. These bodies weren't covered with blankets and all wore dark clothing. He counted them. Seven. Artan moved closer. Even as he stared, horror dawning, another was brought and tossed carelessly beside the rest. One of the guards kicked the body, the other spat on him. It was Sting, with his throat slit. The face cloths had been removed, but Artan would have recognized them anyway.

Beside Sting lay Ice, without his long knives. Then Blade, with a crossbow bolt in his gut and his chest split open in two places. Slash also bore two sword wounds. Dagger and Ripper had been hit with crossbow bolts, though Dagger's throat had also been cut. Edge was missing most of one arm and his chest had been cut in half. Star's head had almost been cut off.

Artan couldn't take his eyes off them. They were his friends. Or, at least, the closest he could call friends. They were the best. The strongest. The most skilled. *How could they be dead?* It wasn't possible.

"Don't look so tough now, do they, boy?"

Artan looked up into the lean face of one of the guards who'd brought Sting out. He wanted to hit him; whip out his dagger, slice him up. His hands wouldn't move.

Snake! Where was Snake? "Is…is this all of them?" Artan forced himself to ask.

"Unless some escaped, this is it." The guard spun on his heel and strode back to the keep.

Snake made it out, he had to have. Artan wanted to throw up. All thoughts of breakfast fled. He forced himself to walk to the gate house; he wanted to run, but he didn't have the strength, nor did he want to attract attention. Snake should be on his way to the cave. Maybe he could tell Artan what happened. Did he have the girl? He doubted Ice and Sting had killed Daric.

Artan made his way down the long, winding road into Tiras, trying to figure out what had gone so terribly wrong.

* * * *

Cenith leaned against the window frame, clenching his fists until they hurt. He'd force them to relax, but it seemed mere moments before his fingernails dug into his palms again.

Kian's room offered a wonderful view of the blanket covered bodies laid out in rows in the courtyard. Even now guards informed their families.

Behind him, Daric tried to comfort his grief-stricken children. Tears flowed freely from all but Daric. Silence would reign, then a broken voice would mention something he or she loved about Kian, or something he'd done. Cenith remembered many of the stories. He'd been a part of them. Daric's family had been there most of the morning, except Elessa. Strong, imperturbable Elessa had been inconsolable. She now lay in a drug-induced sleep in a guarded room on the fourth floor.

Before Daric had come to break the news, Cenith had managed to snatch a couple hours sleep in the chair. It hadn't prepared him. Nothing could. His emotions raged from numb shock to blind anger, all too familiar from when his father died. He glanced back at his lifelong friend. Kian was asleep. Just asleep. He'd wake up any minute, laugh, and tease Cenith about how he'd fooled him, again.

No, not this time. What am I going to do without him? Kian had been his rock when he needed to lean, his ear when he had to talk. Daric listened, but Kian had truly understood him. *Maegden and Talueth! I miss him already!*

Tyrsa hadn't known Kian long enough to discover the wonderful person he was…had been. Cenith needed them to like each other. That would never happen now.

Tyrsa. His strange wife who still hadn't woken up. *Gods and goddesses! I hope no one blames her for this mess.* He didn't want to bother Daric with this right now, but he'd ask Ors to keep his ears open for rumours.

After hearing Daric's tragic news, Cenith had moved Tyrsa to his old rooms just down the hall. He couldn't handle her mysteriousness and Kian's loss all at once. The Companions had taken the news of Kian's death as hard as anyone.

Cenith hated to keep them on guard, yet they'd refused to let anyone else watch over Tyrsa. Especially Jolin. Tired to the bones, he had still tried to take the first shift. Cenith ordered him to bed and set up a rotation so they all could get some sleep. Even if there were more assassins in the castle, Tyrsa should be safe with four Companions on watch in the rooms and four regular guards outside, and it would allow him time to try to deal with this new tragedy.

Ors had caught up with him on the way to Kian's room. They'd lost twenty-six men, including Kian. Eight assassins killed, one captured, and the piece of scroll had been stolen along with an unknown amount of gold. Probably whatever the thief had been able to stuff into his pockets. Since the scroll wasn't found on any of the bodies, they had to assume at least one intruder escaped. Ors ordered a thorough, room-to-room search, in case he was still in the keep.

Movement brought him back to the tragedy at hand. At a signal from Daric, each child kissed Kian's brow, said a prayer in Calleni, and left the room. Avina and Jennica waited outside the door for the youngest twins, Chand and Chayne, to say their prayers, then took them away.

Daric sat in a chair by his son's bed, elbows on his knees. He'd washed and changed out of the blood covered uniform he'd worn earlier. The keep physician, Garun, had attended his wounds. It hadn't helped much; Cenith had never seen him look so old.

"There's a saying in Callenia." Cenith could hardly hear Daric's voice. "There is no word for one who has lost a child, for there is no pain so great, no loss so extreme, that one word would suffice."

Cenith moved beside him and placed his hand on Daric's shoulder. What could he say that would comfort him?

"I'll have to talk to Elessa about where to bury him," Daric said.

"He can have Father's bier in our burial cave. Kian is my friend. I can offer no less."

Daric gave him an odd look, sort of a cross between disbelief and surprise. "Not only is Kian not of your line, he's not of noble blood. What would people say?"

"That he was my friend and that I honour him. He deserves to be there, Daric. Unless there's something in your beliefs that would disallow it. Or if Elessa doesn't approve."

Daric shook his head. "None that I know of, and I doubt Elessa will refuse it. I don't know what to say, except, thank you."

"I'll have another bier built for Father, closer to my mother. We haven't even sent anyone out to retrieve him." That would have to be done soon, which forced Cenith to accept another fact. Life went on, no matter how much you hurt. It had continued after his father died, it would continue now.

A knock at the door stopped whatever Daric had to say. Ors stuck his head in. "Sorry to intrude, My Lord. We need to have a discussion. If you'd like us to go elsewhere…" This last was directed at Daric, who shook his head.

Cenith waved him in and Ors closed the door.

"I spoke with Bailen," Ors said, leaning against the door. "The stable is a total loss, but they were able to keep the fire away from the North Barracks. The keep wall is scorched, though that can be cleaned." He wiped his nose on his sleeve before folding his arms across his chest. "Two horses died, the others seem fine. They're in the training ground right now, but we can move them to the paddocks outside town later. Old Gavril's missing. He may have been sleeping in the loft again, or he may be drunk somewhere. We'll have to wait and see."

Cenith just nodded. The loss of two more horses hurt. As for Gavril, Cenith sent a prayer to Talueth and Maegden both that he'd found somewhere else to pass out last night.

"We discovered where the assassins were hiding," Ors continued. "The dungeon. The place was littered with their mess. They must have been there for a few days, waiting on your return." Ors scratched his balding head. "Still can't figure out how they got in. The kitchen's the only way through to there. They shouldn't have been able to sneak past the guards, even before we doubled them."

"Is that bastard still tied up in the storage room?" Daric asked, his voice as hard as the rock his face had become.

"All nice and uncomfortable. Would you like me to question him?"

"No. I want that honour. Make sure he has food and water. I want him strong enough to take a lot of punishment. Just give me a couple of days to deal with…this." Pain darkened Daric's eyes.

Cenith ached for Daric, and himself. *A couple of days? It's going to take me the rest of my life to find a way to deal with this.*

Ors nodded. "By the way, Buckam is still standing outside the door. Looks more than a little strange in that black shirt, work trousers, and muck in his hair. Not to mention those knives he's clutching like they were made of gold. I thought he was supposed to be working in the kitchen. Unarmed."

"Things have changed with our former Bredun guard," Daric said, his voice quieter than normal. He waved both of them closer. "He warned us of the intruders, captured one of them single-handed, saved my life, obeyed every order I gave him quickly and efficiently…" Daric let out a slow breath. "If he has deceit in his heart, he's hiding it damned deep. Everything he's done this night has thwarted Saulth, not helped him. I believe Lady Tyrsa is right, his heart is true."

"Do you think we should follow Tyrsa's wishes and make him a Companion?" Cenith asked. Judging by the shocked look on Ors face, he hadn't heard that part. "Tyrsa requested it."

Daric nodded. "Find someone to teach him how to use those knives. Apparently he already has some skill." Daric met the guard-commander's gaze. "Ors, I know this is your decision, but trust me on this. Or rather, trust your lady. Send the lad to the baths, then to bed. When he wakes, find him a uniform and kit and get him started right away."

Ors moved back to the door and put his hand on the knob. "Against my better judgement, I shall do as you request."

"Objection noted." Daric returned his gaze to his son's body before Ors had even opened the door.

"There's no sense in my hanging around here," Cenith said. "Nor should you. I'm going to check on Tyrsa."

"I don't want to leave him." Daric's next words came out as a whisper. "I can't."

"Elessa will wake soon." Cenith put a hand on Daric's shoulder. "She needs you more than he does. And you need sleep."

"You're right," Daric sighed. "I'm doing no good wallowing in self pity. I'll take your advice and join Elessa. Maybe I'll be able to find some sleep."

Cenith had nothing to say. He ushered Daric out the door with one last look at a friend, a brother, he could never replace.

Chapter Twenty-Three

Cenith stood silent at the foot of his bed while Laron adjusted the collar of his tunic. On typical mornings, he and his valet discussed the day's schedule, Laron's growing family, or any of a number of topics. Not this morning. One hour remained until noon, when they officially laid Kian to rest.

Two days had passed since the attack and Cenith's emotions still controlled him…anger, grief, and overwhelming helplessness. He could feel Laron's unease at the break in their normal routine, but Cenith couldn't help it.

He should talk to someone; he'd learned that after his father died. It wasn't good to hold in grief, but the only people Cenith felt comfortable speaking to about this were Kian and Daric. They'd always been there for him in times of trouble. Kian lay ready for burial, and Daric had hardly said two words to him since the morning of the tragedy. He had his own grief to deal with.

Cenith couldn't discuss this with Tyrsa, enigma that she was. Not only would she not understand, she remained unconscious in his old bed down the hall. He warred between concern for her, curiosity over just what had occurred, and relief that he didn't have to deal with it while grieving for Kian.

"That's got it, My Lord," Laron said, brushing a piece of fluff from his right sleeve.

Cenith had chosen to wear what was supposed to have been his wedding outfit, a black, short sleeved, fine velvet tunic, trimmed with silver, over a dove grey silk shirt. Black, light wool trousers, tucked into mid-calf leather boots, completed the ensemble. Cenith usually preferred to dress himself, but for occasions like this, Laron had a knack for making him look his best, as befitting his status as Lord of Dunvalos Reach.

Laron pulled a cloak out of the wardrobe. "The glaziers say the new windows should be ready in a week, My Lord."

Cenith just nodded at the valet's attempt to start a conversation. Boards covered the holes where his bedroom windows used to be. New drapes hid most of the boarding. The blood stained carpet had been removed and an old one lay in its place until a new one could be woven. The staff had worked night and day cleaning blood from the halls, though the carpets there would have to be replaced as well. One could almost pretend that nothing had happened. *Almost.*

"I'll pass on the cloak, Laron. It's a warm day." Cenith moved into the sitting room and took a chair by the cold fireplace, wanting only peace and quiet to reflect on what was to come.

Laron followed him. "Will there be anything else, My Lord? A glass of wine, perhaps?"

"Yes, please. Then that will be all."

Laron poured him a glass of the Cambrel, then quietly left. He couldn't have made a better choice for the mood Cenith was in.

Cenith sipped the wine, swirling it around his mouth. Tyrsa's drawings caught his eye. The servants had scrubbed the hearth several times, yet the pictures remained. Somehow, the ashes forming them had turned hard as stone, no amount of scrubbing or chipping could remove them. Cenith told them to stop trying. More of Tyrsa's strangeness.

Just as he lifted the glass to his lips for another sip, a commotion sounded down the hall. A familiar voice shrieked his name.

Cenith groaned. "Not now." Yet he couldn't help but be relived she'd finally woken up. He swallowed the rest of the wine in one gulp.

His door slammed open. Tyrsa dashed in, dressed only in an ivory nightgown, her eyes wide with panic. Jayce, Keev, Fallon, Dathan, and a harried looking maid followed. Cenith didn't bother standing up.

"Cenith!" Tyrsa ran to him and almost jumped onto his lap, clinging to him so hard he could barely breathe. "I couldn't find you! I was in a strange place. You weren't there!"

"Tyrsa..."

"There's a lot I have to tell you, but I don't remember it all. There was a cliff, and voices, and pain, and...I don't remember the rest."

"Tyrsa, you're not making any sense." Cenith tried to pull her arms away from his neck without hurting her. "Relax, please! Let me breathe!"

Chuckles sounded behind him.

"I don't suppose any of you know what she's talking about?" he asked, not letting his hopes rise.

"No, My Lord." Cenith recognized Fallan's voice. "Mara was trying to get some broth down her when My Lady woke up. She wouldn't talk to anyone but you."

"I was scared and I hurt." Tyrsa relaxed her grip, easing Cenith's breathing.

He realized she didn't have Baybee with her. Had he become more important than the doll? Cenith could only hope. "Do you hurt now?"

Tyrsa shook her head.

"Are you hungry?"

She had to be, after two days. "Yes."

"Mara, could you bring a tray, please? She's going to want more than just broth. Could you also find another girl to help? We're going to have to get her ready for the funeral and we've less than an hour left."

"Yes, My Lord." The door opened and closed.

"I'll git th' broth from t'other room," Jayce offered. "She kin git started on that." He left.

"Tyrsa, listen to me." Cenith pulled her arms from around his neck and took her face in his hands. "You've been asleep for two days."

Tyrsa's eyes almost popped out of her head. "Two days? That's a long time!" Days she now understood, months and years she still had trouble with.

"It is, but we can't worry about that right now, nor what happened the other night. We can discuss that later. Right now, you need to eat and get dressed. We have someplace to go."

"But I have to..."

"No, Tyrsa. It has to wait." Cenith kissed her forehead. "Please. This is too important. Kian is dead." Gods, that hurt to say! "Do you understand?"

By Tyrsa's puzzled look, he'd have to say she didn't.

"Kian has gone away, like I almost went away." Her look didn't change. Cenith closed his eyes. How do you explain 'dead' to someone who's never seen it before?

Tyrsa put her hand on Cenith's chest. When he opened his eyes, she said, "You hurt, in here." She looked at the Companions. "They do too."

"Yes, because Kian is gone."

"Then tell him to come back."

Oh, the painful innocence in those words! Cenith pulled her to him. *Gods! If only I could bring Kian back!* "I can't. It doesn't work that way." He pushed her away and took her by the shoulders. "Listen to me, Tyrsa. When Mara comes back, eat as fast as you can. The girls will help you get dressed and then you'll come with me. When we get where we're going, I want you to be quiet. No talking. No words. Understand?"

Tyrsa nodded, her eyes still wide. Jayce arrived with the broth and Tyrsa drank it down. When Mara returned with the tray and a girl named Nika, Tyrsa ate without a word. The only hitch occurred when she went into their bedroom to change.

"The windows! What happened to the windows!" Tyrsa flew out of the room in a panic. It took Cenith several minutes to calm her down.

She emerged from the bedroom shortly after wearing a dress of dark grey light-weight wool with sleeves that hugged her arms to the elbow then widened to hang to the level of her knees, revealing a deep blue lining and the tight fitting sleeves of an ivory coloured linen underdress. A belt of entwined silver leaves circled her narrow waist. The rounded neckline revealed just enough of the pretty bosom that lay beneath to intrigue, while the bodice fit her snug enough to hint at more. Black leather slippers completed her outfit. Her long, corn silk hair had been brushed until it shone. So black, it seemed to have blue highlights.

This was the first time Cenith had seen Tyrsa in a dress tailored specifically for her. The seamstresses must have worked long hours to have this dress ready now. He should be telling her how marvellous she looked, kissing her, wishing he could take her out of it. Cenith could say nothing. He felt nothing, except Kian's loss. He cared for her deeply, but it lay buried under grief. Tyrsa smiled. He wished he could return it, and that he didn't have to tell her to stop smiling.

Cenith took her hand and led her to the door. Fallan opened it and they entered the hallway to find it lined with the remainder of the Companions. Dressed in their uniforms of midnight blue and silver, they each gave the couple a bow as they passed, then fell in behind in two rows.

He and Tyrsa walked down the main stairs to the second floor and along the hallway to the Grand Staircase. Six feet wide at the top, it curved out and down to twelve feet at the bottom. Ornate oaken banisters lined the sides. Made entirely of grey and white veined stone, it commanded the right side of the Great Hall, the room where banquets and council meetings were held.

Two fireplaces, both lit with small fires took up most of the flanking walls. Tables sat in rows near them, ready for the guests when the funeral ended. Cenith couldn't even think about eating, nor could he blame it on the butterflies that had plagued him in Edara. His gut just felt dead.

Cenith led Tyrsa and the Companions out the double oak doors, into the wide hall. There he stopped and bent down to speak to his wife. Though she hadn't said one word, he needed to remind her. "You have to be quiet now, do you understand? You can't say anything until I tell you."

Tyrsa nodded, her pixie-face confused. He squeezed her hand before leading her out the main doors. Murmuring people filled the sun-bright courtyard; soldiers, the dukes who could travel here in time, local noblemen and their families, the servants who didn't have immediate duties, and as many townsfolk as could find a place to stand. More soldiers lined the parapets. Every member of the guard not on duty, and some who were, put in an appearance.

Between the well and the gate house sat a wide, raised dais with Kian's litter in the center, his family standing around him. A colourful array of flowers bedecked both the canvas litter and the dais itself, belying the solemnity of the occasion.

The crowd quieted at Cenith and Tyrsa's approach, parting to form a wide path to the dais. Everyone stared at Tyrsa. She leaned closer to him, clutching his arm. This was the first look the general populace had of their new lady since her arrival just a few days ago. He squeezed the hand he held, hoping to reassure her.

Cenith approached the dais, sorrow in his heart, lead in his feet. All the words he'd rehearsed fled like a flock of starlings at a hawk's shadow. He stopped a few feet from the stairs of the dais.

The Companions carried on around the platform, six to a side. In perfect precision, they flanked the dais and performed a parade stop. In unison, they turned to face Kian, saluted, drew their swords, and held them upright before them, standing at perfect attention; even Buckam, who stood closest to Cenith. They performed the maneuver flawlessly, making Cenith wonder when they'd found the time to practice. As one, they lowered their swords so the points rested on the ground. The Companions shifted to the 'ready' position, feet apart, one arm behind their backs.

In an attempt to hide his surprise, and welling tears, Cenith bent down to tell Tyrsa to wait there for him. He took longer to straighten up than he should. Once more composed, he climbed the four steps to the top of the dais and stood at Kian's head, Daric to his right, Elessa to his left, the children lined up along both sides of the litter. Avina held Rade, who seemed to understand the solemn occasion and, for once, didn't squirm to be put down.

Elessa, sporting a colourful bruise on her jaw, had tears in her eyes, yet a hint of a smile lightened her sorrowful expression, brought on, perhaps, by the honour the Companions gave Kian. Daric's features resembled the stone of the keep walls.

Cenith looked down into the face of his lifelong friend. Still, no words came. What would Kian tell him? The same thing he'd told him after his father died. *You are Lord of Dunvalos Reach now. Your people expect you to be strong, to do your duty, no matter how tired you are or how much you hurt. It's not fair, but that's the way it is.* And that's the way it was now. Cenith cleared his throat. From somewhere, he found the words.

"People of Dunvalos Reach. Two days ago the unthinkable occurred. Assassins attacked our home. It was a covert, cowardly attack. One meant to steal away your new lady." Shouts of anger and indignation greeted Cenith's words. He held up his hand until the noise faded. "They failed. But in the attempt, they killed twenty-six of our guards; fathers, husbands, sons. They will all be missed, like Kian." He reached his hand out, almost touching Kian's cheek. His vision blurred. "Eldest son of Councillor Daric and Elessa of Tiras. More than a friend, he was the closest I ever came to having a brother. I can't begin to describe the empty place he has left in all our hearts."

Cenith lowered his hand and paused a moment, gathering his scattered thoughts, forcing his vision to clear. "I could stand here and tell you what Kian was like…kind, brave, loyal, witty…but they're just words. Kian lived those words, and life, to their fullest. And I wish to…" Cenith almost said 'all the gods', but that wouldn't be appropriate here. "I wish with all my soul that he could be standing next to me now. But that's not possible, and I shall have to learn to live without the best friend I've ever known. My tribute to Kian is short, as his life was short, but don't misunderstand. I simply can't find the words to express the loss I feel. Be assured, I'll always remember him with honour, and with love."

He took a deep breath, fighting back tears. "Normally, this part of the proceedings is turned over to a priest of Maegden. However, Kian followed his father's religion, and I have given Councillor Daric permission to conduct the rites according to the Calleni ways."

A quiet murmur rippled through the crowd. It faded as Cenith stepped down from the dais to stand beside Tyrsa. He didn't care what his people thought about the departure from ritual. Seeing Kian laid to rest according to his family's traditions held more import to him.

Daric took Cenith's place at Kian's head. Dressed in full military uniform, his black cloak hung off his shoulders, the mountain insignia of his chosen home rippling in the folds. He spoke in Ardaeli, as a courtesy to the listeners. "Niafanna, Giver of Life, Taker of Life. Cillain, ruler of the skies, the earth, the water. Hear me Mother and Father of all."

Daric intoned the prayers of his desert people, some repeated back to him by his wife and children. He told of how Cillain and Niafanna made the earth and the creatures that lived on it, how it was intended that they exist in peace and harmony.

Peace and harmony. We haven't had much of that lately. Starting with his father's death, Cenith's life had taken a definite about-face from peaceful; and Saulth lay at the heart of it. He couldn't stop believing the Bredun viper had murdered his father, or that he'd tried, and now succeeded, in stealing the piece of parchment. The assassin in the storage room would prove at least that. Cenith's hands curled into fists. *How I wish I could get my hands around Saulth's neck!* He'd have to settle for the murderer in the storeroom.

Cenith had no idea how to torture a man, other than the small, but chilling, demonstration Daric had given him with Buckam. That didn't matter, he'd hurt the assassin one way or another to make him talk. He pictured himself, knife in hand, cutting the man, blood streaming down his already tortured face. Cenith's belly lurched and he let loose a quiet sigh, common sense overruling anger. He clasped his hands together in front of him to keep them from shaking.

He could kill a man in self defence, and had done so in the past, but Cenith couldn't fool himself into thinking he could deliberately harm an unarmed man, tied up and helpless, no matter how angry. Daric would be the one to torture the murderer, though Cenith would be there, regardless, butterflies or not.

Out of the corner of his eye, he caught Tyrsa looking up at him, a quizzical expression on her face. Cenith ignored his wife, directing his gaze to a spot near Daric's feet, hoping she wouldn't say anything. He couldn't deal with her right now. Her role in all this was hardly insignificant, though she couldn't be blamed for it. If not for her, they wouldn't have had to flee Bredun. Warin wouldn't have been killed, for they would have taken the Bredun Road and not run into the bandits—and Kian would be alive, along with most of the other twenty-five guards; for Cenith felt sure if the assassins had only come for the parchment, that terrible night would have played out differently.

There'd have been no need for the intruders to be anywhere but the treasure room. Buckam wouldn't have deserted Saulth, so he wouldn't have seen the assassins enter the keep. The thieves would have killed the two guards, taken what they wanted and disappeared. If not for her.

The people near him shuffled and murmured amongst themselves. Cenith jerked his head up. At some signal he'd missed, the Companions snapped to attention, sheathed their weapons, and faced Daric. The Calleni led his family off the dais. Daric kept his eyes on the ground in front of him, except to give a brief bow to Cenith and Tyrsa as he passed. Elessa and the children did the same. The crowd parted and the stricken family lined up several feet away from the dais.

Three Companions from each side stepped back. Jolin, Dathan, and Fallan from the right; Jayce, Keev, and Barit from the left. Stepping up onto the dais, they flanked Kian's litter. When all were in position, facing front, they took hold of the handles. Jolin, at the nearest right hand corner, nodded once. They carried Kian off the dais. Cenith followed them, indicating to Tyrsa that she should accompany him, though he didn't take her hand. The rest of the Companions fell in behind.

Just before the litter reached Daric and Elessa, the councillor directed his family into pairs and led the procession to the north gate and the burial cave. Other than the family, Cenith and Tyrsa, only high ranking nobles, the Companions, and Kian's friends would be allowed in the cave and at the meal to be served afterwards.

The burial cave lay several yards past the keep wall. It took two guards to roll back the stone sealing the entrance. The same guards entered first to light the torches. Once all were inside, the Companions carrying Kian placed his litter on the bier and stepped back to join the rest of their regiment.

The odour hit Cenith first. Though dry, the cave smelled dank, cloying, and moldy, like old death. Other biers, stretching into the darkness, their occupants permanently asleep under shrouds of varying decay, sat in a stately row behind Kian's. Near him lay Cenith's mother at the head of another row. Though her shroud still hid her bones, the outline of them could clearly be seen. In too short a time, Kian would look the same. Cenith dragged his eyes away from the mother he barely recalled, back to the friend he remembered all too well.

Two objects lay beside the bier, Kian's sword, and a folded piece of cloth, the shroud. Daric picked up the sword and placed it on his son's body, arranging his hands so he held the hilt, blade down. When he finished, Avina passed Rade to him and took her place at the bier, her mother and sisters joining her.

Elessa picked up the cloth and, with the help of her daughters, placed the shroud over her son, pulling it up to, but not over, his face. Rade decided now was the time to fuss, his whimpers growing to echoing cries. Elessa and her daughters returned to their places and she took Rade from Daric, shushing him with little effect. Daric's final prayers for his eldest had to be said over the cries of his youngest. He kissed Kian's forehead, as did each of the family. With a last long look, he pulled the shroud over Kian's face and indicated the ritual had ended. Each attendant approached the bier and bowed before leaving for the Great Hall. Some of the young ladies laid flowers at Kian's feet, others flanked his bier with small urns of incense, both mountain customs. Cenith doubted Daric would mind the gesture. He directed the Companions to wait outside, taking Tyrsa with them.

Daric and his family stayed longer, saying a final, private goodbye. Cenith held back near the entrance until they finished. Elessa collapsed into sobs. The children tried to comfort her. When she composed herself, Elessa caressed Kian's face through the shroud, then turned away. She, the girls, and the younger twins gave Cenith a hug on the way out. The older boys shook his hand. Only he and Daric remained. Daric stood near the side of the bier, his back to Cenith. The Calleni's shoulders slumped and he fell to his knees.

Cenith strode to his side, placing his hand on Daric's shoulder, anguish in his heart for both father and son. "I wish there was something I could do. Anything…to bring him back."

"There's nothing you can do. Nothing I can do." The hopelessness in Daric's voice tore at Cenith's soul.

"Will you walk with me to the Hall? The guests are waiting."

Daric shook his head. "I can't leave. Not yet, but someone has to play the host. Might I prevail on you?"

Feeding the guests wasn't a Calleni ritual, but Ardaeli. Cenith couldn't shrug off all his people's traditions. "Of course. Don't be long. Elessa needs you."

Daric nodded and Cenith left, taking Tyrsa and the Companions back to the Great Hall. It was over. His best friend was dead and laid to rest, but Cenith's heart still ached.

Once in the Hall, he seated Tyrsa at the main table in the front and center of the room, then took his own chair. Daric's family was already there, talking amongst themselves. The place to Cenith's right remained vacant—Daric's seat.

Elessa leaned over the empty chair. "Is he coming?"

"Not just yet. He wanted some time alone."

"I'm so worried about him. He's hardly said anything since…"

Cenith reached over and patted her hand. "Give him time. We all need time."

She nodded and sat back in her chair. Servants placed heaping plates of food in front of those at the main table before performing the same duty for the guests.

The Hall echoed with chatter, but Cenith paid no attention. Nor did he bother with his food. Tyrsa dug into hers as if she hadn't eaten only a short time ago. He doubted she understood what had happened, though she remained quiet and apprehensive throughout the meal. Then Cenith remembered this was the first time she'd eaten outside their rooms.

When most people had finished and gathered into groups to chat, Cenith refilled his wine goblet and stood. He told Tyrsa to remain at the table, ostensibly to keep Elessa company since Daric hadn't made an appearance. Finding a spot in a dark corner near one of the fireplaces, he leaned against the stone, sipped his wine and stared into the fire, wishing he could put all this behind him. The dukes of Rusty Valley and Warbler Ridge tried to strike up a conversation with him, but left shortly after. Most seemed to realize he wished to be left alone with his thoughts, and his grief.

Maybe once Daric interrogated the prisoner and they found out the truth behind all this, things would return to normal. Although, what was normal with Tyrsa around? They still had to find out just what happened with her that terrible night. Cenith had run the entire experience through his mind several times and he still couldn't come up with any explanation.

His thoughts returned to Kian, laughing, sparring with him, the times they'd gone swimming, fishing, hunting…and then his face, too quiet, too pale, disappearing as Daric pulled the shroud over him. With one hand, Cenith rubbed his tired eyes.

"My Lord." A woman's voice broke into his reminiscences. It was Mara, Tyrsa's maid. "I'm sorry to disturb you, My Lord, but Mistress Elessa asked me to tell you that she can't find Lady Tyrsa. She's gone to look for her."

Cenith jerked upright. "Thank you."

The maid left and he set his goblet on the nearest table before searching the room for the Companions. At first glance, it looked like they were all there. He counted again. Two were missing. He let out a long breath. At least Tyrsa wasn't alone.

Keev stood closest. Cenith approached him, interrupting his conversation with a girl, a nobleman's daughter by her dress, though Cenith couldn't place the face. Curiosity flashed briefly over shy Keev, a backwoods boy, speaking to any girl in public let alone the daughter of a noble. Cenith pulled the Companion to one side, apologizing to the girl. "Where's Tyrsa?"

"Jolin saw her leavin' by the main entrance. He's followin' her, Barit with him. He told the rest o' us t' stay here," Keev answered. "He thought she might be headed for th' privy. Felt she didn't need a crowd trailin' after her." He pulled on his earlobe. His brow dipped in a small frown. "They've been gone for a while now, though. Would ye like us t' look for her, m'lord?"

Cenith had never heard so many words out of Keev at one go. "No, I'll do it. You can return to your girl."

A blush crept up Keev's tanned cheeks, but he wasted no time rejoining his companion.

Cenith checked the four public privy's on the first floor. Tyrsa wasn't in any of them. He ordered servants to his quarters, old and new, and to investigate the other floors, just in case. Cenith needed to find her, but he also had to retrieve Daric for Elessa. Trusting the servants to locate his wife, he headed for the burial cave.

Chapter Twenty-Four

Daric's hand ached, his knees hurt, and his thigh throbbed with both the new injury and where a Syrthian guard had split him to the bone, crotch to knee. He'd almost died then. He'd almost died several times, but Niafanna, luck, and sheer determination, hadn't let him. If only Kian could have been as lucky.

My son. My shining star. Niafanna! Please care for him, protect him. He had to believe his son slept in her arms. *I can cope with this if he's with you.*

Daric loved all his children. Each had a special something about them. Avina's bold confidence; the way Jennica smiled, with a coyness that belied the fortitude underneath. The twins, Valin and Taro, identical, yet different in their own ways. Brave to a fault, they'd be skilled and valued warriors once he broke them of their rash behaviour. He couldn't lose another child. It would destroy him.

Ten year old Mina, a proper little lady with a face that would soon steal the heart of every young man in the keep. Nani, just eight and already asking him to teach her how to fight. She'd rather climb trees and catch frogs than play with dolls.

Chand and Chayne, five years old and another pair of mischief makers. The sparkle in their eyes and their too innocent grins made it difficult to punish them for their transgressions. Little Rade, with his sweet baby scent and chubby face, who's climbing abilities amazed him. Elessa continually picked him off tables, cabinets, anywhere he could haul himself up.

But Kian…

He'd set his hopes and dreams on Kian. His oldest son would have replaced him as councillor when Daric's time was done. Daric sometimes imagined he could have been like his eldest son, if he'd grown up in the same nurturing atmosphere. Kian's grin came much easier than his. Too many dark memories clouded Daric's thoughts. Too much pain and loneliness; until he'd met Elessa, the light of his life.

He should get up. He should go to her. Elessa needed him. He needed her, and yet, Daric couldn't move. If he left, that would be the end of it. Kian would be gone. Dead. Sealed in stone.

Quiet voices sounded from outside the cave. A noise from the entrance alerted him he was no longer alone. Footsteps, soft leather on dirt, tiptoed closer. Elessa? No. She wouldn't walk so quietly, not with him. Her steps would be more confident.

Daric waited, keeping his eyes on Kian's shape under the shroud. A moment later, Tyrsa blocked his view. He only had to look up a little to see her face and the confusion and worry that resided there.

"Cenith hurts, but he does not let me help him."

"Can you?" *If you can, would you help me?*

"I don't know." She moved away from him to the bier and pulled the shroud down from Kian's face. "Cenith said Kian was gone, but he's right here."

Daric's heart lurched.

Tyrsa touched two fingers of each hand to Kian's forehead, trailing them down to his chin. "Oh." She put the shroud back. "Cenith said Kian was dead. This is dead?"

Daric could only nod. His heart had taken up residence in his throat. He stared at the ground in front of him, at a tiny stone, pale grey against the dark brown dirt.

Tyrsa came to him, her small foot covering the stone. "I can't help Kian. He's not there. She didn't take him and that's good. The Mother has him. He'll be safe with her."

Daric's head snapped up. The Mother? *Niafanna!* "You know this? For certain?"

"Yes. Does that help you?"

"It does. It helps me a great deal. Thank you." Relief washed over him, easing his heart, his soul. Kian would return to the wheel of life, not be locked away in one of Ardael's hells, or forced to entertain Maegden on his throne for all eternity. *Thank you, Niafanna.*

Tyrsa knelt, heedless of her dress in the dirt. Her manner changed in an instant, more confident, commanding, less…innocent. Most startling of all, her eyes changed from blue to violet. Daric waited, silent, to see what would happen next. Whatever it was, it would be important.

She stared at him for what seemed an eternity before she spoke. "I need you to do something for me." Even her voice sounded different, educated, self-assured.

Never one to rush into things unknown, Daric replied, "If I can."

"I need the scroll. It is important to what I must do."

"And what is it that you must do?"

More footsteps interrupted them. Heavier, male. Tyrsa looked up.

"What in all the hells...?" Cenith appeared beside them, staring at his wife. "Not again!"

Daric held up his hand, forestalling anything else Cenith might have said. "What is it you must do, My Lady?"

"Save the land," she answered. "To do that, I need the scroll. And Rymon."

"Rymon?" Why would she need Saulth's councillor? Daric glanced up at Cenith. Rapt interest replaced frustration on his face.

"He knows how to read it," Tyrsa said. "Please do this for me, Daric. You are the only one who can."

"I will do as My Lady commands." He didn't know how, only that he had to. "Who is destroying the land?"

Regret flashed in her strange eyes. "That I do not remember."

"Can you tell me what happened the other night? When you glowed?" Daric stole another peek at Cenith. Worry now etched the young man's face, his eyes fixed on his wife.

Tyrsa looked up at her husband. "You did not hurt Tyrsa, Cenith. It was her power manifesting. She had to learn to control it, though she does not yet have full command of her abilities. We were told that we would remember things as needed, otherwise it would make us insane."

Relief eased Cenith's young features. Daric hadn't realized he'd been that worried about hurting her.

"Tyrsa's powers. You mean her healing?" Cenith asked.

"She already had that. There are others."

"What others?" Daric asked, almost afraid to find out. It couldn't be just her way with wild animals.

"I do not know yet. They will come when we need them."

"Powers." Cenith scratched his cheek, his eyebrows dipped in a frown. "Magic?"

"Yes. Magic. That is a good word for it." Tyrsa stood.

Daric decided he should too. He took longer to do it; his knees and wounded thigh objected the movement.

"But there's no such thing as magic. It's only in children's stories," Cenith said.

"Magic is everywhere." Tyrsa waved a hand. "You just have to know where to look."

Daric brushed the dirt from his pants. This new Tyrsa communicated much better than the old one. He wished he knew how long she'd be around. There were more important things to discuss than magic. "What is the purpose of the drawings on the hearth?"

"The Mother and Father were teaching us."

Daric froze. "The Mother and Father? Niafanna and Cillain?"

"Yes. They taught us much that we do not remember."

Cenith blinked. "You said this morning there was a cliff, voices, and pain, and that you didn't remember anything else. What's the point of telling you all this just to have you forget it?"

"It would have been too much at once. We would go mad. I will remember for us, as I need to." Tyrsa turned back to Daric. "Please bring me the scroll…and Rymon."

Before Daric could reply, her demeanour changed, back to blue eyes and innocence, back to the old Tyrsa.

She looked at Cenith, uncertainty wiping out the confidence on her face. "Can I touch you now?"

Her question caught Daric, and Cenith, by surprise.

"Of course you can," Cenith answered. "Why would you think you couldn't?"

"All the people stared at me and I was afraid. You wouldn't hold my hand or look at me. I thought you were angry. I didn't know what I did to make you angry." That was a lot of words for the Tyrsa Daric knew. Was that another change from that night?

Cenith held his arms open and she flew to him, hugging him tight. "I'm not mad at you, Tyrsa. I let my grief for Kian take control. I shouldn't have. I'm sorry."

Daric let them have their moment, but more questions remained unanswered. He only hoped this Tyrsa could help. "The drawings on the hearth, what is their purpose?"

Cenith moved Tyrsa into the crook of his arm, making it easier to talk with her.

"They are the symbols of the beings of power." She spoke the words slowly, like a child remembering a lesson.

The beings of power. His gods, Ardael's gods…they *all* existed?

"There were two other symbols there as well," Daric said. "The cup and the tree. What are they for?"

"They are for the Old Ones."

"More fairytales," Cenith said, though the look on his face told Daric he had second thoughts.

"We have stories of the Old Ones in Callenia. Perhaps there's more to it than fairytales."

Cenith looked down at Tyrsa. "Jolin said the cup represented pixies and fairies, while the tree was for the spirits of the mountains and forests. Are these the Old Ones?"

Tyrsa smiled. "Yes! I remember them. Pixies, fairies, and brownies. Dryads, trolls, and…."

Daric put his hand up. "We know. Why are they included with the gods of Ardael and Callenia?"

Tyrsa shrugged. "Because they have power too?"

She was guessing, though she could be right. Just the thought that those creatures might really exist unnerved Daric. From some of the stories he'd heard as a child, they could be violent and deadly. He could only hope they were just fairytales, but Tyrsa had thrown serious doubts on that. "What do the beings of power have to do with your task of saving the land?"

"I don't know." Tyrsa didn't sound concerned either.

"Do you remember your task? And what you asked me to do?"

She looked at him as if he'd lost his mind. "Yes".

"At least she remembers what she tells us when in that state," he said to Cenith.

"Tyrsa, you said there was a cliff and voices," Cenith put in. "I gather the voices were Niafanna and Cillain?"

Tyrsa nodded. "The Mother and Father. I remember that."

"Why a cliff?"

"Because when we were sharing our bodies you told me to pretend I was on a cliff. So I went there."

Daric managed to change his laugh into a cough. *Niafanna! I thought I'd never be able to laugh again, much less so soon.*

Cenith's cheeks flared red in the torchlight. "Maybe we'll discuss this later." He put a finger under Tyrsa's chin and tilted her head toward him. "Can you make your eyes turn violet whenever you want?"

Daric smirked at the quick change of topic.

Tyrsa cast Cenith a fierce frown. "No. I have to ask."

Cenith's frown matched hers. "Ask who?"

"The other one. She's in here." Tyrsa tapped her head.

"Sounds like she has little control over it," Daric said. "I think we should pay attention when it happens."

"Let's just hope one of us is around when it does." Cenith let go of Tyrsa's chin. "Maybe we should alert the Companions about this, and her mysterious powers, whatever they turn out to be."

"Good idea." Daric scrubbed a hand through his hair, stifling a yawn. "I doubt we're going to get anything else out of her."

"I think I'm finally hungry. There's plenty of food left if you're interested." Cenith removed his arm from around Tyrsa and took hold of her hand. Her smile said all sat right with her world again.

"Food sounds good." *For the first time in days.* Daric found himself almost relaxed. His heart still ached for Kian, but at least he knew for certain that Niafanna protected him, and that had gone a long way to ease his mind.

They put out the torches. Jolin and Barit helped them roll the seal stone back into place. With one last look at the burial cave, and a silent prayer of thanks to Niafanna, Daric joined the others for the walk back to the keep.

* * * *

Cenith decided an early bedtime appropriate. He'd hardly slept since the night they'd returned. Tyrsa accompanied him, though she didn't appear tired. She made him stop at his old rooms to pick up Baybee.

Ors ordered four guards outside Cenith's door permanently, two Companions, two regular. This made scheduling the Companions easier and gave them some time off. When Tyrsa left the suite, those same two

Companions would accompany her. The arrangement satisfied Cenith. Saulth could easily make another attempt at kidnapping her. Though he doubted the Bredun lord would try the same thing twice, they had to be on the alert for anything, or anyone, suspicious.

Mara and Laron waited in the sitting room for them. Cenith dismissed his valet while Mara accompanied Tyrsa into the bedroom to help her out of her dress. Several minutes later, the maid came out alone. "Will there be anything else, My Lord?"

"No, that's all for tonight."

She curtsied. "Goodnight, My Lord."

"Goodnight."

Cenith removed his tunic, shirt, and boots. He sat in his chair by the fire, staring at the symbols, now a permanent addition to the hearth. Beings of power. What part did they have to play in Tyrsa's task? Would they help? Or hinder? So far, it looked like Niafanna and Cillain were helping her.

Did that mean his gods were opposed to her task? That didn't make sense. This was their land. Why would they be opposed to saving it? Not that they'd done much to stop the problems afflicting Ardael, despite all the extra sacrifices and prayers the priests sent. What of the Old Ones? Were they the problem? Too many questions, not enough answers. He wondered when the other Tyrsa would put in another appearance.

His wife materialized at his side, her steps so quiet he hadn't heard her. His jaw dropped at the sight she presented. She wore nothing.

"I thought Mara helped you into a nightgown," he said, when he could find his tongue.

"She did. I took it off. I don't need one." Tyrsa climbed onto his lap, not sideways as she usually did, instead she straddled his legs. All the glory of her naked wonder filled his eyes. Wrapping her arms around his neck, she gave him a long, deep kiss.

"You need me," she whispered, close his ear. Her breath sent a shiver straight through to his soul.

"I'm not sure I'm up to that tonight." He checked the colour of her eyes. Blue.

Cenith mentally shook his head. She'd never been this bold before. *And I worried she wouldn't let me touch her?* He wondered just how much Niafanna had taught his mysterious little wife.

Her next move caught him completely by surprise. Tyrsa sat back and undid the laces on his breeches. She slid her hand inside, caressing his manhood. 'No' wasn't the answer she wanted. She leaned forward and kissed him again, trapping his mouth, capturing it, pulling him in with her desire. Despite his exhaustion and her inexperience, her ministrations had the inevitable effect. Cenith put his arms around her, holding her tight. He stood up and she wrapped her legs around his waist, still kissing him. He broke off long enough to carry her into the bedroom.

It seemed mere moments and they were both near their peak. Cenith's vision wavered. Tyrsa's face, twisted in pleasure, turned into a wall of rock, grey and black, broken by cracks and fissures. His bedroom disappeared.

Cenith turned around. He stood, naked, on a path at the edge of a cliff, an all too familiar mountain at his back. No wind blew. No birds or insects sang or chirped. Someone took his hand. Tyrsa. He could feel his manhood inside her; continued to experience the pleasure of their joining. How could she be beside him and still under him?

"Tyrsa, what's going on?"

She smiled. "You told me to let myself fall off the cliff. I wanted to fall off with you." She led him to the edge.

He couldn't look down. His father lay down there somewhere. "This is too strange. Are we really here?"

Tyrsa shook her head. "We are in our bed. This is in our heads."

"Is this part of your new magic? Or could you always do this?"

"The night we shared bodies was the first time. I pictured a cliff in my mind. This one. And then I was here."

"Why this cliff?" There were plenty of others to choose from.

"I remembered it from when we came here, to Tiras." Tyrsa readied herself to jump off.

Cenith pulled her back. "I don't think I can do this."

Tyrsa lost her smile. "But you told me it would be wonderful."

"Yes, but I was speaking metaphorically."

Tyrsa's pretty brow dipped in confusion.

The other Tyrsa knew 'manifest', this one… He rubbed a hand through his hair in frustration. "I meant to only imagine it, not for it to really happen."

"You said it wouldn't hurt. Look." She pointed to a spot over the cliff. "There are clouds down there. This is only in our heads."

As if clouds would break your fall. Cenith took a deep breath and peered over the edge. Clouds. No bodies. Just clouds, with the odd tree top poking through. He closed his eyes. Tyrsa lay under him, squirming in pleasure. Her pretty face displayed all the joy they both felt. Cenith could see her, their bedroom, still feel their movements as they pleasured each other. That was the reality. When Cenith opened his eyes, they stood on the cliff. This couldn't be real. "All right. I'll believe you. But if I die, I'm coming back to haunt you."

Tyrsa's sweet smile returned. Cenith gripped her hand tighter and let her lead him to the cliff's edge. They dove off together, into unimaginable bliss.

* * * *

Resting his feet on his desk, Cenith crossed his arms and leaned back into the chair, letting Daric tell the Companions what they'd learned about Tyrsa. Everything except Daric's errand, and what exactly had caused her powers to manifest.

With all twelve of the regiment, and Ors, in the study, it made for a crowded room. Daric stood just behind him and to the left, leaning against the wall, arms folded in front. Jolin sat opposite Cenith, flanked by Varth and Ead. The rest of the Companions sat, or stood, as the number of chairs permitted. Ors squeezed his bulk into the far corner by the fireplace.

Cenith's mind wandered back to the night before, and that morning. He'd fallen quickly into a deep, dreamless sleep. When he awoke, alive, he'd expected to find himself sprawled, mortally wounded, on a rock somewhere down the cliff. Instead, he lay on his back in his bed, his wife's head on his chest, her arm thrown across his belly. That entire experience would remain between them. He couldn't even imagine trying to tell Daric.

Cenith had let Tyrsa sleep while he mulled over all that had happened the previous day. 'Strange' seemed too mild a word. By the looks on the Companions' faces, he wasn't the only one who thought so.

When Tyrsa finally roused, she'd wanted another go at the cliff. Cenith wasn't sure he wanted to make love that way every time. It would soon lose its excitement; and it had been exciting, heart-stopping, once she'd talked him into it. This was something extraordinary, something to be saved for special occasions. Once he'd explained his thoughts, Tyrsa understood. Making love in a normal fashion, for the first time, had been special in its own way; fun, and deeply satisfying.

While Cenith had dressed for breakfast, Tyrsa searched the bedroom; under the bed, in the wardrobes, even the privy. When he'd asked her what she'd lost, she informed him that he'd lied. He could still hear her indignant words. "You told me sharing our bodies would give me a baby. We have done that three times now and I don't see a baby."

Cenith didn't even try to explain that one. Right after breakfast, he shipped her off to Elessa for a 'discussion', in the company of four regular guards since the Companions had been ordered here. Perhaps teaching Tyrsa for the day would help prevent Elessa from dwelling too much on her dead son.

"I told ye our Lady Orchid was special."

Jolin's voice roused Cenith from his thoughts. He lowered his feet and sat straighter. Time to pay attention.

"You did," Daric said, a hint of a smile cracking the rock his face had become since Kian's death. "Though I doubt even you realized how much."

"Nay, I'll confess t' that. It'll be interestin' t' see what she does next."

"If her eyes turn violet, come find me," Cenith said.

"Or Councillor Daric?" Barit asked.

"Yes, though he'll be leaving soon on a lengthy errand." Cenith put his hand up before the questions could start. "We'll discuss that later."

"Next topic, uniforms." Daric leaned forward and opened the top left drawer of Cenith's desk, pulling out several sheets of paper and some lead.

"We've been thinking about that, sir," Varth put in. "Rather than go to the trouble of making entirely new uniforms, we could just use a tabard."

Cenith rubbed his chin. "That would work. Cost less too."

Fallan cleared his throat. "The Dunvalos Reach crest could be put on the front with a small badge for Lady Orchid over the left breast."

"Do I want to know what will be on the badge?" Cenith asked, with a wry smile.

All the Companions grinned, but it was Trey who answered. "A fairy orchid of course. And the tabard could be white with purple trim to match, if it's not too expensive."

Purple dye had to travel by ship from the north coast of Callenia, then by caravan to Dunvalos Reach. Made from tiny mollusks, a difficult and labour-intensive job, a small bottle of the stuff totalled the equivalent of several miners' yearly wages. From what Cenith had read, thousands of the little creatures died to produce one garment. They needed enough for the trim and badges. A purple flower on a white background? *It shouldn't take a lot of dye. Thank Keana they didn't ask for purple tabards with white trim.* The budget for the guard had already been set for the year. This shouldn't damage it too much. Cenith looked to Ors for his opinion.

"It's not my decision, My Lord," Ors grunted. "They're the ones who have to wear them."

"The money we save on full uniforms should cover the dye." Cenith sat back in his chair, picturing the tabards over the midnight blue uniforms of the guard. They should look impressive. "Daric, send out requests for quotes on twelve white tabards with purple trim and fairy orchid badges. We can manage it, but I'd rather not pay a motherload for them."

"Consider it done, My Lord," Daric said, resuming his position against the wall.

A cheer went up from the Companions. Cenith waited until they settled down before signalling Daric to continue.

"Next on the list...officers."

Cenith had to smile. Daric didn't actually use a list, he kept it all in his head.

"We'd hoped to publicly announce the regiment and its officers at a banquet celebrating my marriage. The attack put a halt to that," Cenith said. "A celebration seems out of place for a while and this is a matter that can't wait. The fewer who know about My Lady's abilities' the better, so the regiment will report directly to Ors, bypassing the guard-captains." Raised eyebrows and puzzled frowns greeted his remark. "But, Ors has enough to do without the added work you fellows will bring, which means we need officers, a captain and two lieutenants. Daric, Ors, and I have chosen Trey and Jayce to be promoted to first and second lieutenant, effective immediately."

Before Cenith could say another word, a second cheer erupted, along with congratulations and slaps on the back to the two new lieutenants. Trey's normally sleepy eyes bolted open. Both his and Jayce's jaws dropped.

Cenith examined each face in the room; even Buckam, almost hiding in the corner opposite Ors, joined in. None of the Companions appeared to be disappointed or upset by the choices, but appearances could be deceiving. His next announcement could easily be met with resentment or disapproval. Cenith hoped not; he didn't need dissention within the regiment. Jolin was well liked among the guard, but who knew where any man's ambition lay.

When the noise finally died down, Cenith cleared his throat. All eyes turned to him.

"The man we've chosen as captain is intelligent, competent, and resourceful, not to mention skilled and brave." Cenith leaned forward, clasped his hands, and rested them on his desk. "I want it understood that it doesn't mean the rest of you don't have those qualities. You wouldn't have been chosen as my personal guard on the trip to Edara if you didn't, nor would I trust you with My Lady's safety. But this man has shown these qualities in full measure."

Cenith stood up. "Jolin, let me be the first to congratulate you on your promotion to captain, effective immediately."

He held his hand out to the new officer, who sat with his mouth open, disbelief shadowing his eyes. The cheers, whoops, and hollers that rocked the room outdid the previous ones by a fair amount, easing Cenith's fears. Jolin sat a moment, then shook his head before taking Cenith's hand. When Cenith released it, Varth, Ead, and anyone else who could reach took over, shaking Jolin's hand, slapping his back, tousling his dark hair.

Cenith resumed his seat and let the Companions have their moment. None of them showed any sign of discontent. He glanced at Daric and Ors. They both studied the men's reactions. Daric shifted his position, looking more relaxed than he had all morning. Ors caught his eye and nodded once. Cenith held up both hands in an attempt to quiet the room. They had more business to discuss, but the Companions showed little sign of slowing down.

"Do you want to spend all day here?" Daric's growl drowned out eleven excited voices—Jolin had yet to say a word. He just sat, blinking, while the others mauled him with congratulations. The voices quieted at Daric's words.

"Back to business," Daric said. His glower put an end to the noise. "As Lord Cenith mentioned earlier, I'll be leaving in a couple of days on an errand, at My Lady's request."

That news brought on murmurs and curious looks.

"She made the request yesterday, during the time her eyes were violet. She asked for the scroll in Saulth's castle, and Rymon."

The murmurs changed to pandemonium as all the Companions tried to voice their concerns.

"One at a time!" Daric bellowed.

"You'll be killed!" cried Varth.

"No one kin break into that place!" Jolin finally found his tongue. "Sir, 'tis suicide!"

"It's more a fortress than a castle," Dathan put in. "An army would have a demon's holiday breaking in."

"One man can go where an army can't." Daric unfolded his arms and stood straight.

"How do you plan on getting through the main gates, not to mention the castle gates?" Barit asked. "I'm sure the guards would be on watch for any attempt to get the parchment back. Are you just going to walk past them and take it?"

"I'm working on a plan."

"Sir?" Buckam moved out of his corner. "I might be able to help. I know the layout of the castle, how many guards are where. I can draw you a plan of the tunnels. It would make it much easier to move around undetected. Now that My Lady is here, there should be no reason for anyone to use them. I doubt anyone but Lord Saulth, Councillor Rymon, Guard-Commander Tajik, and a few of the guard know they exist."

Daric picked up the parchment and lead he'd placed on the desk earlier. "Buckam, you've got yourself a job."

Buckam grinned, took the parchment and lead, and returned to his corner. Cenith glanced at the rest of the Companions. Some didn't bother hiding their suspicions of Buckam, but none said a word.

"I don't think I need to mention that all this is to be kept secret, even from the other guards," Daric said. "If anyone's curious, tell them I'm on a trade mission to Mador. While I'm gone, I need all of you to be especially watchful. We fully expect Saulth to make another attempt at kidnapping Lady Tyrsa. It could come from anywhere. He may even have spies in the keep. Those assassins knew exactly where the parchment was. Watch for anyone acting suspicious. Report to Lord Cenith or Ors, though you do have permission to act if you think it's required. Understood?"

A chorus of 'Yes, sirs' answered him.

Buckam raised his hand and ventured a foot or two out of the corner. "Why does she need Rymon, sir?"

"Apparently he can read the scroll. No one here knows that language," Daric answered.

"That is true, he can," Buckam said. "But he is a frail old man. I do not know if he is capable of making the return journey. If you succeed, there is every chance you will be followed and it will be have to be a fast trip back. Rymon may not survive."

Daric's brow furrowed in a deep frown, making his face appear more like a boulder than usual. He stared at Cenith's desk a moment before answering. "That's a concern, but I'll skin that rabbit when I catch it."

Buckam nodded and returned to his corner.

Cenith leaned forward and folded his hands on the table. "I hope you all realize the job you've taken on. Although there'll be two of you protecting Lady Tyrsa at any given time, you must all be ready to be called upon day or night in case of an emergency, more so than the regular guards. There are things happening here that none of us understands, so it's difficult to be prepared, but prepared you must be."

Every one of the Companions nodded, their faces serious and determined.

"I believe that's all for now, unless any of you have questions," Cenith said.

"Only that we think you're mad for going for the scroll, sir," Trey said to Daric, his frown hiding his brown eyes even more.

"My Lady asked," the Calleni replied, his face grim. "I must obey."

That put an end to the discussion.

"If there's nothing else," Cenith said, "then you're dismissed. You can all have the rest of the day off to celebrate." Cenith had to raise his hand again to quiet the hoots and hollers. "The regular guards can watch my wife. Just make sure that whoever's on guard tomorrow morning doesn't come with a sore head. Jolin, Trey, and Jayce, could you please stay behind for a moment?"

"Aye, m'lord." Jolin stood, as did Varth and Ead. "Companions, dismissed."

As one, they raised their fists to their breasts in salute to Cenith. All but the three named exited the room, already discussing the events of the morning. Cenith sincerely hoped they remembered much of what they'd heard had to be kept secret.

Once the last of the men closed the door behind him, Jolin set his piercing gaze on Cenith. "Other than th' reasons you gave, an' there's plenty o' others who are just as good if not better, why me, m'lord? I'm not a noble, nor a son of a prominent merchant. Just a simple boy from th' backhills."

"Because Daric, Ors, and I have watched you, both on the trip to Edara and before, as well as the night of the attack," Cenith stated. "You took full charge of the regiment, knew your duty, and responded accordingly. All signs of a natural born leader. As for not being a noble, that's goat's dung. There's no rule that says an officer has to be a noble. Two perfect examples are standing right here in this room."

Daric's low birth was known to all of them, but few knew Ors had been born in a small village near the entrance to Black Crow Pass, the son of simple coal miner.

"We're not nobles either, Jolin," Trey put in. He was the son of a shopkeeper, while Jayce shared Jolin's backhills ancestry.

"But..."

Daric left his post against the wall to stand in front of Jolin. "Just accept it and do the best job you can."

Jolin nodded. "Aye, sir, I will. Thank you." He sighed. "I suppose this means I'll be changin' quarters agin."

Daric chuckled. "Officers are always on the second floor. See Guard-Captain Faris about your new accommodations."

"Aye, sir." He scrubbed his dark hair with one hand. "And I'd just got all settled in."

Cenith laughed and directed them to sit. Daric and Ors moved the two now vacant chairs near the fireplace over to the desk so all could be seated.

"I'm concerned about Buckam," Cenith said. "How is he fitting in?"

"Guard-Captain Faris found someone t' train him on those knives he got, so that part's taken care of. As for fittin' in...he's shy and still can't believe m'lady requested him," Jolin commented. "An' some o' th' others make no bones 'bout not trustin' him. As far as I'm concerned, 'specially after hearin' what happened yesterday with Lady Violet, if Lady Orchid trusts him, then so do I."

Lady Violet? An interesting way to distinguish the two Tyrsas. Trey and Jayce both nodded their agreement.

"That's good to hear. Now I just need you to convince the others. There can be no dissention amongst the Companions. Your job is too important."

"Aye, m'lord."

"The three of you will be taking over the scheduling, training, and general maintenance of the regiment," Ors said. "Divide it up however you wish, but I only want one daily report on my desk. As short and concise as you can make it."

"Aye, sir." Jolin added a nod to his response.

"Any questions about your duties, or anything else discussed this morning?" Cenith asked.

"No, m'lord. Least not until all this sinks in," Jolin said, finding his grin.

"In that case, pay a visit to the quartermaster about your pins, then go join your friends at Silk's." Two gold triangles, situated beneath the shoulder badge, signified a captain, one for a lieutenant.

"Aye, m'lord!" All three Companions saluted him.

"Let me be the first to buy you a drink," Trey said to Jolin as they stood.

"I'm second." Jayce opened the door.

Jolin turned to Cenith and winked. "I think I'm glad I've got night shift tomorrow." Jayce pulled him out of the room.

Cenith waited until the door closed before giving Daric a thorough look-over. He wore a black shirt and pants that had seen brighter days, but it was what he had on his feet that caught his attention. "Interesting boots you're wearing. I don't think I've seen those before."

Old and worn, they had thick soles with metal nubs that clicked on the floor. The tops were rolled down to just below the knee, but could cover his thighs if he wished. The foot appeared thicker than it should, particularly the toes and over the instep. Certainly not standard military issue.

"These boots served me well for years, up until I joined your father's guard. There's metal plating in the toes and instep. I thought they might be appropriate for our next task."

That peaked Cenith's curiosity. "Then let's go see what we can get out of our prisoner."

Chapter Twenty-Five

Wagon wheels creaked, crunching small stones lying in their path. Artan held his breath as he waited just inside the entrance to the cave, hiding behind a boulder. The sun shone straight overhead, making it difficult to keep far enough back that he couldn't be seen.

A simple buckboard rolled into view, headed away from Tiras. A family—husband, wife and a small child—sat on the single bench. The man and woman leaned close, discussing something in earnest, while the child, a girl, played with a doll. Canvas covered whatever they carried in the back. The man could be a miner, or perhaps a farmer, stocking up after the long mountain winter.

Artan kept his eyes on the back of the wagon until it passed the limited view from the cave. When he judged it safe, he peered out. The wagon vanished around a bend and he sighed. He'd half expected Snake to come rolling out from under the canvas; but that hadn't happened, nor had it the other dozen times a wagon passed. Several men on horseback, some alone, others not, had ridden by. None were Snake.

Shortly after he'd arrived at the cave, two separate groups of soldiers, one of twenty, the other thirty, had clattered by, in a hurry to be somewhere. Artan was concerned about where they were headed, but Snake's absence worried him more.

With another sigh, Artan scrubbed a hand through his dirty hair before returning to the small fire at the back of the cave and the mutton stew simmering in a leather cooking bag. While in Tiras, he'd stolen the meat as well as some other supplies. He'd made enough for two, just in case Snake put in an appearance.

Artan blew on his hands and held them close to the fire. Though the days were warm enough, the nights still held an echo of winter's chill. The next day would see summer solstice. Yet, even with more sunlight, the cave remained chilly. He had enough blankets to warm him, but hiding in the cave all day kept his hands and nose cold.

Three days since the disastrous mission at Tiras Keep, and no sign of his leader and mentor. *Snake must be hiding out somewhere in the keep, waiting for his chance to escape.*

Artan made three trips back to the stream's exit, both to check for Snake and to pick up the remaining packs. Two of them couldn't carry everything back to Valda. The dead assassins' belongings would have to remain in the cave, though the extra food could be divided between them. The trip would have to be made on foot, but at least they'd eat well. If Snake ever showed up. *I wonder if he lost his way? He could be out there wandering around looking for the cave.* How could he ever find Snake if that was the case?

Artan stirred the stew with a thick wooden spoon. He scooped up a small amount and tasted it. Any more cooking and it might burn. He spooned half of it into a wooden bowl and set the rest aside, close enough to the flames to keep warm, but not so near it would scorch. He sat on his haunches beside the fire and picked up his bowl.

Two hours. I can't wait any longer. That would give him time to eat and pack. Snake could catch up. Artan's orders were to get the parchment and go to the cave. He'd done that. He'd done everything Snake had told him; found a way in, scouted the keep… Snake said to come here, but didn't say what to do if something went wrong, and the mission had gone wrong, horribly so. Artan wished even one of the other assassins had made it. He would have known what to do.

The parchment had to get back to Saulth, no doubt of that. Snake said that was a high priority, but so was the girl. Artan had no way of getting her on his own. Not only had that not been his part of the mission, he was only one person, and an apprentice at that. How could he get her out all by himself? Pretending to be a servant and learning the layout of the keep had been one thing, kidnapping the lord's wife was a blade of another thickness. Snake might know a way, if he ever showed up.
He has to be stuck in the keep. Snake's body hadn't lain with the others.

What do I do? Artan blew on his spoonful of stew until it cooled enough to swallow. *Two hours. I'll wait two more hours and then start back to Valda.*

* * * *

Lunch before witnessing the torture of a man sounded like a bad idea, so Cenith passed when Daric suggested they find some food first.

The Calleni just shrugged and headed for the storage room where the assassin lay, bound and gagged. Ors joined them.

They had to pass through the kitchen to reach the room. The staff paused to give Cenith a bow before returning to their lunch preparations. The smells tempted him to change his mind...venison stew, fresh brown bread, plus an assortment of pastries. Daric and Ors both asked for bowls and filled them from one of the cauldrons hanging over a fire. A thick slice of bread accompanied lunch and Daric scooped up stew with it as he walked out the back door of the kitchen.

"Would ye like a bit t' eat, m'lord?" asked one of the staff, a cute girl with a pert nose, high cheek bones, and a shy smile. She looked about Jennica's age. Cenith didn't remember this one; he usually kept track of all the pretty female servants. He figured she must be new, or had recently grown up enough for him to notice. On his father's advice, Cenith never dallied with the serving girls, but he enjoyed a pretty face as much as anyone.

Tyrsa's bright blue eyes and innocent smile flashed to mind, and he swallowed a brief surge of guilt. He was married, yes, and he wouldn't bed another girl while married to Tyrsa, but did that mean he couldn't look?

"M'lord?"

Cenith's cheeks warmed at her prompt. "Ah, no, maybe later. Thank you." He followed Daric and Ors to the storeroom.

When Cenith finally saw the assassin, he stared at him for a few moments, not sure just what he'd expected. He'd avoided coming here; all he wanted to do was strangle the man and Cenith refused to take the pleasure of the assassin's death away from Daric.

The man who lay on the dirt floor, older than Cenith had expected and clothed only in a dirty pair of small breeches, was just that, a man, albeit a particularly repulsive one. The lump Buckam had given him stood out on his forehead. Scars twisted his face into that of a demon. Appropriate, for the man's heart had to be as ugly. A short, scruffy beard attempted to grow around the scars.

More white ridges, some thicker than others, crisscrossed his lean, well-muscled body. He had to have at least as many as Daric, if not more. Hardly a part of him didn't have a scar of one sort or another. Cenith supposed that hazard accompanied the job. The man lay partially on his right side, facing the door, his bound hands behind him. Proper rope replaced the binder twine Daric had originally used.

Two guards stood in the room, one on either side of the door, Kindan and Jarvic. Both men stood almost as tall as Cenith, solid and dependable. Ors had chosen the assassin's guards well.

Cenith sat on a barrel near the door. He expected this would be a lot messier than Buckam's interrogation and he'd felt queasy enough then. If his knees planned on turning traitor half way through, they wouldn't do it while supporting him.

Daric stood in the assassin's line of sight, leisurely eating his lunch. Ors copied him. The prisoner ignored them. When finished, Daric set his empty bowl on top of a barrel of potatoes. He crouched to the prisoner's left and studied him, his stony gaze steady. The assassin met him, eye to eye, not flinching.

Daric motioned to Kindan. "Take the gag off."

Ors' bowl joined Daric's and the guard-commander took up a position near the man's head. He crossed his arms and stared down his long nose at the prisoner.

Kindan did as ordered and returned to his post. The assassin worked his mouth a moment before he spoke. "Smells like lunch."

"Not for you." Daric pulled his dagger from the sheath hanging at his waist.

"Ah, this must be torture time…and you must be Daric." Scorn added a rougher edge to the prisoner's gravelly voice.

"And you are…?" Daric examined the knife, running a careful finger over the edge.

"Why should I tell you?" The man grinned.

Cenith had to give him credit for a large set of nuggets; though, judging by some of the scars he bore, it probably wasn't the assassin's first time facing torture.

Daric stopped playing with his dagger, his eyes riveted once more on the assassin. "Because I'm asking."

The prisoner laughed. "Good answer. Hardly original, but good." He shrugged. "I am Snake."

Snake spoke the words as if everyone in the room should have heard of him. Daric's expression didn't change one whit. The assassin's grin wavered.

"Appropriate," the councillor turned interrogator said after several moments. "A snake leading a pack of vipers. Dead ones."

Snake's grin disappeared. "You're lying."

Daric touched the point of his dagger to Snake's throat. "I kill people. I hurt people. I ran the guard. I make out documents, accompany my lord on trips, and advise him. But I do...not...lie." He shrugged. "Unless ordered." Daric shifted his weight until he looked at Cenith. "Did you order me to lie, My Lord?"

Cenith shook his head. "No, I did not."

Daric turned his attention back to Snake. "I do not lie."

Snake snorted and gave Cenith a scornful once-over. "That 'boy' is Lord of Dunvalos Reach?"

"He's more than he seems."

Cenith blinked at Daric's compliment. He always felt the ever-learning student under Daric's tutelage—and he had a lot more to learn.

"Huh. I doubt it," Snake grunted and turned his attention back to Daric. "You're lying. My men are better than that."

"Even though two of them died beside you on the wall?"

Snake ignored Daric's question, his scowl firmly in place.

"Kindan, Jarvic..." Daric stood. "Undo the ropes on his legs and ankles. We're going on an excursion."

Snake's arrogance turned first to puzzlement, then to pain as blood rushed into his now unbound feet. He gritted his teeth, taking control until the agony only showed around his eyes. At Daric's signal, Kindan and Jarvic pulled him upright, each taking an arm. Cenith slid off the barrel.

Daric led the way back through the kitchen and down the halls to the main doors, ignoring the stares of the servants. The guards dragged Snake. Cenith and Ors followed. Snake's feeble steps steadied as they walked and the tension around his eyes eased.

Daric had ordered the assassins' bodies moved around the corner of the keep, lined up against the north wall bordering the training ground. Everyone had been told to stay away from the corpses. A rope fence kept the horses now occupying the field away. Cenith's eyes strayed to the north and the charred remains of the stables. Workmen cleared the rubble, readying the site for the new building.

Just before they reached the corner, Daric motioned the guards away and slammed Snake against the wall—right by Kian's window. "How many?"

"Fifteen."

Daric slammed him again. "Now who's telling lies. Your eyes give you away."

Cenith couldn't see anything in Snake's eyes except residual pain and an entire mine full of arrogance.

Snake's grin made a cautious return. "Nice try."

Daric hauled the assassin away from the wall, motioning to Kindan and Jarvic to resume holding him.

They rounded the corner. Daric let Snake drink in the sight. Even though they were now in shade, the assassins looked awful. Their bodies hadn't been treated the way Kian's had.

Eight pale faces sat on corpses that moved as if still alive. Maggots crawled throughout their wounds, eyes, noses, and mouths, writhing masses of white mixed with the darker blowflies searching for a place to lay more eggs. Cenith choked back bile. The buzzing of the flies overshadowed the everyday sounds of the courtyard: the ring of metal on metal at the smithy, the chatter of the guards on the walls as they passed each other, the birds in the trees beyond the curtain wall.

Snake dropped to his knees. The pain in his feet must have caused it; Cenith couldn't imagine the tough assassin was bothered by the grisly scene. Surely he'd seen worse when he killed his victims. Daric waved the guards back.

"We know at least one escaped," Daric said, standing next to the assassin. "How many?"

Snake's voice lost all hint of arrogance. "Ten." He choked the word out. "Always ten. It's my lucky number."

"Not this time." Daric crouched at the assassin's side.

Cenith blinked his eyes in surprise. Snake actually cared about the dead men? Somehow, 'assassin' and 'compassion' didn't go together. Could there be an odd sort of fellowship, even amongst Snake's cold-hearted kind?

"In a couple of days," Daric continued, "these bodies are going to turn an ugly shade of blue-green and the smell will turn even your cocky stomach. Your friends will swell, pushing body fluids out their mouths, eyes, noses, ears, and arses. More insects will find a home here, wasps, beetles…" He shrugged. "We can bring you back every day so you can keep track for yourself. You deal in death for a living. Won't it be fun to watch what happens after a man's throat has been slit? After you've torn his gut open or thrust your sword through his chest?"

Daric's voice and face remained passive, cool, and calm, yet every inch of him screamed outrage, demanded retribution for his son's death. Cenith realized he'd watched this entire performance with no butterflies, even the bile had settled, leaving only a cold curiosity over what Daric would do next. He felt no sympathy for the assassin as he had for Buckam. Snake deserved everything Daric gave him. Probably more.

Daric dragged Snake to his feet. "Take him back to the storeroom."

Kindan and Jarvic each took an arm and frog-marched Snake away. Daric signalled Ors and Cenith to remain behind.

"Do you think he'll talk now?" Cenith asked.

Daric shook his head. "No. As soon as he's back in that room, he'll clam up tighter than a whore when a man's money has run out. Ors, have a squad bury this lot in a deep pit as far from the city as they can. Make sure they use gloves and cover their faces. When all the bodies are in the pit, have them throw the gloves and masks in after them. We don't want any of that stink hanging around."

Ors nodded once and headed for the barracks.

Cenith watched him go before returning his gaze to the bodies.

"Aren't you going to use them to intimidate Snake?"

"I won't need to. He'll break and it won't take days. I've seen his kind before." Daric nodded at the corpses. "And we're going to have a problem with disease if we don't get rid of them." He waved a hand back the way they'd come. "Let's go."

By the time they reached the storeroom, Kindan and Jarvic had Snake sitting on the floor, their swords pointed at him. Daric set his right foot on Snake's sparsely haired chest and pushed until the assassin lay on his back. The boot left its mark on the skin, each metal nub making an imprint. With his hands still bound behind him, Snake had to be uncomfortable; but Daric proved right, every ounce of arrogance returned. Cenith leaned against the wall next to the door, almost eager to see what Daric would do next.

"Now then," the Calleni said, "who hired you?"

Snake grinned. He spat, but missed Daric by several inches.

Daric crouched beside the man, his dagger in hand. He trailed the tip from between Snake's eyes to the end of his nose, but didn't draw blood. "I could cut you here. Peel back the skin from your nose and stitch it to your cheeks. I could stake you out with your friends and let the flies have fun with you. Since you're not dead, the maggots won't enjoy the meal quite so much, but if you stay there long enough the wound will putrefy, and they'll like that.

"Don't you want to know what your friends are going through right now? Feel the maggots crawling in your flesh?" Not a hint of Daric's anger or grief showed on his face or could be heard in his voice. "Oh, but they're dead, aren't they? They aren't feeling any of that. No, they're burning in Char."

Daric's dagger traced the scars on Snake's face, though, again, he didn't draw blood. Cenith almost wished he would. The man hadn't suffered anywhere near enough.

"While you're lying there, I could open your gut." Daric's dagger moved down to Snake's stomach, tracing a line across it. "Done right, there wouldn't be a lot of blood and I could personally introduce you to your liver, kidneys, spleen...whatever you wanted to see. I wouldn't even have to cut them out. You'd live longer that way. The flies and maggots could have a right good time in there."

Despite the sustained haughty attitude, Snake's face paled. He spoke not a word, just glared at Daric as if silently daring him to do it. The former mercenary twirled his dagger and replaced it in the sheath before standing. "But I don't want to do that. It's messy and takes too much time."

The Calleni walked around Snake, his eyes studying every inch of him. His gaze settled on the assassin's hips and he stopped beside the left one. With his toe, he prodded the hip, took aim, and kicked. Judging by the look on Daric's face, he used his full strength, holding nothing back. With the metal in the toes of those boots, that *had* to hurt.

Snake bellowed and squirmed away from Daric. He writhed and kicked his leg for a few minutes before taking control of the pain. He gritted his teeth, hissing in air, and glared at his attacker.

Daric raised an eyebrow. "Hmmm. I missed. Jarvic, roll him slightly to the right. Hold him down. Kindan, take his legs."

The two guards did as ordered while Daric lined up for another kick. This one must have hit harder, for when it connected, Snake exploded. He screamed for what seemed an eternity, shaking off Kindan and Jarvic. When they tried to resume their positions, Daric waved them away. Snake twisted and squirmed, his ugly features screwed up in agony. His face turned ashen. Sweat broke out on his brow and upper lip. He tried to curl up, but his thrashing leg prevented the protective movement.

The door to the storeroom opened. Cenith backed away and the guards drew their weapons. Ors' bald head appeared. Kindan and Jarvic re-sheathed their swords. After that tragic night, no one could relax.

"I didn't want to miss the fun!" Ors had to shout over the assassin's screams.

Cenith resumed his place by the door. He waved Daric over, speaking close to his ear. Ors leaned in close enough to hear. "I've never seen a man react like that to a kick. What did you do?"

"There's a nerve running down the leg. It's extremely sensitive. If I just hit or cut him, it's a momentary pain. It'll ease and he's tough enough to endure it. This way, he's going to be in severe pain for at least three days."

"*Three days*?" Cenith glanced at the assassin, who still writhed and squirmed, kicking his leg, his screams bouncing off the rock walls of the cave turned storage room.

Daric nodded, a glint bringing life to his eyes. "As I said, I know his kind. He's proud of his scars. He wants me to cut him...more for him to show off. There are other nerves I can use if he proves reluctant." Regardless of what Daric had told him and the Companions about revenge that night in the copse, the Calleni garnered no small measure of satisfaction from this.

Ors glanced over at the assassin. "Can't say he doesn't deserve it."

Daric returned to the prisoner. Ors moved back to his section of the wall.

"Kindan! Jarvic!" Daric shouted. "Turn him a little to the left and hold him down!"

Snake's pain doubled his strength and, regardless of their size, the guards struggled to obey their orders. Daric crouched and took the assassin's head in his hands.

"Who hired you?" Daric shouted into his ear.

Despite the tremendous pain, Snake shook his head, his jaw clenched tight. The assassin's left leg turned as pale as his face and a red streak, running most of its length, appeared, then faded, only to reappear a few moments later.

Daric stood and took aim again, this time on the right hip. He connected the first try. Snake's screaming increased tenfold. His mouth stretched so far Cenith feared his jaw would break. A violent thrash threw off Kindan and Jarvic. Both guards landed on their arses. They jumped to their feet, stepping back quickly to avoid Snake's kicking legs.

Daric let the assassin enjoy the pain for several minutes before taking hold of his head again. "Who sent you?"

Snake managed to speak through his clenched teeth, though it came out as more of a croak. "Go…futter…yourself."

Daric shook his head and tsked. Snake thrashed out of his grip. His entire body had taken on the grey cast of his face and legs. Before long, another red streak appeared on the right leg.

"Tie his feet. Securely, but not enough to cut off the circulation," Daric instructed the guards.

They had quite a time of it, trying to capture Snake's writhing legs. Once they were done, the Calleni told Kindan to bring in a chair. It took all three of them to sit Snake down and secure him. Daric ordered them to untie the assassin's wrists and bind them to the arms of the chair. Snake managed to get in a couple swings. One connected with Jarvic's face, bloodying his lip. Daric returned the blow, stunning Snake and giving the guards enough time to carry out his orders. The assassin continued to cry out, though he struggled to hold it in. Tears watered his eyes and sweat soaked his oily hair, forming twisted grey-brown mats.

"Now that you're more comfortable, we'll try again." Daric squeezed Snake's chin, right where he'd punched him, forcing the prisoner to look at him. "Who sent you?"

Snake attempted to spit, but nothing came out. He squirmed in the chair, trying to kick his bound legs. Sweat beaded his chest. Cenith couldn't imagine that great a pain.

He glanced at Ors. A small, satisfied smile creased the guard-commander's lined face. Ors had watched Kian grow up, had helped train him. He must feel Kian's death as much as they did.

Daric untied Snake's left arm and adjusted it until the elbow stuck out. He held it firm while Jarvic replaced the ropes. Dagger in hand, Daric squatted beside Snake. The assassin's pain wracked eyes riveted on the weapon. Daric studied the man's elbow, lining up the dagger four times before he hauled off and struck. Snake's eyes watered until tears leaked down his ruined cheeks. He closed his eyes and set his jaw against the new pain, while his body contorted with the old.

Daric grunted. "Huh. Missed again. Been too long." He struck Snake's elbow twice more before hitting the spot he wanted.

Snake's reaction was just as loud and violent as when Daric hit the nerves in his hips. The assassin's two smallest fingers curled while the others remained straight. Cenith winced. He'd banged his elbow more than once and knew the agony of a mild injury. This must be a hundred times worse.

Sweat glistened over Snake's entire body. His screams pounded into Cenith's ears and leached their way into his brain as the assassin fought against his torture and bonds. The ropes encircling his chest bit deep, rubbing against the ashen flesh, though they didn't break the skin.

Daric sheathed his dagger and waited, whistling a nameless tune. Cenith had no idea how much time passed before Snake could grasp some measure of control. He never stopped writhing, though he finally managed to clench his jaw, the screams changing to loud grunts and moans.

Impressive. Daric had the man in more pain than Cenith could imagine—with not one drop of blood shed. He wondered if his ears would ever stop ringing.

Once again, Daric took Snake's head in his hands. He stressed each word. "Now, I can continue. You have another elbow. There's also a place behind your ear. If I hit you there, that side of your face will explode in a pain so intense you won't be able to touch the skin. The muscles will slacken and your mouth will drool. By the time I do both sides, you'll look like the lack wit you are. Shall we talk? Who hired you?"

Though the glint in Daric's eye disappeared, replaced by a gaze of stone, something flickered in Snake's eyes. Fear?

Through clenched teeth, his voice strained, Snake said, "Promise…me…freedom."

"No!" Daric let go of Snake's head and pulled his dagger.

"Yes!" Cenith pushed himself away from the wall and strode to Daric, taking his arm. "Yes. This might be our only chance."

"I can break him," Daric hissed in Cenith's ear. "Have him weeping for his mother to save him!"

Snake's failing attempts at keeping quiet made it hard to talk. Cenith pulled Daric to the door, ignoring Ors' curious glance. He held up his free hand, indicting to the guard-commander to remain in the storeroom.

Once out in the tunnel, Cenith said, "You didn't hurt his right arm. Do you think he could sign a document stating that Saulth hired him to kidnap Tyrsa and steal the parchment?" He still gripped Daric's arm. "This is the proof we need! We can take it to the council and reveal Saulth for the lying, stealing, traitor he is."

"I want…I *need* that goat futterer dead! He holds responsibility for Kian's death!"

"Snake is one of them, yes, but you already killed the man who took Kian's life. Saulth is the one we want. He ordered it."

Torchlight highlighted a brief flash in Daric's eyes, though ice tinged his words. "He will die too."

Wasn't this backwards? Shouldn't it be Daric forcing Cenith to see past his emotions? "Snake wants freedom. I'll give it to him in exchange for what we need." Cenith squeezed Daric's arm harder, hoping to make him see reason. "After he signs the document, I'll have him escorted to the border." He made a point of stressing his next words. "That is as far as I can guarantee his safety. Then he's on his own."

"And free to take another man's life!" Daric spat.

Cenith set his hand against Daric's chest. "You have an errand to run for my lady in Valda. I can guess where Snake will run to." This was the first time Cenith could remember countering Daric on a serious matter. Would he listen? Could he see past his grief?

Daric's eyes drilled into his. Cenith met his gaze. He kept one hand on the Calleni's chest, the other still gripped his arm. If Daric decided to fight, Cenith wouldn't stand a chance.

After a few tense moments, the glint in Daric's eyes returned. "He won't be able to travel for three days. Even then, sitting a horse will be extremely painful."

Cenith nodded, relief making his words come out in a rush. "No less than he deserves."

He let go of Daric's arm and strode to the back door of the kitchen. Lunch was long finished and the staff now prepared dinner. *Is it that late already?* Cenith's stomach rumbled at the new odours, but food could wait.

The workers cast furtive glances at the back door, the usual bustle of the kitchen subdued. With both the kitchen and storeroom doors open, Cenith could hear Snake's attempts at dealing with his agony. Even with the doors closed, the screaming must be unnerving for the staff.

Cenith grabbed the arm of a boy pretending to peel carrots. The lad's eyes shifted back and forth between him and the open door. "Go to my study," Cenith told him. "Tell one of the guards outside I need parchment, quill, and ink. Bring them to the storeroom. You got that?"

"Y…yes, m'lord!"

Cenith let go of the boy's arm. "Run!"

Dodging the other workers, he disappeared through the opposite door. Rather than endure the frightened stares of the kitchen staff, Cenith returned to Daric. The gleam remained in his eyes and his face had taken on a determined look. Cenith dragged him back into the storeroom, closing the door behind them.

"Listen for a knock on the door," Cenith said to Ors. "I'm expecting a delivery." He ignored the guard-commander's quizzical look. Cenith moved closer to Snake. "You want freedom?"

"Yes," the assassin hissed, his teeth clenched tight.

Cenith leaned near enough to ensure Snake could hear him clearly. "You will sign a document stating who hired you and exactly what you were hired to do. We also want you to tell us how you got in here and where your missing friend is. If you do these things, I'll guarantee your safety to the border of Dunvalos Reach. Past that, I have no jurisdiction and can guarantee nothing. Understood?"

Snake's entire body danced with pain, but he managed a nod. Speaking proved harder than moving his head. Long before Snake finished his tale, the boy returned with the objects Cenith requested. The lad's eyes popped out of his head upon seeing the assassin and Cenith ordered him back to the kitchen.

Once Snake answered all their questions, Cenith used the top of one of the barrels to write out the deposition while Daric leaned over his shoulder. At the bottom, Cenith wrote:

> 'On this day, the 20th of Sixth Month, in the
> year 426, I, Snake, resident of Valda,
> assassin by trade, do swear with all my heart
> and soul that the above statement is true.'

Before he could write the next line, the traditional oath to Maegden, Daric interrupted. "Assassins don't pray to Maegden, only Shival. An oath to Maegden would mean nothing to him. Assassins believe they won't go to Abyss, Frost, or Char. They'll sit at Shival's side instead. Put down 'If these words be untrue, may Shival dull my blade, and make my aim untrue. May she refuse to take my soul.' It's a more appropriate oath for an assassin."

Cenith did so. Daric kept Snake's head steady while Cenith held the document for him to read. When the assassin finished, he gave Cenith a nasty glare.

"Sign it, or I'll give Daric free rein to do what he wants." Cenith glared back at him. "Will you sign?"

"Yes." Snake hissed the word, sounding like a true viper.

Kindan and Jarvic moved the barrel close to Snake's right side. Cenith placed the document on the lid and dipped the pen in the ink well before passing it to the assassin. Daric untied the man's right arm, then suggested Snake practice signing his name a few times on a blank piece of parchment. He twitched so violently, Daric finally had to hold his arm steady.

Despite the pain, and in reasonably legible letters, the prisoner wrote 'Snake, Chief Assassin of Valda, Bredun'. For some reason, Cenith had expected him to sign with an 'X'. He passed the document to Ors while the guards untied Snake from the chair.

"You won't be able to travel for three days. For now, you'll stay here under guard," Daric told Snake. The assassin didn't look happy.

Kindan and Jarvic lay Snake on the floor, a difficult job since he continued to writhe and squirm in agony, screaming when they jostled his legs or arm. They replaced the ropes on his wrists. Snake shrieked again when they wrenched his sore arm behind him. Kindan rolled him on his right side, relieving the pressure on the left arm. The smallest fingers of Snake's hand remained bent.

"He can have water. Don't try to give him food unless he asks for it, though I doubt he will," Daric told the guards. "Your relief should be here soon. Be sure to pass those instructions on to them." He set his gaze on Jarvic and his bloodied lip. "I'll send Garun to tend to that."

The guard shook his head. "Thank you, sir, but don't bother. As you said, it's not long 'til our relief comes."

Kindan and Jarvic took up their former positions. Ors moved out of their way and opened the door, motioning Cenith and Daric through before closing it. They stopped in the tunnel. Someone had closed the kitchen door. They had privacy here.

Ors tapped the document against his left palm. "Would you like me to put this somewhere safe?"

"I don't trust the treasure room anymore, despite Snake telling us his apprentice left for Valda." Cenith pulled a set of keys out of his pocket and chose one. "The right drawer of my desk has a false bottom. Put it in there." He passed the keys to Ors. "Return them to me after dinner. I'll be in my rooms."

Ors nodded, opened the kitchen door, and left.

"That last assassin has a three day head start. There's no way we can catch him now," Cenith said with a sigh.

"If we send a message by bird to the guard station at the foot of the pass to watch for him, we might stop him there. The extra men we sent won't have arrived yet, but there's always a chance," Daric suggested.

A pigeon could fly in a few hours what took a man four days to travel. "Do it." Cenith leaned against the wall and folded his arms; just watching that performance had worn him out. "Did you know there was a stream there?" He jerked his head toward the back of the caves.

Daric shook his head. "I don't think your father did either. I'd never heard him mention it. I assume it was intended for use during a siege, but since there's never been an attack on Tiras, it must have been forgotten. I'll have Ors check it out tomorrow and see if there's some way we can prevent anyone else using it."

Cenith smirked. "So you're worth two hundred gold? You should feel honoured."

Daric grunted, a scowl darkening his stony features.

"I never thought I'd be telling you to be patient," Cenith said, studying him. The Calleni's eyes were bloodshot and his shoulders drooped. Cenith wasn't the only one who needed a good night's sleep. Daric snorted. "Neither did I."

"I'm off to find Tyrsa and dinner. We're eating in our suite. Will you and Elessa join us? She can give Tyrsa more cutlery lessons." Daric shook his head. "Dinner sounds good, but I think I need to spend time with my family. I'll stop by later. There's still some things we need to arrange before I leave."

Cenith understood. He squeezed Daric's shoulder and they went their separate ways.

* * * *

A tiny waterfall trickled down the mountain near the cave before joining a larger stream in a ditch at the side of the road. Artan washed his bowl in it, scrubbing the wood with his fingers until no more of the stew remained.

Two hours. I'd planned on two hours. The afternoon sun had wandered long on its path before dipping below the mountains. Now twilight shrouded the valley and the hidden sun tinted gathering clouds pink and gold before Artan gave in and ate the last of the stew. Still no sign of Snake. *What do I do?* He washed his spoon and the leather bag before heading back to the cave. The fire had burned down to coals.

Artan packed his bowl, spoon, and the cooking bag; his movements slow and reluctant. He'd already stuffed as much food as he could fit into both his and Snake's packs, and tied two blankets each to the bottoms. He fastened the straps and set his pack near the entrance. Snake's, he kept separate from the others. When the assassin finally showed up all he had to do was pick up his pack and leave. He could catch up sooner.

Dread lay like a rock in the bottom of Artan's stomach, battling the stew sitting there. Several reasons for Snake's absence rolled through his thoughts, the same ones that had come to him repeatedly over the last two days. The ones he'd refused to think about forced their way through the others. *What if he's been captured? Or worse, he's dead?* Possibilities he had to face.

That left Artan alone. He kicked dirt over the little fire, smothering the coals. Wisps of smoke wafted up, disappearing into the darkness overhead.

He had to leave, make his way through Eagle's Nest Pass. Ice said he'd been through there once, several years ago. No one manned the old station at the head of the pass, though thirty guards protected the one at the foot. Two days journey to the pass, travelling by night, then another two to its exit. Artan couldn't wait any longer. He had to complete his part of the mission. Snake would catch up as soon as he could.

Artan shouldered his pack and, with one last, lingering look at the belongings of his mentor and dead comrades, he spun on his heel and strode out of the cave.

Chapter Twenty-Six

"So, spring follows winter, then summer and autumn," Cenith said to Tyrsa, who sat in her favourite place, his lap. At least tonight she wore clothes. Just as well, since he expected Daric and Ors anytime. "When winter starts again, it's been one year."

Tyrsa nodded. "I watched the white stuff…snow…fall from the Book Room. That was the best time for making pictures on the window."

"How did you do that?"

She shrugged, more a quick lift of her thin shoulder, a gesture he'd never seen her use before. "I blew on the window and it turned...different. The pictures didn't stay, but it was fun."

An image of two young faces reflected in glass, one light, one olive-toned, intruded on Cenith's thoughts. Two friends drawing shapes in the fog their breath made on the balcony door—ages ago, when he had no cares, no responsibilities, and no grief.

Cenith forced his pain back to the corner of his heart where Kian now resided so he could focus his attention on the lesson at hand. "Elessa taught you about the months today, so we can move straight to the days of the week."

"She said when the moon goes from full and round to not there and back again, that's one month. And it takes nine of those to grow a baby." She tilted her head. "If there are names for days, do months have names? Elessa didn't tell me if there are."

"Easy ones to remember. First to Twelfth." Cenith took a sip of his wine, a fruity white from Syrth, not as tasty as the Cambrel, but pleasant in its own way. "First Month starts the new year on winter solstice, the shortest day. Today is the longest. Even after the sun disappears behind the mountains, the sky will stay light for a long time. I'll show you."

Cenith indicated she should stand and led her to the balcony doors. The wide, iron-railed platform ran the length of his suite. He extended one hand, encompassing the view before them. The original lord had chosen the keep's position well. The sheer mountains behind prevented attack from that direction while the steep road from the town to the keep, only wide enough for two wagons to pass, would make it difficult for a frontal approach. Those defences had never been tested, but in these troubled times, it was reassuring to know they were in place.

The lord's suite faced east, giving him a clear view of the town of Tiras, now readying for sleep in the valley below. The surrounding peaks, always tipped in white, reflected the last of the sun's rays; red, gold, and pink, a particularly spectacular scene.

Clouds gathered to the northeast, a sure sign of rain by tomorrow, but the colourful mountain view took Tyrsa's breath away. "I didn't see this from the Book Room. It was already dark when I got there."

She couldn't have seen this view from that window anyway. Cenith couldn't wait until Maegden's Lights appeared. They graced the sky regularly around the spring and autumn equinoxes, but the Father of the Gods sometimes displayed his colours at other times of the year. He let her drink in the sight for a few minutes before taking her back to the chair. "Now, the days of the week are named after the gods and goddesses. The first is Maegden's Day, which is today."

Tyrsa pointed to his symbol on the hearth. "That's him."

"Yes. Then comes Talueth and Tailis, the twins. Sailors prefer to start a voyage on Tailis' day, while children born on Talueth's are considered lucky. Many couples prefer to marry on her day."

"What are twins?"

Cenith sighed. He didn't want to be all night at this. "That's when two babies are growing in your belly at the same time. Valin and Taro are twins, so are Chand and Chayne. It doesn't happen very often, and having two set of twins in one family is even more rare."

"Two babies?" She put her hand over her stomach. "I don't see how there's room for one."

Cenith kissed her frown away, relieved he hadn't been forced to explain where babies come from. "The fourth day of the week belongs to Siyon. Because he's the God of War, battles fought on that day have a better chance of success. The fifth is Ordan's, the smiths' day."

Tyrsa pointed to the symbols as Cenith named the gods.

"The sixth is Keana's. Spring planting is started on this day. Trades and deals made on Keana's Day are more binding. Anyone who breaks a bargain made then is considered to have no honour and no one else will deal with him." Cenith finished his wine, wishing Daric would come.

"And the last day is Aja's?" Tyrsa asked.

Cenith nodded. "Only people who consider themselves extremely lucky make deals or start anything new on his day. He can be fickle and you never know which way the dice will roll. Many people take it as an excuse to do nothing."

"Do you?" Tyrsa's pretty brow furrowed with curiosity.

He shrugged. "I don't worry about it. I do things when they need doing."

Perhaps it was Daric's Calleni influence on his upbringing or that Cenith simply didn't take the gods as serious as others. He sent prayers to them on occasion, especially lately, but he'd learned over the years that not just Aja could be fickle. Cenith, like his father, didn't sit back and wait for them to answer.

"What about her?" Tyrsa pointed to Shival's symbol.

"No one worships Shival except assassins. There's rumours of a death cult who honour her, but I've never seen any sign of it here. A day of Shival's own would be a bad one indeed."

A knock came at the door just as Tyrsa opened her mouth to ask another question.

"Enter," Cenith called.

Daric came in and nodded a greeting to them before occupying the other chair. "How was your dinner?"

"The pork was burnt and the biscuits dry. The carrots were too crunchy and the potatoes overdone. I don't want to even discuss the gravy." All of it kept trying to come back up. "Fortunately there were plenty of pastries left over from lunch."

"I couldn't eat all my meat," Tyrsa said. "It was hard to swallow."

"Snake's screams must have put Jarven and his crew off more than I realized," Daric grunted. "Maybe we should have moved him to one of the caves at the back."

"Who is Snake?" Tyrsa asked.

"I'll tell you later." To Daric, Cenith said, "I doubt it would have made a difference. He made quite a racket."

"I just checked on him. He still is." Daric's mouth twitched into a small smile.

The assassin's screams continued to ring in Cenith's ears, jarring his thoughts and putting him on edge. He suspected he'd be hearing them for days. "We could have Garun give him something for the pain."

"We could." Daric's smile disappeared. "Do you really want to?"

Considering all the trouble the man had caused? "No, I suppose I don't."

Daric sat back and folded his hands over his stomach. "There are some things that need seeing to before I go. I've been to the message tower and had a bird sent to Aleyn." He crossed his feet at the ankles and sighed. "Now that we have the garrison manned at Eagle's Nest Pass, we'll need messages sent there. The bird master says he'll set it up, but it'll take time.

"I also took the liberty of sending messages to your nobles informing them of a council meeting to be held at your leisure," Daric continued.

The annual spring council meeting had been delayed while Cenith made the trip to Edara and back. He held in his groan. The meeting always started with complaints and ended the same way, sometimes taking days to complete. The nobles who lived in the keep and town clamoured for a full explanation of both the Edara meeting and what had happened the night of the attack. Cenith had put them off, using his grief as an excuse. He couldn't keep that up much longer.

"How about next Maegden's Day? That gives everyone a week to get here. I can answer all the questions at once and won't have to repeat myself. It might also be a good time to officially introduce Tyrsa and announce the Companions. I wish their tabards could be ready by then."

"I haven't even had time to send out the requests for quotes. I'll take care of it in the morning." Daric stretched his legs out to the fire.

The balcony doors still hung open and the night air cooled the room, a gentle breeze enticing the flames to flicker and dance. Daric no longer wore his old boots or clothes, just a simple tunic of light wool and matching trousers, both in black. Other than his military uniform, the Calleni rarely wore any other colour; he claimed it a preference left over from his mercenary days.

"Speaking of," Cenith said, "I can't see Ors taking over for you while you're gone. Is there anyone else who can write up documents and run your usual errands? If I'm to hold a council meeting, I'll need someone to help with the preparations."

"I'd planned on discussing that with you." Daric scratched his chin before settling further into the chair. "Elessa said while we were travelling, Avina followed Kian everywhere, pestering him to show her how to do different aspects of the job. He not only showed her, he let her do some of it. As long as you don't mind a female acting as cleric, I think she'd do fine. Just be patient and explain exactly what you need. She'll catch on quick."

"I don't mind. Avina's a smart girl. I think she'd do a good job."

"I'll leave a list for her. That should help." Daric slouched further into the chair and put his hands behind his head. "A search party leaves tomorrow." He didn't have to say for whom. "The stone masons should have the new bier ready before they return. I won't be back in time for the funeral."

Cenith just nodded, praying to Maegden that Daric would return. He had no illusions about the danger this 'errand' posed. Tyrsa wriggled on his lap. His wife weighed so little that Cenith had almost forgotten she was there.

Another knock sounded at the door. Ors entered at Cenith's command.

"I'm returning these…" Ors tossed Cenith's keys to him, "and I've a couple of things to report, My Lord." Ors leaned on the back of Daric's chair. He held a bundle of black cloth under his arm.

"The rubble from the stable is almost cleared away. One of Bailen's crew found charred bones in the wreckage. Human. Looks like Gavril was in the loft after all. No one's seen him in his usual places, so we're assuming it's him."

Daric grunted. Sadness pulled at Cenith's heart. He remembered the old drunk from his youth. Shiftless alcoholic though he was, Gavril had always had a kind word, a smile, and an odd assortment of advice for his lord's son.

"What's under your arm?" Cenith asked.

"More trouble. Morren reported one of his cleaning staff missed his shift yesterday for the second time in a row. The man's noted for sipping more than he should and he put it down to him being passed out or sick. Not the first time it's happened, but when he didn't show up for the evening shift, Morren sent a maid to his room. She came back screaming about blood and that the assassins had come back, so he sent for me."

Alarm shot through Cenith. Daric jerked upright, startling Tyrsa.

Ors held up one hand. "He's been dead for three days. Found him sprawled on his bed wearing only his small breeches."

Cenith breathed a quiet sigh of relief. Daric twisted in his chair so he could look at Ors. Tyrsa leaned forward slightly, one hand on Cenith's shoulder and all her attention on the guard-commander. Cenith wasn't sure she should be hearing this.

"The man's clothespress had been gone through and I found these under the bed." Ors shook out the cloth bundle, holding up black pants, shirt, and a cloth mask—the same clothes the assassins had worn.

"So that's how our missing apprentice escaped. With Buckam blocking the kitchen, he walked out looking like any other citizen of Tiras," Daric growled. "He's a clever one."

"Clever enough to find a way past the guards, increased or not," Ors said, folding the clothes back into a bundle.

"That's the trouble with extended peace," Daric put in. "You grow too lax."

"There are two more people dead?" Tyrsa asked. "Like Kian?"

"Yes," Cenith answered since Daric appeared unable, or unwilling.

"Who is doing this?" Tyrsa demanded.

"Saulth told some bad men to do it. Snake is one of them," Cenith explained.

"Saulth. The man you said is my father." Her face took on a fierce glower. "He's a very bad man."

"I won't argue that point." Cenith had to find some way to make him pay.

"That's all for me," Ors stated. "If you don't mind, I'll say goodnight. I've been so busy over the last few days, my wife's complaining she's forgotten what I look like."

Cenith and Daric both wished him a goodnight.

After Ors left, Daric said, "I should go too. It's been a long day."

"Make a point of sleeping in tomorrow. I am. You'll need your strength for your errand." Cenith looked at Tyrsa. Her innocent smile returned. No sign of Lady Violet. He shifted his attention back to Daric. "How's Buckam doing on the maps?"

"I ran into him on the way up from the kitchen." Daric stood and rested a hand on the back of the chair. "He hadn't started yet. Apparently he spent his time at Silk's with the Companions. I hope that means they're accepting him. He seemed happy enough and swears he'll be done before I leave."

Cenith nodded.

"I told you Buckam's heart was true," Tyrsa said.

Cenith watched her closely to see if her eyes changed. He hoped they would. Lady Violet might have some advice on just how to get into Valda castle.

"That you did, My Lady." Daric gave her a short bow and a smile. "With that, I shall bid you good night and peaceful sleep."

"Same to you," Cenith responded. When Daric had left, he returned his attention to Tyrsa.

Her smile widened and her eyes lit up. Cenith knew what she had on her mind. After informing the guards they were not to be disturbed until they awoke, he scooped her into his arms and ravaged her sweet lips.

* * * *

Wet bushes didn't sit high on Artan's list of places to hide. Or sleep. City born and bred, all this sneaking around in trees and rocks had proved difficult at best. Two days of rain hadn't helped.

Dry caves proved non-existent when he needed one. Artan had found two yesterday soon after he'd started out. Time was of the essence now and he couldn't take advantage of them. He found an empty cabin, but again, it had been near the start of his nightly trek, and he couldn't take the risk of some other traveller wandering in.

Once he'd made his decision, Artan wanted to get back to Valda as soon as possible. While he travelled, he tried to think of other reasons Snake hadn't put in an appearance besides the two that nagged at him. Perhaps Snake had to use Black Crow Pass. He could have snuck out the same way Artan had. If that was the case, then he could still meet up with him in Valda.

Worrying about Snake didn't solve the dilemma now facing him, though. Artan hid on the wrong side of the garrison protecting the entrance to Eagle's Nest Pass. Perhaps several years ago the place was unmanned. He stared down the road at the building itself. The three-story, squat, stone tower looked abandoned at first glance, but a small glimmer of light in the dirty windows, not to mention the men patrolling, said otherwise. A long, low shed stretched back along the road, making the tower appear to possess a tail. Whickers and the stamp of hoofed feet named it a stable.

By the dilapidated condition of the tower, these men might be one of the groups of soldiers he'd seen ride by five days ago. With a silent groan, Artan realized if he'd left right away he'd have avoided the mess he now found himself in.

He wiped his face with his wet sleeve. The rain had stopped an hour ago, yet the bushes he squatted in continued to soak him, as did the tiny rivulet running under his feet as it made its way down the incline from the pass. Not that it mattered; his clothing hung heavy from two nights of walking in miserable weather. He choked back a sneeze.

Artan had only two sets of clothes and they were both soaked. He'd discarded the clothing he'd used while scouting the keep before the raid and left his blacks in the dead servant's room. Once on the plains, if he could get one good day of sunshine, he could dry both himself and his clothes.

Artan swatted at a mosquito. Now that the rain had stopped, dozens of the pesky bugs swarmed around his head, along with a few biting flies, adding to his misery. He crouched in the thick patch of bush, keeping his head down. The trees had disappeared half a mile back, leaving bushes that varied in height from one to five feet for him to hide in. Fortunately, the taller bushes prevailed and the shallow ditch formed by the rivulet gave him a little more room. His feet had been wet for two days, what were a few more hours?

Lingering summer twilight would soon turn to full night, giving him a chance at sneaking past the patrol. Artan had been watching their movements since he arrived two hours before, creeping through the bushes as close as he dared. More than twenty feet remained between him and the tower.

He could only guess at the number of soldiers inside; more than a handful, judging by the windows showing candlelight. Four patrolled outside, though no soldier Artan knew would call it 'patrolling'. They leaned against the tower, relaxing while they chatted.

Despite the guards' seeming inattention, this excursion would require all of Artan's skills. The road narrowed from twenty feet to ten, right at the point where the garrison sat and the pass began. The tower was built against the mountainside, blocking the eastern route. He'd have to be half mountain goat just to get around it, let alone accomplish the feat without someone seeing him. He had no choice but to try to squirm through the eight foot expanse of bushes on this side, keeping away from both the road and the sheer mountain the brush abutted.

A crescent moon remained hidden by cloud, though if the sky continued to clear that would change. The sliver wouldn't cast much light, but Artan preferred complete darkness. The clothes he'd stolen from the dead man in the keep, a dark green tunic and brown pants, would help hide him in the bushes, but his light hair would stand out, as would the metal buckles of the leather pack on his back. He'd have to keep it slow and time his movements to when the guards paid the least attention.

Artan glanced at the sky. *It's now, or not at all. This might take all night.*

Holding his breath, Artan studied the ground in front of him. He duck walked four feet, keeping an eye on the guards. No reaction. He repeated the movement three more times and now crouched almost directly across from the garrison.

Artan sneezed. He just managed to cover his mouth.

"I heard somethin'," one of the guards said, standing straight. "I think it came from th' bushes over there." He pointed close to where Artan squatted.

Sweat broke out on Artan's brow.

"What did it sound like?" another guard asked.

"A cough."

The soldier standing next to the first one grunted. "Probably a mountain cat. Feel free to investigate if you want."

"Mountain cat?" the first one asked, echoing Artan's thoughts.

Wild animals hadn't entered his mind. Just what he needed, something else to worry about.

"Let's wait an' see if I hear it agin." The first soldier drew his sword, but moved closer to the tower door.

The other guards chuckled and resumed their conversation. Nonetheless, Artan waited a long time before trying the movement again. To be on the safe side, he paused almost as long between each try.

His ordeal did take most of the short night, but now Artan lay fifteen feet on the opposite side of the garrison. The bushes here didn't grow as tall, forcing him to crawl. The rivulet running underneath added more weight to his soggy clothes. He dragged himself another four feet and waited.

Wiping his brow, he snuck a peak back at the guards; different ones since the change two hours ago. They hadn't moved. Artan risked another movement then rested his head on his arms. He wanted sleep, and a safe place to do it, but that lay somewhere up ahead. He hoped. The border of bushes had shrunk from eight feet to six. He lifted his head enough to risk a front view.

The moon chose that moment to reveal itself, and what lay before him. Artan's heart sank. Not ten feet ahead the bushes thinned, shrinking to almost non-existent, leaving a long gap before the road disappeared around a bend. He glanced back to the tower and up at the eastern sky. Was that a glimmer of pre-dawn brightening the snowy peaks? He couldn't wait; he had to take the chance. *Damned short nights.*

Creeping close to the end of the bushes, he discovered the little ditch continued to follow the road. If he stayed as low as possible, it hid almost half of him, except for his pack, sitting on his back like a turtle. Mud coated his clothing and matted his hair, turning him a shade of non-descript brown, better for blending into the shadows of the mountain.

Artan rolled onto his side and shrugged out of one strap of the pack, then repeated the maneuver for the other. Leaving the pack where it lay, he crawled a few feet forward. Wiggling his right foot, Artan looped it through one of the straps. Now, as he crawled, he could drag the pack after him.

In this manner, and always checking the patrol, Artan made it past the bend. Ensuring he could no longer be seen, he sat and heaved a long sigh of relief. He uncorked his water bag and drank deeply.

He could only allow himself a brief rest. The sun would soon rise and he had to find a place to hide so he could get some sleep. He rubbed his eyes and dragged himself to his feet, shouldering his pack. Alternately jogging and walking, Artan distanced himself from the garrison.

The mountain dropped away into an expansive, dark ravine to the left; the right side remained steep and barren. To make travelling worse, the road narrowed further, to the point where two horses couldn't pass. If he ran into anyone now, he'd be dead. *No wonder I haven't seen any travellers since well before the garrison.* Wagons couldn't travel this route, even those on foot or horseback had to use caution. Especially at night. As the road twisted and climbed, the air grew cooler and he walked in wispy clouds of fog. He hoped that would change as the sun rose.

By the time the sun reached its zenith, the clouds had almost disappeared and the sun worked hard at drying the sweat and mud that coated his face. He dragged himself further up the path to a spot on the mountainside, a dark blemish against the lighter rock. It proved to be a gouge in the mountain, one deep and wide enough to hold him and his pack. No cave, but it would do. *Thank Shival!*

A tiny waterfall leaked down the inside and trickled to join the rivulet he'd crawled through. Artan rested his pack against the back of the depression, high enough to use it for a pillow. The parchment sat in its frame, in the pack, cushioned by wet clothing. He briefly wondered how it fared. *Probably better than I am.* Sitting on his haunches, he rested his head and closed his eyes, too tired to eat. *Just a few hours peace, please Shival, that's all I ask.*

* * * *

Ors leaned on his saddle horn, holding the reins of another pony. He chewed on a piece of long grass. "Four days of 'Can't you at least untie my hands?', 'I need to rest', and 'I want water'." He grunted, then spat on the ground. "You'd think him a nobleman."

Aleyn, astride a black mountain cob, chuckled. They stood on the southern end of the half-mile wide, forested valley that opened onto the Bredun plains and saw the beginning of the trail leading to Eagle's Nest Pass. The forest leaked out of the valley and stretched to the east and south, home of the vale where Lord Cenith had been attacked.

The shrinking form of Snake lurched its way across the ridged scrubland separating the valley from the grasslands. When they'd first sent an agonized and disgruntled Snake on his way, he'd hobbled hunched over, his breathing laboured. Walking hadn't appeared to ease his discomfort any; he stopped frequently to rub his legs. Ors had seen men years older move faster.

Snake disappeared in a dip then reappeared on the next ridge. An instant later, he vanished again. The assassin had fallen several times before finding his legs. Ors swore the goat-lover had spent more time glancing back to see if anyone would follow than paying attention to where he walked. Any wonder he kept tripping.

"I think he fell again," Aleyn commented, his voice uncaring. A few minutes later, Snake stood on the top of the same ridge.

"Yep," Ors chuckled.

A groan sounded from one of the six guards who'd formed Snake's escort, sitting astride their horses several paces back. They'd placed bets on how many times Snake's legs gave out. Someone just had lost.

"I can't believe the demon-futterer demanded to keep his horse," Aleyn said, shaking his head.

"Not to mention him wanting us to supply him with food and water. He's lucky we gave him clothes." Ors snorted loudly. "Lord Cenith guaranteed his life to the border, nothing else."

Daric had been right; riding proved less painful for the assassin than walking, but not by much. Ors straightened up, stretching his back. He rocked from side to side in the saddle for a few moments, attempting to bring some life into his arse; a small discomfort when compared to what Snake endured. He chuckled again. Aleyn cast him a questioning glance.

"Just thinking about the last four days. You missed all the action, stuck down here at the bottom of the pass. It got quite entertaining actually." Ors lifted one arse cheek and scratched. "The goat-turd kept passing out. Sometimes he'd fall off his horse, sometimes he wouldn't. Provided another way for that lot to pass their money around." He aimed his thumb at the soldiers behind him. "The big question came when we stopped for the night. If he was unconscious, do we take him off the horse? Or leave him to see how long he stayed on by himself? The second night he almost made it 'til dawn."

Aleyn laughed and they resumed their vigil. A light breeze wafted past, drying some of the sweat forming on Ors' head and brow. He took a blue handkerchief from his pocket and wiped the rest away. Folding it into a bandana, he tied it around his head.

Ors glanced at the sun, now reaching its zenith. "Lord Cenith should be starting the council meeting soon," he commented, more to pass the time than out of real interest.

"This is the first one on his own, isn't it?" Aleyn said, his squinting eyes still on Snake. "And without Councillor Daric."

"Yep. He'll do fine. Grown up a lot in the last few months. Even more over the last week or so." Ors tapped his fingers on his thigh in rhythm with the tune running through his head; one he'd heard recently in a tavern, about a woman taking revenge on the man who'd scorned her.

The assassin now appeared no more than a blotch on the horizon. Ors shaded his eyes with one hand, then judged the distance Snake had travelled. He turned his head to the right and raised his voice. "You can come out now, he's past the border."

Daric, dressed in black armoured jerkin and trousers, led Nightwind from a nearby stand of alder. All trace of allegiance to Dunvalos Reach had been removed from both man and horse. A long coil of hemp rope hung from the saddle.

The Calleni had left a day before Ors, earlier than planned, stating he wanted time to rest and fill Aleyn in on the events of the last several days. Ors put it down to uncharacteristic impatience, since the additional guard they'd sent down would have known most of the tale.

Keeping himself hidden behind Nightwind's head, Daric drew near. The big bay danced with the need to run and the Calleni had to keep a tight hold on his bridle.

"Too bad we didn't catch your escapee." Aleyn turned back to Ors. "As I told Daric, the pigeon arrived during the night. It wasn't until morning that I read the message. I split my men into three shifts, but ten soldiers over a half-mile isn't a very effective net. Your extra men came too late." He leaned over and added spit to the same spot Ors had chosen earlier. "If the cur left the morning of the attack, he should have come through the same day I received the message."

Daric stared in the direction the assassin had gone. Aleyn mopped his brow. Ors used his sleeve to wipe more sweat from his bald pate. The late morning sun shone warmer here than in the shadows of the mountains. Though it had rained in the hills, the plains had seen five days of steady sun. The farmers needed it. Too much rain and too many storms had hindered their crops. Rot and disease loomed over the horizon.

Ors briefly wondered how the farms around the Kalemi and Asha Rivers fared with all the horrendous flooding. The mountain people depended on the plainsmen for their grain and flour. If the prices rose too high due to shortages, it affected everyone.

"Haldis thought he heard something night before last, right in that stand." Aleyn's nod indicated the one Daric had hidden in. "He and another guard checked it out and found nothing, so we came back in daylight. There were tracks, but they could just as easily have been theirs from blundering around in the dark. But if that was our boy, he sure took his time going through the pass."

"He may not even have come this way," Daric said, stroking Nightwind's nose. His eyes remained locked on the no longer visible Snake. "It was a guess. If he left by Black Crow, we'll never find him."

Ors couldn't help wondering if the violet–eyed Lady Tyrsa knew the assassin wouldn't be caught and that's why she asked Daric to go on his dangerous mission. "How did Buckam do on those maps?"

"Better than expected," Daric said. "He not only drew the tunnels, he's given me the entire layout of the castle, marked all the guard's positions, and how many to expect at night."

"Well, you know my opinion on the whole thing. I just hope he's not leading you into a trap."

Daric grunted and slid his hand along his horse's neck, moving back enough to mount.

"Time?" Ors asked.

The Calleni nodded.

"I'm surprised you didn't leave sooner," Aleyn said. "He's been past the border for a while now."

"Sound carries easily here. I don't want your women and children hearing any of it." Daric's icy voice added an extra chill to his words.

Aleyn's face paled.

Ors smiled. "Good hunting."

Daric nodded to them both, then let Nightwind have his way. Dirt flew from the bay's hooves as he sped across the scrubland bordering the plains.

Ors grinned. "Go get 'im."

To be continued in Tyrsa's Choice, Book 2 of The Jada-Drau.

About the Author

Sandie Bergen lives on an island in the Pacific; Vancouver Island to be exact, idyllic and perfect in its own way. She lives with Charlie, her husband of thirty-two years, and three muses, otherwise known as cats, MacDuff, Harmony, and Molly. She has two grown children, Amanda and Aaron. Sandie has been writing for years, mostly for personal enjoyment. The Jada-Drau is her first published novel though she had two ghost stories with Whispering Spirits Digital Magazine, as well as stories published with Worlds of Wonder Magazine and Flash Me Magazine.

About the Cover Artist:

Ron Leming has been a professional writer and artist for over 25 years, with publications in markets such as Fangoria, Space and Time, Year's Best Horror IV, Outlaw Biker, Mayfair, Ironman, Gauntlet, several Chaosium role playing games, DVD covers for Zombiegeddon, Slaughter Party, Minds of Terror, book Covers for JF Gonzales' the Beloved, Victor Heck's Book of Legion and many others. His book, the Gutbucket Quest, co-written with Piers Anthony, was published in hardback in May of 2000 and released in paperback in May of 2001. He was also the editor of the Damnations anthology and of the infamous parody genre newsletter, the Daily Bonestructure. He's the co-author of the screenplay for the horror film Carnies. http://www.carniesmovie.com

His friends and mentors have included Erle Stanley Gardner, J.N. Williamson, Robert Bloch and Piers Anthony. Originally from Ventura, California, and homesick, he presently lives in Amarillo, Texas, being an old hippy in an unhip world, looking for honest graphics work, and looking for love.

About the Cover Designer:

Stephen Blundell lives in Brisbane, Australia with his wife Joanne and three year old son, Michael. His illustrations have graced many book covers and interiors from horror to historical fiction. He is currently working on his own novel as well as his zombie comic "Before The Ashes". His art can be found at www.djdyme.deviantart.com and he can often be found on Facebook where he regularly posts new images.

LaVergne, TN USA
25 February 2011
218031LV00001B/12/P

9 780982 929568